THE DEVIL'S MOUTH

A Novel

THOMAS WILLIAMS

D1304754

WORD PUBLISHING

NASHVILLE

A Thomas Nelson Company

Library of Congress Cataloging-in-Publication Data

Williams, T. M. (Thomas Myron), 1941–
   The Devil's mouth : a novel / Thomas Williams.
     p. cm. — (The seven kingdoms chronicles ; v. 2)
   ISBN 0-8499-4267-5
   1. Middle Ages—Fiction. 2. Princes—Fiction. I. Title.

PS3573.I45562 D48 2001
813'.54—dc21

2001017610

Printed in the United States of America

01 02 03 04 05 PHX 9 8 7 6 5 4 3 2 1

WHAT READERS AND REVIEWERS HAVE SAID
ABOUT THOMAS WILLIAMS'S FIRST NOVEL,

ThE CROWN OF EDEN

"Put Tom Williams up there with C. S. Lewis and J. R. R. Tolkien. His first book is a 'great' of the fantasy world."

—*The Houston Chronicle*

"Magnificent language, stunning imagery, and compelling symbolism . . . worthy of the most critical reader."

—Ellen Gunderson Traylor, author of *Song of Abraham*

"We are privileged to enjoy Tom's skill with a story."

—Max Lucado

"Tom Williams has written a Tolkien-like fantasy in *The Crown of Eden*."

—*Chicago Sun-Times*

"Williams's tale of the ongoing struggle between light and darkness carries a strong moral and religious message that makes this high fantasy adventure a good choice for libraries in search of Christian-oriented fantasy."

—*Library Journal*

"Williams delivers a romantic tale examining such topics as fate, free will, and the power of good and evil. Both fantasy and romance readers will enjoy this first adventure in the Seven Kingdoms Chronicles series."

—*CBA Marketplace*

"The book has the basis for fantasy fiction—believable plots, greater-than-average characters, good vs. evil. But unlike many Christian fiction books of the past, the Christian elements of Williams's book are not hokey or forced."

—*The Amen Page*

"... a masterfully told fantasy comparable both in style and wisdom to the works of George Macdonald, C. S. Lewis, and J. R. R. Tolkien. The book is filled with spiritual truths and deals with a number of challenging issues on an allegorical level. It is a book to be read slowly, and to be savored."

—*Christian Library Journal*

"If you like fantasy, it will completely gratify your expectations. Brilliantly written! Thomas Williams is a modern C. S. Lewis and John Bunyan rolled into one."

—Emily Alger on Suite101.com

"My wife and I were overwhelmed by this book. I don't know when I have enjoyed anything so much. Warning: once you start it you will find it hard to stop. I let several things go and read it over a couple of days. It's a fine piece of work."

—Dr. Thomas A. Langford,
Retired Dean of the Graduate School,
Texas Technological University

"Deserves to be on the same shelves alongside the tales of Narnia and Middle Earth."

—*Gospel Tidings* (denominational monthly)

"An intriguing fantasy of love and adventure that takes place in a world of hidden identities, secret motivations, and the unfolding of a divine prophecy."

—Joseph Bentz, author of *A Son Comes Home*

LIST OF CHARACTERS

MAJOR CHARACTERS:

Prince Lanson—Son of King Kor of Lochlaund.

Evalonne—Daughter of a tradesman in Lochlaund.

King Kor—Widowed King of Lochlaund.

Sir Maconnal—Knighted tutor to Lanson.

Bishop Hugal—Head of the Kirk of Lochlaund.

Gronthus—Accorder of the Kirk of Lochlaund.

Lady Lamonda—Niece of Bishop Hugal.

Alenia—Serving woman in Macrennon Castle in Lochlaund.

King Aradon—Young King of Meridan.

Queen Volanna—Aradon's wife.

Vallia (Mossette)—Infant daughter of Aradon and Volanna.

Brendal—Displaced fugitive from the Kingdom of Valomar.

Morgultha—Power-lusting witch. Hundreds of years old.

Father Clemente (or *Father Vitale*)—Angelic bearer of wisdom.

Avriel—Wandering minstrel.

SECONDARY CHARACTERS:

Sir Llewenthane—Knight of Meridan. Aradon's outspoken friend.

Sir Olstan the Silent of Meridan—Aradon's friend and aide. Mute.

Sir Denmore of Meridan—Aradon's general.

Sir Eanor of Meridan—Aradon's diplomatic envoy.

Lady Kalley of Meridan—Sir Olstan's wife.

Lord Kenmarl of Oranth—Friend to King Kor and Sir Maconnal.

Dwag—Slow-witted servant on Lord Kenmarl's estate.

King Umberland—King of Vensaur.

Dunwig—Innkeeper of the Red Falcon Inn in Oranth.

Golwen—Wife of Dunwig.

Gwynnelon—Serving girl at the Red Falcon Inn.

Lurga—Serving girl at the Red Falcon Inn.

Glynnora—Wet nurse in the service of Morgultha.

Lograine—Evalonne's friend in Macrennon.

Sir Werthen—Knight of Vensaur. Friend to King Umberland.

Branwydd—Overseer to Lord Kenmarl's estate in Oranth.

Sir Cramalon—Knight bearing treaty to King Kor.

Lady Griselda—Friend of Lady Lamonda.

Lord Caldemone—Knight in Vensaur.

minor characters:

Lord Aldemar—Advisor to King Aradon of Meridan.

Dalkane—Guard at the prison in Oakendale Castle of Valomar.

Kalnor—Follower of Morgultha who helps Brendal escape.

Moburne—Friend of Prince Lanson and fellow trainee.

Rogarre—Friend of Prince Lanson and fellow trainee.

Corandon—Wheelwright in Lochlaund.

Sir Kenegal—Knight of Lochlaund's Hall and advisor to King Kor.

Sir Wexfeld—Knight in Sir Cramalon's delegation.

Sir Karramore—Knight in Meridan's Hall.

Sir Prestamont—Knight in Meridan's Hall.

Sir Halliston—Knight in Meridan's Hall.

Lady Eleannore—Wife of Sir Llewenthane of Meridan.

Lady Florimel—Wife of Sir Denmore of Meridan.

Rynon—Kidnapper employed by Sir Brendal.

Bwark—Kidnapper employed by Sir Brendal.

Ganwold—Archer under Lanson's command at Ensovandor.

Mariella—Twelve-year-old daughter of a baker in Brancester.

Lady Dulessa—Chaperone for Lanson and Lamonda.

Hollek—A farmer in Oranth.

To Gene Shelburne

tbe seven KINGDOMS

PROLOGUE

t was the great conqueror Perivale who first united the Seven Kingdoms into a federation powerful enough to defeat the evil Morgultha in her war to conquer the island. After his victory, Perivale was proclaimed high king over all the Seven Kingdoms. Though his reign began well, it ended in shame as pride corrupted him and brought him to a death that remained shrouded in mystery for over a hundred years.

Without Perivale's strong hand at the helm, the confederation crumbled into separate, warring kingdoms, and those kingdoms soon fell headlong into anarchy and license. Order disintegrated into chaos, and thievery, murder, rape, and revelry came to be the way of things. The roads linking the kingdoms became infested with outlaws and predatory animals, and many of them reverted to mere trails or were reclaimed altogether by the forests and wilderness. Trade came to a halt and prosperity withered on the vine.

In the wake of Perivale's fall, it was the kirks of the kingdoms that rose up and saved the island. The kirk, long a powerful presence in each of the Seven Kingdoms, was a body of believers dedicated to upholding the laws, perpetuating the rituals, preserving the revelations, and illuminating the will of the Master of the Universe.

To reverse the island's slide into oblivion, the kirks applied stringent measures. They enforced strict observance of all the ancient rituals and the regular partaking of sacraments. They set down precise laws for food preparation, banning spices and savory ingredients. Certain foods, such as pork, they banned altogether, and fasts became frequent. They prohibited the drinking of ales, wines, and all but the weakest of meads, except for certain ritualistic uses by the kirk itself. The kirks forbade all offensive and profane language, as well as any kind of labor on Sundays. They silenced all music except for chants and dirges. They removed harps, lyres, and other instruments from their own worship and rituals. They forbade dancing and feasting (except for solemn holy feasts) as well as jesting and games. Men and women who showed affection in public, they pilloried, and outright immoral behavior they punished by death. In general the kirks turned the kingdoms away from the lure of beauty and pleasure to redirect the focus of their citizens back toward duty and order.

As the years passed and kings rose up in the separate kingdoms to take on the task of maintaining order, most of the kirks relaxed their firm hand and restored liberty to the people as they grew able to manage it. Kirkmen returned to their original purpose of illuminating the ways of the Master. Music, poetry, story, and dance began to find their place again in the Seven Kingdoms. Spices returned to the kitchens. Alehouses opened their doors. Minstrels began to circulate among the towns and villages, and wine presses resumed their work. Courting men and maidens no longer feared to hold hands in the village streets. In most of the kingdoms, a healthy balance was struck between individual liberty and public order.

The kirks in two of the kingdoms, however, were appalled at the revival of these dangerous liberties. The rubble of Perivale's fall had convinced the bishops of Lochlaund and Rhondilar that freedom was the seed from which license and destruction sprang. These kirkmen were convinced that the way of the law was the way of the Master. It was clear to them that the island's other five kingdoms were slipping into apostasy, and their own two kingdoms were the last remaining fortresses of truth. It was up to them to hold the battle line. They insisted that to relax one more finger of the iron hand by which they had ruled the people would weaken the grip of the law, and in one generation the will of the Master would be lost forever in the Seven Kingdoms.

These bishops were greatly vexed that the ill-advised relaxing of the collective kirks had already allowed many dangerous freedoms to creep back across the borders of Rhondilar and Lochlaund. Though they could not prevent the return of frivolous music, wine and ale, and savory foods, they vowed to stop any further erosion of the pious path upon which they had so diligently set the feet of their people. In Rhondilar, the kirk was so weak that such a policy had little effect. But in Lochlaund, the kirk was much stronger and the kings weaker. The kirkmen of Lochlaund sought ways to staunch the hemorrhage of freedom and retain the grip on the lives of the people they had won in the days of chaos.

Of course, the slippage back to freedom did not reach into the halls and abbeys of the Kirk of Lochlaund itself. It retained the old ways for the conduct of all its own officials. Bishops, monks, priests, and other kirkmen were not to touch any fermented drink, participate in any frivolity, eat anything savory, sing any joyful song, or have any contact with women. Though the kirk could no longer impose all these restrictions on the rest of Lochlaund's citizens, it enforced as many of the old ways as it could on the entire populace. The Lochlaund kirk demanded attendance to rituals and sacramental observances, prohibited all labor on Sundays, forbade public affection between men and women, and imposed the death penalty on every sinner condemned for immorality.

Those freedoms that had already seeped into their kingdom as a result of the unfortunate relaxing of the neighboring kirks, the kirkmen of Lochlaund looked upon with a frown. They did all in their power to paint them as sins unworthy of the Master's followers. They warned the people continually of the dangers of pleasure, urging them to emulate the practices of kirkmen as the ideal and take frequent vows of abstinence and celibacy. Men and women who did not abstain at least from some pleasure were deemed less worthy of the Master's favor and in danger of his wrath (though one could always ensure the safety of one's soul if, after any indulgence, one would add a few farthings to the kirk's coffers).

As the years passed, the souls of Lochlaund's citizens grew weary and bent under the burden of accumulated rules and accumulating guilt. They looked often from the prison of their lives, gray and bleak with the banishment of beauty, and saw their brothers and sisters in neighboring kingdoms walking tall in the sunlight of freedom. Like the Hebrew slaves in ancient Egypt, the people of Lochlaund longed for a deliverer.

PART I

EVALONNE

CHAPTER ONE

The Condemned Woman

he accorder Gronthus knocked lightly on the door of Bishop Hugal's chambers. When he heard the voice inside bidding him to come in, he entered. The Bishop of Lochlaund, a portly man with a heavy jowl and skin that had seen little sunlight, was sitting at his oaken desk. He was robed in the long gray of his order, and the cowl was pushed back from his head, revealing a pate pallid as a lump of tallow sparsely covered with wisps of hair just beginning to turn gray. The only sound was the scratching of his quill on the parchment in front of him. He did not look up from his work as Gronthus entered the room.

"We have the woman, your grace," said Gronthus.

"Bring her in," said Hugal without lifting his eyes.

Gronthus left the room and returned moments later, followed by two guards holding between them a young woman. Her only covering was a frayed sheet, wrapped loosely around her body. Her wrists were chained in front and her head was bowed, her long, disheveled hair hanging about her face, hiding it in a cavern of darkness. The guards thrust her toward the bishop and stood back. The woman did not look up, but struggled as best she could with her chained hands to keep the sheet tucked securely about her.

Bishop Hugal finished the line he was writing before he looked up at the young woman. He gazed at her as she struggled with the sheet and slowly licked his lips. "What is the accusation against this woman?" he asked.

"She is accused of adultery, your grace," replied Gronthus.

"How do you plead, woman?" asked the bishop.

She did not reply, but great tears began to fall from the cavern of her hair like raindrops from a dark cloud, splashing on the floor at her feet.

"What evidence of her guilt do you have?" Hugal asked.

"We caught her in the very act," said Gronthus. "We have been watching her for weeks and have discovered a pattern of deception that has been repeated many times. We followed her from her own home to the house of the man she seduced. She always arrives shortly after his wife leaves for the market. If she sees a white rag hanging from his window, she knocks on his door with a basket in her hand to give the appearance that she is an eggseller. The man takes her inside, and she leaves a half-hour later. Today we followed her and waited until she had been inside for some ten minutes, then we entered and found them together in his bed. We wrapped her in his bedsheet and brought her to you just as we found her. There is no doubt as to her guilt, your grace. The woman should be put to death."

"What do you have to say for yourself, woman?" said Hugal.

Still she made no reply, but her shoulders began to convulse as tears bathed her chained hands and splashed to the floor.

The bishop sighed. "Well, if you offer no defense for yourself, we shall judge you by the evidence presented. You have committed a great evil and must face trial for it. We will stand you before King Kor as soon as it can be arranged."

For the first time the woman looked up. "King Kor is a good king, he is. Don't ye think his majesty might show a bit of mercy to a poor one like me?"

"The king will follow the recommendation of the kirk," replied the bishop, "not only because it is the law, but because he is a personal friend of mine." Hugal could hardly resist boasting of his standing with the king, even to the lowliest of Lochlaund's citizens.

At the wave of the bishop's hand the guards lifted the woman to her feet, and he watched as they led her toward the door. The sheet loosened and slipped, exposing her white, slender back. Hugal's breath came deeper as he gazed. When the door closed behind them, he picked up his quill and resumed his writing.

On that same afternoon as King Kor held audience on his throne, Bishop Hugal entered the great hall and stepped ahead of the line of supplicants awaiting their names to be called. He walked the length of the room, lined on either side with clusters of knights and noblemen watching the proceedings, and breathing as if he had just run a race, stood before the king.

"Your majesty, we have a matter needing your immediate judgment. The accorder Gronthus has apprehended an adulterous woman we have been watching for weeks. In our continuing effort to bring such cases to a swift conclusion, I ask you to hear the case now."

King Kor hesitated, and for the briefest of moments his brow knotted, giving him a look of defiance that Hugal had not seen before. But the look passed and the king said, "Very well, bring the woman in."

At Hugal's signal the doors of the hall opened and Gronthus entered, followed by two guards holding the young woman between them. She was still clad only in the ragged sheet, still shackled, and still hanging her head in shame. She neither struggled nor looked up as they forced her down the hall and thrust her toward the foot of the dais before King Kor. She sank to the floor as if her legs had turned to sand.

"State the charges, Bishop Hugal," the king said.

Hugal rehearsed to King Kor the account of the woman's sin and arrest. "We left her dressed just as Gronthus found her so you could see that our evidence is unassailable. The woman is obviously guilty. She has flouted the law and pursued pleasure in defiance of the Master of the Universe. She must be condemned to death."

"What is your name, woman?" asked Kor. But the woman, quivering with fear and shame, could not reply.

"You have heard the charges against you. How do you plead?" continued the king.

Still she did not reply but stood with her head bowed as convulsive sobs wrenched her body.

King Kor seemed uneasy. He shifted his position and ran his hand across the back of his neck. "Gronthus, the bishop has told us that the woman was caught in the very act. Obviously, the man was caught as well. Why is he not standing before me?"

"Your majesty," replied Gronthus, "the man bears less guilt than the woman because she enticed him. She sought him out, not vice versa. And you know the teachings of the Master on the relative guilt of men and women: Adam's sin was reckoned lesser than Eve's because the woman enticed him."

"Nevertheless, it takes two to commit this particular sin. And who really knows how this little arrangement began—whether the woman enticed the man or the man seduced the woman? Who knows whether the guilt of one is greater than that of the other? The one clear thing here is that two sinners were caught in the act, but only one was brought to trial. Am I the only one who senses a bit of unfairness in that?"

"Your majesty," said Bishop Hugal, "your sense of fairness is most commendable, but you make your task too complex. The law is simple and clear. It tells us without ambiguity that adulterers must be put to death. Whether other adulterers run loose on the street who should be condemned as well is beside the point. The point is we have a guilty woman before us who deserves nothing less than death. It is that simple, sire."

"It is not that simple. I am increasingly troubled by the Kirk of Lochlaund's disregard of fairness and mercy. How can we claim to administer justice if we ignore fairness? As King of Lochlaund, I choose not to follow the recommendation of the kirk in the case of this woman. I grant her clemency. She may go free."

Bishop Hugal arose immediately, utter consternation clouding his heavy face as he sputtered, "Your majesty will forgive me for pointing out that the king is not above the law. In the Seven Kingdoms even the monarchs of the nations are subject to the laws of their kingdoms and, especially, to the laws of the kirk."

"But surely neither the kirk nor the state has a law against mercy."

"There is no law against mercy, but there are limits to the application of it—limits set and enforced by the kirk. In the chaos that swept the Seven Kingdoms after the death of Perivale over 120 years ago, the kirk stepped in and became the arbiter of moral law in all the Seven Kingdoms. To prevent the rise of anarchy in the absence of a strong, centralized government, the kirk has insisted on the strict enforcement of morality, punishing violators uniformly as a deterrent to sin. Clemency breeds disrespect of law."

"Nevertheless, the law must be applied evenly," the king insisted. "Where such impartiality is lacking, I choose to grant clemency."

"The king will forgive me if I point out that the kirk has long assumed the right to veto clemency in matters of morality," said the bishop. "Fortunately, you and I have always been in agreement on such matters, and the issue has never arisen to divide us. I would regret to find that your judgment today marked the first time the Kingdom of Lochlaund pitted itself against the Kirk of Lochlaund."

King Kor rubbed his sweating palms on his robes. "The kirk merely assumed this right. It does not bind me, because it was never written into law."

"It has become law by precedent of a hundred years. To defy it is to place oneself in jeopardy of heresy."

Everyone in the hall gaped in stunned silence at the unexpected drama unfolding before them. Beads of sweat now glistened on Kor's brow, but his voice was firm and strong. "Bishop Hugal, do you mean to tell me that the kirk considers an act of mercy to be a heresy?"

"Yes. When it is performed in defiance of the judgment of the kirk."

The king's face turned red, and he stood and pointed a finger at the bishop. But before he could speak, a voice rang out from a cluster of assembled noblemen watching from the side of the hall. "Your majesty, would you allow me to approach the throne?"

"Lord Kenegal may approach the throne," said Kor as he lowered his hand and resumed his seat.

Kenegal mounted the dais, knelt beside the throne, and spoke in low tones that only the king could hear. "Your majesty, forgive me for intruding into this debate. But as a longtime advisor to the throne, I wish to express a concern before you continue."

"Say on, Lord Kenegal."

"More than a century of precedent and usage has given the kirk's right to veto moral decisions of the kings the status of de facto law. It now has force of authority equal to laws that are passed and ratified by the Hall of Knights. I know that you have sometimes chafed under the kirk's insistence on rigid justice, but I wonder if now is the best time to mount a challenge."

"When is the best time to begin administering justice with mercy? I think I have waited too long already."

"I fully understand, sire, and your desire for mercy is most commendable. But I see two reasons for choosing a time more opportune than now to pit yourself against the kirk. First, what would happen if you choose to defy the kirk in this matter today?"

"It's possible the kirk would declare me a heretic."

"Precisely," replied Kenegal. "And if I know Bishop Hugal, such a declaration is not merely possible but probable. As you know, just as the king appoints the bishops of the kirk in his kingdom, the kirk has the right to depose a heretical king. If the Kirk of Lochlaund exercises its right to conscript the armies of the Seven Kingdoms to depose you, are you confident that Lochlaund has the military power to defend your throne?"

The king's eyes narrowed at the question. "No, I'm certain Lochlaund could not stand against the amassed armies of the Seven Kingdoms. But should I let even my own safety be a factor in choosing whether to administer fairness?"

"Of course not, sire. I commend you for your courage and selflessness. But your own safety is not really the issue here. Think of the well-being of the kingdom. What would a conflict now between the kirk and the Kingdom of Lochlaund say to King Aradon of Meridan? How would it play into his dream of a united Seven Kingdoms? Would he look at Lochlaund as a renegade kingdom too full of internal strife to enter the confederation? Do you want this one judgment you render today to put Lochlaund at risk of being left on the outside looking in as the other kingdoms unite and build this island into a mighty alliance of unprecedented prosperity?"

King Kor sat silent for the space of seven breaths, his brow knitted as he stared unseeing at the great oaken doors at the far end of the hall. Finally, with a tired gesture of his hand, he waved Lord Kenegal away. "No doubt you are right." Looking suddenly haggard and drawn, he sighed like a deflating blacksmith's bellows as he turned to Bishop Hugal. "The throne accedes to the wishes of the kirk. Do with the woman as you will."

The bishop's face took on a look of self-satisfied triumph as he turned to the crowd and boldly declared, "It is the will of the kirk, acting under laws prescribed by the Master of the Universe, to condemn this woman to be cast into the Devil's Mouth."

"No! Please, not that!" the woman wailed. She looked up at Bishop Hugal, her face contorted in anguish. "I know I done wrong, but not that wrong. Take a sword and cut off my head clean like, or put a rope on my neck and hang me from a tree, but please, your grace, don't feed me to the Devil's Mouth. Please!"

"You should have thought of the consequences before you gave in to your lusts," the bishop replied. "You are of the devil and to him we shall return you. Take her away."

The woman sank to her feet sobbing and wailing, trying to wipe her tears with her chained hands.

Without another word the king arose and left the hall by a door to the side of the throne. Gronthus nodded to the guards, and they lifted the weeping woman to her feet and half dragged, half carried her out of the hall. Bishop Hugal, standing at the foot of the dais, watched the undulation of the sheet playing about the contours of her hips as the little procession disappeared through the wooden doors of the hall.

*

King Kor sat deep in the cushions of the oaken chair in his chambers, staring into the fire that flickered in the hearth. In the flames he saw the writhing form of the woman he had just condemned. Her anguished wails echoed in his mind as if from the caverns of hell. He tried to think of other things—his son Lanson, the confederation treaty with Meridan—but to no avail. Why could he not get the woman out of his mind? Her guilt was certain, and he had sent others to their deaths for the same crime. Why were such sentences becoming so abhorrent to him?

As he sipped from his goblet of wine, a knock came at his chamber door and Bishop Hugal entered.

"Oh, come in, Hugal. I had forgotten it was Tuesday. Take a chair and I'll have a page bring a pitcher of water for you."

Bishop Hugal sat down, casting a longing glance at the king's ale as his mouth salivated at the aroma. After a moment of awkward silence, he spoke with a hint of coldness in his voice. "What were you trying to do today, sire? Never have you taken it upon yourself to cross the kirk with your judgments."

"Oh, get off your high horse, Hugal. We've known each other too long for you to ruffle your feathers simply because I happen to call in question one of the kirk's practices."

"I hardly call the death sentence for a grievous moral sin merely one of the kirk's practices," Hugal snorted. "It is at the core of our control of morality in the Seven Kingdoms. Your attempts to substitute your own ideas about mercy for the demands of the law would undermine justice on this island. The kirk cannot yield this principle. But you have known that as long as we have been friends. Why the sudden change?"

King Kor sighed and shook his head. "I hardly know myself, Hugal. Yes, throughout my reign I have strongly supported the kirk in all its dogma and practices. But I'll admit that lately I've had second thoughts about the kirk's lack of mercy. No doubt all those we have condemned deserved to die, yet it seems to me that many were genuinely repentant and might well have turned from their evil had we granted them clemency."

The bishop sat rigid in his chair, his face set like stone. "Begin granting clemency and you can be sure that immorality will run rampant. The strictness of the penalty is the only deterrent against the pursuit of beauty and pleasure."

"And that's another thing," said Kor. "The kirk tells us that beauty and pleasure are intrinsically evil, created by the Master of the Universe as lures to test whether mankind will resist temptation and remain dedicated to him. But don't you sometimes wonder whether beauty and pleasure are really evil? Is it possible the kirk has missed the meaning of them somehow?"

"I can hardly believe what I'm hearing, sire." Hugal's voice rose as he glared at the king. "Surely you know such thoughts are heresy."

"Is merely thinking and wondering heresy?"

"Yes!" Hugal's fist came down hard on the arm of his chair. "There is no need to think further on the laws of right and wrong as determined by the kirk. They are true and correct, and any variance from them is evil. The kirk must hold us accountable, not only for what we do, but for what we think as well."

"And who holds the kirk accountable?"

"The Master of the Universe himself, of course. His laws are absolute and immutable, and the kirk must adhere to them utterly."

"But as a kirkman you know how difficult it is to understand and interpret many of these laws. How can you always be sure whether the kirk understands them and upholds them as the Master wills? Aren't errors of interpretation possible? Isn't it a good thing to examine our beliefs and convictions again and again to assure ourselves that we are truly aligned with his will?" The king gazed at the bishop with eyebrows raised.

"It has already been done, sire. Scholars over centuries have delved into every detail of the law and amassed huge bodies of work examining every facet, every nuance, every jot and tittle of every ordinance the Master ever gave." Hugal punctuated his words by jamming his forefinger into his fleshy palm. "We have the truth, now. It has been handed to us shaped to perfection like a finely cut diamond. Our duty is to accept that gift without looking askance at it as if we lacked appreciation for the labor that went into giving it to us."

"Surely no one has a lock on all truth," the king said as he leaned toward the bishop. "We all have our own blinders. We can become entrenched in our own interpretations shaped by our individual experiences and prejudices. Perhaps we need a constant check on our view of truth to be sure it is solid."

"I must say I have never heard you talk this way before, and I admit that I am alarmed. But I'm inclined not to lay it all to your charge. I suspect you have been listening to a voice that has planted these seeds of doubt in your mind." Hugal leaned toward the king and looked directly at him. "Tell me frankly, sire, are you expressing ideas you have heard from the mouth of Sir Maconnal?"

"You know that Sir Maconnal is a most learned and valued advisor to the throne." The king sipped his wine and gazed into the fire.

"And I suspect that he is also a heretic, though I've not been able to prove it," replied the bishop. "Tell me what he says to you and let me judge whether he has departed from the teachings of the kirk."

"No, Hugal." The king set down his wine goblet and spoke firmly. "I would not violate your friendship by repeating your private conversations to him, and neither will I violate his. Indeed, in spite of the dangers, which you have so eloquently described, I value hearing all sides of an issue. I am convinced that merely hearing and considering options contrary to what the kirk teaches is not heresy. We should be judged not for our exploring the truth but for the rightness of our decisions."

"I can appreciate your loyalty to your friends, sire. But in this case it is misplaced. You may not know that Maconnal was expelled from an abbey in Rhondilar before he came to Lochlaund."

"Yes, I know that. But his expulsion was not for heresy; it was because he raised questions the abbot did not want to face."

"What he questioned was the validity of some of the kirk's teachings. And it concerns me greatly that this man now has access to your ear. Not only that, he is tutoring your son, Lanson, who is the heir to your throne. This is most disturbing. As you know, I've objected to Maconnal before, and I now object to him again. He may be the most dangerous man in Lochlaund."

"Hugal, are you trying to rule Lochlaund by dictating my every decision? Already today I have relented and given you the sentence you demanded for the adulterous woman. I will not give you the right to determine my counsel. I will continue to listen to Sir Maconnal just as I will continue to listen to you. But neither you nor he will make my decisions for me." King Kor pushed himself up from his seat and began to pace the room.

Bishop Hugal looked hard at the king and opened his mouth to speak but thought better of it. He would let the matter drop for now. Settling himself comfortably into his chair, he gazed into the fire and the two men began to talk of broader topics as they had done every Tuesday evening for more years than either could count. He valued his close access to the king not only for the prestige it brought him, but for the influence he was able to wield in shaping the policies of the kingdom. He was even on the verge of securing from the king a promise to betroth Prince Lanson to his own niece, Lady Lamonda. In spite of the alarming new direction of the king's thoughts, the bishop saw no need to push the man further tonight. Why risk severing his ties to the throne while the issue of the betrothal was yet unsettled? If he could get his niece on Lochlaund's throne as queen, he would have his yeast in the loaf and his influence over the kingdom would be virtually unlimited.

Hugal eased the tension between them by turning the conversation to the topic he knew was most dear to King Kor's heart—his son, Prince Lanson. At the mention of the young prince, the king relaxed, settling back down into his chair and becoming his old self again. Like a farmer seeding a field, Bishop Hugal often dropped into the conversation glowing accounts of the accomplishments and virtues of his niece Lamonda, ever building in the king's mind a picture of the perfect match between the crown prince and the most virtuous, upright girl in the kingdom.

Before the hour grew too late, the bishop took his leave and returned to his chambers in the abbey at the edge of the city of Macrennon. Long after the departure of his longtime advisor, the king sat in his chair, utterly still, gazing into the flickering flames as the cries of the condemned woman reverberated in the chambers of his mind.

CHAPTER TWO

THE EXECUTION

ronthus watched with arms folded. His eyes, set deep under frowning brows, glared from his gaunt face as guards placed the condemned woman in a two-wheeled cart hitched to a single ox. His lips drew down in revulsion at the sight of the woman's bare skin as the sheet slipped from her shoulder. The guards bound her hands to the front rail of the cart to force her to stand and signaled the driver to begin the short drive to Black Mountain. Gronthus and his two guards got into a horse-drawn carriage that followed the cart bearing the woman. The cart lumbered across the castle drawbridge through the high street of Macrennon. A crier walked in front of the ox calling out for all to hear, "Thus be it done to the immoral, the impure, and those who give themselves to sinful desires. They shall be returned as this woman to their father the devil."

People on the street turned to stare at the condemned woman. A few mothers hustled their young children away like hens shielding chicks from a snake. Others pointed to her and whispered to their daughters, making of the woman an example to frighten all thought of sin from their young lives. Many young men and women, ever eager for a spectacle, fell in behind the wagon, intending to follow it to Black Mountain, where they would gape in fascinated horror at the ghastly means of execution long employed by the Kirk of Lochlaund.

Among those who followed the cart was another young woman,

barely eighteen years of age, with eyes of emerald green, a full head of long hair, deep red as the summer coat of a fox, and a striking womanly form. Her name was Evalonne, the daughter of a wheelwright in Macrennon, though both of her parents were now dead. Unlike the others, she followed the cart neither from morbid curiosity nor for the spectacle of horror. She followed because an inner anxiety compelled her—the cause of which she had not yet revealed to any soul.

When the procession reached the edge of the city, Evalonne looked ahead and saw Black Mountain looming above the green fields and slopes of the countryside, stark and bare against the sky. Although Lochlaund was a country of high green mountains and lush valleys, Black Mountain, less than two miles from Macrennon, was the dominant feature of the landscape visible from the city. It commanded attention not merely because of its height but because of its ominous aspect—a craggy mound of slate-colored stone, cracked and fissured, upon which no greenery would grow. Today a dark shroud of heavy clouds obscured its peak.

Though Evalonne had lived in Macrennon her entire life, and the mountain was as much a part of her everyday experience as her own hand, today she shuddered as she gazed at it and instinctively clutched the pendant hanging at her breast. The pendant was of silver, an elegant dove, exquisitely carved. It had been given to Evalonne by her late mother on the day Evalonne had first committed herself to obey the will of the Master of the Universe. *"The dove is a symbol of purity,"* her mother had said as she lovingly placed the delicate chain bearing the pendant around her daughter's neck. *"May this dove lie forever upon your own heart and be a true reflection of your Master's presence within."* Evalonne's eyes moistened and a wave of panic surged through her as she remembered her mother's words.

As the procession approached the mountain, Evalonne looked up to see three or four winged creatures, black and huge, which she knew to be the giant bats that hovered about the area.

"Have you heard any of the legends of the Devil's Mouth?" Evalonne started at the question and turned toward the source of it, a young man little older than herself. He had sidled over to walk beside her and now gaped at her like a hungry dog at a piece of meat.

"I've heard enough of them," she replied and turned away. Many stories about Black Mountain, the source of which had long been lost, had been passed down through countless generations. Evalonne was in no mood to hear the tales again, nor did she want the company of this gawking young man, or any man. But he was not so easily deterred.

"The best legend says that in ancient times, long before the history of man, the Master of the Universe bound the devil deep within the fiery core of the earth after the great war in heaven. The fallen angel bellowed and fumed in his flaming prison, causing great upheavals far above on the surface of the earth. Hundreds of centuries later the peak of Black Mountain burst open and became a fountain of fire, spewing the anger of the devil from its hollow cone. Ever searching for a way of escape, the evil one saw in the opening the very opportunity he had been awaiting."

The boy was a good storyteller, and though Evalonne kept her head forward as they walked on, she could not help but listen to him and secretly hoped he would continue.

"Borne from the bowels of the earth on streams of molten rock and liquid flame, the evil one was vomited into a valley on the mountain's west side. Immediately he immersed himself in Loch Lorithan, the lake with no bottom at the far end of the valley. It took a year and a day for the cooling waters to quench the fire in him, and after he stepped onto the shore, he turned and looked into the mirror of the water and saw himself for the first time since his banishment from heaven. He stood for a day and a night in utter shock, then covered his face with his hands, and from his throat arose a groan that shook the mountains. Eons in the fiery prison had left him horribly scarred. His face, once beautiful above those of all the Master's creatures, was now a nightmarish horror that even his own eye could not bear to look upon. His hands, once strong and well formed with skin like velvet, were now twisted, misshapen claws."

Evalonne ventured a sidelong glance at the man and found that he was gazing at her unabashedly as he told his story.

"Burning with hate against the Master of the Universe, the devil left the lake and sat himself down on the slopes of Black Mountain.

He sat for another year and a day, never moving, staring into the north, still as stone, his eyes glaring with hate against his oppressor. Having been accustomed to great heat, and burning fiercely inside with plottings of vengeance, he did not notice the residual molten stone as it oozed down the mountainside about him. He never moved as the magma covered him entirely from head to foot, hardening as it cooled, encasing him in a stone shroud. But unlike most who wear shrouds, he was far from dead. When his scheme for revenge was fully formed, he stood from his sitting place and the stone shell burst from about him. All but that which encased his head, which he lifted from his shoulders with his own hand as if removing a helmet and tossed behind him where it settled on a ledge near the base of the mountain.

"The devil marched away from Black Mountain until he encountered a serpent, then legged and winged. He conspired with the serpent to trade bodies, then lifted the creature's great wings and flew south and eastward to the newly created Eden to work his fateful plot. Meanwhile, over eons of time, the empty casing the devil had removed from his head filled with silt and rubble washed down from the mountainside by the rains. This filling hardened into stone, and in time the shell itself crumbled away, leaving a hideous casting of the image of the devil's head. Look, even now you can see the devil's breath."

Evalonne looked to where the young man pointed and saw the cloud of silver steam billowing from a source just out of sight around a bend in the road. "Thank you for your story," she said as she increased her stride to remove herself from the boy and get alone with her own thoughts.

"Wait, there's more," he called after her. But she did not look back, and turning up his palms in a silent gesture of defeat, he did not pursue.

As the cart with its train of followers rounded the bend of the road to the north side of the mountain, all could see the image of the fabled stone. It protruded above an outcropping perhaps a hundred feet up the craggy slope of the mountain, roughly rounded to resemble the shape of a ghastly human skull. Two deep holes of similar size, more or less circular in shape and set side by side, gave to the skull the appearance of eye sockets. One of these eyes was obviously only a shallow indention in the stone, for one could see the rocky surface of the back of it. The other was black and deep, penetrating into the depths of the mountain itself. As she looked, one of the huge bats flew from the eye, and with little movement of its great wings, circled above the approaching procession. A jagged, horizontal opening to a cave roughly forty feet wide and eighteen feet high formed the mouth of the face—the infamous Devil's Mouth. A cloud of steam, which often could be seen from the edge of the city, billowed in a continual but uneven stream from the mouth—"the devil's breath," according to the legend.

Again Evalonne shuddered and wondered if she could go on. Would she be able to watch what would happen when the procession reached the stone skull? *I must do it,* she thought and continued to follow the cart bearing the condemned woman.

On reaching the north side of the mountain, the cart left the main road to follow the sloping trail that angled back and forth up the outcropping toward the skull formation. The followers could now hear the hiss of the billowing steam. As they began to climb, Evalonne looked up at the stone skull, its dreadful face now looming above the advancing party. She blanched at the sight and turned quickly away. She had never been so close to the hideous formation, and the sheer size of it was overwhelming. The dark mouth gaped huge and wide, the irregular stones along the lower lip looking like enormous teeth. Three or four erratic streams of greenish wetness issued from between the teeth and ran down the ledge that formed the skull's chin, giving the face the look of a drooling monster. Evalonne stared at the enormous face, vile and foreboding, and could not help thinking it must possess some sort of evil sentience.

She wondered what must be consuming the poor girl's thoughts as they approached the awful mouth. The prisoner swayed to the uneven lurching of the cart, her head bowed in shame—or grief or fear. Or likely all three.

The cart reached the ledge just below the mouth and came to a halt. Gronthus, with his two guards, stepped down from their carriage. As the accorder lit a torch, the guards untied the condemned woman's hands and, each taking one of her arms, dragged her stumbling to the steps that led up to the black cave. Evalonne's heart came into her throat. She felt all the fear the woman showed as the convicted adulteress wailed in terror and pulled back against the guards, who forced her up the stone steps and into the mouth. Gronthus stood waiting with the torch held aloft, his face hidden in the black shadow of his cowl, giving him the look of death itself.

The woman peered into the cave, and her eyes widened in terror as she saw the black pit gaping in the floor of it—the throat of the Devil's Mouth. The hole was a jagged, funnel-like fissure in the stone floor, roughly round, steam rushing from it with a moan like that of souls cast into outer darkness. The roof of the cave was damp from the perpetual bathing of the steam and the floor about the pit puddled with scum-covered pools.

According to the legends, the throat of the Devil's Mouth was the entrance to an underground maze of complex caves and passages, at the center of which lived the Dark One himself. Many a condemned violator of the kirk's laws had been fed into the Devil's Mouth in the generations since the kirk had invoked the punishment, but none had ever returned. Evalonne wondered what really happened to the victims. Were they killed instantly by the fall? Or did they plunge downward until the tunnel narrowed, wedging them in until they starved? Perhaps they were merely injured by the fall and died slowly in pain. Or maybe the legends were true, and they wandered in a subterranean maze until they reached the Evil One, who devoured them.

However, according to the legends, return was possible. They said that if one were wrongly accused, guardians sent from the Master of the Universe would meet the victim deep inside the maze and lead him out of it. The cave was said to be filled with countless passageways, tunnels, and stairways, some leading nowhere, others leading to unimaginable horrors, but only one leading to escape through the right eye of the devil's skull. Anyone cast into the Devil's Mouth who later emerged from this eye was to be deemed innocent and freed from the penalty of law.

Because of this theoretical possibility of return, a ritual vigil of one night followed every feeding of the Devil's Mouth. The vigil watchers were usually relatives and friends of the condemned, who gathered on the ledge beneath the mouth and watched for their loved one to emerge from the skull's right eye. The watchers brought ropes and ladders to aid the descent of the survivor from the eye socket to the ledge below. But the ritual was merely one of form, for no one fed to the Devil's Mouth had ever returned. And over the years, vigil watchers had become fewer and the watch less diligent, until the kirk had often found it necessary to conscript watchers, or even pay two or three, simply to maintain the legalistic practice.

Gronthus signaled with a slight tilt of his head, and the two guards pushed the woman toward the pit. "No!" she shrieked. She twisted and strained against their grip as they shoved her to the edge of the steaming fissure. Within the darkness of his cowl, Gronthus grinned at the woman's cries. She was reaping what she had sown. Justice was being served.

"It is wanton pleasure that has brought you to this," he cried out. "Think of that pleasure now as you look into this pit. It has lost its luster, has it not?" But the woman, now screaming and sobbing hysterically while twisting and pulling against the grip of the guards, heard nothing of what he said. The sheet had slipped to the ground, and the woman stood naked before the pit. Gronthus's grin turned to a scowl of disgust as he looked upon the devil's most insidious snare, the beauty of woman.

"Do your duty," he said to the guards. Ignoring the woman's screams, they grasped her firmly to prevent her now frenzied attempts at escape. They lifted her above the black maw and dropped her into the belching steam. Her piteous scream reverberated across the plain beneath the mountain as she hurtled downward into the pit.

Evalonne clapped her hands to her ears. She could not stand the woman's shriek of terror. She stood wide-eyed and trembling after the sound ceased while the others who had come looked at one another, appalled but fascinated by the horror they had witnessed.

Gronthus stepped to the edge of the skull's mouth and addressed the crowd standing on the ledge below. "Take heed, citizens of Lochlaund. What you have witnessed this evening is the certain fate of all who depart from the way and break the laws of the kirk. Let all beware and walk the narrow path."

As Evalonne listened to the kirkman she grasped the pendant at her neck. Her fingers trembled as they traced the elegant shape of the silver dove. The people began to leave the ledge, but she stood silent for a moment longer, still feeling all the terror and panic of the woman's cries as if they were her own. She felt her fear and guilt as well, for she knew that what she had just witnessed could easily become her own fate.

Evalonne was with child, and she was not married.

CHAPTER THREE

THE MINSTREL

hen Evalonne's trouble started, it did not seem like trouble at all. Indeed, her life had blossomed bright and beautiful as a summer rose.

The only child of a successful wheelwright in the city of Macrennon, Evalonne grew up happy and loved. No stone or shadow had marred her smooth, sunlit path until just under a year earlier when her parents had both died within the same day, the victims of a riding accident. The loss left Evalonne bereft but not penniless. Her father had set aside a sizable dowry to ensure his daughter a good marriage to some diligent tradesman. In fact, he had already chosen the young man and shortly before his death had begun negotiations with the boy's father. But as Evalonne's parents returned late at night from the dinner at which the betrothal was discussed, some movement in the darkness spooked their horse. The frightened animal galloped headlong off the bridge that spanned the Crynne River, then swollen from spring floods, and the couple drowned in the rushing water.

As it turned out, the young man's father had also been negotiating for the daughter of another tradesman, playing one offer against the other to get the best dowry. When Evalonne's parents died, the boy's father immediately contracted with the father of the other woman, who wed his son a fortnight later.

Soon after the death of her parents, Evalonne sold her father's shop to Corandon, a wheelwright from the village of Kranthar in southern Lochlaund, who wanted to set up for business in the more populous city of Macrennon. Corandon offered a fair price for the adjacent cottage in which Evalonne's family had lived, but she chose not to sell. The house gave her a sense of stability, which she sorely needed at the time. Her parents, who had moved to Lochlaund from Rhondilar, had no known kinsmen, so Evalonne was left alone except for her friend Lograine, a young woman of her own age whom she had known since childhood.

For several days after the death of her parents, Evalonne did nothing but stay in the cottage mourning their loss. Lograine visited often to comfort her and urged her to attend the rare village dances and minstrel performances, but Evalonne did not yet have the heart for it. However, as time passed, the weight of her grief diminished and she began to venture out with her friend, though more to look for work than for entertainment. She wanted to earn enough money to sustain herself in food and clothing so she could leave intact the dowry her father had left her.

Evalonne's mother had taught her to bake pastries, and she had become very good at it—good enough that she soon found work at a baker's shop within a ten-minute walk from her cottage. The recent wedding of the baker's daughter had left an opening in the shop. Evalonne applied herself diligently to her work and was content.

At least, for a while.

Near the end of a day in early spring, a year after her parents' passing, when Evalonne was cleaning and putting away her spoons and pans, the sound of cheering and applause welled into the shop from the public square outside the front window. Spring had made her somehow restless this year, for the bleakness that had settled on her like morning fog after her parents' death had finally lifted, and the desire to enter the flow of life was strong in her. She removed her apron, splashed water on her hands and face, and went out to see the cause of the cheering.

Men and women clustered like swarming bees around something on the square that was hidden by the press of the crowd. From the center of the cluster arose a masculine tenor voice, rich and vibrant like the sound of an archangel, she thought, filling the evening air with a melody of spring. Perhaps it was her vulnerability after her long drought of joy, or perhaps it was because it was spring, or because she was young and the fire of life was coursing through her veins. Whatever the reason, she stopped and listened, transfixed by the magical sound. Then, drawn like a butterfly to a blossom, she made her way forward through the crowd and gazed upon the source of the heavenly music—a minstrel, tall, young, and blond with eyes sparkling like sunlight on a blue sea. She stared entranced as he strummed his mandolin and sang:

> *The maiden's winter was long and cold,*
> *And no man warmed her lonely nights,*
> *But spring bloomed fair and one grew bold,*
> *To woo the maid to love's delights.*
> *His lips oozed words of endless love,*
> *And won her soul and mind and heart,*
> *He swore by heaven's throne above,*
> *And vowed he'd never from her part.*
> *They laughed and loved the summer long,*
> *And through the days of harvest red,*
> *Until a new maid came along,*
> *And turned her lover's fickle head.*
> *She tried to keep him with her charms,*
> *But love had flown her fragile hold,*
> *He left her grieved with empty arms,*
> *To face the winter long and cold.*

When the song ended the minstrel smiled broadly and bowed to his cheering audience. Evalonne had never seen teeth so white and even. He tightened the strings on his mandolin, putting his ear close as he plucked them until satisfied. He sang six or seven more songs then sat and told the gathered crowd the great love story of Aradon and Volanna of Meridan. Evalonne knew the story vaguely, but she had never heard it as this man told it, spinning with fine words and expressive gestures the high romance of the princess and the blacksmith whose love was doomed by their own honor until heaven gave them what they would not take for themselves. Evalonne listened transfixed, giving her heart wholly to the young heroine of the story and clasping her hands with joy as the princess and her blacksmith-become-king were finally wed.

The minstrel sang a final song. Then he smiled, bowed to the crowd, and held out his hat to be filled with coins as the men and women dispersed. Evalonne did not notice the hat; her eyes were transfixed by the tumble of blond waves that sprang free as it was removed. The young man's eyes flickered about the crowd, his white teeth glistening in a broad smile as he continually nodded and mur-mured his thanks to the many who dropped coins into his hat. His eyes fell on Evalonne and locked with hers for a moment before she blushed, looked away, and turned to go. But the minstrel quickly poured his coins into his pouch and followed her into the crowd, keeping her red hair in his sight until he caught up with her.

"Good maiden, could I have a word with you?" he called. Evalonne's heart leapt as she heard his voice behind her, whether in fear or hope she could not tell. But unsure that he was addressing her, she neither turned nor stopped.

"You—you with the hair like the setting sun; why do you run from me? Stop for a moment, I pray you."

Evalonne stopped and turned, and the sparkling smile of the young man at such close range made her knees tremble. "I hope you will not think me untoward," he said as he removed his green hat, "but I could not help but notice your deep attention as you listened to my story. I've not been telling it long, and I thought it might have been a bit rough."

"I have never heard anything more beautiful," replied Evalonne.

"I thank you for that," he said, charming her yet again with his smile. "But it's hard for me to tell just how the story is being received. I need to hear it through another's ears. Forgive me if I seem to im-pose, but perhaps you would be willing to dine with me this evening and give me a few pointers on how to improve it."

Evalonne blushed with pleasure at the young man's invitation, yet she felt she should refuse it. She knew her father, a devout mem-ber of the Kirk of Lochlaund, would never have approved of her attentions to a minstrel or to any man who so appealed to her senses. And this man did appeal to her senses. Already captivated by his voice and songs and smile, she now found herself unnerved by his attention and fumbled for an answer. In her hesitation, he simply took her hand and said, "Come on." Grateful that he had taken the decision out of her hands, she followed willingly enough as he led her down the street through the lanes of vendors, many of them now beginning to take down their stalls as the streets darkened.

They walked until they came to the booth of a fowler who made it his habit to remain open as long as people were leaving their shops. The minstrel bought a roasted hen, a loaf of bread, and a jug of ale. The two of them sat at a street-side table in the vendor's area, already lit by torches against the coming night. The minstrel drew a cloth from his knapsack and spread it on the table. He took his knife and sliced the hen into several pieces, placing two or three in front of Evalonne.

"Go ahead and eat," he said when she made no move to take the pieces.

She blushed and smiled. "I feel strange dining with a man I met just moments ago and whose name I do not even know."

"Of course," he laughed. "Forgive me for not introducing myself. I am Avriel of Sorendale. And who might you be?"

"I am Evalonne of Macrennon," she replied.

"Evalonne," repeated Avriel, caressing the name with his velvet voice. "It is a beautiful name, and thus fitting to the one who wears it." Evalonne glowed at the compliment. "And what do you do in Macrennon?" he asked.

"I work with the baker whose shop is on the square," she replied.

"Have you lived here long?"

"I have never lived anywhere but Macrennon, nor traveled more than twenty miles from it. It must be wonderful to journey about the Seven Kingdoms and see their wonders."

"Indeed it is," said Avriel. "I have seen Braegan Wood, the swamps of Maldor, the harbors of Vensaur, and the silver mines of Valomar, crossed the Dragontooth Mountains many times, and even performed in the great hall of Morningstone Castle for the new King Aradon of Meridan and his queen Volanna."

"Have you?" said Evalonne, her eyes wide in wonder. "Are Aradon and Volanna as beautiful as people say?"

"To be sure. King Aradon has the countenance of a young god, and Queen Volanna is widely acclaimed as the most beautiful woman since Helen of Troy. And when I saw her not more than a fortnight ago, I heartily endorsed that assessment. Looking on her beauty leads one to understand the thought behind the ancient myths of strong men being weakened or blinded or turned to stone by the beauty of goddesses. But now as I look into your eyes, green as a sun-lit meadow and framed by the glistening flame of your hair, I think Meridan's queen may have met her match." Evalonne blushed deeply and continued to listen enraptured as the minstrel filled her ears with tales of his travels and the courts, battles, and kings and queens he had seen.

While they talked and laughed, or rather Avriel talked and Evalonne laughed—as she had not laughed in many months—the tall, angular frame of Gronthus walked slowly down the street. As he passed the laughing couple, he eyed Evalonne with cold sternness. She saw his eyes drop to the dove pendant on her neck, and her fingers went to it involuntarily. Was he questioning whether this symbol of her commitment reflected the truth of her life? Though simply dining with the minstrel was not in violation of any precept of the kirk, she felt uneasy about his seeing her with him. Evalonne became subdued for a time, but Avriel took no notice, and soon after Gronthus had passed, the stories of his travels had her talking and laughing freely again.

"The tale of your life is wonderful," she said.

"Indeed my life is wonderful. I am a dandelion seed riding the wind, drifting who knows where to plant a little happiness and bring a little joy into lives that know too little of either."

"But don't you ever tire of always traveling from one town to another with no home of your own? Don't you ever long for a place where you can feel rooted?"

Avriel sighed. The smile left his face and his eyes took on a far-away look. "Yes, I do feel that longing. Often. But what would be the point of a home without one to share it with?"

"Someday you may meet such a person."

"Someday I may," he said, looking soberly into her eyes until she dropped them and blushed yet again.

Evalonne hated for the night to end, but darkness had fallen two hours ago, and she told Avriel that she must go home. He insisted on escorting her to her cottage. They walked slowly, Avriel still spinning tales of his travels as Evalonne laughed and listened in rapt attention.

They arrived at the cottage, and as she unlocked the door Avriel said, "I am engaged to sing tomorrow night at the dinner of the tradesmen's guild. Perhaps you would accompany me."

"I would be most pleased," she replied, no longer hesitant.

Avriel bowed deeply and pressed his lips to the back of her hand. Then with a final smile, he turned and left. He walked down the road whistling the tune of the abandoned lover, and Evalonne watched until he disappeared into the night. She closed the door and lit a candle, aware of the exquisite burning that lingered on her hand from the touch of his lips. The warmth remained as she undressed and slipped into bed, soon to dream of the golden-haired minstrel with the voice of an angel and eyes like the sea.

On the following evening Evalonne sat at a table with Avriel at the Macrennon tradesmen's dinner. She wore her best skirt and bodice, and her face glowed with a radiance that turned the head of every man in the hall. As on the night before, she lost herself in Avriel's easy conversation and bright smile. And when it came time for him to sing and play as the guests dined, she found herself utterly transfixed by his mellow voice soaring among the rafters of the hall, weaving in and out of the chords of the mandolin like a hummingbird among blossoms.

Afterward he escorted her to her home, and once more his stories of love and laughter added magic to their path. They arrived at her cottage, and instead of the kiss on the hand she had hoped for, he took her in his arms and kissed her full upon the lips. She resisted briefly, then yielded to the ecstasy of his embrace as her own arms found their way around his neck.

"May I see you again tomorrow?" asked Avriel, his arms still about her waist.

Too breathless to speak, Evalonne smiled at him and nodded as she regained her composure. He began to draw her to him again, but now unable to trust her own will, she gently removed his hands and placed a warm kiss upon his cheek. "Until tomorrow," she said, smiling as she opened the door, slipped inside, and closed it against the unbearable thrill of his gaze.

That night the young minstrel with the voice like honey again filled all her nighttime dreams. And the next day as she walked to the baker's shop, she felt so light on her feet that she almost skipped the whole way. At work as she kneaded the dough on the board before her, she found herself singing the songs she had heard him sing while visions of his golden hair and manly form danced in her mind. As the day approached its end she looked often at the sun, dropping so slowly into the trees she thought it must have got tangled in their limbs. But evening came and she removed her apron, combed her hair, freshened her face, and went out into the square, where a crowd had already gathered around the minstrel. Again she listened, freshly entranced. She found herself humming along with his songs and clapping her hands with the rest of the listeners at the rhythms of his mandolin. Afterward they dined again at the booth of the fowler, and she opened her own life to him. She told him of her happy childhood and her devastation at the death of her parents, and how desolate her life had been in the lonely cottage until he came along.

The next evening followed the same pattern, as did the next. Then came the wonderful night when after they had dined, Avriel took Evalonne for a stroll on the moonlit road at the edge of the town. They ambled along, chatting happily until they came to the spring of Moralane. He led her to a stone at the edge of the pool, where they sat together, his arm about her waist and her head against his shoulder as they pitched pebbles into the pool and watched the ripples expand and fade in the sparkling moonlight. For a time neither spoke, listening to the croaking of the frogs and the chirruping of the crickets as Evalonne glowed in the warmth of his closeness.

"Evalonne," he said, his voice low and sweet. "I have something to tell you." He paused and drew a deep breath. "I love you, Evalonne. I have known many women in my travels, and many have cast their eyes at me. But none has ever captured my heart as you have. I love you and I want to wed you."

Tears of happiness welled up in Evalonne's eyes, and she could not speak.

"I know you have no dowry," Avriel continued, "but it does not matter. I cannot imagine my future without you. We don't need money, really. I have heard you sing, and you have a wonderful voice. I could teach you my songs and we could travel together as minstrels. I know it is much to ask of a woman but—"

"But we will not need to live as minstrels," said Evalonne. "I do have a dowry, and I have my parents' cottage. My father left enough that we can live until you find work here in Macrennon."

"You have a dowry? I would never have guessed it. Why do you work at the baker's?"

"I did not want to lose what my father had saved for my marriage."

"That is wonderful, and it will indeed mean that we can live a settled life. Wandering about the Seven Kingdoms is really no life for a woman. I think I can see the hand of the Master of the Universe in our union."

"I think so too. But if I had no money and no cottage, be assured I would have followed anywhere you chose to take me. Home for me will always be where you are."

After sealing their commitment with a deep kiss and warm embrace, they walked back toward the village, first hand in hand, then arm in arm, watching their single shadow reach ahead of them in the moonlight and stopping often for more of such embraces and kisses, each deeper and warmer than the one before. When they reached the cottage, Evalonne's face was flushed, her blood pulsing through her body. Once again Avriel wrapped her close in his arms and kissed her long and hotly.

Evalonne tried to pull away. "I must go in now."

But Avriel did not release her. "Let me come in with you."

Evalonne felt a surge of fear as the stern face of Gronthus flashed across her mind. But after more kisses and more intimate caresses, the kirkman's face faded away and she realized that she wanted Avriel to come into her house. Her conscience made one last effort to warn her of the danger, but its voice was now so weak and distant that she found it easy to shut out, leaving no other voice but the pulsing call of her own desire. *You are as good as married anyway,* the voice whispered. *You have vowed to wed; what does it matter if yielding to him comes before or after the words of commitment?*

Shutting the door to her conscience, she opened the door to her cottage and led Avriel to her bed. He did not leave until shortly before dawn.

On the next evening Evalonne joined Avriel near sundown on the square, where he was singing as usual to the gathered crowd. As she watched and listened, she felt a warmer, closer bond with him than she had known before. The longing to touch him and hold him was strong in her, as if, in some sense she could not articulate, her body had found in him its own completion. *This must be what it means to become one with a man,* she thought and wondered why the Master of the Universe frowned upon such bliss.

Avriel finished his songs and stories, and again his upturned hat grew heavy with coins from the appreciative audience. As the crowd dispersed he came smiling toward her, and she thought heaven had descended and enveloped her with its splendor. They strolled toward the fowler's booth, laughing happily until again Evalonne saw the gray-robed form of Gronthus approaching, his cold eyes boring into her soul like shards of ice. She shuddered, clutching the dove at her breast. Did he know their secret? Of course not. There was no way he could know. But perhaps he did know. Perhaps he could read something in her face that told her story like a book. She knew she felt different; perhaps that difference showed in some way that such men could see. But Gronthus passed them by and Evalonne breathed again.

"What is wrong, Evalonne?" asked Avriel.

"Oh, uh, nothing really," she replied. "I . . . I just felt a little chill."

"I can be your remedy for that," he said as he reached to put his arm about her.

"No, not now," she said, moving away and turning to see if Gronthus was looking. But she did not see him, and they made their way to the fowler.

"Listen, Evalonne, I have an idea," said Avriel as they sat to eat at the vendor's table.

"When I was in Sorendale a month ago I saw a wonderful little farm. It was for sale. The farmer is getting old, his wife is gone, and he wants to move in with his son in the town. The farm has a cottage much like yours but nestled in a grove of shade oaks. The barn is almost new, and a stream runs between it and the cottage. A plank bridge crosses the stream into a small wooded area where I saw abundant hare, squirrel, and partridge. It has three fields of good soil, and the man will sell his oxen with it."

"It sounds perfect for us," said Evalonne. She could picture herself baking at the hearth in the morning, weeding the garden and feeding the animals by day, and sewing and mending by the fire in the evening as Avriel sat and sang to her.

"It is perfect for us. I just met a friend who was in Sorendale ten days ago, and he told me the farm is yet for sale. The problem is that your dowry will pay only half the price the farmer is asking."

"Won't he take less?"

"I'm sure he will, but not that much less. However, I have an idea. Since we will not need your cottage here in Macrennon, you could sell it to Corandon. The proceeds would bring our total close enough to his asking price that I'm sure he would take it. What do you think?"

A stab of panic shot through Evalonne at the thought of giving up the last link with her old life and moving to a country she had never even seen. But she was on the threshold of a new life, and no ties from the old should hold her back. It would be foolish to let the farm slip away because she would not let go of a memory.

"Yes, of course I will sell the cottage," she answered. "Corandon will buy it in a moment. I will offer it to him tomorrow."

"Excellent! I will take the money and go immediately to Sorendale, purchase the farm, and return to you in a month. Then we will wed, pack up your things, and be off to our new life."

Evalonne agreed to the plan, and on the next day she sold her cottage to Corandon and gave the proceeds to Avriel, along with a small oaken box reinforced with iron that contained her dowry. After many kisses and caresses and promises for a quick return, Avriel left that same day for Sorendale.

CHAPTER FOUR

A CHANGE OF FORTUNE

he wheelwright Corandon bought the furnishings in Evalonne's cottage as well as the cottage itself, sparing her the difficulty of storage and carting them to Sorendale. Evalonne packed her clothing, quilts, blankets, and some kitchenware into a single trunk and sent it to the cottage of her friend Lograine. Lograine's father had been dead for many years, and she lived with her mother, who was happy to have Evalonne with them.

On the first day of the week all shops and marts in Lochlaund closed their doors or suffered a sizable fine for flouting the law of Sabbath. Evalonne sat on a stool in Lograine's cottage, her elbows on her knees and her chin in her hands as she gazed out the window. But she saw nothing of the few people out strolling or the rare carriage that rolled down the lane. Her thoughts had taken her to Sorendale and into the picture of the little farm that Avriel had painted in her mind. She saw the daub-and-wattle cottage as clearly as if she were there—a trim, sturdy little house with whitewashed walls and roofed with fresh golden thatching, snuggled in a nest of sturdy oaks with their green leaves rustling in the breeze. She imagined herself at that cottage window, looking out over fields of rich amber grain, rippling like a banner as the breeze caressed the ripened heads. The brook wound its way just past the barn between the fields and the yard where the chickens and geese, clucking and honking, scratched and pecked at worms and bugs hidden in the green grass. In her mind's eye a call from the edge of the woods on the far side of the stream turned her attention to yet another golden-topped image to match the grain and the thatch of the roof in this Eden of hers. Avriel, his glistening locks lifting in the breeze, was walking across the bridge holding up two grouse he had killed with his bow. He ran to her, pitched the birds on the table, and swept her into his arms . . .

Evalonne sighed.

"Evalonne, where are you?" Lograine's voice intruded on her idyll.

"I was in Eden," she replied with yet another sigh.

"Oh, Evalonne, I hope it is Eden. But you have seen this place only in your dreams. You know of it only what your minstrel has told you. What if the fields are filled with stone and the cottage a broken-down shack? Or worse, what if it is all a fantasy of his own creation?"

"Why must you always look for the worst?" said Evalonne. "You've done all you could to smother our plans with a cloud of gloom ever since you heard of them."

"I'm only trying to get you to look at reality instead of living in this dream weaver's fantasy world. Yes, I am afraid for you. I've told you before, you let all this happen too fast. This wandering minstrel from who knows where sweeps into town, sings a few songs, and tells a few stories that weave you into his spell. In little more than a fortnight he has promised you the moon, talked you out of your dowry and your home, and now has left on a promise to return and carry you into Eden. Yes, I am afraid for you, Evalonne, very afraid."

"That is because you don't know Avriel."

"I don't know Avriel, but I do know minstrels."

"You can't throw all minstrels into the same pot. Each person must be judged on his own merits, not on those of his class."

"The very fact that he has chosen to be a minstrel tells me much about him. He is in the frivolous business of entertainment. You know what the kirk says about love songs, poetry, and pretty stories— they are sirens that lure us away from commitment to the Master. I'm surprised that an upstanding girl such as you would fall for a man in such a trade."

"Do you sometimes wonder if the kirk is right about songs and stories and the love of a man and a woman? There is so much joy in them it's hard to think them all evil."

"Evalonne! How can you say such a thing? You know it would be a slap in the Master's face to live a life of joy after the sacrifice he made for us. We should live in perpetual mourning and shame for the agony he endured."

"But he made everything, which means all beauty comes from his hand. And it cries for us to respond with joy and laughter and love. Doesn't it seem strange that he would create such beauty and joy, then deny us the experience of it?"

"Surely you don't need me to answer that. It's basic to all the kirk teaches. Beauty is a lure to test our love for the Master. To find joy in it is to succumb to its enticement."

Once more Evalonne felt a stab of guilt pierce her heart as the shadow of Gronthus's glare darkened her mind. It was true. The lure of beauty had quickened her desire, causing her to seek her own happiness and turn her back on the Master. "You are right, of course," she muttered and turned again to the window. It was easy for Lograine to adhere to the doctrines of the kirk; the kind of joy that had invaded Evalonne's life had never knocked on her friend's door. She would argue differently if her heart had ever soared as Evalonne's did now. As to her friend's warnings against joy, they had little effect. Lifted as she was by her dreams, Evalonne could no more keep joy from her heart than a mountain could keep sunlight from its peak.

Her routines settled into a rhythmic pattern as she counted the days until Avriel's return. She arose shortly after sunup, breakfasted with Lograine and her mother, then walked to the bakery. As her hands mixed the batter and kneaded the dough, her mind roamed the fields of her farm in Sorendale. In the evenings she dined with Lograine and her mother, helped with the chores, and slipped into bed to dream that she was wrapped in the arms of her singing angel. Often she wondered how Avriel was faring. She never fell asleep without first uttering a heartfelt prayer that the Master would guard him and keep him safe for her.

Thus the days passed, and on the evening before Avriel was to return, Evalonne could hardly sleep. She tossed and turned through the night and awoke long before the rooster outside her window called the daylight to the horizon. She lay in her bed until the gray of dawn diluted the darkness in the room, then quietly arose and donned her best dress, moving about silently to avoid awakening her hosts. She spent more time than usual combing out her hair and tied it with a ribbon the color of her eyes. She cooked breakfast for Lograine and her mother and, after eating, walked to the baker's shop with her heart soaring in anticipation.

As she worked she looked out the window often, hoping to catch sight of her lover approaching. He did not come during the day, but when her work was ended she hurriedly threw aside her apron and ran out to the square, searching everywhere for his golden head among the crowd. She roamed the square until sunset, then walked home with a heavier tread. Exhausted from her long day after a sleepless night, Evalonne spoke little at dinner and went to her bed shortly after. She was disappointed that Avriel had not come, but she convinced herself not to be alarmed. She knew it was impossible to predict the exact day one would return from a journey of such length.

On the next day she again dressed her best and watched the door of the bakery with even greater expectation. Surely he would come today. But again she went to bed disappointed. On the third day she watched not merely with hope but with a touch of apprehension as well. A tiny seed of panic had lodged in her mind and sprouted tentacles into the rest of her body, tensing her muscles and throwing her a little out of rhythm as she went about her work. She stumbled once on the uneven floor, spilling half the flour from the crock she carried. Later a bowl slipped from her hands and shattered on the floor. The baker's wife glared at her but said nothing, as Evalonne was a good worker and the shop's business had increased by a quarter since customers had discovered her blueberry pies.

On the fourth day her sense of panic doubled. Her fingers trembled and she had moments when tears welled up unbidden. *Why doesn't he come?* she wondered as she looked out the window for the twentieth time. It was early afternoon before she dared to look out again. But when she did, her heart stopped, her eyes grew wide, and her hands clapped to her mouth to keep from squealing with joy. There was Avriel walking onto the square, his mandolin strung across his back and his blond hair waving from beneath his green cap with its point flopping about his left ear. His back was to her as he looked about the crowd. *He's looking for me!* she thought. Heedless of the time, she flung her apron aside and ran from the shop, oblivious to the glare of the baker's wife. She stopped at the edge of the square and scanned it to see where Avriel had gone. She spotted him walking away toward the far side of it.

"Avriel!" she cried as she picked up her skirt and ran after him. "Avriel!" He did not turn but kept walking. "Avriel, here I am," she said as she came up behind him. He stopped and turned. Her jaw dropped, her hands went to her cheeks, and her smile disappeared. He was not Avriel. "Oh, I'm sorry," she said. "I . . . I thought you were someone else."

He touched his hat and smiled. "No, I am not someone else. But then neither are you. We both are simply us, aren't we? And that being the case, since someone else is not here, I see no reason why I can't buy you a mug of ale."

"Oh, no. I'm sorry. I must find the man I was looking for."

"Too bad," sighed the stranger as he turned to continue on his way. Evalonne trudged back to the shop, wiping her eyes and biting her lip to keep from sobbing.

"What could have happened to him?" wondered Evalonne that evening at dinner.

Lograine reached over and gently touched her arm. "He could have been delayed in Sorendale," she said.

Evalonne looked up at her friend, whose face reflected a concern she was not voicing, and panicked. "I'm afraid something has gone wrong, Lograine. He could have been hurt or robbed or even killed." Her voice trembled as she spoke.

"Oh, there's no need to think the worst. Perhaps the farmer would not accept Avriel's offer."

Evalonne nodded hopefully and replied, "Yes, that could be it." Then another worry assailed her. "But wouldn't he have returned to tell me?"

"He might have done any number of things. He could have gone looking for another farm or he could have—"

"He could have sung several nights in Sorendale villages to raise the additional money he needed," Evalonne said.

"Yes, of course, he could have done that," Lograine agreed, though her voice conveyed no conviction that she thought it likely.

That night it was long before Evalonne closed her eyes. When she did sleep, it was fitfully, and she awoke often to find her pillow damp with tears.

When a week had passed and Avriel still had not returned, Lograine began to make inquiries in the town. She learned from a friend in the tradesmen's guild that Avriel had asked a number of questions about Evalonne the very day after he met her. He had learned of her dowry and her ownership of the cottage from the wheelwright Corandon, who was disgruntled at her refusal to sell. When Lograine told Evalonne what she had heard, the poor girl was stunned. Avriel had seemed genuinely surprised when she told him of her dowry on the night they agreed to wed. Was it possible that he had deceived her? She went to bed that night burdened with misgivings and doubts and woke often with a cold weight of dread pressing upon her heart. But she convinced herself that even if he did know of her dowry, he had come to love her for herself alone. Her hope was wounded, but she nursed it and fed it like a desperate mother nurturing a sick child, refusing to let it die.

Two nights later Evalonne arrived at Lograine's home to find her friend waiting for her at the table. Her face was grim, and she looked at Evalonne through eyes filled with deep concern and compassion. "Evalonne, sit down. I have very bad news."

Evalonne sat, a feeling of dread gripping her belly like a claw.

Lograine reached across the table and took her friend's hand in both of her own. "Today I saw a minstrel walking toward Macrennon Castle, and I stopped him to ask a few questions. As luck would have it, he knew Avriel and had seen him recently. I am very sorry to tell you this, Evalonne, but Avriel never went to Sorendale."

"He never went to Sorendale? But why? What happened to him? Is he hurt? Where is he?" Evalonne asked, her eyes wide with apprehension.

"When he left here he went straight to Vensaur. He has a woman there, and he is now living with her in a lavish style that would be impossible unless he had come into money."

Evalonne stared in shock as Lograine continued. "The minstrel told me that this kind of thing is typical of Avriel. He has women in half the villages in the Seven Kingdoms. And he has left a trail of broken hearts which he has cast aside like discarded apple cores."

Evalonne could not speak. She now looked into the face of the terrible truth she had kept at bay: Avriel would not return. The dam of her emotions broke and tears flowed in torrents. Lograine sat up with her deep into the night, comforting and soothing her as she tried to come to terms with her loss. For the next three days she was sick with grief and could not stir from her friend's home. Finally she mustered the will to return to the baker's shop, but the bloom had faded from her cheeks and the smile from her lips. The sunlight that had bathed her life in joy now shone bleak and pallid. She went through the motions of work, but nothing seemed worth the effort or had any meaning when it was accomplished. All creation had lost its luster. The magic was gone. The songs of birds were now just noises and the flowers in the field mere blotches of meaningless color. She wondered if life was worth the energy required to live it.

But soon Evalonne found that the loss of her dowry, her cottage, her singing angel, and her Edenic farm were not the worst of her troubles. Within a week she suspected that she was with child, and in another month she was sure of it.

On the evening after this unthinkable discovery she left the shop at the usual time, and as she made her way across the square toward Lograine's cottage, she looked ahead and saw Gronthus approaching. Her heart sank. His unrelenting gaze burned into her, and she instinctively ducked her head, clutched the dove on her chain, and hurried on by. *Why does he look at me that way?* she thought. *Could he possibly know?* No doubt her own sense of guilt read more into the kirkman's glance than he could have intended, she told herself to quell her rising terror. But on the next night Gronthus hovered about the square again, and once more he eyed her as she crossed it and hurried on to Lograine's cottage. When she saw him standing in the same place on the third night, Evalonne feared that his presence on the square each evening at the particular time of her homeward walk was no mere coincidence. Surely he suspected something, and she knew it would be only a matter of time before her own body would expose to him her guilty secret.

Impelled by the cold stare of the accorder, Evalonne half walked, half ran to Lograine's cottage in a panic. She knew her life was not yet in danger, but it soon would be. When her belly began to swell she would not be able to hide her sin from the hawklike eyes of the bishop's nooseman.

"Lograine," Evalonne said as she entered the cottage and closed the door behind her. "Where is your mother?"

"She went to be with her sister tonight. She has been ill, you know. What is wrong? You're as pale as if you had seen a ghost."

"I have a problem. We must talk."

"Of course," replied Lograine. "Sit down and tell me what is wrong."

Evalonne sat at the table across from her friend and looked about the room as if she expected to see the eyes of Gronthus peering at her from the dark corners. "I am in serious trouble, and I don't know what to do about it."

"Tell me what it is. You know I will do whatever I can to help."

"I . . . I am with child," she blurted as she buried her face in her hands and began to sob.

Lograine said nothing for a few moments, then asked, "Are you sure?"

"Yes," Evalonne replied, her voice weak and wavering as she wiped away her tears. "I have known for several days."

Lograine stared hard at her friend before she answered, her voice colder now. "This is serious indeed. Did he force you?"

"No."

"How could you have done this, Evalonne? How could you have let this man have his way with you?"

"We were in love—that is, I was in love and I thought he loved me. We were soon to be wed, and I wanted so much to please him, and I—"

"And you threw aside your honor and sinned against the Master of the Universe." Lograine pushed away from the table and leaned back, her arms folded and a look of scorn in her eyes at this incredible revelation.

Evalonne simply nodded and buried her face in her hands as once again she convulsed in sobs.

"When you begin to swell, Gronthus will arrest you, and you will be thrown into the—" Lograine nearly hissed.

"Don't say it!" cried Evalonne. "Please! I can't stand the thought of it. And Gronthus is eyeing me already. I'm sure he suspects something."

"I'm sure he does. He watched you keeping close company with that minstrel. Why shouldn't he suspect something? You brought this on yourself, you know."

"Yes, I know," Evalonne said meekly, not daring to look at Lograine again.

"Well, you can't keep staying here."

"I know. I can work perhaps a couple more months before my condition is detectable. That will give me time to save a little money for travel. Then I will leave Lochlaund."

"You intend to stay *here* until you begin to show? How can you even think of doing this to my mother and me? When Gronthus realizes we have been harboring you, we will be found guilty as well. If our friendship means anything to you, you must leave now, Evalonne."

"But I have so little money, I could not get—"

"You should have thought of that before you let that bloodsucker into your bed. You can't do this to us. You may stay here tomorrow night, but on the next day, you must find another place to live. I'm sorry, Evalonne, but you did bring it on yourself."

Evalonne was stunned. She had not imagined that her friend would be anything but helpful in her time of desperation, but now she was forcing her out of the house. Though she had no other place to go, she numbly assented. She was now beyond panic. When clinging to the edge of a precipice, one does everything possible to find a handhold. But once the fall begins, there is no further need to grope for safety. The plunge must take its course. She bade Lograine good night and went to her bed.

The next morning she arose long before sunup, gathered from her trunk as much clothing as she could carry, and rolled it tightly inside two blankets. She also packed a fire flint and a wallet full of nuts, bread, and dried meat, leaving coins on the table in payment. The sun was minutes away from rising as she slipped from the house and walked in the gray dawn to the bakery. She looked carefully all around as she approached the square. She did not want Gronthus to see her carrying her pack. He was nowhere about, so she crossed the square and went to the back of the shop, where she hid her bundle behind a stack of firewood. When the bakery opened, she entered and went about her work as usual.

Shortly after noon she heard a clamor outside the shop and went to the door to see the cause of it. An ox-drawn cart was coming down the street bearing no burden other than a woman, chained to the front rail and wearing nothing but a sheet. Evalonne could not see the woman's face, for her head was bent forward and her thick hair hung all about it. Behind the ox cart rolled a carriage bearing the accorder Gronthus, robed and hooded in dark gray, and two guards. Behind the carriage walked a gathering trail of followers.

Evalonne had seen such processions before and knew the meaning of them. The woman had been condemned of some crime of immorality—likely adultery, judging by the sheet—and Gronthus was escorting her to her death at the Devil's Mouth. Without taking her eyes off of the woman, Evalonne removed her apron, left the shop, and joined the procession. She could not have said why she chose to follow the woman to her doom. Horror gripped her at the thought of witnessing this precursor to her own fate, yet she felt drawn to watch it. Perhaps it was the bond of sisterhood she shared with the shamed adulteress, isolated by her guilt on an island barren of compassion. Evalonne understood, and her heart went out to the woman. *She and I are one,* she thought. Though she did not know the woman's name, she would follow and with each step beg the Master of the Universe to show her the mercy she could not find among her fellows in this terrible hour. She joined the procession to the mountain and witnessed the execution, speaking softly to the Master until the guards dropped the screaming woman into the pit.

The sun had set when Evalonne returned to Macrennon. She walked directly to the baker's shop, now closed for the evening, and retrieved her bundle from behind the woodpile. Having nowhere to live and knowing it was foolish to stay in Lochlaund, she began walking in the darkness toward the southern edge of the city. Lochlaund's neighbor nearest to Macrennon was the Kingdom of Valomar. But since the roads to that kingdom were always busy, she thought it safer to take the less traveled route southeast to Oranth. So she headed south, hoping to cross into that kingdom and out of Gronthus's jurisdiction in perhaps five days. She had told no one that she was leaving, for she knew that as one who had violated the moral code, she could trust no one with her intentions. Anyone would feel justified in betraying her to the authorities. This way she could be out of Lochlaund before Gronthus or the constable knew she was gone.

As she walked through the lanes of Macrennon, light from the cottage windows kept her way from being utterly dark, but they also mocked her loneliness, wrapping families and loving couples in a glow of warmth denied to her. When she reached the edge of the city she paused, her heart pounding as she looked out into the darkness. No moon shone tonight, and she found herself daunted by the blackness of the looming hills and mountains of the highlands. Yet she had no choice but to go on. Leaving the light of the city behind, she stepped onto a road she could barely see.

For a while the road wound its way between rolling fields sown with corn and wheat. The first farmhouse she saw, nestled in a grove of trees, brought a stab of pain to her heart. Through the window, glowing orange in the light from the hearth, she could see the outlines of a couple cuddled together on a bench, gazing into the fire. The sight of such domestic bliss stirred the grave of her slain dream and her eyes began to swim with tears. *Why, Avriel, why?*

After a while the farms became fewer as the road began to rise into the hills. It became flanked on each side by a thick forest of trees growing up the steep slopes and looming tall and black against the nighttime sky. With a shudder Evalonne wondered what sort of creatures or felons hid within these darkened woods. Soon she descended a hill, and looking behind her she could no longer see anything of the town. Her fear began to rise. The night was still and quiet. The only sound was the chirping of crickets in the trees, the distant croaking of frogs in some stream, and the scrape of her own shoes upon the road. She felt vulnerable and exposed, as if inviting some feral animal to tear her apart or some roadside thief to rob and ravish her. She had heard tales of such things. In Perivale's day knights had patrolled the roads of the Seven Kingdoms, sweeping them clean of such dangers. But in the hundred or so years since, such patrolling had been abandoned, surrendering the roads to the domain of the wilderness, and no one, especially a woman, dared travel them alone.

But what need have I to be afraid? she thought. What could any highwayman do to her now that really mattered? Two of the three things she could lose had already been taken. Her maidenhood had been breached, and she had no more money to be stolen. All that could be taken from her was her life, and she wondered if it was really worth saving. With no money, no family, no home, no friends, and no one to love her, her existence had become a wasteland in which all joy had withered and died.

Suddenly the cry of a forest animal split the air. Evalonne instinctively ducked and looked wildly about her, but she could see nothing in the darkness. Terror overcame her now that the possibility of death was actually upon her. She wanted desperately to flee, but she dared not run into the woods, and running on the road would be futile. Unable to stand on her quaking knees, she sank to the road and rolled into the thicket beside it. She curled into a tight ball and waited for the sound of paws or hoofs or wings to descend upon her. Although she heard nothing more, she dared not get up. In time sleep overcame her fear.

CHAPTER FIVE

escape

valonne awakened at dawn, cold, stiff, and hungry. In spite of the pain in her back and hips, she stood and walked on until the sun drove the darkness away. The woods were less daunting in the morning light, and she was not so afraid to go into the trees a little way where she sat and ate a breakfast from her pack. She drank from a nearby stream and bathed her face in it before continuing on her journey. Soon, however, she wished she had not eaten. Being with child had unsettled her digestion, and her stomach forced her to stop more than once as it rebelled against the food she had taken.

The hills grew steeper as the morning progressed, and in her weakened condition, following the winding road up their slopes left her panting with exhaustion. She felt better in the afternoon and managed to walk all day, stopping only to rest or hide from other travelers. She feared meeting anyone, as she did not want to arouse suspicion or become a victim. Whenever she heard the beating of distant hooves, she hid among the trees until the traveler passed. But the farther she got from Macrennon, the fewer travelers she met.

The sun was hovering above the treetops in the west when Evalonne began to think about where she would spend the night. She knew little woodlore but instinctively thought she should look for a place on the bank of a stream. She decided to turn from the road at the next brook or river and follow it until she found a protected place to sleep through the night. Thus musing, she did not notice the drumming of hooves in the distance behind her. When she did hear the sound, she spun about and saw galloping toward her a mounted horseman, huge and black bearded, a rusted lance in his fist and a tattered cape flapping behind him. Instantly she scrambled from the road and dashed into the woods. But the man had spotted her. He reined his horse to a halt, leapt from the saddle, and lumbered into the trees after her.

On the verge of panic, Evalonne thrashed and flailed her way through the thick brush into the depths of the forest, heedless of the limbs and briars that snagged her dress and tore her flesh. Not daring to look back, she plunged on until she began to trip and stumble as exhaustion overcame her. Soon she could run no longer and dropped to the earth behind a thick gorse bush. She did her best to curb her wheezing gasps for air and listened for any sound of her pursuer. For a moment she heard nothing but the noises of the forest, and she began to think she had eluded him.

Just when she thought it safe to get up from her hiding place, she heard the rustle and thud of the man's boots and lifted her head to peer through the leaves. He had stopped some forty paces away, and her heart pounded like a fist on a door as he turned all about, looking for any sign of her with fierce eyes glaring from beneath matted straggles of filthy hair. He stooped and picked up several stones the size of plums and began to throw them into the bushes around him. Getting no response out of the first two bushes, he turned toward the one hiding Evalonne and hurled a stone toward it. The rock penetrated the leaves and struck her sharply on her upper arm. She bit her lip to keep from crying out. After tossing stones into the remaining bushes, the man uttered an obscene oath as he slung the last of the stones to the ground and stalked out of the forest.

Evalonne waited until she could no longer hear the clomp of his boots, then rose from her hiding place, trembling with the aftershocks of terror. The narrow escape had brought her to her senses, and she fully realized now that in spite of her despair and the ruin of her life, she wanted to live. She could not bring herself to return to the danger of the road and plodded on through the forest, maintaining her southeasterly direction by keeping the sun to her right.

Nightfall was less than a half-hour away when she came upon a stream crossing her path. She followed it eastward, looking all the while for a safe place to stop for the night. She found a hollow in a vertical bank set back from the stream about ten paces. Using her flint, she built a fire in front of the hollow. She sat down by the blaze and ate another meal from her pack, then curled up in the narrow space, covered herself with a blanket, and tried to sleep. For a while the sounds of the forest kept her awake. She heard a distant howl, which she took to be a wolf, and once she listened with her heart in her throat as some creature rustled the brush at the edge of the stream just out of range of the firelight. But soon exhaustion conquered her fear, and she fell asleep.

When the first light of dawn broke through the trees, Evalonne tried to rise and found her body as hard to move as a stone. Her legs and hips were stiff and sore from their unaccustomed exercise, and she groaned as she stood and grasped the ledge for balance. Her stomach churned as if she had eaten something alive, and soon she lost her dinner from the night before. She heaved several more times, even though she had nothing left to disgorge. She crawled to the stream and drank, then sat panting and sweating beside the trunk of a tree. When she thought she could stand again, she got up, shouldered her pack, and continued on her way.

She began to angle toward the east, hoping to pick up the road again and follow it into Oranth. She reached it at midday but kept to the woods alongside of it to avoid further unwanted encounters. She skirted the village of Morrowton and found another stream south of the town, which she followed until dark. Again she built a fire and slept by the stream, and again she awoke to dreadful nausea the next morning. When the sickness eased somewhat, she struggled to her feet and began to walk, though she plodded more slowly and had to rest more often.

She avoided the village of Furthing and, unable to find a stream before the sun set, camped in a sheltered place among fallen stones at the bottom of a mountain ledge. She checked her pack and found that she had food for only three more days, so she ate nothing that night. Nevertheless, she was sick again the next morning and retched for half an hour, though her stomach had nothing to yield. Much weakened, she forced herself to get up and plod on. Before noon she was hungry, but instead of opening her pack, she ate the red berries from bushes she found growing by the side of the road.

For three more days she walked southward, sometimes in the woods, sometimes on the road. She ate little, partly because of her continuing nausea and partly to conserve her food supply. By late evening on her fifth day, she came to a broad river, which she took to be the Sunderlon, and her heart leapt with the first hope she had felt since leaving Macrennon. When she crossed this river she would be out of Lochlaund and into Oranth—out of peril and into sanctuary. As there was no bridge, she would ford the river where the road met it. But she was hungry, her strength was waning, her feet ached, and she thought it best to stop and eat before she attempted the fording. She sat in the shade of a great oak and rationed herself half the remaining food, leaving enough for one more meal. As she ate the last bite and looked toward the wide river, she did not want to get up and go on. But once more she forced her weary legs to stand, shouldered her pack, and after looking both ways to be sure no one was coming, stepped into the road and walked toward the river.

She waded into the shallows, expecting the water to be no more than waist deep at the center as it was in most fords. Unfortunately, she did not realize that the Sunderlon had been swollen by heavy rains and flowed higher than normal. The water reached her waist before she was a third of the way into it, and she lifted her pack higher to keep it dry. Soon the water was chest-deep, and she carried the pack on top of her head. After a few more steps, she became alarmed. Not only was the water shoulder-deep, the current was swift and strong. She felt it tugging at her dress, causing her feet to slip sideways on the bottom. She managed to keep her balance for a few more steps, but when she stepped off a ledge no more than two or three inches high, the water was just deep enough to increase her buoyancy to where her feet could not find purchase on the bottom. She felt herself swept along, flailing wildly as she lost her balance.

The first thing she thought of was her pack. She righted herself and looked to see it floating downstream, and immediately she plunged forward to swim after it. She made good headway and would have caught up with the pack quickly had not an eddy between two boulders caught it and propelled it far ahead of her again. The current near the boulders flowed so swiftly that Evalonne had to slow herself to keep from being dashed against the stones, and by the time she maneuvered around them, her pack was many yards ahead. But she could not let it get away. It contained everything she owned—clothing, blanket, fire flint, comb, and her little bit of food. She thrashed desperately toward it.

Evalonne became aware of a continuous roar, which she realized she had been hearing dimly ever since coming to the ford, though it was much louder now. It became louder yet as the current bore her swiftly along with bits of bark, twigs, leaves, and small limbs streaming beside her. She looked up and saw her pack, still many yards ahead. It tumbled along for a moment, then suddenly disappeared. *What happened to it?* her mind raced. *Did it sink?* Then with horror she realized the truth: it had plunged over a waterfall—the source of the roar that now thundered in her ears. She tried hard to stop, thrashing backward with her hands and arms, but the current was too strong to resist. She clutched at a passing branch, but it snapped off in her hand. She began to swim desperately toward the near bank, hoping to reach it before she plunged over the falls. Though she put all her strength into each stroke, the current swept her downstream much too fast. She could see that she would not reach the bank. Her only chance was a round stone protruding from the water like the shell of a giant turtle some ten feet from the bank and right at the edge of the waterfall. She redoubled her effort, stroking with all the power she could muster. She clutched at the rock, grasping it for a moment, but the raging water thrust her to the side and her hand began to slip. Just when she thought she would be swept away, her fingers raked across a ridge in the stone, which she was able to grasp and stop her slide. She pulled herself onto the rock and lay across it gasping for breath.

She peered over the edge of the falls and drew back in a wave of vertigo, clutching the stone as if it were made of gold. She felt the stone move. It was tipping toward the falls. In desperation she looked about her. The bank was too far to swim to, and no other stones were within reach. She looked up and saw the limb of a pine tree hanging just over her head. She scrambled to her knees and tried to stand on the stone, causing it to tip precariously toward the waterfall. She jumped, grabbed for the limb, and caught it, swinging in midair as the stone teetered beneath her and tumbled over the edge. She clung to the swinging branch as she watched the rock crash into the torrent below. Slowly, placing one hand over the other, she moved along the limb toward the bank. Her fingers began to lose their strength, and she wondered if she could maintain her grip until she hung over solid ground. She was only a few feet from safety when her fingers gave way and she plunged into the current. She landed at the edge of the bank and managed to grip a root protruding into the stream, by which she pulled herself up to solid earth. She crawled up the bank to safety, where she collapsed in a sodden heap, drawing her breath in deep, rapid gasps.

The forest about her was almost dark before she could breathe normally again. She thought she would rest a moment longer before finding a place to curl up for the night. She began to shiver in her wet clothing and drew up into a ball, hugging herself with her arms. As the darkness deepened, so did her despair. Her pack was gone, and now all she owned was the dress she was wearing. She had nothing else at all—no family, no friends, no home. And she was now a fugitive from the Master of the Universe. *I am reaping the harvest I have sown,* she thought. What else could she expect? Over and over since she could remember, she had heard that sin was a glittering lure that led to a pit of grief, agony, isolation, and death. It was true. She had no excuse. She had been warned.

But the punishment seemed far in excess of the crime. Why should those brief moments of stolen joy have led to the loss of everything in her life? Was this the Master's idea of justice? To create pleasures and passions, the fulfillment of which seemed to touch the essence of one's being, then forbid the experience of them? Was it his idea of justice to jerk the pleasure away from one who succumbed and plunge the offender into hopeless despair? *I could not bring my worst enemy to this,* she thought. *Why does the Master of the Universe do it to me?* Tears streamed from her eyes as she hugged herself in misery, as if she were her own source of comfort. Soon she fell asleep in spite of the chill and the roar of the waterfall, never moving from the place where she had fallen.

Evalonne slept fitfully and awoke many times in the darkness, shivering in her wet dress, but she had no means of warming herself. Her blanket was lost with her pack, as were her fire flint and two changes of clothing. She might have made herself a bed in the leafy ground cover beneath the trees, but even if she had known to do such a thing, she lacked both the energy and the will to get up and do it. She remained drawn up into a tight knot and drifted fitfully in and out of sleep throughout the night, shivering all the while.

She awoke as the first shafts of sunlight sifted among the trees and rose weakly to her feet. Her dress was still damp and she was chilled to the bone. Her throat was so sore that swallowing was painful, and she coughed and sniffled frequently. She thought briefly of going downriver to search for her pack, but in her weakened condition descending the ledge into the valley was unthinkable. And she knew she had little chance of finding it. Soon she was sick again and fell to the ground retching and coughing in dreadful spasms. She lay shivering for several minutes before she got up and trudged back toward the road through the dew-covered grass. At least she had come out of the river on the south side and would not have to cross it again.

She had been on the road for less than an hour when the mountainous woods gave way to rolling hills of fields and meadows, punctuated by groves of oak and elm. She saw sheep and cattle grazing, and distant cottages surrounded by pens and sties and barns. She did not know how bedraggled she looked. Her red hair was matted and tangled, sprinkled with leaves and twigs and caked with dirt. Her dress was splotched with mud where she had lain on the ground and was flecked with twigs and bits of dried leaves. The hem was ragged and tattered, the sleeves torn and frayed where briars and nettles had snagged them. Her mind had been so dulled by the fitful night and stuffy head that she had forgotten to wash her face, and dirt still clung to her cheek where it had pressed against the ground during the night. She encountered more travelers on the road now, but all were farmers or herders and she had little fear of them, though all eyed her with curiosity. Her unkempt appearance could not hide her innate beauty, causing some of the men to gaze at her with a gleam that would have made her wary had she been more alert. But Evalonne, coughing harder, feeling weaker and more dull headed with each step, hardly noticed the stares.

Shortly after midmorning her nausea subsided and she began to feel hunger. Several times she veered aside into roadside groves to look for berries, but she found none. The day wore on, and without food she grew ever weaker as she stumbled on southward into Oranth. When night fell, she curled up beneath a tree beside the road and fell asleep almost instantly. She awoke deep in the night, shaking in the grip of a chill and coughing deeply. She slept little the rest of the night. When dawn broke she struggled to her feet to resume her journey, but after her morning bout with nausea, she was too weak to continue. She was able to walk only a few steps before crumpling to the ground beside the road, where she lay coughing and trembling violently. She would have given a year of her life for a cup of water to wet her cracked lips and cool her parched throat.

Perhaps I am dying, she thought, and for an instant the possibility cheered her. She had ruined the life the Master had given her, and she could see nothing in her future except more of the misery that now afflicted her. Immediately the thought turned into a horror, however, as she remembered the vivid pictures of the eternal fires of punishment that kirkmen had painted in their sermons. Such was her future if she died now. She must get up and go on. She must live. She struggled to get to her feet, but weakness and dizziness overcame her and she sank back to the ground like a wilting flower.

She lay beside the road, breathing hard as if she had run a race, and opened her eyes to see the hazy form of a young man approaching. He was singing, and she recognized the voice. Avriel! She tried to rise, but her weakness would not allow it. He came to where she lay, smiling all the while. He held in both his hands an enormous jug of water, which he lifted frequently to his lips and drank from deeply, splashing and dripping the precious liquid all about him.

"Please," Evalonne said. "Please give me just a swallow of your water and I will forgive all you have done to me."

Avriel said nothing, but the wide grin never left his face as he tipped the jug and took a long drink. Then looking at Evalonne with a mocking smile, he deliberately poured the water on the road and dashed the jug in pieces against the ground. Water ran everywhere among the shards of pottery, some of it streaming off the road in little rivulets. But none came toward Evalonne. She strained desperately toward a little puddle forming a few feet from her, but she could not reach it, and it sank into the earth, leaving nothing but a spot of brown dampness. Avriel laughed and went on his way singing:

> *She tried to keep him with her charms,*
> *But love had flown her fragile hold,*
> *He left her grieved with empty arms,*
> *To face the winter long and cold.*

Something between a groan and a whimper escaped her lips as she opened her eyes. There was no water on the road, no broken shards, no puddles of mud. She looked in the direction Avriel had gone, and there was no sign of anyone at all. A fit of coughing overtook her as she sank back to the ground. Shivering violently though the day was warming, she fell into a fevered sleep.

CHAPTER SIX

THE INDENTURE

he sun was high overhead when Evalonne felt the delicious splashing of water on her face as caressing hands spread the coolness to her cheeks and forehead. She knew she must be dreaming again, but it did not matter. She would not open her eyes for fear of awakening and driving the soothing ecstasy away.

"D'ye think she be alive?" said an honest masculine voice somewhere above her as she felt her head being lifted and a cup of water placed to her lips.

"Aye, but she be terrible sick," said a feminine voice that Evalonne took to be the mate of the masculine. She opened her eyes and, with some effort, focused them on the face hovering above her, a plain but concerned visage of a woman of about thirty.

"Please don't be a dream," whispered Evalonne.

"We be as real as ye are, but not as sick," said the woman. "Here, Hollek, get this girl onto the wagon. We be takin' her into Larenton."

Hollek came into Evalonne's view, a burly man with a thick black beard and clear blue eyes. He picked her up as if she were a child and laid her gently on the blanket his wife had spread over the hay in the bed of their wagon. The woman knelt beside her and held her hand as the man mounted the board and drove the wagon down the southward road.

"We'll take ye to Larenton's inn," she said as the wagon rolled along. "They'll put ye up proper like until ye get yerself on yer feet again."

It was late afternoon when Hollek's wagon stopped at the door of the Red Falcon Inn. He carried Evalonne into the dining hall, setting her gently in a chair near the hearth. A stout middle-aged man with thinning hair and a grizzled beard strode forward, followed closely by his wife, a heavy, aproned woman with her hair tied into a scarf.

"Welcome to the Red Falcon," said the man, his broad smile showing a missing front tooth. "Me name's Dunwig and I be the proprietor here. Do ye want a supper or a room? Or both? Or will it be two rooms, perhaps?"

"Nay, we'll not be stayin' here," said Hollek. "We're on our way to Wallenton, and we found yonder lass sick near death beside the road. We brought her to you."

"I hope she's got money to pay."

"By my reckonin' she's got nothin' but the clothes on her back, and they's not much."

"Well, I don't know as I can take her on, as much as my old heart goes out to poor unfortunates like her. If I had my way, I'd feed and put up every sick traveler that darkens my door and charge them nothin' at all. But I've had a run of such cases lately and it's nigh to breakin' me. Why, just last week we kept a man four days who had sickened on his own pork roast. Didn't charge him nothin'."

"That's right. We didn't," Dunwig's wife piped in.

"No matter, we're leavin' her here," said Hollek. "She's got even weaker since we picked her up. I hardly think she would survive the ride to Wallenton."

"Ye can't do that. Not without payin' something," said Dunwig.

"Yes, we can," Hollek's wife insisted. "Ye know the custom in Oranth. No inn ever refuses help to the sick or injured, whether or not they can pay."

"It's a custom, not a law," said Dunwig, "and I'm not willin' to push myself into poverty by relievin' someone else's. I get some kind of pay up front or out she goes."

Hollek reached into the pouch at his belt and removed a coin, which he slapped into the innkeeper's hand. "Do what ye can with this, and after that, dig deeper into your heart and find a touch of human kindness there. Good day, Dunwig." Hollek and his wife left the inn, and the scowling Dunwig looked toward Evalonne, who had not moved from the position in which Hollek left her.

"Well, I suppose we're stuck with ye for the moment," he muttered. "But ye'd better mend fast, because I'll not be long keepin' a nonpayin' guest." Evalonne gave no sign that she had heard but slowly slipped from the chair onto the floor, where she lay still as a fallen log. Dunwig called for his porter to carry her to a cot in the scullery. "No use wastin' a good room I can charge to someone else."

The inn's chargirl, a smallish woman named Lurga, took off Evalonne's tattered dress, bathed her, and slipped a light shift over her body. For three days, she spoon-fed broth to her. On the fourth day Evalonne was awake and fully aware of her surroundings for the first time since Hollek had brought her in. Her morning nausea had diminished, but frequent fits of coughing still wracked her, and she was too weak to walk without support.

The next morning the innkeeper's wife, Golwen by name, saw that Evalonne was still lying on the cot and went immediately to her husband. "That girl's been eatin' our food long enough. What the man paid would hardly have covered three days, and she's been here four. It's time you sent her on her way."

"Shut your mouth, woman," growled Dunwig. "I'll not be turnin' her out yet."

"And why not, I'd like to know? Ye were dead set enough against takin' her when she was brought in. What has changed yer tune?"

"I don't have to explain my thinkin' to ye."

"If ye're thinkin' what I think ye're thinkin', ye better do some explainin'."

"Have ye looked at the girl lately?" said Dunwig. "She didn't look like much when she was brought here, but she cleaned up good. She's a rare beauty, she is—got a face and shape on her to rival Venus herself. Get that red hair combed up and put her in the right kind of dress and she could bring us some good business. Gwynnelon's not what she used to be, ye know. We'll be better off nursin' this one back to health and puttin' her to workin' for us."

"And what makes ye think she'll agree to doin' the kind of work ye're thinkin' of?"

"It's easy, woman," Dunwig grinned. "She's indebted to us, ain't she? And we've already gone through her clothes to know she's got no money. I'll put her to work payin' off her debt."

"But she don't owe us enough to make it worthwhile messin' with her. The couple who left her here paid ye for well nigh three days, so she don't owe ye but for one. That won't keep her here for long enough to matter. I say turn her out and be done with it."

"She don't know what's been paid or what's owed. She was beyond hearin' a thunderclap when the man gave me the money. And none of the other servants were around to know any better. She'll have to believe what I tell her." Dunwig grinned in unabashed pride at his little plan, and his wife responded with a toothless grin of her own. She had to agree that it had within it a touch of brilliance.

Lurga brought Evalonne's own dress to her, now clean though wrinkled and tattered, and she donned it and began to walk without assistance. She was able to stay up longer and walk farther each day, and by the end of the week she thought she had regained enough strength to try a walk outside without Lurga's help. She coughed little now, her appetite had returned, and eating the solid fare of the inn put color back into her face. Dunwig watched her go out the door and circle the inn once before she returned to her cot, where she collapsed, red faced and breathing hard. He followed her into the scullery, took a chair, and sat next to her cot.

"I see ye're doing much better," he said. "I be glad of it."

"Yes, and I owe you a great debt of gratitude," replied Evalonne.

"Oh, think nothin' of it. We was only doin' what the Master would have us do. It does me ol' heart good to know that all the care and medicines we been lavishin' on ye has brought ye back to health."

"Medicines? I didn't know. How long have I been here?"

"Well nigh two weeks. And the barber has been by most every day till ye started gettin' better, prescribin' all kind of concoctions and herbs and special soups. We were lucky to find all the ingredients to the stuff he required."

"I'm so sorry I have put you to so much trouble," Evalonne said. "The problem is that I cannot pay you. I have no money at all."

"Think nothin' of that, woman. We did hope for a little payment to defray just a bit of the cost of all we did, but we'd have done it anyway. However, there is a way ye could, uh, pay us back if you're of a mind to do a little work. I've been needin' another servin' girl here at the inn."

Hope sprang in Evalonne's heart like a blooming flower. It seemed the Master had guided her to exactly what she needed. "Yes, I'll be happy to work for you."

"Good, good." Dunwig smiled his gapped smile and rubbed his hands together. "We'll need to do this thing proper by the legal laws of Oranth, of course. I'll pay ye the same wage as my other servin' girl. Since ye owe me money already, I'll draw up papers of indenture and have them ready for you to sign tomorrow."

Evalonne agreed, and Dunwig left the scullery grinning and rubbing his hands together. She walked about several more times that day, each time a little farther than before. That evening she was very tired, but she knew she was gaining strength and went to sleep buoyed by the first hope she had felt in weeks. She was safely out of danger from Gronthus, and she had a place to sleep and a means of earning her livelihood.

The next morning after she had breakfasted and walked twice around the inn, Dunwig called her to the back of the room. A yellow parchment lay on the table filled with lines of writing. He sat her down and said, "I'll summarize the terms of the indenture for ye. To dispose of yer debt incurred to me over the past two weeks, includin' food, bed, fees to the barber, service from the maid, the cost of medicines, and ingredients for potions, ye will agree to work for me for three months. Yer work won't be all that hard. It will include servin' the customers of the inn with all their needs. I have other servants to empty chamber pots, clean rooms, and wash linens. Now, during these three months, I'll be providin' ye a room with a bed, all yer meals, and two complete changes of clothin'. Since everything ye earn will be goin' toward the debt ye already owe, ye'll not be able to pay for the clothes and the ongoin' room and board. To pay me for continuin' all these advantages while ye're workin', I figure the indenture should be extended to six months. What do ye say to that?" Dunwig handed the parchment to her.

As Evalonne looked over the contract, her first thought was that six months was a long time to serve for a mere two weeks of care. But she had no idea of the cost of medicines or fees to barbers. Besides, the thought of leaving the inn to go looking for better terms was unthinkable at the moment. After her recent experiences in Lochlaund, her travels across the country, and her illness, the security of the inn and steady work had the look of heaven to her and overshadowed any disadvantage. And she would have a place to live at least until she had her baby. She handed the parchment back to Dunwig. "I agree to your terms," she said.

"Good. Very good," said Dunwig. Then he turned and bellowed, "Golwen, come here." When his wife came to the table, he picked up a candle and held it above the bottom of the parchment, letting a few drops of wax drip onto the paper. "You need to witness the woman's signin'," he said to her as Evalonne leaned forward and pressed her dove pendant into the soft wax and, with Dunwig's quill, scratched her name beneath it. After Dunwig and his wife signed the parchment, he opened a drawer in the desk and took out a smooth ring made of a quarter-inch band of iron curved in a circle six inches in diameter. It was hinged on one side and open on the other, with a lock at the open end.

"Lean forward and I'll put this on yer neck," said Dunwig.

Evalonne let out a little gasp. "I didn't know I would wear a slave's collar. Really, I'd rather not," she said. "I assure you, I will meet your terms without it."

"I know ye think that, and I hate to put it on ye," Dunwig said, shrugging his shoulders. "But it's the law here in Oranth. And many an indentured person has begun with good intentions that somehow slipped away when the work got hard or the road looked invitin'. But wearin' it won't be so bad. Look at it. It's all smooth and shiny like—not rough and rusty so's it would chafe yer fine skin. Bend over, woman."

After a moment's hesitation, she bent over and allowed Dunwig to lock the ring onto her neck. She felt it with her fingers, and the first apprehension about what she was doing began to burrow in her mind.

"Here's yer first outfit." Golwen handed her two folded garments—a dark red skirt and a white blouse. "The other will be ready in a couple of days. I'll have Gwynnelon show ye to yer room where ye can bathe and change. Ye might as well start earnin' yer keep today."

"Gwynnelon," she shouted, and immediately a woman appeared wearing a tattered, stained dress and a filthy apron. Her brown hair was long and ragged, her eyes hollow, and her pallid cheeks sunken like an eroded field.

"Yes, mum," said Gwynnelon.

"Evalonne here will be takin' over the servin' from ye. Startin' tomorrow yer job will be cleanin' the rooms, washin' the linens, emptyin' chamber pots, drawin' water, shovelin' the stables, and washin' pots in the kitchen. Lurga has more than she can handle. Evalonne will be roomin' with ye at the top of the stairs. Now take her to the room and draw her bath. After she's bathed and changed, spend the rest of the day teachin' her to do yer job."

Gwynnelon blanched at her mistress's words and looked at Evalonne with obvious resentment. But she dropped her head and muttered, "Yes, mum."

Evalonne was shocked at the squalor of the room. At least a dozen brown roaches scurried into hiding when the door opened. The planking of the floor creaked, and she felt the crunch of dirt as she stepped inside. The walls were of crumbling plaster, mottled with mildew and stained from leaks in the roof. Spider webs hung in all the corners, and one rafter, riddled like a sponge with termite channels, sagged ominously. The bedframe was of unfinished pine and the mattress a stained and shapeless bag of straw.

Gwynnelon, never uttering a word, brought in a tub and, making several trips to the well in the yard, filled it with water. After bathing, Evalonne slipped into the skirt and blouse. The top was much too small, hung uncomfortably off her shoulders, and was cut precariously low. She had never seen a blouse that revealed so much flesh, as such clothing did not exist in Lochlaund. She tried to pull the fabric high enough to cover more, but to no avail. Unwilling to leave her room with most of her bosom exposed, she peeked out the door and called for Gwynnelon to bring her scissors and needle. Gwynnelon said nothing but left and returned with the requested items. "Ye'd best hurry, mum. They be waitin' for ye downstairs."

Evalonne quickly cut enough fabric from her old dress to make a vest of sorts that covered her exposed area. When she finished she dashed down the stairs and came into the dining hall, where Dunwig sat at a large table laughing and bantering with several drinking men. All became silent and looked toward her as she entered the room. Obviously they had been waiting for her to make her entrance.

Dunwig looked at her, first with surprise, then his brow knitted in anger as he strode toward her. "What in thunder is that thing ye're wearin'?" he bellowed.

"The blouse is too small, sir. It would be indecent to wear it without—"

Dunwig grabbed the edge of the vest and ripped it from her body. The men at the tables cheered and hooted and made various unintelligible animal noises as Evalonne quickly covered herself with her hands and hung her head in shame. The men all laughed, and Gwynnelon laughed with them. Utterly mortified, Evalonne ran out of the hall and up the stairs and locked herself in her room. Dunwig bounded up behind her and pounded on the door.

"What d'ye think ye're doin', woman? Get yerself out here and do yer job."

Evalonne did not answer, and Dunwig kicked open the door, splintering a panel from the lower part of it. She cowered in the corner, still trying to cover her bare flesh with her hands. He jerked her roughly to her feet and half dragged her down the stairs and into the hall where the men applauded and cheered at her return.

"You get to work accordin' to our agreement or I'll be takin' the whip to ye," said Dunwig as he shoved her toward the kitchen. Evalonne knew she had no choice, and under Gwynnelon's begrudging tutelage, she set about her work in great shame and discomfort, trying in vain to pull the skimpy blouse closed as much as possible as the men gawked and leered.

Raised in the atmosphere of strict propriety in Lochlaund, Evalonne was shocked at the behavior of the men in the inn. Most of them were openly boorish and lecherous, pawing at her as she passed among their tables, making crude remarks and even cruder suggestions. She bore the talk silently and managed to twist and pull away from much of the pawing and pinching. But as it continued, her shock dissolved into anger, and more than once she set down a patron's cup so hard its contents sloshed on the arm that groped toward her. She jerked her arms roughly away from the greasy fingers that clutched at her and slapped at the hands that tried to lift her skirt. Most of the men just laughed and went on with their drinking.

"Wench!" boomed a voice from the far side of the room. "Wench, can't ye hear me? Come over here."

Evalonne took her pitcher of ale and went to where the man sat, a yellow-bearded farmer with a barrel chest and arms like ham hocks. "What do you want?"

The man said nothing but, grinning, held out his cup and turned it upside down, letting the remaining few drops of ale drip to the floor. He turned the cup upright again, but as Evalonne began to pour from her pitcher he jerked the cup away and the ale splashed to the planking.

"Haaah!" he said as he pawed at her with ale-sticky hands. "It's not ale I be wantin', but somethin' much sweeter."

Evalonne angrily shoved his hand aside and turned to walk away, but he grabbed the back of her skirt and pulled her roughly into his lap. He thrust a coin in front of her face and said, "Let's be goin' to yer room, wench."

She hit the man's hand, causing the coin to spin through the air. "Let go of me!" she cried and began to pummel his head until he cursed and knocked her to the floor.

"Dunwig!" he bellowed. The innkeeper came running while all the inn's patrons turned to watch. "Is this the wench ye've been braggin' was the tastiest this town has seen? I tell ye she's more witch than wench. She's refusin' to do what ye brought her here to do."

"Get up from there," growled Dunwig as he grabbed Evalonne's arm and jerked her from the floor. "What do ye mean, refusin' a customer?"

"He asked me to do something immoral."

Laughter erupted from every throat in the inn. Dunwig took her by the shoulders and shook her like a rag doll. "I told ye that yer job is to serve the customers of my inn with their needs. Are ye tryin' to go back on the terms of yer indenture?"

"But I thought you meant serving them food and ale. I had no idea you meant—"

"Oh, come now, woman. Ye weren't born yesterday. Ye know what servin' wenches do at inns."

"No. I did not know. In Lochlaund—"

"Well, ye know now! And ye've already signed an agreement of indenture. Ye'll do yer job or I'll have the constable take ye to the magistrate." He punctuated his threat by shoving Evalonne hard away from him. As she stumbled backward, someone extended a foot and she sprawled hard on the floor. Again the men burst into laughter.

She lay on the floor as crude jeers rang in her ears. She had been cruelly tricked. She had unwittingly contracted to be a harlot, with all proceeds going solely to Dunwig. For a moment she thought of refusing and allowing fate to take her wherever it would. But she remembered that she was with child, and the thought of being turned out into the wild to fend for herself again filled her with cold dread. Slowly she got up from the floor, glaring at the grinning yellow beard all the while. Without a word she walked up the stairway to her room, her heart throbbing with hatred and despair as the drunken man stumbled along behind.

CHAPTER SEVEN

ᎠᎬᏚᏟᎬᏁᎢ ᎥᏁᎢᎣ ᏂᎬᏞᏞ

unwig had calculated well. The presence of Evalonne at his inn soon doubled his business. As word got about of the rare beauty serving at the Red Falcon, men from miles around flocked to it like flies to honey. Evalonne's life became one of shame, squalor, hard work, and unmitigated abuse from the inn's patrons. As the days turned to weeks her soul became calloused to protect itself from pain as does a foot that trods on sharp stones. Each day she grew more angry and sullen, feeling trapped like a caged animal in a life that showed nothing on the horizon except more shame and bitterness.

She had no friends. Gwynnelon, with whom she shared a room, made no attempt to hide her hatred. The woman had been supplanted and relegated to the dirtiest, most menial work, and she often had to wait for her bed until late in the night when the last man left Evalonne's room. Usually on such nights Gwynnelon would curl up on a pallet in the scullery and doze until she heard clumping down the stairway that signaled she could return to her own cot. But on many nights she was so exhausted she never heard the footfalls and did not awaken until the cook's broom prodded her in the morning.

Evalonne grew more and more weary of the long days and longer nights. Often midnight had long past before she was left alone, and when Dunwig pounded on the bedroom door at dawn, she learned to arise quickly and get downstairs to serve breakfast or feel the bite of his rod on her back, though in his beatings he took care not to leave permanent marks on her flesh that would spoil her appeal to his patrons. Soon exhaustion began to take its toll, especially in the mornings. Circles formed under her eyes; she moved slower and with less of her natural grace, mixed orders, dropped plates, and spilled ale with greater frequency. Although Dunwig and Golwen had no qualms about squeezing from her every hour of work they could get, they could see that this tree that bore them golden apples was beginning to wither. They removed Evalonne from breakfast duty and allowed her an extra hour of sleep in the mornings. They put Lurga with Gwynnelon to serve at breakfast.

One morning Evalonne arose and stood before the tiny cracked mirror on the wall of the room. As she washed her face and combed her hair, Gwynnelon came to the door and said, "If ye want to look into a mirror that shows yer future, look at me."

Surprised that the woman had initiated a conversation, Evalonne did indeed turn and look at her.

"How old do ye think I am?" asked Gwynnelon.

"I would say no more than forty," Evalonne replied. She did not mean to be cruel; she actually thought she was flattering the woman.

"I be twenty-six, though my soul is a hundred. Ye see my face? See the lines, the baggy eyes, the hollow cheeks? It's all a picture of what ye'll be like in four or five short years. It's a mean life, it is. It's hard enough on the body, wearin' it down like ruts in a road. But it's death to the soul. Ye soon forget ye're human. Ye feel like ye're a piece of meat or a jug of ale—somethin' for men to devour to slake their appetites. Nothing more. They forget ye the moment their thirst is quenched, and don't care if ye're alive or dead.

"I hated ye when ye first came here. Ye reminded me of what the years had stolen from me. Yet in that hate ye gave me a gift. At least by hatin' I was feelin' somethin' for the first time in years. But now my hate is dyin' just like everything else about me. I'm not hatin' ye anymore. In fact, seein' ye look in that mirror like I used to do should make me pity ye, but it don't do that, either. I look at ye and I know where yer road is takin' ye—right to where I'm standin' now, and I feel nothin'. I'm already dead inside."

Without waiting for a reply, Gwynnelon left the room, and Evalonne turned back to the mirror. She stared into it, and imposing Gwynnelon's face over her own, she saw herself as she would be in a few short years—haggard and drawn, thin and lined. She knew that this was indeed her future, but at the moment she could see no way out of it. Someday soon she would look for a way of escape, but for now, leaving the inn was unthinkable. It was a hell, but it offered food and shelter, which she sorely needed to protect the life within her.

Evalonne had begun to notice the first swelling of her belly. For a while the fullness of her skirt hid it easily enough, but of late the swelling had crept upward to her waistline. As she looked at her profile in the mirror, her hand on her abdomen, she wondered how much longer she could hide her condition.

In another week she found she could no longer button the waistband on her skirt. She cut off the button and reattached it a few inches closer to the buttonhole before she went down to the kitchen. She noticed that Golwen eyed her strangely much of the day, and with a woman's intuition for such things, Evalonne knew the innkeeper's wife suspected the truth.

Usually she fell asleep minutes after the last man left her room, but that night she lay awake wondering what Dunwig would do when Golwen told him of her suspicions. Evalonne had known this day would come, but she had refused to think on it. Her life was bleak enough without borrowing trouble from tomorrow.

In the morning Dunwig met Evalonne at the bottom of the stairway and drew her to his table at the back of the dining hall.

"Ye have deceived me," he said, his face a scowling mask of anger.

"I have not," Evalonne spat back.

"Ye are with child. Why didn't ye tell me?"

"You didn't ask. How would I have known it mattered?"

"Of course it mattered! Are ye daft, wench? I had a right to know that for half the time of yer indenture ye'd be of no use to the men who come to this inn."

"Just as I had a right to know what kind of use these men were to make of me," she spat.

The scowl left Dunwig's face, and he settled back in his chair and grinned. "Very well, then—go. Ye have deceived me; ye think I have deceived you. We'll simply void the indenture and ye can leave." He reached into a drawer, drew out the contract, and tore it in half. "Ye're free. Go on, get out. Leave. Begone."

Evalonne gasped in panic at the ripping of the parchment. What would she do? Where would she go? Life at the inn was hellish, but life outside it meant certain death, not only to her but also to her unborn child. She could not face the thought of being hungry, cold, and sick again, especially with a baby on the way. "No, please, don't send me away. I can do other work, and there's enough of it. Please."

Dunwig looked at her and rubbed his chin. "I didn't hire ye for other work. And now the men won't—"

"The men are too drunk to care, or even notice for a while. I can serve them for at least another month or more. You will lose nothing until then."

"Well, I don't know . . ."

"You can extend my indenture to whatever length you think fair. Please, Dunwig, I beg of you."

"Very well. I will write up a new contract. But only if ye agree to extend the terms of indenture to one year from today."

"Another year? I didn't think it would be so long."

"Listen, wench. I'm doin' this only from the goodness of my heart. Ye'll be worthless to me durin' your indisposal. I'll need yer services after the babe is born to make up for my losses while I'm feedin' ye for nothin'. If ye don't like the terms, ye can be on yer way."

"No! I . . . I mean yes. Another year will be good, sir. Thank you, thank you." Her voice quivered with relief. She felt she had just averted a fall from a deadly precipice. On the next day she signed the new contract and continued her work.

When Evalonne grew too large to attract the inn's customers to her bed, Dunwig placed Gwynnelon on serving duty again and set Evalonne to the dirtiest and most menial tasks. She scoured pots, hauled buckets of water from the well, emptied chamber pots, scrubbed sheets, towels, and clothing in the river, and even scooped manure from the stables, all the while enduring the taunts of the inn's patrons. In time she grew too large even for many of these tasks and, along with the taunting, endured complaints from Dunwig and Golwen for the cost of keeping her while she did so little work.

Then the day of her delivery came. Toward evening she was carrying two buckets of water from the well, hung at either end of a wooden bar laid across her back. She had just entered the kitchen when a pain hit her that doubled her over. She dropped the bar and the buckets clattered to the floor, splashing water over half the kitchen. Dunwig ran to the kitchen and, seeing Evalonne sprawled on the wet floor, struck her hard across the back with his rod, ranting at her.

"Get up from there, ye clumsy wench. Look what ye've done!"

But Evalonne could not get up, as another spasm gripped her with such intensity that Dunwig's cruelty went unheeded.

"I think the baby's comin'," said Gwynnelon. "We'd best get her abed. And she'll be needin' someone with her."

Dunwig spat a curse. "All right, ye can get her to bed. But don't ye be stayin' with her. Ye got yer work to do down here. I'll not be havin' two of ye slackin' at the same time. I'm runnin' an inn here, not a sick house." Muttering another curse, Dunwig turned on his heel and stalked from the kitchen while Gwynnelon and Lurga lifted Evalonne to her feet and managed to get her up the stairway to her bed. Not daring to disobey Dunwig, they quickly returned to their work. However, Gwynnelon brought a basin of water and several rags, which she set beside Evalonne's bed, along with a pitcher of water and a cup.

Alone in the dark room, Evalonne moaned and writhed with each spasm of pain. As the frequency and intensity of the contractions increased, her moans became cries that rang throughout the inn. Gwynnelon and Lurga paused in their work and looked at each other, but they became industrious again when Dunwig walked in and glared at them. Not a half-hour later, a terrible scream filled the inn and all activity stopped.

"The wench'll drive away every customer we got," Dunwig growled.

"She needs help. We've got to do something," Gwynnelon pleaded.

"She kept to herself about bein' with child—let her keep to herself deliverin' it. It'll be a lesson to the wench."

"But if she don't get help, the babe could die," said Gwynnelon.

"It would be the best thing that could happen. We don't need a brat squawlin' around this place."

Another scream pierced the air, and Gwynnelon threw down her broom and ran up the stairway. She had seen babies delivered before and knew something of what to do. She arrived just in time, for the babe was emerging as she entered the room. Evalonne was a lather of sweat, panting like an animal, and she looked at Gwynnelon through eyes wild with fear until a spasm of pain contorted her face and another scream tore from her throat. A few minutes later a baby girl was born into Gwynnelon's hands. She tied the cord, cleaned up the child, wrapped her in a blanket, and laid her on the bosom of the exhausted mother. She cleaned Evalonne and wiped her face with a damp towel before hurrying back to the kitchen to face the wrath of Dunwig.

Upon seeing her tiny daughter's face, a beam of light began to penetrate the darkness of Evalonne's world. Through a haze of exhaustion, she stared in wonder at the child now in her arms, tenderly unwrapping the blanket to count every little finger and toe. The baby was perfect—the most perfect thing she had ever seen. So perfect that Evalonne forgot the hours of agony she had just experienced. She forgot the bitterness that had ravaged her heart for months. The little creature at her breast brightened her life like a sunbeam from heaven and helped her to forget, if only for this moment, the squalor and shame that were her life.

"You are beautiful," she whispered as her lips spread into a true smile for the first time since Avriel had deserted her. "I will name you Luciella," she cooed to the babe. She remembered the name from an old ballad, and a monk of the kirk had told her that it meant "light." For the next two days Dunwig required nothing of Evalonne, and the little room, for all its shabbiness and filth, became a haven, its corners brightened by the joy she felt at the tiny bundle in her arms.

But early on the morning of the third day, Dunwig pounded on her door. "Do ye intend to slug abed the rest of yer days? I be needin' help downstairs. Ye've dawdled long enough."

Evalonne did not care. He could be as cruel as he wished, but he

could never take away her happiness now. She felt she could endure
any pain as long as she had her baby to love and protect. She con-
verted a crate into a crib and placed her child in a safe corner of the
kitchen while she went about her work, checking the crate often to
be sure all was well. When Luciella awoke hungry, Evalonne sat in the
kitchen and nursed her. Occasionally when the child cried between
feedings, she would pick her up and walk her outside or about the
kitchen, cooing and singing all the while until the babe quieted.
Dunwig complained and threatened her each time she tended to the
baby, but it did not matter. Even Dunwig could not dent the immen-
sity of her joy—more joy than she could ever remember having.

In the evenings when her work was done, Evalonne took Luciella
up to her room, where she spent hours gazing at the perfect little face
in the candlelight and clasping the delightful little creature to her
breast, cuddling, singing, laughing, and talking to her in a voice over-
flowing with love.

Within a few weeks Evalonne got her shape back, and Dunwig
put her to serving the men again. When a man was in her room,
Gwynnelon or Lurga kept Luciella. But no matter how late the hour,
when the last customer left, Evalonne would not sleep until she had
spent another half-hour or more just gazing in love and delight at the
little wonder that had graced her life.

Three months passed, seeming like three days to Evalonne, so
consumed was she by her new duties as a mother, and so full of happiness. Little Luciella was smiling now, and she knew her mother by
sight. When Evalonne nursed her, the child would gaze up at her with
wide blue eyes, often pulling away from her task to break into a
toothless smile that set Evalonne's face to glowing like a heaven full
of stars. Late at night when Evalonne took her from Gwynnelon's
weary arms, the baby would gurgle and coo and smile at her mother's
songs and caresses until Evalonne could hardly bear the ecstasy.

Life at the inn was no easier: men still pawed and pinched and
badgered her with their crude talk. Golwen still railed and glared at
her, Dunwig still stormed and cursed and occasionally struck her
with his rod, but none of this mattered anymore. Evalonne moved
about in the world of the Red Falcon and went through the motions

of its life, but it was not where she lived. The inn was a hall of shadows in which her body functioned by rote, letting her habits and instincts take over her movements while her mind and soul soared to the bright sunlit world of her Luciella. A prayer of gratitude to the Master of the Universe often passed her lips. She had paid a fearful price for the gift of her daughter, but her life took on more meaning than she had ever imagined possible.

But Evalonne's joy was not to last, for she was soon to be bludgeoned by a heavier blow than she had yet endured. On the morning that ended her happiness, she did not awaken until the sun was well above the grove of trees outside her window. Gwynnelon had arisen at the crack of dawn, as usual, and was already downstairs serving breakfast. Evalonne was grateful for the extra hour of sleep and stretched luxuriously before getting out of her bed and peeking over the edge of Luciella's crib.

"And just why are you sleeping so late, lazybones?" she cooed.

Luciella did not move.

"Little sleepyhead. It's time to start your day," she sang, tickling the babe's cheek with her fingertips. Still Luciella did not move, and Evalonne became alarmed. She picked up the child and found her limp and cold. "Luciella, Luciella! Wake up! Wake up!" But Luciella did not wake up. Her face was cold and gray, and she was not breathing. Evalonne clasped the tiny body to her breast and began rocking back and forth, singing a lullaby as tears streamed down her cheeks.

A half-hour later Gwynnelon opened the door to her room and said, "Dunwig's wantin' ye downstairs now. Ye better come before he's up here after ye."

"I can't come down today. My baby's sick," Evalonne wailed and went back to her rocking and singing. Gwynnelon could see that something was amiss—Evalonne's continual rocking, the tremulous voice in which she sang, the tears streaming down her cheeks—then she saw the baby's face, gray and cold, and the woman's heart chilled.

"Evalonne, let me see your baby," said Gwynnelon, stepping into the room.

"No! Go away! I can take care of her myself. Leave us—please!" Evalonne held the body tighter and drew away from Gwynnelon.

But Gwynnelon had seen enough. "Evalonne, yer child is dead. I'm so sorry. Let me take her for you, and you can—"

"No! She's not dead!" cried Evalonne. "She's just sick, that's all." She went back to her rocking and singing.

Gwynnelon quietly slipped from the room and closed the door. She told Dunwig and Golwen what she had seen. "Well, I guess we'll have to do without her for the day," muttered Dunwig as he went back to his work. But that afternoon when Evalonne still had not come out of her room, Golwen insisted that the three of them must go up and take the baby's body from her. "It be for her own good," she said. Evalonne screamed and resisted with all her strength, collapsing on the floor and wailing as they carried her child away. Gwynnelon brought her food and water and left her alone, sleeping that night on the cot in the scullery.

For three days Evalonne did not leave her room. On the second day Dunwig glowered toward the top of the stairway and muttered, "How long does that wench expect to hide up there? We got work to be done around here. If she don't come down today, I'll throw her into the street." But Golwen firmly insisted that he wait another day at least.

Evalonne sat alone in the room, staring at the empty crib. She seldom moved. Most of the food Gwynnelon brought daily she left untouched. Nothing, not even eating, was worth the effort it took to do it. Life itself was not worth the effort it took to live it. She wanted to die, but the taking of her life required more exertion than she was willing to give it.

She had been warned. That she could not deny. All the teachings of the kirk had exposed the futility and ultimate despair that comes from yielding to the lure of beauty. But she had never known the power of beauty until it had stormed her own heart in the entrancing form and voice of Avriel. It was overwhelming. Under his spell her eyes had been opened to beauty in its many guises—the mountains, the sunset, the nighttime stars, the smile of a baby. And each stirred an unknown longing in the deepest part of her heart, as if the Master of the Universe had put a hint of himself into everything beautiful. Could such beauty really be an alluring facade for evil? Was it truly the nature of the Master to lure men and women with beauty that seemed to resonate with the call of his own voice, then punish them for following? Would a good master create a hunger for delight, then condemn one for pursuing it? Was the Master of the Universe so capricious?

Yes, she had to answer. Her own experience had proven the kirk to be right. The Master thought it good to tease his creatures with visions of infinite joy, only to snatch those visions away and punish the hands that reached for them. She had grasped, and now her hands were empty. Her heart was empty of love, her life empty of meaning. Ever since she could remember, her parents had drummed into her the importance of full allegiance to the Master of the Universe. Now she asked herself, *Is such a Master worth my allegiance?* As she stared into the empty crib, the answer became clear. She would no longer pretend to follow him. Life had been a struggle to resist all that made life beautiful and live in a gray world bound by his smothering rules. She would abandon this regimen and henceforth live solely by her own wits. She would make her own rules—rules that would benefit her, not some ideal that could not be lived and should not be lived. For any world that made beauty evil and the drab, joyless life of the kirk good was a world of a malevolent Master not worth serving.

Evalonne gripped the dove pendant at her throat, tore it from her neck, and flung it out the window. Expelling a long sigh of relief, she sat back on her bed, free of the kirk, free of all obligation to the Master. Anger still seethed within her, and grief still weighted her like a tumor. She knew it would never leave her, but she resolved to go on in spite of it. She could thrust it aside and close it up in some corner of her heart and live with it in the same way one lived with a missing limb or blind eye.

She stood up, washed her face, combed her hair, and went downstairs to take up her work. Dunwig met her as she walked into the kitchen. "Ah, so ye've decided to start earnin' yer keep again, have ye? I guess ye know I'll have to extend yer indenture another two months to make up the time ye've been slackin'."

Evalonne turned on him in fury. "You fat bloodsucking leech! You will do no such thing. Your business has doubled since I came here, and I've not seen an extra penny for it. You'll double my wage and give me half the take of the men who come to my bed."

Dunwig stepped back a pace, visibly startled by her change of demeanor and the vehemence of her response, but he quickly strove to recover the upper hand. "Ye're insane, wench!" he bellowed. "I'll turn ye out in the cold before I let ye rob me like that."

"As you will," said Evalonne as she removed her apron and walked toward the door.

"Wait!" called Dunwig. "I don't know what's got into ye, woman, but don't go bein' so hasty. Let's talk this out like reasonable people."

Evalonne turned back and stood before him, her eyes glaring hard and her fists on her hips. In the end he agreed to increase her wage by half and pay her forty percent of her takings from the men. She agreed to extend the indenture by one month.

From that day forward she performed each task with cold efficiency. Her bitterness bred in her a new determination never again to be a victim. She vowed to get her destiny under her own control and never trust another or give herself to anyone. Her pain began to form a callus around her heart so hard the world would never hurt her again. Her hate became a shield she held between herself and the men she served. She no longer put up with pawing or groping from those who could not pay for her services, and if they persisted, she dipped their stew from yesterday's pot and watered their ale even beyond Dunwig's normal dilution. She made certain that those who would later come to her room had full purses on them, and she saw to it that they got the strongest ale from cups that were never empty. The more intoxicated they were, the less they demanded of her and the easier it was to control them. And to rifle their purses afterward. She gave the men what they paid for but no more. She did not even try to hide her contempt for them and demanded of them her own price, not merely what Dunwig charged. And if they did not pay, they would find their purses a few coins lighter next time they counted. She squirreled the money away, intending to buy out her indenture months early and save enough to move on to a larger town where she would set up her own business.

PART II

Lanson

τhe ReLease

The man sat upright, still as a marble statue. His seat was a rough pine bench set against a cold stone wall. His right hand rested in his lap, his left fist clenched into a tight knot. His eyes stared expressionless as a dead man into the darkness that enveloped him. He did not even feel the beetle that crawled across his bare foot; nor did he hear the slight, dry scraping in the straw as the bug pushed its way through it. The sun had set two hours ago, taking away the thin shaft of light that had beamed through the high, narrow window of his cell. But day or night did not matter. The man's mind burned hot with the same fevered thoughts whether in daylight or darkness, cold or heat, health or illness. It did not matter to him that he was imprisoned in one of the most humane dungeons in the Seven Kingdoms, or that he was well fed, warmly clothed, and even given books and parchments from time to time. In fact, it hardly mattered to the man that he was in a prison at all. His confinement was not the source of the anger that burned in his belly like molten iron. All the prisoner's waking thoughts were focused like sunrays through a broken bottle on the hated face of one man—Aradon of Meridan.

The man's throat tightened and his breath became a guttural rasp as he ran his left thumb along the scar on his right hand that marked the absence of his thumb and two fingers. Two years ago he had been jousting and dueling champion of the Kingdom of Valomar. A little over a year ago he had been a key conspirator in a plot to gain control of the Seven Kingdoms. And the plot had almost succeeded. He had worked the plan of the necromancer Morgultha. Thwarted in her first attempt to take the Seven Kingdoms, bitterness still smoldered hot in her black heart. She was determined that this time she would succeed. Under her direction, the prisoner had begun to take over governments of the villages on the outer edges of Meridan, the largest of the Seven Kingdoms. When many of the border villages were taken, he had begun to move inward, stealthily usurping established authority in town after town and replacing it with men loyal to him.

All had gone well until a chance stroke in a duel with a blacksmith-turned-warrior had left him with half his right hand missing. The blacksmith, Aradon by name, had then bound him and sent him to Meridan's regent, Lord Aldemar, for disposition. Aldemar had sent him back to his home kingdom of Valomar to be tried for conspiracy by the great King Tallis. And now he was condemned to molder in a cell of the garrison of Valomar's Oakendale Castle for twenty years.

"Aradon will pay for this." The words came tight and guttural through the man's clenched teeth as though forced from a cauldron of intense pain.

Soon the prisoner sighed deeply and slipped from the bench to the straw mattress on the stone floor. He pulled the woolen blanket around him and began to drift into sleep, once again fondling his favorite dream. The dream followed its now familiar pattern. He sat on the throne of Valomar, as Morgultha had promised he would. At his command, Aradon was brought groveling before him. But instead of condemning the blacksmith to death, he had the guards hold out both of the man's hands as he drew his sword and lopped them off. Then he watched with satisfaction as the man lay writhing and screaming on the floor.

As the dream faded, the prisoner suddenly awoke. He thought he had heard a soft scraping in the passageway outside his cell. He lay quiet and listened. In a moment he was sure of it. Someone in the corridor was creeping toward his cell. The prisoner remained quiet, hardly breathing as the sound ceased at his door. His ears strained to hear any sign of movement.

A whisper, barely audible but unmistakable, came through the darkness: "Brendal."

The prisoner rose to his elbow and turned toward the sound. "Brendal, it's me, Dalkane, your guard. You are about to be freed."

Brendal heard the scrape of the key in the lock and the clank of tumblers followed by the groan of the seldom-used hinges. Dalkane whispered a curse at the noise. When the creaking stopped, he held still as he listened for stirrings from the other cells. Hearing no cause for alarm, he entered Brendal's cell and continued his whispered instructions.

"At this moment a man is waitin' at the postern gate to take you away. You must make haste, but first you must do as I tell you. Here, take this club."

Brendal saw a hand extend from the shadow and he reached toward it. His left hand closed on a rough but rounded piece of wood. He ran his fingers along its length and found it to be about two feet long.

"Now you must hit me on the head so I will not be held responsible for your escape. Your father once did me a good turn, and I'm simply repayin' the debt. Go down this corridor till you reach the end, turn left, and follow the next corridor to the postern gate. Your friend Kalnor is waitin' for you across the moat with a fresh horse and a change of clothin'. Now, club me and be gone. Not too hard. On my bald head even a light blow will leave a beastly mark."

Brendal wasted no time asking questions. He lifted the club with his good left hand and brought it down on Dalkane's head, but not lightly. It was a blow from which the guard never awakened. Then by the dim light of widely spaced wall torches, he made his way through the corridors and out the postern gate. He swam the moat and found Kalnor waiting where Dalkane said he would be.

Brendal quickly changed into the dry clothing Kalnor gave him and mounted his horse, and the two men rode into the streets of the city. It was past midnight and the streets were empty and dark except for an occasional oil lantern hung from a post. To Brendal's ears the sound of the hooves on the cobbled pavement rebounded from the walls of the darkened buildings like hammers on anvils, and he wondered if the whole town wouldn't be awakened. But Kalnor, riding just ahead of him, seemed unconcerned. They passed beneath the weathered sign of the Green Rooster Alehouse, swaying slightly in the night air. The tavern's windows were now dark and the door closed, but the smell of stale mead and ale brought to Brendal memories of many evenings of song, laughter, and wenching with his friends and fellow knights. But those days were now gone.

They rounded a corner onto a lane narrow and straight. Suddenly Brendal's spine chilled and he drew his horse to an abrupt halt. Ahead stood a mounted watchman, clearly visible under the orange glow of a streetlamp.

"Don't worry about him," said Kalnor. "He's been paid."

Brendal urged his mount forward but kept his good left hand on the pommel of his sword. From long habit he was wary of lawmen, despite Kalnor's assurances. But as they rode past the gate, the watchman gave no indication that he even saw them, and soon they were out of the city riding the barely visible road toward Blackmore Forest.

Six men met them as they entered the shadows of the woods, all former aides to Brendal in his days of usurping village governments in Meridan. The eight men followed a trail deeper into the forest until Kalnor veered from it and led them through the brush to a sheltered hollow where they built a fire and made camp. One of the men got a wallet of salted pork from his saddlebag while another got a skin of ale, and when all were seated around the fire, Kalnor began to tell Brendal of all that had happened since he was imprisoned.

But Brendal held up his hand to stop him. "First I want to know one thing. Where is the blacksmith Aradon?"

Instantly the men stopped chewing their pork, and there was no sound but the crackling of the fire. They looked at one another uneasily until Kalnor drew a deep breath and said, "You won't be liking what I must tell you, Brendal. Aradon the blacksmith from Corenham was crowned King of Meridan some fourteen months ago. And he has wed your former betrothed, Valomar's Princess Volanna."

Brendal felt his stomach clench like a fist at the news. "How did this come about?" His voice was cold as iron. "King Alfron's son Prince

Lomar was to have been crowned king and Volanna was to wed him."

"It's a complicated story, but I'll try to simplify it. Lomar died—no one knows how, likely the victim of witchcraft, so we hear—and it was proved that Aradon was really the son of King Alfron and rightful heir to the throne."

Brendal sat stunned as he absorbed the incredible news, hate and jealousy seething through every nerve of his body. "There is more," said Kalnor. "In accordance with the prophecy of the uniting of the Seven Kingdoms, King Tallis, now Aradon's father-in-law, has brought the Kingdom of Valomar under Aradon's leadership. Two other kingdoms have already agreed to follow—namely Oranth and Rhondilar. They seem eager to align with Aradon because they think a confederation of the Seven Kingdoms will increase trade, and they hope to share in the bounty of the prophesied golden age. The remaining three kingdoms, Lochlaund, Sorendale, and Vensaur, still maintain their independence, though King Kor of Lochlaund and Umberland of Vensaur have both shown willingness to negotiate with Aradon about joining the confederation."

"It must not happen. It simply must not happen," growled Brendal, his good hand crushing his cut of salt pork. "What of Morgultha? Where is she?"

"Morgultha has fled Maldor Castle and now hides deep in a cave in the root of a mountain at the edge of Braegan Wood," answered Kalnor. "It was she who commanded your rescue, and we are taking you to her now."

Brendal slept little that night.

The next morning the men broke camp and continued their journey to Morgultha's hiding place. They traveled from dawn until sundown for five days before arriving at the mountain where she hid. Kalnor led them through a maze of boulders and into a hidden cleft between two peaks in the northern range of the Dragontooth Mountains. After an hour of riding single file, they entered the cleft and wound their way through a narrow passageway bounded on each side by steep ledges. Looking forward, Brendal saw a vast cloud of black, undulating forms rise into the air ahead of them.

"What is that?" he asked.

"Bats," replied Kalnor. "Morgultha's giant bats. I've heard she has them trained like hounds to do her own will."

The riders continued in the cleft until they came to an opening in the mountain wall shaped roughly like a giant keyhole. Still riding single file, they entered the black mouth of the cave. For a moment they could see nothing at all, but as they advanced, the darkness gave way to the light of torches set in the walls of the passageway. The corridor led them ever downward until, after a quarter-hour of riding, it opened into a cavernous room, also lit with torches, which revealed rows of stables along one of the walls. The ceiling was black with uncountable hanging forms, some of them twitching and swaying. *Morgultha's bats,* thought Brendal with a shudder.

Kalnor and his riders halted and dismounted. Silent servants dressed in the same gray as the cavern walls appeared as if from nowhere. They took the horses and led the men past the stable doors into a twisting corridor lined on each side by a forest of stalactites and stalagmites, many of them grown together in columns of grotesque, organic-looking forms. In minutes the trail widened and ended at a pool of water, where the servants told the men they could bathe. After the bath, they were given gray robes, which they donned and then followed the gray servants to a dining hall where their meal awaited. Afterward the servants showed them to their sleeping quarters, a single room of hewn stone lined on either side with cots. "You will see Morgultha in the morning," the chief of the servants told them as he closed the door. The clank of a bolt echoed through the caverns, telling them they were not here merely as Morgultha's guests.

The next morning the gray-clad servants awakened Brendal, Kalnor, and their men, and after serving breakfast in the dining hall, the chief of servants took Brendal alone to meet Morgultha. He led Brendal through a maze of corridors to a double door carved from two slabs of black marble, each at least sixteen feet high and six feet wide. The doors were set in a wall of rough-hewn stone, and in front of them stood guards clad in breastplates and helmets of a dull gray metal and armed with axes mounted on six-foot shafts. At a word from the servant the guards stood aside, and without a sound the doors opened inward.

Brendal stepped into a room so darkened that he could not see walls on any side. Directly before him lay a long table of the same polished black marble as the doors. The table was about seven feet wide and stretched away from him to a length of perhaps sixty feet. The only light in the room was a greenish glow from a small brazier set on the far end of the table, and the only movement was the flicker of that green flame and the wisp of gray smoke flowing off to the left. Behind the brazier, at the end of the table facing Brendal, sat Morgultha, still as stone, her long, thin face framed in a black hood and glowing green in the lurid firelight. Her eyes, almost as pale as her face, stared unblinking at Brendal.

The gray servant withdrew and the huge doors closed behind him. "Sit down, Brendal," said Morgultha, her voice low and cold as a winter draft. Brendal took the chair and faced the impassive countenance at the far end of the table. "You have failed me," she said, her voice clearly audible in spite of the distance and echoing in the cavernous hall. "I gave you a task and offered you a kingdom for its accomplishment. You had ample opportunities, but you squandered them all. You had the heart of the crown princess in your hand, but you let her slip away. I thought you had recovered from that error when you began to take over the villages on the outskirts of the Kingdom of Meridan, but you, the jousting champion of Valomar, let a stripling blacksmith overcome you and ruin you forever as a warrior. You have disappointed me, Brendal."

Brendal felt his stomach clench again at the mention of Aradon, but he forced his anger down. "Don't try to intimidate me, Morgultha. You have failed as well. You let Perivale defeat you and lost the Crown of Eden to him, along with your own right hand. Besides, it was not my hand that almost won Meridan for you; it was my head. And apparently you need that head again or you would not have risked the lives of seven men to free it."

"You think too highly of yourself, Brendal. The lives of those men mean nothing to me, and neither does yours. As to whether I need you again, that is yet to be seen."

"Don't take me for a fool. You would not have brought me here unless you needed me. So enough of this pretense. Tell me what you want of me."

"As I said, you have failed me twice. Yet I freed you because I am willing to give you one last opportunity to redeem your past incompetence and prove yourself worthy of the reward that can yet be yours."

Brendal shot up from his chair. "Morgultha, I will not abide these accusations. I—"

"You are in no position to make demands. I have taken you from Valomar's prison and I can return you there. Indeed, I have prisons of my own right here in the roots of this mountain. In fact, you are my prisoner at this moment. You cannot leave until it pleases me to dismiss you. So get control of your rage, sit down, and hear what I have to say."

Slowly Brendal eased back into his chair, glaring all the while at the pale, heavy-lidded eyes glowering balefully from above her angular cheekbones. Robed in black as she was, her face seemed to float in the darkness like a disembodied wraith. "Now," said Morgultha, "listen carefully to me. You have heard already that the blacksmith Aradon wears the Crown of Eden and is now King of Meridan. However, the prophesied uniting of the Seven Kingdoms has not yet been achieved. Three kingdoms have yet to move into Aradon's alliance, and there lies our hope. We must do all we can to prevent these kingdoms from aligning with Meridan. I can do only so much myself. Too many in Meridan know who I am, and they will be watchful and wary of me. With some disguising I can risk the roads in the mountains and farmlands, but I must stay clear of the villages. I need you to be my front. If you are successful, I will hold to my original agreement and give you the throne of one of the kingdoms, Valomar if possible. If you are not successful, I will have your head."

At Morgultha's threat Brendal's anger erupted like a nest of startled hornets, but he held himself in check as he glared at the immobile face before him, thinking she now seemed much closer than before. "Very well," he said. "I will listen to what you have to say, though I will promise nothing until I have heard you out."

"I will humor your delusion that you have a choice and give you the gist of my plan. Since we have no army, we must resort to subtlety. Lacking power, we must use leverage. All it takes to control the greatest ship is to turn the rudder, which we can do even with the few men we have. We must act on three fronts. And fortunately, on one of them little action is needed for the moment. King Morgamond of Sorendale has no love for Aradon and seems safely resistant to the Seven Kingdom federation. We can leave him alone for now and direct our attention to the other two fronts. We must stop King Kor of Lochlaund and King Umberland of Vensaur from aligning their kingdoms with Meridan. And we haven't much time. Both are presently inclined toward him and have begun negotiations. Our best hope is to find a way to get our few numbers into those two castles to depose the kings. And we must do it without attracting Aradon's attention."

"Why shouldn't we attract Aradon's attention?" asked Brendal. "Why not capture the two kings in palace coups and hold them hostage to our demand that Aradon relinquish his quest to control the Seven Kingdoms?"

"Because Aradon has nothing to relinquish. The three kingdoms that have joined his confederation came to him voluntarily. He has steadfastly refused to resort to persuasion or coercion. So he has nothing to undo. Holding kings hostage would be futile for he has taken no action that he can withdraw or recant.

"We must do our work quietly without arousing undue attention because we do not want to provoke Aradon into war. Although he will not coerce his fellow kings to bend to his own will, he might protect them from outside interference. And if he did come against us in war, we would not have the power to stop the amassed armies of the three kingdoms already aligned with him. The idea of a hostage does have merit but it must be the right hostage to apply the right leverage."

"No doubt you have already identified such a hostage," said Brendal. Morgultha seemed much closer, as if the long table were shrinking as they talked.

"I have indeed chosen a hostage," she replied. "Aradon has a new daughter not yet six months old, who may be all the rudder we need to wreck his ship on the shoals."

There was no doubt about it. Morgultha now sat only a few feet in front of Brendal. He could see the narrow black pupils in her pale eyes, and a chill ran up his spine. He did not know if her apparent nearness was an illusion designed to intimidate him, or if by some uncanny magic she had actually shrunk the table. "If you want me to engineer a plot to kidnap the infant and bring her to you, my answer is yes. I would like nothing better than to be the cause of grief to her parents."

"No," replied Morgultha. "I have that scheme well in hand. A servant of my own works already in Morningstone Castle and sometimes serves Queen Volanna as wet nurse. She is biding her time, gaining the trust of the royal couple and learning the passages and rhythms of the castle before she makes her move. The babe will be in my hands in a matter of weeks."

"Then what do you need of me?" asked Brendal. "As you said, control the life of the babe and you control Aradon. All else is superfluous."

"I know better than to hide all my gold in one pot," replied Morgultha. "We must work on the other two fronts as well. If we fail on one, we will succeed on the other. Your task is to carry out plots I have already devised to overthrow kings Kor and Umberland, and you must do it quickly."

"Very well. Show me what you have in mind," Brendal said. Morgultha now sat so close he could have reached out and touched her, though he shuddered at the thought of doing such a thing.

Morgultha spent that day and the next two explaining the details of her plots. She went over maps and diagrams of the castles of Kor and Umberland, and told Brendal everything her men had learned about the agreement Kor was drafting for confederation with Aradon. On the fourth day she outfitted him with weapons, armor, and a horse and assigned to him a company of seventy men. When Brendal was set to be on his way, Morgultha called him into her presence at the long table once more. She did not invite him to sit but spoke as he stood at the far end. "Do not forget the terms of your service to me, Brendal." Her lips curled into something like a snarl, exposing her long white teeth. "When you ride out of here you may think yourself free, but you are still my prisoner. You are on trial and I am your sole judge. Succeed and you win a kingdom. Fail and you lose your life. And should it come into your head that you might simply ignore your fealty to me and escape, remember that the men I have given you may be under your command, but their first loyalty is to me. They are not only your servants; they are your jailors as well. Now, be on your way."

Without a word Brendal turned from Morgultha and left her presence, seething with anger. Who was she to impose such a test on him? He would indeed implement her plots in Vensaur and Lochlaund, but if he was successful, why shouldn't he ignore Morgultha and her ambitions and take the reign of the Seven Kingdoms himself?

Brendal wasted no time. Within two weeks King Umberland of Vensaur mysteriously disappeared while on a hunt with men of his court. Lord Caldemone, who replaced him immediately, sent letters to Aradon rejecting any further discussion of the subject of confederation. Shortly afterward it became widely known that Brendal had escaped his prison in Valomar and had been invited to take up residence in Lord Caldemone's castle. Many observers who knew Brendal from his days in Meridan harbored a strong suspicion that if the truth were known, he might be the one who held the real power in Vensaur, while Lord Caldemone was merely a puppet.

On learning of Brendal's presence in Vensaur, King Tallis of Valomar immediately sent to Lord Caldemone a request for extradition of the escaped prisoner, but his letter was not even answered. Within another two weeks Brendal easily convinced the stalwart but politically inept King Morgamond of Sorendale to reject confederation with Meridan and align with Vensaur.

These unexpected developments caused great concern among the leaders of the other kingdoms. While there was no evidence that Brendal was involved in any way, a strong suspicion grew in the minds of many observers that he was the mastermind behind the actions in Vensaur and Sorendale, and some surmised that he was trying to form his own empire in opposition to King Aradon. Soon afterward Aradon's advisors gained evidence that Vensaur and Sorendale were building up their armies. But as long as such actions were taken in the names of the legitimate rulers of those nations, no one could find legal cause to move against them.

ℒ⁊

After these events became known, the forty-two members of Meridan's Hall of Knights met to debate the subject of the confederation of the Seven Kingdoms. Some of the knights, led by Sir Llewenthane, urged King Aradon to wage immediate war to bring the three recalcitrant kingdoms into line. Through his network of intelligence sources, Aradon knew that the common people in the three kingdoms were unhappy with the changes that had been imposed. And he was fairly sure that Brendal was behind the building of the armies of Sorendale and Vensaur. Llewenthane urged Aradon to attack immediately before Brendal became too strong to overcome. But Lord Aldemar and Aradon's general, Sir Denmore, urged the young king to continue his policy of diplomacy. After listening thoughtfully to his knights and advisors, Aradon chose to stay on the diplomatic course. If the alliance was to re-form, he insisted that the confederation would be voluntary, not coerced. He would not become the aggressor and violate the independence of the sister kingdoms by waging war without provocation. He would trust the prophecy to fulfill itself in its own good time.

ᴅᴜᴛʏ ᴀɴᴅ ᴘʟᴇᴀsᴜʀᴇ

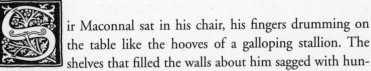ir Maconnal sat in his chair, his fingers drumming on the table like the hooves of a galloping stallion. The shelves that filled the walls about him sagged with hundreds of volumes of books and scrolls, all carefully cataloged and ordered. Lochlaund's library was second only to that of King Tallis in the Seven Kingdoms, and King Kor was justly proud of it. The musty smell of dust and old leather filled the room. Four or five books, all with leather cases and gilded lettering on the spines, were stacked on the table at which Maconnal sat. Another volume lay open in front of him, its yellowed pages mottled and crinkled, filled with neat rows of carefully wrought black letters with red and green flourishes decorating the initial capitals. But the man was no longer reading. He glanced yet again at the empty chair opposite him and continued to drum his fingers. "Where is that boy?" he muttered. After another five minutes, he rose abruptly from his chair and strode from the library, his dark blue cape billowing behind him. He hurried down the spiral stairs and marched down the corridor in front of the great hall and out of the castle keep into the grassy bailey.

Already Sir Maconnal could hear the sharp, bright clang of blunted swords coming from inside the stone fence that enclosed the practice yard in front of the armory. As he approached the fence he saw the shapely backs of two young chargirls, their baskets of clothes on the ground beside them. Their elbows rested on the top of the fence as they chatted and giggled while watching the young men dueling within the enclosure. The object of their attention was a tall, well-formed man with dark, thick hair crowning a clean-shaven face of strong masculine features. The young man had outmatched all previous challengers, and his present opponent stumbled and retreated before strokes that flashed in the sun like lightning. When the girls heard the approach of Sir Maconnal's footsteps, they turned, blushed, quickly gathered their baskets, and hurried on to the wash house.

Sir Maconnal flung open the gate and marched up to the duelers. "Prince Lanson, are you aware of the time?" he said to the young man.

Lanson wiped his glistening face with his sleeve and closed his eyes in chagrin. "I am very sorry, Sir Maconnal. I have no excuse. I was preparing for the Surrifax tournament, and I simply let the time get away. I will follow you back to the library right now."

"Not until you bathe and change," said Maconnal, scowling at the prince's soaked tunic. "I'll not have you dripping sweat on your father's books. To be sure your attention doesn't wander again, I shall wait for you. I had the foresight to bring a book to pass the time as you bathe."

Sir Maconnal followed Prince Lanson and the half-dozen young men with him as they returned their weapons to the armory and headed for the bathing fountain, stripping off their clothing as they ran, leaving a trail of tunics and leggings from the dueling yard to the pool. Laughing and bellowing in sheer good humor, the young men jumped into the water and began to thrash about. Maconnal sat on a nearby bench shaded by an old oak and opened his book.

"Lanson," said one of the men, "did you see the two chargirls watching you? Winsome lasses, both of them. And by the gleam in their eyes I'd say you would have little trouble getting either of them into a hayloft."

"Our pure and pristine prince is not interested in such things," said another. "He'd rather curl up with a book than a girl any day. Right, Lanson?"

"You know better, Moburne," replied Prince Lanson as he scrubbed his arms. "It's not a lack of interest; it's simply the lack of a wife."

"Lanson, is it true that you have never tasted the joys of a woman?" asked another.

"Of course. The Master of the Universe expects of us to wait until we are wed, does he not?"

"Oh, I know that's what is written, but it's too hard a command for a healthy man. The urge outstrips the will, and there are few who can resist."

"You mean there are few who try to resist," replied Lanson. "If you vow to resist, abstinence becomes a matter of your integrity."

"There you go again, Lanson. You beat us about the yard with your blade, then beat us over the head with your kirky chastity. I don't know whether you are becoming the greatest swordsman in the Seven Kingdoms or the greatest monk." Moburne punctuated his complaint by splashing a spray of water into Lanson's face.

"We'd best not speak so loud," said one of the men, looking all about the pool. "What if someone overhears us and reports us to the accorder? We could be hauled before the bishop and put in stocks for the sort of things we're saying."

"Oh, don't be so timid, Rogarre," said Moburne. "There's no one about to hear us but Maconnal, and everyone knows he's far from being a slave to the kirk."

"Anyway, Lanson won't have to wait much longer. I hear that Bishop Hugal has clenched a match with King Kor to wed our prince to the bishop's niece," said one of the men.

"You mean Lamonda?" said Moburne, his eyebrows lifted in disbelief. "Lanson, are you really going to marry that cold fish?"

"No wonder he'd rather love a book," said Rogarre.

"The match has not been finalized," said Lanson as he scrubbed his thick hair.

"Why not? Is she demanding a contract that you will live in separate chambers?"

"Or that you extend your vow of celibacy through the duration of the marriage?"

"Or that you make a eunuch of yourself?" The men all laughed as Moburne grabbed a couple of floating reeds and splashed toward Lanson, crossing and snapping them like scissors.

"Perhaps it won't be such a bad match after all. Lanson and Lamonda will spend so much time reading the old kirk scrolls and discussing theology they won't have time for anything else."

"Perhaps you misjudge the girl," said Lanson as he swam toward the edge of the pool. "She may not be as cold inside as she appears on the surface."

"I should hope not, or you may be risking yourself to a serious case of frostbite." The men all laughed and Lanson hurled his bathing rag at Moburne's face, where it splatted with deadly accuracy.

"And what's worse, Lamonda never laughs at Lanson's jokes," said Rogarre.

"No one ever laughs at Lanson's jokes."

"In fact, as I think on it," continued Moburne, "I've never seen the woman laugh at all—or even smile. Have you ever seen her laugh, Lanson?"

"Who wants to wed a giggling imbecile?" retorted Lanson. "Is it such a bad thing to have a wife who takes life seriously?"

The prince grew quiet as they all climbed out of the pool and toweled themselves dry. Some of his friends' barbs had struck home. Although he was a year over twenty and many lords and kings had tried to match him with their daughters, he had resisted marriage simply because he had not found a woman who inspired him to a life-time of commitment. Indeed, he was not even certain he knew ex-actly what that woman should be like.

But of late his father, King Kor, had begun to speak to him of his duty to provide an heir for the Kingdom of Lochlaund. "If you don't find a wife soon, I shall have to do it for you," his father had warned. When another a year had passed and Lanson still had not found a woman to his liking, Kor had become impatient and began to make arrangements with his friend Hugal, Bishop of Lochlaund, for the hand of his niece Lamonda.

Although Prince Lanson could muster no enthusiasm for the match, the thought of resisting it brought him pangs of guilt. For by all tangible measures, Lamonda was the ideal mate. Under the tutelage of her uncle she had become a serious student of the scrolls of the prophets and the writings of the sages of old. She held the laws of the Master of the Universe to be firm and inviolable and followed diligently all the practices and traditions of the Kirk of Lochlaund. Lanson dutifully agreed with all who told him how fortunate he would be to have such a committed and upright woman as his mate. But the match troubled him, and he knew his friends had put their fingers directly on the reason. He had never seen an ounce of warmth or good humor in the girl. He knew that warmth and good humor were not the core ingredients to a sound marriage, and he felt guilt at desiring such self-serving peripherals when the woman possessed fundamental attributes for which he should be grateful. Nevertheless, uneasiness about the match continued to plague him.

He donned his clean clothing, bid farewell to his companions, and walked with Sir Maconnal to the castle keep and climbed the stairway to the library. Again he apologized as he took his seat across the table from his tutor. But Maconnal waved it off, opened the book before him, and got right into the lesson.

"Today we begin a new subject—our relationship to the kirk and the Master of the Universe. According to Merculian, what is the highest duty of man?"

"To do the will of the Master of the Universe, of course," answered Lanson.

"Of course," muttered Maconnal. "And why is it so terribly important to the Master that we obey his laws?"

"He is testing us to see if we are fit for his reward of heaven," Lanson replied.

"So he looks on us as trained dogs to see how many hoops we are willing to jump through to earn a place in the eternal kennel, eh?"

"It's not like that. Our obedience simply brings glory to him."

"So you think obedience to law is a sop to the divine's craving for adulation. Has it ever occurred to you that all laws might be given for our own good, that all acts of obedience result in a natural benefit to us? In fact, that his instructions are designed to show us how to side-step evil and be deliriously and ecstatically happy?"

Lanson sat for a moment trying to place the words of his tutor into the matrix of his understanding. They seemed entirely the wrong shape and would not fit. "But, Maconnal, doesn't duty require that one put aside happiness for some greater good?"

"Give me an example," said Maconnal.

"Well, there is the matter of my impending betrothal to Lady Lamonda. Frankly, I hardly even like the woman, much less love her. But duty to my kingdom demands that I wed a woman fit to be queen, and the good of the kingdom is a greater thing than my happiness."

"Are you sure the Master will be pleased when you treat the gift of marriage as a duty?" Maconnal challenged.

"The marriage contract is filled with duties," replied Lanson. "Protection, self-sacrifice, providing shelter and food, begetting children. When we look beyond these duties and seek the pleasures of marriage, we succumb to earthly desires, which draw us from our devotion to the Master. We must neither seek nor expect happiness on this earth. Life is a vale of tears and happiness a vanity of self-seekers."

"Are you saying we should avoid being too happy?"

"That's what we read in the scrolls. When the ancient prophet Suribad found himself becoming too joyful, he would curb the tendency by wearing hair shirts, walking barefoot on sharp pebbles, eating raw insects, and driving pins into his flesh."

"That should have done the trick," Maconnal replied. "But tell me this. By depriving himself of joy did Suribad reflect the nature of his Maker?"

"I think he did. The Master grieves continually at our failure to obey him, and we have no right to be joyful while he is grieving."

"Do you think grieving over us consumes all his emotions? Tell me where the idea of happiness came from? Is it from the Master of the Universe or from the Dark One?"

"All frivolity is an impertinence to the Master. It must come from the Dark One."

"Really now, are happiness and joy impertinences? Is it possible that you have things inverted? Has it ever occurred to you that the Master of the Universe laughs?"

Lanson stared speechless at Maconnal. Such an idea had never entered his head.

"I can see that you think me a heretic," said Maconnal. "Not so, my young prince. It's true that the kirk of today would hardly endorse what I've just told you, but the kirk has drifted from its original understanding of the nature of the Master. Haven't you read that all creation was pronounced good? Before they turned from the Master to themselves, Adam and Eve lived each day in sheer delight, laughter, and ecstasy, and that is the life the Master intended for all humanity forever. In spite of your uprightness, you do not know the Master as well as you think you do. You might learn more about him if you attended a few less masses and a few more dances."

"Sir Maconnal, you are speaking things so close to blasphemy that I'm not sure I should listen."

"Shut your ears if you will, but first let me give you one bit of advice. Before you bind yourself to Lamonda, answer the question Moburne raised. Is there a spark of humanity buried anywhere beneath her icy exterior?"

"Well, I hardly know how one would go about finding out."

"I will tell you how. No matter how cold and resistant, women want men to act as men and break down their defenses. It is part of the game. Look at the mating dance of birds—the female seems always to be fleeing the male, but never so far that he can't catch her. Lamonda may be dancing away to whet your urge to pursue. Perhaps she is simply waiting for you to break down her defenses."

"Maconnal! What are you saying? You know I have vowed not to—"

"No, no, my dear, upright prince. I'm not suggesting anything improper. But would it sully your vow to take the girl in your arms and kiss her? Her response might tell you whether there is any reservoir of warmth in her soul. I suggest you try it. And the sooner the better."

"I . . . I don't think I know how to kiss a girl."

Sir Maconnal leaned back in his chair, placed his palms to his forehead, and sighed. "I see that I have failed you. I have trained you well in all the matters of kingcraft—statesmanship, economics, diplomacy, military strategy, and law—but I have sorely neglected the most important thing: love. I should have known the bishop's sermons would poison your view of love. The kirk has reduced the man-woman relationship to a duty fenced by restrictions aimed at smothering joy and pleasure. And in doing this, it has slapped the face of the Master of the Universe."

Lanson started as if his own face had been slapped. He stared with amazement at his tutor. "How can you speak such things against the kirk? Don't you know that heretics have been condemned for less?"

"You misread me, Lanson. I'm no heretic. I, too, have a strong commitment to the Master of the Universe, and in many ways it takes the same form as yours. Like you I kept myself from intimacy with women before I married. I never steal; I honored my parents; I abhor a lie; I was faithful to my wife. But in spite of what the kirk teaches, I have learned to believe that the Master intended us to experience pleasure and joy. Now, it is true as you suggested earlier that duty sometimes means the denial of pleasure. But denial was never the Master's original intention. And even so, the reason we are called to make such denials is so that good may abound to others. Sometimes a few must go hungry so that all may have food. The strong must share their power with the weak. But the kirk has made duty and sacrifice ends to themselves and the total focus of our relationship to the Master, forgetting that the ultimate purpose of duty and sacrifice is to foster a greater attainment of joy for all."

"But he gave us mountains of rules and laws," said Lanson, gesturing to the rows of books on the shelves about them.

"All meant to help us avoid the pitfalls that keep us from joy. Law curbs our selfish tendencies and warns of obstacles to delight. Three-fourths of the books in this room are filled with laws not given by the Master but appended by the kirk. Seeking to become holier than the Master himself, the kirk has made pleasure an evil and added a mountain of rules to block our experience of it. The kirk has bound us to rules where the Master intended us to be free to enjoy."

"Are you saying the kirk and the Master of the Universe are at odds with each other? I can hardly believe that you can just march in and tell me that generations of teachings by holy men of the kirk are wrong."

"But I can read the original scrolls and compare them with the writings of later fathers just as you can yourself. Here is what they will show you. The kirk has armored us so heavily in rules that we cannot move. Originally the Master gave us only a core outline of law. He also gave us a mind and an innate sense of right and wrong by which we could apply it. But man feels insecure without rules. We tend to grasp for rules like an infant grasps the finger thrust into its hand. When the kirk fathers became ever more uncomfortable with behavior that did not square with their own sense of propriety, they began to encrust the Master's law with rules of their own that they enforced as strictly as law itself."

Maconnal took note of Lanson's furrowed brow and closed his book. He knew he had given his patient all the medicine he could take in one dose. "The lesson is over for the day. I'll meet you here tomorrow."

"Father is sending me to Valthorne tomorrow to help negotiate water rights with King Tallis for building a dam on the River Tynor. He thinks I should learn such things."

"He is right. I had forgotten. You won't be back for more than a week, and before you return I will leave for the southern continent to negotiate another trade agreement for your father. So lessons are off for a few weeks. But I think I have given you enough cud to chew until I return—and an assignment as well."

"An assignment?"

"The kiss, Lanson, the kiss. Kiss the woman and see what happens. I will expect a report when I return."

"Well, I will think on it. But one thing more, Sir Maconnal. Until you mentioned it moments ago, I did not know that you had been married. May I ask if your wife—"

"I'm sorry, my prince, it's a thing I cannot presently speak of. Perhaps someday I will answer you, but not yet."

"Of course. Forgive me for asking." Both men stood and Maconnal bowed to the prince, who turned and left the library.

Maconnal slumped again into his chair and ran his hand through his brown hair, just beginning to gray at the temples. He gazed out the window, seeing nothing of the lush green of Lochlaund's hills as pictures from his own past played through his mind. Lost in his reverie, he sat unmoving until from the corner of his eye he saw one of the books move from the table. He started. "Oh, it's you, Alenia," he said. "I didn't hear you come in."

"Of course not. You never know I'm around. I'm the silent, invisible ghost of the library." Alenia was a fair woman in her mid-thirties with light blond hair, eyes of deep brown, and full, sensitive lips that could look solemn as a priest or laugh at the slightest provocation. She had been a maid in Macrennon Castle for half her life.

"What are you doing here?"

"Do you think these books sprout legs and jump back on their shelves after your lessons? If I didn't lug and hoist them, every book in this room would be piled on this table." She took the heavy volume to the nearest shelf.

"Don't put it there," said Maconnal. "No wonder I have to hunt all over the library for every book I want. Place it where it belongs."

"How about if I just leave them on that table so you'll have them all at your fingertips?"

Maconnal wondered why the servant—a castle favorite—was being so difficult. Suddenly he suspected the reason. "Alenia, can you read?"

"No, I cannot," she sighed. "I wish I could. I had an aunt who could read, and she said every book was a door to another world where one could find mysteries and adventures enough to broaden any life."

"Your aunt was right. Why don't you let me teach you to read?"

Alenia's eyes brightened as if lanterns had been lit inside them. "Oh, would you really do that for me?"

"Of course. In fact we could start now. I cut the prince's lesson short today and have a little time to spare. And since he will be out of the castle this week, we can take his daily lesson time to continue."

The maid Alenia thanked Maconnal profusely and sat at the table across from him. An hour later when the lesson was over she finished replacing the books—this time under his watchful direction. After he left the library she dusted and swept the room from top to bottom, as she had done for all of the twelve years Maconnal had taught there, but with a lighter step and a song on her lips. It was the first time he had ever acknowledged her existence.

☙

Prince Lanson was to dine privately with his father that evening. As he climbed the stone steps to the king's chambers on the second floor, his mind wrestled with the startling thoughts his tutor had thrust into his head. The prince and his father had always been close, a closeness that had increased to a mutual bond of fierce loyalty after the death of the queen some five years ago.

King Kor was seated and waiting as Lanson entered. After greeting his father, the prince took the seat opposite him at the table. Servants brought a dinner of roasted hen, leeks, a thick vegetable soup, and brown bread, and the two men fell to their plates as they exchanged news of the day and discussed the king's expectations from Maconnal's negotiations. When Kor had scooped his last spoonful of soup, he pushed himself back and looked at his son.

"Well, Lanson, it seems that you will soon be a bridegroom. Today Bishop Hugal and I worked out the last of the details of your marriage contract with Lady Lamonda. His clerk will look over the terms for a few days and justify his existence by changing a word here and there. Then we will sign the agreement and proceed with the wedding."

Lanson hesitated long before answering. "Father, I must admit that I'm not as happy about this news as I feel I should be."

King Kor raised his eyebrows in surprise. "Why not, Son?"

"I hate to admit that it matters, but . . . don't you think Lady Lamonda seems a little cold and prim?"

"Surely you don't want a wife who is frivolous and flighty. And you must think of the future. Someday she will be more than a mere wife. She will be Queen of Lochlaund, and Lamonda is an upstanding young woman who will take that duty seriously."

"Oh, I have no doubts on that point. But I have come to hope for something more in a wife, and I'm not sure I see it in Lamonda."

"Nevertheless, you have a duty to perform to your kingdom, Son. And I am certain that Lamonda will fulfill her duty to you as well and produce an heir to the throne of Lochlaund."

"I'm sure she will, Father. But I can't help but wonder if it is wrong for a man to desire something more from a marriage than duty—what Maconnal calls the ecstasy of love between a man and a woman."

"You know what the kirk says about such things."

"Yes, but do you sometimes wonder if the kirk has it exactly right? Is it possible that the kirk has made laws and imposed restrictions where the Master never intended?" Lanson had hardly believed the arguments his tutor had heaped upon him, but now he cast them toward his father to test their strength.

King Kor sighed before reciting to his son the official kirk doctrine. "You know that long ago the kirk found it expedient to put a fence around pleasure because pleasure is a seductive harlot that lures men and women away from the Master of the Universe."

"But if pleasure is created by the Master, it must be good, for nothing evil can come from him. And if good, there can be no sin in desiring it."

"I cannot deny that the Master is the maker of pleasure," responded Kor, "since he is the maker of everything. But consider well what the kirk has taught us—that he created pleasure as a test for man. If a man can maintain his commitment to the Master in spite of the lure of pleasure, that man will receive the Master's reward."

"Does not the Master want us to experience joy? Is all pleasure strictly forbidden? Must we admit to nothing pleasurable in the marriage relationship?"

Kor was quiet for a long moment as he stared out the window, a distant look in his eyes. "Son, I will admit to you that in spite of what the kirk tells us, I have come to think that some limited pleasure may be legitimate. Yet a man must not indulge in too much of it or let it carry him away."

Lanson could see that his father was troubled by uncertainty on the matter, and he let the subject drop. His father's doubts gave Maconnal's arguments greater force in the young man's mind. After turning the talk to hunting and the upcoming water rights negotiations, Lanson embraced his father and took leave of him to return to his own chambers.

After Prince Lanson departed, King Kor sat gazing out the window of his chambers, his elbows resting on the arms of his chair and his fingers laced beneath his chin. His son had pushed against a door in his mind that hid thoughts he had not dared express since his confrontation with Bishop Hugal over the sentence of the adulterous woman less than a year ago. The king sighed. The woman's pleas for mercy still rang in his mind. He heard them every night as he lay down to sleep and every morning when he awakened. Though he was king of a sovereign nation, he felt locked inside a prison. He could not move in the direction his conscience pointed. The rigid laws of the kirk constrained him like dungeon bars. In condemning the adulterous woman, he had chosen to sacrifice his conscience for the good of the kingdom. Or so he had told himself. But when he was alone and the woman's screams reverberated in his skull, he often wondered. Had he really backed down to Hugal for the good of the kingdom? Or was it simply for fear of the consequences of crossing the kirk?

He thought bringing Lochlaund into the Seven Kingdom federation of King Aradon would go far to diminish the stranglehold of the kirk over the people of Lochlaund. When he had mentioned the idea (but not his reasons) to Hugal a few months ago, the bishop was clearly alarmed, as Kor had known he would be. The kirkman had argued against it vehemently. The kirk was not strong in Meridan. Aradon was an untrained king—indeed, a mere blacksmith. He would be a puppet to his father-in-law King Tallis of Valomar, whose disdain for the Kirk of Lochlaund was well known. But having backed down to Hugal on one matter of conscience, the king was determined not to repeat the mistake and held his ground. The week after, he had sent an emissary to King Aradon to begin negotiations. He noted that in subsequent meetings with Hugal, his friend was noticeably cooler, though strangely, he never brought up the subject of confederation again. Kor could not help but wonder what steps the bishop was taking to oppose the move.

King Kor had never discussed his questions about the kirk with his son, and he reminded himself to do it soon. However, he found comfort in knowing the prince's education was in the hands of the scholar Sir Maconnal. Perhaps the tutor would instill into Lanson the courage to follow his conscience, even if it meant standing against the kirk. Taking what comfort he could from the thought, he sighed again and wearily pushed himself out of his chair and retired for the night.

CHAPTER TEN

NIGHT OF INFAMY

rince Lanson sat at the long elevated table next to his father, King Kor. The treaty with Meridan was to be signed tonight, and about seventy diners filled the hall. A core of lords, diplomats, and knights of Lochlaund, along with their ladies, comprised about forty of these, while Aradon's delegation, unaccompanied by their women, made up the rest. Lady Lamonda sat at Lanson's right, and to the left of King Kor sat Sir Cramalon, chief of Aradon's delegation. Other officials, both of Meridan and Lochlaund, sat at the tables below the dais. The food had not yet been served, but servants bearing large ewers moved among the tables, keeping the tankards full of wine and mead.

Prince Lanson sat with his back rigid and his expression impassive, unconsciously reflecting the attitude of the woman sitting next to him. Lamonda was a pretty woman, or at least, she could have been had she chosen to enhance her best features. Her eyes were a clear gray, but no kohl darkened the lashes. Her unreddened lips were sometimes full, but only when she opened them to eat or speak. The rest of the time she kept them pursed into a thin line. Her chestnut hair was pulled straight back and bound in a complexity of russet ribbons and bands the same color as her dress, which was high of collar with a loose bodice and a plain, straight skirt.

"Sir Eanor sends his regrets that he could not be here, your majesty," said Cramalon. "He was bitterly disappointed when the illness hit him and he could not leave his bed."

"I do wish the man could have come," replied Kor. "Eanor crafted the treaty, and I must say he was very fair with me. But such is the way of the world. It seems that the harvest is often denied to its planter."

Lanson looked around the hall and wondered at the large number of men Aradon had sent to the ceremony. "Sir Eanor must be an exceptional man," he said. "At the crafting of the treaty in Meridan, only he and four other men met with our delegation. Tonight you've brought thirty or more. Does it take so many to replace Eanor?"

Sir Cramalon laughed, a hollow sound without humor that stretched his mouth very little. "Nay, your highness. King Aradon had initially made plans to attend the signing himself, but he was called to other duties at the last minute. He insisted on sending thirty men as a token of the great honor he wished to show to Lochlaund's king."

"We thank you for your honor," said King Kor.

Lanson, not completely satisfied with Cramalon's answer, opened his mouth to speak again but felt an elbow nudge his right arm. He turned toward the glaring eyes of Lamonda, who leaned toward his ear and whispered, "I see no need to be rude to our guests."

"I am not intending to be rude. But it doesn't take thirty men to sign a treaty, and I cannot fathom why King Aradon sent so many."

"Sir Cramalon just told you—to do honor to Lochlaund. Let it rest."

"Is it such a great honor to feed and quarter thirty men when a half-dozen would do?"

"I'm shocked at you, Lanson. Have you no bone of hospitality in your body? I should think—"

At that moment a short trumpet fanfare filled the hall announcing the entrance of the servants bearing the evening's feast. They marched in single file, each carrying a dish or a bowl filled with vegetable soups, savory pies, pheasants, salmon, dates, and nuts. Menservants followed, bearing on their shoulders broad boards heavy with steaming platters of spitted pork and beef.

When a whole roast pig appeared in front of Sir Cramalon and King Kor, Cramalon immediately wrenched a leg from the carcass and began to gnaw and tear at it with much slurping and smacking, oblivious to the quieter, cleaner manners of his host, who sliced off a piece with a knife and placed it on his plate. Lanson looked about the hall and noticed that all of Aradon's delegation ate with the same animal sloppiness. It was not the first time he had seen men eat with their hands and toss the bones to the floor, but it was the first time he had seen such manners in men of the courts of Meridan, Valomar, or Lochlaund, which had for over a generation adopted a code of more refined etiquette from the nations across the Narrow Sea. Again he felt that something seemed amiss. He turned to Lamonda and said, "Are you as surprised as I am that the manners of Aradon's delegation seem so boorish?"

"What can you expect of a kingdom ruled by a blacksmith?" she replied.

"King Aradon's story is quite remarkable, isn't it?" said Lanson. "Actually the son of King Alfron but raised as a blacksmith to hide him from the schemes of Morgultha. The Master's providence at work."

"Of course, but a blacksmith king is sure to be more blacksmith than king. The reputation of the court of Meridan will be set back for a generation."

"Perhaps it took a blacksmith to forge an ironclad treaty with my father," said Lanson with a grin. With a sniff and a toss of her head, Lamonda returned to her plate. Lanson tested another subject.

"Apparently my father and your uncle have brought us close to a wedding."

"So it seems," she said without looking up.

"Are you pleased?"

"I will do my duty."

"I don't doubt it for a moment, but is duty all you expect from our marriage? Do you hope for joy at all?"

"Of course. We will have the joy of knowing that our union serves the Master."

"And that is a fine joy indeed. But since he created us male and female, do you think—"

"I think it inappropriate for a man to discuss such things with a woman. We will encounter such necessities all too soon when we are wed."

Lanson turned back to his plate and remained silent as he ate. *This will not do,* he thought. *Moburne is right; the woman is a cold fish.* Suddenly he thought of Maconnal's assignment. As the dinner progressed he grew more and more determined to try his tutor's advice. He knew he might not find a better opportunity than tonight. The idea of kissing Lamonda made him a little uneasy, and he wished his tutor were here to give him moral support, maybe even a few pointers. When many of the guests had finished their meal and began milling about the room, he turned to Lamonda and said, "Would you care to accompany me to the balcony?"

Without showing any enthusiasm for the idea, she stood and took his arm, and they walked across the hall to the balcony. Soon they were standing together in the fresh night air overlooking the city of Macrennon.

"Isn't the moonlight on the city beautiful tonight?" said Lanson.

"It looks very cold," she said and drew her shawl about her.

He looked at her profile. In spite of her refusal to enhance her eyes or redden her lips, she had good features and smooth, healthy skin.

"In fact, you are beautiful in the moonlight yourself."

"If you intend that as a compliment, you miss your mark. Don't you know that beauty is a snare that tempts man's emotions to abandon his reason?"

Disheartened by such a response, Lanson decided to think no more. Before she could know what he was about, he took her in his arms and kissed her full on the mouth. Lamonda neither responded to the kiss nor resisted it, but remained unmoving as a gatepost until Lanson released her from his embrace. She stood passively, her arms hanging inert at her sides, her eyes staring at him with cool reproach. Lanson was exasperated. He wished this woman would show some kind of passion either for or against the kiss. He wished her eyes would flash fire instead of chilling him with their stone coldness. He wished those hands would either hold him close or slap him in the face—anything but hang limp at her sides like dead eels drying in the sun. He could have kissed a marble statue and enjoyed it more.

"Why must you be so cold and unfeeling?" he asked.

"Just this morning a young woman was pilloried for doing what you just did. And rightly so, because to take pleasure in such sensuality is the first step on a stairway that can lead nowhere but down."

"And how do you expect to bear children to me without first indulging in a little pleasure?" Lanson surprised himself by taking up Maconnal's line of argument.

"We must act on the basis of duty, not pleasure," she replied. "It is not the act that engenders children that is sinful; it is the enjoyment of it."

"Why would the Master of the Universe make the act so pleasurable if he didn't intend us to enjoy it?"

"Surely you know the answer to that," she replied. "It is his way of testing men and women to see if they have the will to resist what man has in common with the low animals. Males may be beastly enough to pursue this pleasure for its own sake, but women must be strong enough to exercise uprightness and keep male lust in check. When we are wed, I will do my duty and endure your nuptial advances to bear your offspring. But I do not expect to give or receive pleasure from it. And neither should you if you want to please the Master of the Universe."

"I'm beginning to think it unlikely that I will," he sighed.

Though Lamonda was merely parroting the doctrine of the kirk, Lanson felt greatly disappointed to hear the woman who would become his wife endorse it so firmly. He hoped she would adopt the tacit enjoyment of conjugal companionship as most couples did in spite of the kirk's official disapproval of it. Not at all encouraged, he escorted Lamonda back to the dining hall. He could hardly wait for the banquet to end so he could get away from this iceberg of a woman before she froze his emotions into permanent numbness.

✒

After the banquet, the men moved to a smaller room adjoining the hall for the signing of the treaty. Bishop Hugal summoned a carriage and sent his niece to her chambers in the abbey. The twelve remaining women removed themselves to a sitting room to visit as they waited for their men to finish the kingdom's business.

Everyone was well fed and spirits were high. As the men milled about finding chairs, Sir Cramalon rapped his sword hilt on the table to get their attention. "Men of Lochlaund and Meridan, tonight we will be blending not merely two kingdoms, but two peoples. To symbolize this blending, I suggest that our two delegations should not seat themselves in separate groups. We should mix and sit among each other. We need to come to know one another as people, not merely as kingdoms." The knights and noblemen of both kingdoms reshuffled themselves according to Cramalon's suggestion. Lanson took his seat on the front row facing the table where the treaty would be signed. A burly, dark-bearded knight sat beside him and introduced himself as Sir Wexfeld.

When all the men were seated, Bishop Hugal arose and spoke. "Lords and knights of Meridan and Lochlaund, tonight we have the privilege of witnessing a historic moment in the annals of the Seven Kingdoms. As we assemble here, we walk in the footsteps of the Master of the Universe, taking one more step toward fulfilling a prophecy he gave to the Seven Kingdoms over one hundred twenty years ago. No mere mortal can fathom the vast good the Master will bring when we submit our wills to him and walk the path he has illumined with his word. I applaud the goodwill and foresight that has brought Kings Kor and Aradon to this agreement and given a new sense of brotherhood to our two kingdoms."

As the bishop took his seat, King Kor and Sir Cramalon rose from their chairs and took their places at the table facing the assembly. The full attention of every man was upon Kor as he dipped the quill into the inkwell and held it poised above the parchment, ready to sign.

At that moment a terrible doom struck—a doom so insidious that historians wrote of it years afterward as the most infamous deed ever witnessed in the Seven Kingdoms. Before King Kor's pen touched the parchment, the ring of thirty swords sliding from their scabbards filled the air. Sir Cramalon thrust his blade deep into the belly of the king. At the same instant each of the knights of the visiting delegation plunged his sword into the heart of the Lochlaund knight sitting beside him. Lanson had jumped to his feet in alarm the moment Cramalon had drawn his sword, and he had taken a step toward the table when he saw the sword of Wexfeld sweeping toward him. He ducked and felt the blade brush through his hair just as he saw his father double over and fall to the floor. The king's face contorted in agony and blood flowed over his hands as they clutched the sword protruding from the folds of his robe.

This unspeakable horror filled Lanson's vision for only an instant. He jumped aside just in time to keep Wexfeld's backstroke from slicing through his neck. As he whirled away he drew his own sword and faced his opponent, but Wexfeld was no longer alone. Other members of Cramalon's entourage had done their butchering more efficiently, and six or eight of them now stood beside Wexfeld, their swords pointed toward Lanson as they approached.

Knowing he could not hold off so many men at once, Lanson backed his way out of the room and turned to run down the corridor. The swordsmen came bellowing after him. He leapt down the stairway, rounded a corner, and made for the high arched door that opened onto the bailey. As he reached it he stopped short. Standing in the doorway were eight or ten men whom Lanson did not recognize, facing him with swords drawn. Behind them he glimpsed a dozen or more bodies lying on the flagstones and at least six more alien swordsmen stepping over them, coming toward the door. The thought flashed through Lanson's mind that so many invaders could not have achieved such quiet and easy access without an accomplice inside the castle. But he didn't have time to dwell on the possibility. Trapped in front and pursued from behind, he turned and ran headlong toward a marble sculpture of an ancient gladiator his father had brought from the southern seas. The statue was more than life-size and set on a high pedestal just under the railed balcony that overlooked the hall. The assassins followed close on his heels.

When Lanson reached the sculpture he half leapt, half pulled himself to the top of the pedestal, scrambled up to the warrior's stone shoulders, and made a flying jump toward the balcony, just managing to grasp the rail. He dangled precariously, his fingers groping for a hold. Most of his pursuers turned back to the stairway, leaping up the steps to meet their prey on the balcony. Two or three stood under his dangling feet, jumping and slicing at them with their swords as they waited for him to fall. He firmed his grip and pulled himself over the rail. His pursuers were only steps away as he ran with all his strength to the nearest window and leapt into the darkness outside.

Lanson plunged two stories into the water of the moat and swam furiously toward the far bank. He heard several thin splashes on either side of him and realized they were arrows. He reached the bank, clambered out of the water, and ran headlong toward the thick stand of trees thirty yards away. He reached the woods and disappeared into the welcome blackness of it.

CHAPTER ELEVEN

The Castle Coup

ith King Kor and the ranking noblemen of Lochlaund now dead, Cramalon commanded twelve men to follow him to the sitting room where the women waited for the meeting to end. He opened the door and gave them the terrible news that their men had been killed. Ignoring their shock and sudden cries of grief, he nodded to his men, who drew their swords and entered the room. He closed the door and stood outside until the dying screams of terror and agony told him the slaughter was over. Then he went to find Bishop Hugal and report to him the success of their mission.

Cramalon took control of Macrennon Castle, placing his own guards at the gates and all the watch points. He had King Kor secretly buried in the castle garden under a freshly plowed plot of earth. To keep the death of Kor from arousing King Aradon's suspicions, Cramalon had Bishop Hugal draft a missive, which he sent throughout the city of Macrennon. The letter told the people that their king had survived a mutinous attack by his own men, who had conspired against him to prevent his signing the treaty with Aradon. But the king had been gravely wounded, and recovery—if he did recover—would be slow. He would be confined to his quarters for some time to come. The message went on to say that Cramalon's men, who had bravely avenged the king at the cost of some of their own lives, had volunteered to guard King Kor and Macrennon Castle until the king recovered enough to re-form his government and restore order to the

kingdom. The message went on to say that the estates of the mutinous noblemen had been confiscated and their wives banished from
the kingdom.

On the night following the slaughter, when the blood had been
mopped from the floor, Bishop Hugal breathed a satisfied sigh and
mounted the stairway to King Kor's chambers. To maintain the fiction that the king was alive, Cramalon had given the king's chambers
to the bishop, explaining to all who needed to know that Kor had
requested his longtime friend to stay with him during his recovery.
Hugal unlocked the oaken door and entered the room, walking past
the curtain he and Cramalon had hung to shield Kor's empty bed
from any eyes that might peer in from the chamber door.

Hugal gazed at the bed, which was spread with a woolen cover-
let embroidered with King Kor's coat of arms, a lion rampant on a
field of red. He ran his thumb along the bedpost, intricately carved
with broad-leafed vines intertwining with dancing dryads. He sat on
the bed and breathed another sigh of deep satisfaction at the softness
of the down-filled mattress. At that moment a knock sounded at the
chamber door. Hugal slid the bolt and opened the door a mere crack.
A servant had brought his dinner.

The bishop looked at the tray and said, "Where is the king's wine?"

The page explained that he thought the meal had been prepared
solely for the bishop. "It is for the king," said Hugal. "In his condition, the wine will do him good. And don't bring just any wine—pick
out a bottle of red Rhondilar wine. Do you understand?" The page
bowed and ran down the hallway, returning minutes later with a large
bottle of the red liquid. The bishop received the delivery and locked
the door behind him.

After finishing the meal, Hugal sat back in the great cushioned
chair and delighted in the warmth emanating from the stone hearth
at his feet. He looked over the letter he had received days ago from
Brendal Seven Fingers, which explained in detail how King Kor and
his nobles were to be killed by Brendal's own men posing as King
Aradon's delegation. The bishop laughed quietly at their easy success
and tossed the parchment into the fireplace. Only two flaws marred
the plan. The first was the absence of Sir Maconnal, and the second—

which was far worse—was that Prince Lanson had escaped. Hugal's grin faded and his brow furrowed as he thought of these loose dogs in the kennel. But he could take care of Maconnal when he returned from his mission. And he had no doubt that Brendal's men would soon find the prince and put an end to him.

To divert his mind from the disquieting thought, Hugal rose from the chair and ambled about the room, admiring the lifelike artistry in the tapestries that hung from the dressed stone walls. His eyes gleamed and his lips moistened as his fingers, Midas-like, could not resist caressing the golden pedestal of the candelabrum that stood beside the king's bed. He examined the candlesticks on the king's oaken desk and the sconces on the wall. He touched one of the sconces with his fingers, delighting in the feel of the burnished gold. Suddenly he jerked back in fright. The sconce moved away from his touch as the section of the wall on which it was mounted swung inward, revealing a darkened passageway.

Hugal calmed his racing heart. Such hidden passages were not unusual in a king's chambers, for kings often met a need for quick escape. It occurred to him that he might find such a passage useful himself. He took the small torch from the sconce and stepped into the opening. He found himself on a landing with steps leading downward to his left and upward to his right. He followed the downward steps first, which led him to a first-floor hallway and on to the postern gate of the castle. He returned and followed the upward stairway, which opened into several outlets in the upper floors of the castle, including the tower room.

As the bishop returned to the king's chambers, he forgot the fugitive Lanson and smiled with satisfaction at his discovery. He poured himself a goblet of the fine Rhondilar red wine the servant had brought, downed it quickly, then poured another and downed that as well. After the third cup, he yawned widely, undressed, and, with a long sigh of self-satisfaction, eased his bulk into the king's bed. He drifted into sleep thinking that if he planned his moves carefully, these chambers could become his permanent residence.

Perhaps it was the wine, or perhaps the enfolding billows of the feather bed, or the fine meal he had eaten shortly before retiring.

Whatever the reason, Bishop Hugal was still sleeping the next morning when the guards let into the room the chambermaid Alenia, who daily cleaned the king's chambers. The bishop did not awaken as the door opened and the woman tiptoed into the room. The only sound was Hugal's deep breathing, blowing like a March wind through an arrow loop beyond the curtain, a sound that the woman took to be the king's own labored breath. Alenia stood still for a moment as her lips moved in a silent prayer for the king's recovery. King Kor had been kind to her, and she had been loyal to him. She took extra care to remain noiseless as she removed the dishes and cups from Kor's table and knelt to sweep stray ashes from the hearth. She chose not to clean the fireplace, fearing the scooping of the ashes would awaken the wounded king.

As Alenia set fresh logs behind the andirons, she noticed a piece of charred parchment in the back corner of the fireplace. She picked it up and looked at it. She could see that it was a letter, but the words had no meaning to her, for she could not read. *Maconnal will remedy that soon enough,* she mused. The thought sent a warm thrill through her body. She wondered if the document might be something of importance to the king that had accidentally fallen too near the fire. She folded it and tucked it into her bodice, intending to give it to him at the first opportunity when he grew well enough to receive it. Alenia left the chamber, quietly closing the door on the sleeper, and went about her daily chores. That evening as she undressed, she found the parchment, which she had forgotten, and tucked it into a basket with her scarves and stockings. Soon she forgot that it was there at all.

When Bishop Hugal awakened, the sun had been streaming into his window for almost two hours. His head felt stuffed with cotton, and his eyes rebelled against opening to the intrusion of the sunlight. With a groan he pushed himself to a sitting position, stood, and stumbled to the wine pitcher. He poured himself a cup, downed it in three swallows, and dropped heavily into the king's chair. He looked into the fireplace, now dressed with fresh logs, and suddenly his eyes widened and his mouth curled into an angry scowl. He stomped to the door, unbolted it, and flung it open.

"Who came in here?" he bellowed at the guard, wincing at the sound of his own voice.

"Only the chambermaid, your grace," replied the guard.

"Why didn't you awaken me?"

"You gave me no such orders, sir."

"You idiot! Do I have to tell you everything? No one is to come into this room at any time without my explicit permission. No one! Ever! Do you understand me?" Hugal glared at the poor guard.

"I do, your grace, and I will obey. My apologies, your grace. It will not happen again."

"It had better not," snapped the bishop. "If anyone gets past this door again without my permission, you will find yourself in a garrison cell for a year. Now, who was the chambermaid?"

"Alenia, your grace."

"Summon a page to deliver this message to the lord chamberlain. The chambermaid Alenia is to be reassigned to duties in some other part of the castle at once."

"It will be done immediately, your grace."

Hugal closed the door, and as he poured himself another cup of wine, he remembered with a sinking in the pit of his stomach that Prince Lanson was still at large. Even after two more cups, the scowl had not yet left his face.

CHAPTER TWELVE

The Nightmare

rince Lanson plunged through the forest with long, lumbering strides, heedless of the branches that whipped his face and the stones that bruised his toes. He ran until his breath tore from his throat in hoarse wheezes. When he was too winded to continue, he walked until he could breathe well enough to run again. He could see little. The forest was black except for dim outlines of branches and stones created by the moonlight filtering through the leaves. Though he heard no footsteps behind him, he dared not slacken his pace. He ran all night, stopping only when necessary to catch his breath or lap water from one of the brooks that webbed the woods.

Finally the blackness of the night gave way to dawn, and through occasional breaks in the trees, Lanson could see the sky beginning to glow purple and orange. He knew he could not continue much longer without rest. He found a hollow at the base of a rock ledge hidden from the forest by a cluster of fallen boulders, where he curled up and closed his eyes.

Exhausted as the prince was, sleep did not come easily. The unspeakable horror he had witnessed flooded his mind. Over and over he saw his father crumple to the floor with a sword in his belly and the grimace of death upon his face, and Lanson clenched his teeth in anguish as tears streamed from his eyes. It was his own fault. He had known something was amiss. Aradon had sent too many men merely to sign a treaty, and their manners at the table should have told him these men were not diplomats. But how could he have guessed Aradon would send butchers? No matter. He had known something was wrong and he should have been wary enough to prevent the slaughter. At the very least he could have stood by his father's side, prepared to defend him against whatever danger arose.

The prince writhed in anguish on his bed of sand as these dark thoughts cycled over and over through his mind. Finally sheer exhaustion plunged him into sleep, but he found no relief there. He dreamt that he was on the parapet of Lochlaund's castle overlooking the city of Macrennon when he heard screaming in one of its streets. He looked in the direction of the sound and saw men and women running in panic from some huge, living shadow that was creeping after them. In a moment he could make out the form of the thing, and his blood ran cold. The creature was monstrous. Its body was that of a lizard perhaps fifty paces long and covered with gray-green scales. Down the line of its back grew a ridge of spines like stone sails on a galleon. Its head was that of a gargoyle, evil and demonic, with a mottled green tongue sliding in and out of its cavernous mouth. The eyes glowed orange under heavy brows as if lit from within by the fires of hell.

The creature showed no interest in the people who fled before it but made straightaway for the castle. Lanson saw the drawbridge rise as the thing approached, but it did not matter. The monster slithered into the water, and Lanson heard timbers splitting and ripping away as it clawed first through the drawbridge, then the portcullis. He ran from the tower parapet down the stairwell to the second floor and toward his father's chambers. As he approached, Lanson saw that the creature had arrived before him. His father's door had been shattered, and a massive, scaly tail protruded from the doorway. The prince entered with his sword drawn, but he was too late. The hideous head turned toward him, its jaws dripping blood as it licked its foul lips with its putrid, speckled tongue.

Lanson awakened in a sweat and trembling. He sat up, drew his knees to his chest, and laid his head on his crossed arms as great sobs convulsed his body. He had failed his father, and he would never see

him again. Happy images from the past flooded his mind—his father
teaching him to play chess, letting his son beat him every other game
to build his confidence; riding in the hunt at the king's side; the great
hall ringing with his father's laughter over some jest; his arms around
Lanson on the night his mother had died. Such moments would
never come again. It was more than Lanson could bear.

But in minutes the wave of grief passed—though it returned with
force again and again for many days—leaving behind it a great mono-
lith of anger engraved with the name of Aradon. *The Seven Kingdoms
has greatly misjudged Meridan's new king*, thought Lanson. *The man is
ambitious and treacherous beyond belief. Not content with a mere federation of independent kingdoms, the tyrant intends to rule the island himself with an iron hand. He must be stopped. Whatever the cost, Aradon
must be stopped. And I will do all in my power to stop him. My father
must be avenged.*

Lanson rested his chin on his arms and plunged himself into
thought. How could he stop Aradon in his quest to dominate the
Seven Kingdoms? He thought of Brendal Seven Fingers, whom his
father considered an ambitious, vengeful power seeker not to be
trusted farther than a man could heave a horse. Apparently King Kor
had sewn his buttons on the wrong suit. He had misjudged Brendal
as well as Aradon. Aradon was the treacherous one and Brendal,
apparently misunderstood as those who resist the tide often are, was
the one man who knew the would-be high king must be resisted. As
the Seven Kingdoms fell into Aradon's camp, Brendal's resistance had
begun to look futile. But perhaps Lanson could help turn the tide. If
he joined Brendal and proclaimed the truth about Aradon throughout the Seven Kingdoms, the rush toward Aradon might yet be
checked.

Sitting in the sand with his back to the wall of the hollow, the
fugitive Prince Lanson of Lochlaund determined that he would make
his way southward to Ensovandor Castle in Vensaur where Brendal
was residing. He would offer his sword to help overthrow King
Aradon of Meridan.

Lanson checked his assets. Fortunately he did not lack money, for
he had on his belt a fat leather pouch of gold and silver coins. He had

a fire flint and his sword, but no weapons for hunting. He must find a village where he could purchase a bow and a quiver of arrows. He thought of purchasing a horse as well but decided against it. A horse would prevent his hiding effectively in the woods. He had no doubt that Aradon's men were searching everywhere for him, which presented another problem. He could not show himself in the villages to buy anything at all—horse, clothing, food, or weapons. His princely clothing marked him like a target. He must find some way to get rid of them before he dared venture into any village.

Lanson was not a woodsman, but he had absorbed a little wood-lore while hunting with his father and the king's huntsman—enough to know of certain edible roots and berries and where to find them. For now he would settle for berries, and he found several bushes easily. He filled his pockets with the red morsels, which he ate as he continued to walk southward.

He walked throughout the day, sometimes pushing his way through thickets, sometimes following the trails of animals or hunters. As night approached he found a small clearing by a stream well hidden by thick trees and a boulder the size of a house. By now he was weary of eating nothing but berries and decided to try his luck catching trout. He had seen his father's huntsman catch them with his bare hands in the brooks of Lochlaund, but Lanson could not get the hang of it and gave up trying after a half-hour. He found a cluster of mandrake plants and, using his sword and a sharp stone, dug out several roots and washed them for his evening meal. He built a small fire, removed his clothing, bathed in the stream, then warmed himself dry by the flames as he ate the mandrake roots. *This will not do for long,* he thought. He dressed, curled up by the fire, covered himself with his cape, and drifted into sleep.

No sooner had he done so than, once again, the devouring dragon lumbered into his dreams. Lanson awoke with a start, trembling and feeling his grief afresh. He built up the fire and stared into it. The face of his father gazed longingly at him from the flames as from an infinite distance. Then the face contorted with pain as it had on the night of his death. The fire jumped and flashed like liquid light as tears flooded Lanson's eyes. His father's face dimmed to be replaced by the hated form of Aradon writhing in the blaze. After a while Lanson returned to sleep but only to dream again.

He arose at sunup and continued his southward journey. In half an hour he came upon a road he recognized as leading to the village of Blaiseburn. He avoided the road itself but traveled parallel to it, thinking he would skirt the village and watch for some safe opportunity to purchase food, clothing, or weapons. He judged himself to be little more than a mile from the town when he heard the sound of splashing in a creek ahead. He crept silently toward the stream, taking care to remain hidden from whatever might be making the noise. As he approached he could see a man bathing where the stream widened into a deep pool. He crept closer and, remaining crouched behind a bush, noted that the swimmer was about his own size. The man's clothing, along with a bow and a quiver of arrows, was piled in the tall grass some ten paces from the water. Lanson could hardly believe his good fortune. Here at a single bazaar were all the commodities he needed.

His course of action became immediately clear. He would take the goods and leave a little money in their place for payment. He retreated from the scene and found a long, fairly straight dead limb. Then, lying flat in the tall grass, he began to crawl toward the clothing. He watched until the swimmer turned away, then reached with the limb, hooked his new wardrobe on the stub of a broken branch, and drew it toward him. He repeated the procedure and became the new owner of the man's bow and quiver, as well as his boots. Then he drew from his pouch a silver coin—at least twice what the man's clothing and weapon were worth—and pitched it to the place where the clothing had been piled. He inched his way back to the bush and, crouching low, disappeared into the forest.

Prince Lanson went deep into the woods before he stopped and changed into the bathing man's plainer clothing. He had considered leaving his own suit in exchange but thought better of it, knowing his princely garments could give Aradon's searchers a clue to his direction. He walked on until he found a crevasse about eight inches wide in a stony patch of ground. Using a long stick, he stuffed the suit deep into the crevasse and covered it with sand.

Now dressed in the garb of a common citizen, Lanson thought he could risk a visit to a village inn to buy himself a proper meal. He was more than ready for one. He made his way through the woods until he came to the village of Blaiseburn. He was pleased that his nondescript clothing apparently hid him well. No one paid particular attention to him—except for a couple of young women with flushing cheeks and fluttering lashes who stole sidelong glances as he passed.

He asked directions to an inn and made his way up the street toward it. At fifty paces away, Lanson suddenly stopped short. Three soldiers stood talking with one another at the inn's door. They were not of Lochlaund's army, and Lanson did not recognize the blazon on their shields. He had to assume they were Aradon's men, either looking for him or already occupying the villages of Lochlaund. He turned aside, pretending to examine trinkets at a jeweler's stall, then retraced his steps out of the village and into the woods. A meal at an inn was now out of the question. He had no choice but to avoid all villages until he crossed the border out of Lochlaund.

Lanson spent the next four days walking in the edge of the woods along the base of the Dragontooth Mountains. He fed himself with small hare, squirrel, grouse, and trout he shot in the streams. He crossed into Meridan and snaked his way through the mountains until he reached Braegan Wood. He had heard from stories and legends that Braegan Wood was haunted and treacherous, but he stayed within the edges of it to remain hidden until he could reach the southern border of Meridan and cross into Vensaur.

Lanson now craved a seasoned meal and news of his homeland. The farther he traveled from Lochlaund, the safer he began to feel about venturing into a village. He was now a kingdom away from Macrennon, his beard and hair had grown, his face was browned by the sun, and his clothing gave no clue to his princely identity. In the late afternoon of his sixteenth day of travel, he came to the mountain village of Stoneledge at the western edge of Braegan Wood and went directly to the Hathfield Inn, an alehouse on the main avenue. He had heard Sir Maconnal speak of the inn as a place where he always spent a night on his journeys to the coast.

The barmaid served him a meal of mutton stew and a mug of ale and would have served him more had he lifted his eyes to meet hers. As he ate he listened to the talk of the patrons at the tables around him. Most of it was of goats, market prices, weather, and women, and Lanson paid little attention. But his spoon stopped before it reached his mouth when he heard a grizzled goatherd two tables away speak his father's name. Lanson rested his spoon and listened.

"They be lookin' for him, they are," said the goatherd.

"Did the proclamation say why the prince disappeared?" asked his companion.

"Nothin' at all. Just that King Kor of Lochlaund is lookin' for his son, Prince Lanson. He wants his boy back home, he does. And he's willin' to pay a handsome price to get him. A hundred crowns just for word of the boy's whereabouts, and five hundred to see him safe and sound to Macrennon Castle. Enough to set a man up for life, it is."

"Indeed it is. But it's still a mystery to me why the prince disappeared."

Lanson listened carefully, but the conversation drifted back to the price of goats in Corenham and he turned his attention again to his stew. He heard nothing to indicate that the men knew of Aradon's slaughter of Lochlaund's nobles or his takeover of his father's castle, which would have been fodder for talk in every tavern in the Seven Kingdoms. From what he did hear, Lanson understood fully what had happened. Aradon's usurpers had hidden the fact that his father was dead and were conducting the affairs of the kingdom in King Kor's name as if he were alive. He knew the meaning of the proclamation issued to locate him as well. It was obvious that Aradon's men were searching for him, but he knew their motive had nothing to do with parental concern. He must remain in hiding.

Lanson assumed that all the men of his father's court had been slain. He had seen some of them die with his own eyes, and in his rush to escape the slaughter, he could not remember seeing any one of them alive after the attack. But it had happened so fast he could not be sure of anything. He wondered whether Bishop Hugal survived. It was possible that even Aradon's men would have spared a cleric.

He breathed a prayer of thanks that his tutor Maconnal was out of the country when the deed was done, but he suddenly realized that his friend would be in danger when he returned. He must find a way to warn him. He knew a little of Maconnal's routes and habits on these journeys. In a matter of days he would land at a harbor in southern Meridan and travel northward on horseback to Lochlaund. In addition to his regular stop at the Hathfield Inn, Lanson knew that when Maconnal's travels took him through Oranth he sometimes spent a night or two at the Kenmarl Estate in the south of that kingdom. He and Lord Kenmarl were childhood friends. Lanson decided to leave a message for the tutor here at the Hathfield, urging him not to return to Lochlaund but to seek sanctuary at Kenmarl.

Thinking it best not to stay the night at the inn, Lanson paid for his meal, wrote his message to Maconnal, sealed it, and left it with the innkeeper. Then he left the village to find a sleeping place in the woods. He built his fire and sat staring long into it, burning with hatred and schemes for vengeance against the treacherous Aradon. When he fell into sleep, the recurring nightmare of the devouring monster plagued him yet again.

CHAPTER THIRTEEN

ThE ABDUCTION

hen Sir Eanor, head of King Aradon's six-man delegation to sign the treaty with King Kor of Lochlaund, did not return to Morningstone Castle on the appointed day, King Aradon was not greatly concerned. The road between Corenham and Macrennon was long and in disrepair, making exact travel times hard to predict. He waited two more days before sending Sir Olstan the Silent and three other knights toward Lochlaund to search for Eanor and his company. Sir Olstan returned six days later bearing tragic tidings. They had found the bodies of Sir Eanor and his men piled in a ravine a quarter mile off the road just over the border of Lochlaund. Eanor's company had been robbed of everything, including their clothing, weapons, horses, money, and food. The treaty parchment was missing as well. It was clear that the delegation had never reached King Kor. Olstan and his knights had spent most of a day building a cairn over the bodies before returning to Morningstone.

Tears streamed from Aradon's eyes when he heard of Eanor's death, and he insisted on bearing the news to his widow himself. Two days following Olstan's report, the king presided over a memorial assembly in the great hall for Eanor and his party and delivered a heartfelt eulogy for his loyal friend and counselor. On the following day he called for a meeting of Meridan's Hall of Knights, along with his chief advisor and interim chancellor, Lord Aldemar.

"Noble knights of Meridan's Hall," said Aradon. "You have heard

Sir Olstan's report of the insidious murder of Sir Eanor and the five knights of his diplomatic party. At this moment we do not know who committed this crime or why they did it. I have convened this meeting of the Hall to get your insights on the meaning of it and your counsel as to what action we should take. The floor is now open for discussion."

Sir Karramore stood and addressed the king. "Your majesty, it occurs to me that since the uniforms and the treaty itself were stolen from Eanor and his men, the murderers may have had deception in mind. They may have used these items as tokens of authenticity to make King Kor believe they were Meridan's designated representatives."

The seated knights nodded and several of them affirmed Karramore's supposition. Sir Halliston arose and said, "But what kind of deception would they have wrought on Kor? And to what purpose? Is it likely they would have taken the treaty to him to be signed? That would only serve our purpose and make the murders meaningless. Isn't it more likely they wanted to prevent the signing? I suspect they simply killed our men and ran away."

"Perhaps they rewrote the treaty using the authentic one as a model. They may have added terms they knew to be unacceptable to Kor so he would refuse to sign it."

"Had such a thing happened we would have heard from Kor long before now."

"But why would they do any of these things?"

"We can't answer that question until we know who they are."

Thus went the debate for an hour or more as all the knights shared their collective wisdom in an attempt to make sense out of what seemed a meaningless tragedy. The men examined every facet of their guesses as carefully as if they had real evidence, just as a dog will worry a dried bone when he has no real meat to chew. But the speculations were leading nowhere, and Aradon began to think of adjourning the meeting when a page slipped into the hall and brought to him a parchment scroll tied with a leather thong. The king unrolled the scroll and read it as the debate continued. Then he stood and called for silence.

"I have in my hand a proclamation from King Kor, just this moment received. It answers some of the questions you have raised but poses others in their stead. I will read the letter to you." The hall fell quiet.

"From his majesty Kor, King of Lochlaund, to his majesty Aradon, King of Meridan: Be it known that whereas Aradon, King of Meridan, has failed to honor his sacred agreement to send a delegation from Meridan to Lochlaund to sign a treaty of federation agreed to and drafted in previous councils, I, King Kor of Lochlaund, do hereby renounce the terms of the agreement and declare our intent to confederate with the Kingdom of Meridan null and void. Be it known that the people of Lochlaund find in this breach of promise an insult to our trust in your honor. Furthermore, we deem that this breach holds within it an implied threat of ill will that could mean peril to our nation, and we deem it prudent to take steps to strengthen our security against Meridan and its allies. Therefore we shall pursue confederation with the nations dissenting from the uniting of the Seven Kingdoms under Aradon of Meridan. In accordance with this resolution we have dispatched a delegation to Sir Brendal, presently of Vensaur, to pursue terms of affiliation. Signed by my hand with regret at your breach of promise, Kor, King of Lochlaund."

For the space of seven breaths the only sound in the Great Hall of Morningstone was that of King Aradon rolling up the scroll. Then Sir Llewenthane stood, his face burning almost as red as the thick shock of hair on his head. "Sire, this letter is an outrage. What right has King Kor to act against the Seven Kingdoms without an inquiry as to why our delegation never arrived? If he aligns with Brendal, the uniting of the Seven Kingdoms is in great peril. We must march into Lochlaund and stop King Kor immediately."

The venerable Lord Aldemar rose from his seat, standing straight and tall. "I believe it is premature to abandon our diplomatic course on the basis of a single incident, however treacherous or tragic. Although it seems that King Kor is acting rashly in turning toward Brendal, his letter makes it clear that he acts on the basis of a misunderstanding. It also tells us that he had nothing to do with the deaths of our delegation. I advise that we hold to our course of persuasion. It may be that when he knows the facts, his temper will cool."

"How long must we hold that course, Lord Aldemar?" replied Llewenthane, waving his hand in a gesture of exasperation. "If we do nothing but talk while the unaligned kingdoms fall to Brendal, we can be sure we will see more of the kind of treachery we have just suffered."

"We cannot be sure of that," said Aradon's general, Sir Denmore, a tall man of about thirty with dark hair already graying at the temples. "We do not even know who murdered Eanor or why. It may not have been Brendal's men. For all we know they were simply killed and robbed by a band of highwaymen."

"That is possible but not likely," replied Llewenthane. "And it has nothing to do with the point. The point is, Kor is defecting to Brendal and the Seven Kingdoms are divided. With the kingdoms that have joined us already, we can defeat Brendal now. But what of later when he spreads his lying poison that we dealt deception to King Kor? Other kingdoms will turn to him instead of to Meridan."

"The other kingdoms must be free to do as they see fit," said Aldemar.

"But they have been deceived," cried Sir Llewenthane. "We must put a stop to Brendal's lies. And the best way to do it is to separate his mouth from his lungs by passing a sword through his neck."

"You are right. We must correct the deception. But we can do it peacefully by sending a delegation to King Kor, explaining to him why Meridan's delegation never arrived in Lochlaund," replied Aldemar.

"Talk! Talk! Talk! That's all we ever do," boomed Llewenthane. "And while we work our mouths, kingdoms leak from Meridan's bucket into Brendal's. He gets stronger as we get weaker. If the Seven Kingdoms are to unite at all, we must call together our army and march now before he gets too strong to resist."

In the end Lord Aldemar's view prevailed, and King Aradon chose Sir Halliston to journey with a party of five men to Lochlaund and explain to King Kor how Meridan's emissaries had been murdered bearing the treaty of confederation. Meridan would hold to its diplomatic course. Aradon would not force the prophecy by violating the sovereignty of the independent kingdoms. However, in the name of prudence he charged Sir Denmore to intensify his efforts to gain intelligence on the activities of Brendal.

After the meeting adjourned and the knights began to leave the hall, Sir Llewenthane stopped King Aradon. The big knight's eyes flashed fire from under knotted brows. "Why do you keep me around?" he said, frustration constricting his usually booming voice. "You never listen to anything I say or follow any of my advice."

"It's true that I don't always follow your advice," replied Aradon, "but I do always listen to what you say."

"Why do you bother? I'm a lone breeze blowing against forty winds."

"I would be the poorer if I didn't have opposing views presented with passion and lucidity by a man whose loyalty is as certain as that of my own hand. You force the Hall to look at all sides of every issue. Your boldness in proclaiming your thought without fear of opposing opinion or political implications is rare and sorely needed. And if we fail, you will become the most valuable of our lot."

"But it seems so futile to sit and do nothing while your enemies are mounting forces against you."

"You must understand, Llewenthane, that I cannot use the tactics of our enemies. Though I may command the power, I cannot coerce the other kingdoms to join Meridan. In some ways good is more vulnerable than evil, for while evil can employ any tactic that works, good cannot violate its own goodness without becoming evil."

"But when our cause is right, surely we must take advantage of every possible opportunity to prevail," replied Llewenthane.

"If we resort to the tactics of evil even in a righteous cause, it doesn't matter who prevails, evil wins. An evil path cannot bring you to a good destination." Aradon stretched his arm about the wide shoulders of his friend as they walked out of the room. "Come on, the women are waiting for us."

Aradon's general, Sir Denmore, and his aide and confidant Sir Olstan the Silent joined the two men as they walked down the corridors to Little Hall, the private dining chamber where Queen Volanna and Lady Kalley waited with two other women. As the men entered the room, Sir Olstan embraced his new wife, Lady Kalley, and Sir Llewenthane and Sir Denmore greeted their wives, Lady Eleannore and Lady Florimel, with equal warmth.

Queen Volanna came to Aradon bearing in her arms their five-month-old daughter, Vallia. Springs of affection welled up within the young king as he gazed at his wife approaching. Her extraordinary grace and beauty touched him even more deeply now than when they had wed fourteen months ago, for now he knew her beauty to be an exact reflection of her inner self. And he felt perpetual awe at the sight of his infant girl, who turned her unsteady little head and beamed on him a toothless smile of happy recognition that warmed him like sunrays from heaven. His daughter leaned eagerly toward him, and he took her from Volanna's arms. Her chubby little hands could resist nothing within reach. Aradon laughed with delight as she tugged at a lock of his golden hair but, finding it firmly rooted, picked at the golden threads on his wine red robe instead. Shortly afterward the nurse Glynnora came to take Vallia to the nursery for the evening.

"You need not feed her tonight," said Volanna. "She nursed not half an hour ago, and I thought the little glutton would never get enough. Lay her in her crib and she will probably sleep until I come up."

"As you say, your majesty," said Glynnora, curtsying as she took the child. "And how long will you be?"

"Not more than three hours," replied Volanna, too trusting by nature to think the question a strange impertinence for a servant. Glynnora curtsied again and took Vallia from the room as Volanna turned and sat with the others at the table.

The four couples relaxed in the easy company of one another as the servants brought in their meal. As they ate, the women insisted on hearing about the council's deliberations. Denmore told them of Kor's letter and Aradon's decision to refrain from using Meridan's military might against Kor or Brendal.

"Does anyone know just how Brendal escaped King Tallis's prison?" asked Kalley.

"Not with certainty," replied Denmore. "But we know he had help from outside. And he killed a prison guard in the process."

"I wonder if Brendal has not renewed his alliance with Morgultha," said Volanna. "Couldn't she have arranged for his escape?"

"I have wondered the same thing," said Aradon. "Morgultha has lusted for control of the Seven Kingdoms for at least 150 years, and she fought hard to get the Crown of Eden before the prophecy could be fulfilled. It's unlikely that she will give up her ambition as long as there is breath in her body. Naturally she would know of Brendal's desire for vengeance and would use it to keep the kingdoms from uniting."

"Is it true that she is hundreds of years old? How is such a thing possible, and why isn't she all withered and wrinkled?" asked Kalley.

"Long ago she made an alliance with the disembodied dark spirits that have roamed the earth since the days of the great flood," said Aradon. "They taught her the secret of preserving her body from aging. What she gave them in return I cannot imagine."

"Then she must be immortal," said Eleannore.

"Not really," Aradon replied. "She will not die a natural death, but she can be killed just as any other human. A sword thrust or an arrow would do it."

"I wonder where Morgultha is now?" said Florimel.

"No one has reported seeing her since Olstan and Volanna encountered her at Maldor Castle about two years ago. But I don't believe for a moment that she has abandoned her quest for control of this island."

"You don't suppose she would have returned to Maldor Castle, do you?" asked Kalley. "She should feel very much at home there with all the swamps and spiders and dead trees."

"No, she is not at Maldor," replied Aradon. "I have that ruin inspected monthly, and there has been no sign of any human activity there."

"I think you are right. Morgultha is likely the power behind Brendal now," said Denmore. "Some of the moves he has made lately seem too subtle for him. My guess is that she is providing the mind and he is providing the muscle."

"I still don't see why we can't make Brendal's head a stranger to his shoulders—with integrity and honor, of course," said Llewenthane, shooting a dark glance toward Aradon. "At least we should take him prisoner and throw him into Perivale's dungeon until the flesh rots from his conniving bones."

"I'm sorry, Llew, but it's too late for that. Just today I approved the mason's plans to plug and seal Perivale's dungeon. Such a foul pit has no place in a civilized kingdom. Work will begin this very week."

"What a waste," muttered Llewenthane.

Olstan, mute from birth, made a series of hand signs to Kalley, who turned to Aradon and said, "Olstan wants to know what you will do with Balkert. We know that King Tallis chained him in Perivale's dungeon—in fact, in the very cell where Lomar had you chained. And I myself am wondering if you will take him out before you seal the dungeon, or will you let it be his tomb? He doesn't deserve better, you know."

Aradon laughed. "No, I'll not seal Balkert in Perivale's dungeon. In fact, I had him moved shortly after my coronation. On Lord Aldemar's recommendation, I sent him into exile on Felon's Island."

"Felon's Island!" Kalley shuddered. "I've heard of it—a tiny, rocky place full of murderers, thieves, and rapists. They either learn to work together to till and forage for survival or they kill each other off. And I'm told that both go on all the time. What a horrid place!"

"It doesn't sound that different from any other place," said Eleannore. "We all learn to work together or we kill each other off. It's the choice facing the Seven Kingdoms at this very moment."

The others voiced their agreement, and the conversation turned to more mundane matters. The men talked of tournaments and horses, falcons and hunting, while the women spoke of music and minstrels, dancing and poetry, fabrics and tapestries. Two hours later the table had been cleared of food and dishes, and laughter and banter flowed as freely as the mead from the servants' pitchers. The little party was at its peak when suddenly a page entered the hall, wide-eyed and pale. All conversation stopped as the boy hurried to Aradon with news that shook him and his queen to the very core.

"Your majesty, your daughter has disappeared."

Volanna's hand went automatically to her heart as Aradon stiffened. "What do you mean, disappeared?"

"We don't know, your majesty. A chambermaid came into the nursery and found the crib empty and the nurse Glynnora gone. She didn't think much about it at first, but when she returned a half-hour later, things were still as they were. No baby, no nurse. She sent me immediately to tell you."

"I thank you," said Aradon as he stood. "No doubt there is some explanation that will give us no cause for alarm, but we will check the nursery immediately." He and Volanna hurried from the room as their friends followed. They checked the nursery and found things as the page had described them. They searched their own connecting chambers, the hallways, and all the rooms on the floor. Now alarmed, Sir Denmore immediately alerted the castle guards, who systematically began to search every chamber and corridor in the castle. Llewenthane, Eleannore, and Florimel began to question the servants. Olstan searched the infant's room for any sign of foul play.

As the night wore on and the guards found no trace of the child or the servant, Volanna's face took on a look of stricken desperation as she began to realize the enormity of the crisis that was unfolding. Kalley sat with her, holding her hand and assuring her that all would be well. Aradon stormed through the castle like a wild man, pounding on doors, looking under beds and inside chests, kicking aside chairs and even unstacking crates and bags of grain and flour in the buttery.

Shortly after midnight Denmore brought two castle servants to Aradon—a charwoman and a kitchenmaid—and bade them tell the king what they had seen.

The charwoman curtsied nervously. "Your majesty, I seen the nurse Glynnora carryin' the princess down the hallway from the nursery, and—"

"When was this?" asked Aradon.

"Early in the evenin', sire. Not long after she tooken the wee one from the queen. She was walkin' fast like and lookin' around like she was afraid of bein' seen, if you know what I mean."

"Which way was she going?"

"Toward the main stairway, your majesty. I didn't think nothin' of it at the time. She could have been goin' to the kitchen or to the linen chamber for all I knew."

"I thank you for your information." Aradon turned to the kitchen-maid. "And what did you see?"

"I saw the same woman, Glynnora by name, walkin' fast down the hall outside the kitchen. I was servin' you and your friends in Little Hall, you know, and it wasn't more than a half-hour after your dinner was startin'."

"Did you see where she went?" Aradon asked.

"No, sire. But she was walkin' in the direction of the postern gate. I didn't think nothin' about it at the time. Most servants who don't live in Morningstone Castle leave by that gate at night when their work is done."

"Was she alone? Was she carrying anything?"

"She was alone, sire. And yes, she was carryin' somethin'. She had a fair-sized bag or bundle, which I didn't see too clearly. I was busy like, you understand, and not payin' good attention. What she was doin' didn't seem unusual at the time. I'm very sorry, your majesty."

"You have committed no fault and bear no blame. I thank you for what you have told me. If either of you think of anything else that could help us, or hear of anyone else who might have seen anything amiss tonight, please come to me immediately. You may go with my thanks." The two servants curtsied and left the room.

At that moment Sir Olstan entered, followed closely by Lady Kalley, Queen Volanna, and the other four members of their evening party. "Your majesty," Kalley said, "Olstan has discovered something important. Half the clothes in Vallia's chest are missing, along with two of her best blankets and a woolen headpiece." Olstan interrupted his wife with a series of rapid hand signs, which Aradon could read almost as well as Kalley. "He says these missing items indicate that Vallia has been kidnapped, which is a terrible thing. But it also shows that whoever took her intends to take care of her, which is a good thing."

"The child may have been taken as a hostage," said Llewenthane.

"Which means we should get a message of ransom terms very soon," said Denmore.

"And it means you need not be desperate," Lady Eleannore added. "We now have strong evidence that the child will be cared for, and if she is being held for ransom, her safety is valuable to her abductors. Of course you can't help but worry, but your anguish need not be desperate. The child will be kept safe." The distraught parents were grateful for this thread of hope and clung to it like a drowning man to a floating twig.

"There is nothing more you can do tonight," said Denmore. "The best thing is to get some sleep and we will search beyond the castle in the morning."

"How can I sleep when I don't know what has happened to my baby?" said Volanna, her voice wavering and her eyes full of anguish.

"Nor can I," Aradon agreed. "I will continue to search around the postern gate and into the woods beyond. I will sleep when I must."

"And I will join you, sire," said Llewenthane.

"As will I," Denmore added, and Olstan's hands signified the same resolve.

The ladies stayed up with Queen Volanna as the four men spent the rest of the night searching all about the walls of the castle and the paths leading down Morningstone Hill. When morning came Denmore conscripted men to extend the search into the streets, inns, and taverns of the city of Corenham. He sent criers throughout the city and messengers into the nearby towns offering a reward for news of the missing princess. Meanwhile Aradon and his three friends explored many of the known trails into Braegan Wood, but their search was unavailing.

They returned to Morningstone Castle in the evening, and after taking their dinner again in Little Hall, the exhausted king and queen went up to their chambers. Yet for much of the night sleep evaded them. In their despair they clung to each other, their minds filled with images of their little Vallia with her chubby legs and wide, innocent eyes the color of the roof of heaven. Was the child safe? Was she warm? Had she indeed been abducted? They refused to utter the thought that their child might never be found, though its shadow lurked in the dark corners of their minds. More than once great sobs overtook Volanna as Aradon held her close, tears streaming from his own eyes. More than once she drifted into sleep only to be assaulted by dreams of Vallia wailing for her as she wandered through the utterly empty castle unable to find the baby or the source of her cry. Each time she awoke she determined not to sleep again. At least awake she could stop her thoughts when they became too despairing to bear.

The days wore on and the search continued, but no clue to the child was found. Nor did they receive any letter of ransom or political demand. The royal parents drifted through each day on a great sea of despair. They arose each morning facing the impossibility of living through the day without hearing some word of hope, yet when that word did not come, they lived to face the same impossibility on the next day. They found some relief in returning to their duties, Volanna with an ache that never left her breast and Aradon with a distant look in his eyes that told all who saw him that his soul was elsewhere.

CHAPTER FOURTEEN

MOSSETTE

he nursemaid Glynnora made her way down Morningstone Hill as quickly as she could in the near darkness. She was fortunate that the path was well worn and easy to follow. Across her shoulder she carried a bag stuffed with all she would need to care for the princess Vallia for the next several days, and in her arms she carried the sleeping princess herself. She reached the base of the hill and hurried toward a copse of trees that hid a merchant's cart with a driver waiting on the board. She climbed into the cart and said with lowered voice, "Let's go." The driver flicked his whip lightly over the horse's back and the cart moved down the road.

He drove due west, and soon they plunged into the blackness of Braegan Wood. Though the towering trees shut out most of the starlight, the driver knew his way and the cart traveled along the narrow road for a little more than two hours. Glynnora cradled the baby in her arms, and the creaking and rocking of the cart were just enough to keep the little princess asleep. Dawn was less than two hours away when Glynnora saw ahead a dim glow of light reflecting on a circle of tall oaks. As the cart approached she could see the fire that caused the glow and barely make out the outlines of five men standing or sitting about the fire. The driver brought the cart to a stop and said, "The road ends here. The trees ahead are too thick for my cart."

Glynnora stepped down, still carrying the sleeping Vallia, as the driver turned the cart about and retraced the trail out of the woods.

The nursemaid kneeled near the fire and laid the baby, now beginning to whimper as she awakened, on the grass in front of her. "Bring me the bag," she said as she began to remove the infant's clothing. She drew out plainer, more ragged garb of homespun linen and dressed the child in it. One of the men gathered up the discarded pieces of royal apparel and flung them out into the darkness.

"What's the matter with ye, man?" said Glynnora. "D'ye want to mark a trail for Aradon's men to follow? Ye can just go find the babe's garb and put them in the fire. And be sure every last thread of them burns." She picked up the crying infant and began nursing her.

The man did not move. "Are we goin' to let this hardmouthed woman order us about?"

"She's right, Bwark. We can't leave a trail behind us. Do as she says."

Bwark glared at the speaker, Rynon by name, then turned and stalked into the darkness to find the scattered garments. He brought them back and threw them angrily into the flames. "What we're doin' is no job for a woman. I don't see why we need to keep this bossy female with us."

"If ye can feed the child I'll gladly leave her with ye and be on my way," said Glynnora. "Otherwise, stop the foul wind that's blowin' from yer mouth."

"And we need her for another reason," said Rynon. "When travelers or villagers see us on the road, they'll be less suspicious if the woman is with us. Five men carryin' a baby is not a common sight."

At that moment the howl of a distant wolf pierced the darkness. Some creature stirred in the bushes about them and bounded away into the forest. "These woods chill my blood," said Bwark. "I've heard tales of monstrous creatures stalkin' in them. I'd just as soon be out of here by mornin'."

"We'll not be out of here for another day," said Rynon. "We must avoid open roads as much as possible, and the forest will cover us all the way into Vensaur. When we reach the edge of the woods in Vensaur, Brendal will have a cart waitin' to bring us to him."

"I'll be restin' a lot easier when we get to Vensaur," replied Bwark. "Aradon wouldn't dare follow us there."

"An anguished heart cares nothin' for the boundaries of king-doms," Rynon replied. "The desperate father in Aradon may overcome the king in him. Besides, Aradon's are not the only eyes we're evadin'. Brendal wants the royal babe brought to him without Morgultha knowin' anything of it."

"Does he, now?" said Glynnora. "I might be havin' somethin' to say about that, bein' myself in the service of Brendal only because my mistress Morgultha lent me to him. Ye know that Morgultha and Brendal are plottin' this thing together. And when we've delivered the child to Brendal, I'll be returnin' to my mistress to give the tale of our success."

"You will do nothin' of the kind," replied Rynon. "You may as well know now that when we get to Vensaur, you will be held at Brendal's castle until he draws the Seven Kingdoms under his own banner. He has no intention of sharin' the crown with your Morgultha. And with this child in his hands, he's got a bit in Aradon's mouth to turn him any way he wants."

"Fine thanks Brendal shows Morgultha for freein' him from prison. He is a fool even to think of betrayin' her," spat Glynnora. "She'll blow him aside like a dried leaf, just like she's done men with twice the brains as him, not that that's sayin' much."

"This Brendal you call a fool has already taken over Lochlaund, Vensaur, and Sorendale, and now has Aradon quakin' on the throne of Meridan. And he did it all without Morgultha's help. Why should he share the throne with her? She sits hidden away somewhere in a dank cave, tappin' her foot while Brendal does all her work. She's like a spider squattin' at the center of a foul web, gorgin' her ambitions on the blood of men. It's time someone stopped her, and Brendal is just the man who can do it."

"Not with my help, he won't," Glynnora plucked the child from her breast and immediately the little princess began to cry. "I'll not go back and tell my mistress I had any part in this treason of Brendal's. You can find yourself another wet nurse." She laid the wailing Vallia on the grass, then stood and began to walk into the forest.

"You are goin' nowhere." Rynon put his sword to the woman's

neck. "Either that child will drink your milk or this sword will drink your blood."

Glynnora opened her mouth to reply when Bwark's scream split the air. All turned and stared in terror. At the edge of the clearing stood a dim, transparent form. As they watched with jaws hanging and knees trembling, the apparition slowly took on solidity until a robed man, tall and white haired, stood before them. He took a step toward the fire and panic seized the six conspirators. They turned and bolted through the forest leaving the princess Vallia on her back in the grass crying, her arms and legs flailing in the air.

The ancient man stepped into the empty clearing, picked up the infant, and drew out a skin of milk from his long robes. He uncorked the skin, stuffed a bit of twisted rag into the opening, and put it to the child's mouth. Immediately she stopped wailing and sucked vigorously on the soaked rag, gazing all the while without fear into her benefactor's smiling face. After she had taken her fill, the man held her until she drifted again into sleep, then he laid her gently on a bed of soft moss between the encircling roots of a huge oak tree. He sat on a stone nearby and watched over the child as the fire died and the darkness deepened.

Prince Lanson awakened suddenly and peered into the darkness. He was sure he had heard a sound. But he lay still and listened a moment longer and, hearing nothing, decided he had dreamt it. His fire was merely embers now, and he got up to toss a few more logs upon it, looking into the dark forest all the while for any clue to what he had heard.

He lay down again, pulled his cape about him, and drifted into sleep. Soon the monster of his nightmares stalked yet again through the streets of Macrennon and clawed through the door of his father's castle. As always, he ran to his father's chambers only to arrive too late, as the monster had devoured the king and now turned on him. But this time the dream took a different twist. The moment the hideous creature lumbered toward Lanson, a tall man, white haired and bearded and clad in a long robe the colors of earth and leaves, suddenly stood straight and unmoving between him and the monster. The creature raised itself to all the height the room allowed, opened its fanged jaws, and roared until the castle trembled. The robed man stood his ground, not even moving except to raise toward the creature a sword with a blade of fire white as lightning. The monster bellowed in rage as it jerked backward and clambered to the far corner to get away from the flaming sword, but to no avail. With a flick of the man's wrist, the sword blasted the creature and dancing flames licked about its body until it collapsed into a heap of ashes that hissed and smoldered for a few seconds before lying inert on the castle floor.

The man sheathed his flaming sword and turned toward Prince Lanson. Lanson looked into the face of his rescuer and gaped in wonder at what he saw. Though the man's hair and beard were pure white, his face bore no evidence of age except for the look of great wisdom in eyes clear and deep as the sea. The skin itself was smooth and supple as that of a man Lanson's own age.

"What—who are you?" asked Lanson.

"I have many names," the man spoke in a voice resonant as a bell, "but you will know me as Father Clemente. Come. I have somewhat to say to you, Lanson, son of Kor."

Father Clemente led him out of the castle and into the woods. Though they seemed to walk for only a few minutes, Lanson found that they had arrived at the very place in Braegan Wood where he had camped for the night. He recognized the fire with the two fresh logs just beginning to burn and found himself now clad in the clothing he had got from the unwary swimmer. Father Clemente sat on a stone near the fire and bade Lanson sit on another nearby.

"King Lanson—for you are now rightly king over Lochlaund though your throne is not yet ripe for the claiming—I have come to give you this word: You will soon do a great service for the Seven Kingdoms. You will destroy the evil that would destroy the land. And you will shut the gates of hell, securing the future of this mighty island for generations to come. But hear this, King Lanson: the gates of hell can be shut only by one who has seen them from the inside."

"I have no idea what you mean by any of this," said Lanson. "You must explain it to me."

"I give you only the word, not the meaning," said Clemente. "The meaning of the word becomes clear in the fulfillment of it, not before."

"I think I can guess the fulfillment," said Lanson. "Undoubtedly I will kill King Aradon and thereby rid the land of the evil that would destroy it."

Clemente looked steadily at Lanson. "You are filled with rage and hate for the man."

"And why should I not be? The man is a vile murderer who has the Seven Kingdoms fooled into believing he is the prophesied savior of the island. Someone must expose this snake for what he is and bring him to justice."

"But there is a power stronger than justice, Lanson. The power of forgiveness will put an end to more evil than justice possibly can. Justice ends evil by executing its perpetrator. Forgiveness ends evil by removing it like one removes an embedded fang, freeing the victim from its poison. Forgiveness, not revenge, is the fountain of peace."

"I cannot let my father's death go unavenged. Surely it is right for me to require the life of the man who killed him."

Father Clemente sat quietly for a moment, and Lanson, unable to meet the man's steady gaze, stared at the grass between his feet. Suddenly he jumped up. A snake was crawling over his boot. He grabbed a small log from those he had gathered for the fire and turned to kill the reptile, but as he raised the club, he saw that it was not a snake at all but merely an unusually large but harmless night crawler such as any fisherman would hunt for bait. Feeling sheepish, he tossed the stick onto the fire.

"Beware, Lanson. Things are not always what they appear to be. You must keep your mind pure to see the truth behind the appearance." Without another word Father Clemente arose from his stone and walked into the darkness. Lanson stood for a moment watching with wonder as the black night swallowed him. Then he lay down once more and wrapped himself in his cloak.

He was not quite asleep when the sound that had awakened him earlier came again. He started and opened his eyes. For several minutes he lay still and listened. The sound came once more—the cry of some distant animal, he thought. He listened a moment longer and, hearing nothing, pulled the cloak about him and closed his eyes. The cry sounded again and Lanson sat up and threw off his cloak. He was almost certain the cry was that of a human infant. In another moment he was absolutely sure, for the sound became more intense and sustained, like the cry of an infant who was hungry or afraid.

Lanson got up and, taking from the fire a limb that was burning at the tip, held it before him as a torch and made his way cautiously toward the cry. Soon he came to the great oak with the twisted roots and found the baby cradled there in a bed of moss, now screaming as if her heart would break. He looked about for any sign of another person, then set the burning limb against a stone and picked up the crying infant. He cradled her in his arms and held her close, speaking gently to her all the while the way he had seen nurses comfort the children of noblewomen in Macrennon Castle. Finding the linens wrapping the child to be soaking wet, he removed them and enfolded her in his own cape. She blubbered and snubbed a few minutes more, then quieted in the security of Lanson's arms and the sound of his soothing baritone voice.

Why is this child here? he thought. *Who are her parents? What could possibly have caused her to be abandoned deep in Braegan Wood?* Still holding her close, he walked about the great oak looking for anything that might answer the riddle. Several feet from the tree he found a leather bag with a shoulder strap attached, filled with two or three changes of clothing and several linen rags. As he walked about he felt the child relax in his arms and realized she had fallen asleep. Apparently she had been fed recently or hunger would have kept her crying.

Lanson had no experience caring for an infant, and he racked his brain for solutions to this tiny, sleeping kink in his plans. Somewhere a pair of anguished parents must be searching desperately for her. Or perhaps her parents had been somehow killed or wounded in the forest. Perhaps they had been robbed and left for dead. Lanson determined to widen his search when morning came. If he could not find the parents, he would find some way to feed the child until he could leave her with someone who could care for her. And soon. He knew she would be hungry when she awakened in the morning.

He looked down at the baby's face, now peaceful and angelic in repose. He remembered the ancient story of Pharaoh's daughter finding the Hebrew baby floating in a basket on the River Nile. He said to her, "Like that lonely Egyptian, I don't know who you are or from whence you came. Until I discover your real name, I will call you not Moses but Mossette, because I found you in the moss of the forest." But unlike Pharaoh's daughter, Lanson had no intention of keeping the infant any longer than necessary. He was on a mission and the baby would hamper him greatly. And each step of his journey would undoubtedly take her farther from her home and guardians. He carried the baby back to his fire, settled down beside it with his back to a tree, and cradled the sleeping little Mossette in his arms.

As he waited for dawn to break, he recalled his vivid dream of the strange man who had called himself Father Clemente. What did the man mean by saying Lanson would "shut the gates of hell"? How could he not expect him to desire revenge against Aradon? His memory of the man was so vivid that he began to wonder whether it was a dream at all. But what else could it have been? The dream had begun back in Macrennon Castle and ended here in Braegan Wood, and the man had fought the dragon of his recurring nightmare. Certainly it was a dream.

Lanson looked down at little Mossette. She still slept soundly, and he felt strangely flattered that the little creature would trust him enough to sleep so contentedly in his arms. He lay back against the tree and waited for morning.

CHAPTER FIFTEEN

The Reluctant Nursemaid

orning came before Lanson was ready for it. Dawn had barely broken when the thrashing of little arms and legs against his chest brought him awake. Mossette began to cry and he held her close, hoping she would settle back into sleep. When she continued to cry and flail, he got up and walked with her, singing softly. But the more he walked the louder she wailed. Finally he sighed, "Very well, little one. I will get your breakfast."

He sat again on the stone, uncorked the skin of milk, held the squirming and crying child as still as he could, and poured the milk into her mouth. The result was disastrous. Mossette choked and coughed and cried alternately. Lanson stood immediately and held her by the heels, thinking to drain from her throat any milk that had choked her. She coughed and sputtered for a few moments, then began wailing in earnest. Obviously he had used an improper feeding method. He sat again, laid the kicking and screaming infant on his lap, wetted his finger with milk, and thrust it into her mouth, wiping the milk against her tongue. He repeated the procedure three or four times before Mossette began to respond and suck the milk off his finger, crying less and less with each application. Finally she got into the rhythm of the process and ceased her crying, her round little mouth and pink tongue working in anticipation of each approach of the tasty finger.

Lanson thought Mossette had consumed enough long before she did. Each time he tried to stop she cried until he resumed the feeding. But finally she began to lose interest and he stoppered the milk-skin. The sun was well up and he should have put a few miles behind him by now. He could not afford the time the child was taking from his journey. He must find someone to keep her soon.

Lanson kicked dirt onto the embers of his fire, slung Mossette's bag over his shoulder, took the baby in his arm, and set off once more through the woods. For most of the morning Mossette wanted to be held upright so she could look about the forest. She cooed and gurgled, staring wide-eyed as they passed among the ancient oaks and towering conifers soaring toward the heavens from patches of wild-flowers and green seas of grass. Lanson often found himself talking to her and pointing out animals and flowers, or singing nursery ditties in a lilting voice. Sometimes he looked at her and found her smiling for no apparent reason other than sheer delight at the colors and sounds of their journey. By midmorning, however, he could feel her little body relaxing as the steady rhythm of his stride and the warming of the day lulled her into sleep.

A half-hour later Lanson came to the western edge of Braegan Wood, where it met the lower slopes of the Dragontooth Mountains. He dared not take the road that ran southward between the forest and the foothills but stayed back within the trees and traveled parallel to it. Soon he came upon a hut, huddled among the trees some hundred paces off the road. Lanson made for the hovel, which was surrounded by crude sheds and cages. A half-dozen goats grazed from the grass at the edge of the clearing, and a few dozen chickens scratched and clucked around the outside of the cabin. Three or four large sows lay in the mud within a pen made of rail fences.

Lanson approached the hut and called out, "Is anyone here?"

Soon the wrinkled face of an old woman, white haired and stooped, appeared at the door and glared at Lanson. "Who be ye and what d' ye want here?"

"I am a wanderer who happened upon this abandoned babe in the forest last night. Perhaps you know whose she might be."

"I know nothin' about any lost child."

"Is there a family or a mother along this road who could have lost her somehow?"

"Like I told ye, I know nothin' about any lost child."

"Well, I just happened to find her. She is not mine, and I can hardly care for her on the long journey ahead of me. Perhaps you could keep her until someone—"

"Nay, I'll not be takin' the child. I'm an old woman, and I can hardly care for the animals that keep me in eggs and milk."

"Surely it would not be for long," said Lanson. "Someone is certain to come looking for her, and you are not far from where I found her. It's a shame for me to carry her miles away from where she was left."

"No matter, I'll not be takin' her, and that's that, young sir." At that moment Mossette began to awaken, crying as she had cried to begin the day. "The babe is hungry," said the woman. "Have ye fed her?"

"Of course I have fed her," replied Lanson. "Though it took me well nigh an hour."

"How did ye feed her?"

Lanson explained how he had found the skin of milk beside the child and the slow process of letting her suck the milk off his finger. "She almost choked to death when I tried to pour the milk into her mouth."

The woman glared at Lanson as if she thought him an imbecile, then looked into his bag. "Why didn't ye use these rags?"

"I did use them to wash her face and her, uh, well—"

"Men are so stupid. Let me show ye how it's done." The old woman found a clean rag, twisted it, and stuffed it tightly into the mouth of the skin. She sat on the step at her door, took the infant in her arms, and put the rag, now soaked with milk, to her mouth. Mossette worked at it for ten minutes or less, then pulled away and turned her head when the woman tried to put it to her mouth again. "The babe's had all she needs," she said as she handed the child back to Lanson.

Shaking his head, Lanson made no move to take her. "You are so good with the child, I think I shall leave her with you and travel on. I'm sure you would not have her long. Someone is certain to come looking for her soon." He turned and began walking away.

"Young man," the woman called after him, "I'll not be keepin' this child. If ye leave her with me, I'll take her to the road and set her out until either someone comes along and picks her up or she starves to death."

"I don't believe you would do such a thing," called Lanson over his shoulder as he continued walking into the woods. But she got up from the step, picked up the baby's bag, and with her short, shuffling steps, carried the child to the edge of the road. Lanson stopped and peered from behind a tree as she set Mossette on the grass, dumped the bag beside her, and returned to her hut. Lanson watched for several minutes, and Mossette began to cry. He waited for the woman to emerge from her hut and come after the baby, but she did not. Mossette's cry became a wail, but still there was no sign of the woman. He waited several minutes more. Then, with a sigh of exasperation, he went to the child, picked her up, and soothed her. He glanced at the cottage, where he saw the old woman watching from the window, a smile of satisfaction on her face as she turned away. Lanson sighed and, carrying the baby, continued his journey.

For two days he walked southward through the woods, keeping near the road, each day traveling less than half the distance he had covered before he had found Mossette. The feedings went faster now that he knew the trick of the soaked rags, but early on the second day she had awakened crying and nothing he could do would stop her. She would not eat, and she drew up tightly when he held her close. He tried to feed her, but she turned aside when he offered her the milk. And when he sniffed at the soaked rag, he understood why. The milk had soured. No doubt the poor child suffered from a stomachache. Lanson had no idea how to treat the malady, but he stopped for the remainder of the day and watched in anguish and pity, gently stroking Mossette's tight little belly as she cried herself to sleep. He watched her as she slept, and with his bow he killed a hare that wandered within range and roasted it for his own meal. He knew he would have to find fresh milk for Mossette, and quickly. Or better yet, someone who would take her off his hands.

Before evening approached, Lanson decided to move on. He dared not wait longer to search for milk. Again he traveled at the edge of the woods alongside the road at the foot of the mountains. Darkness had descended and the night was deep before he came upon another human habitation—a stone hut with a thatched roof standing alone at the edge of the woods. No light came from the windows or smoke from the chimney, though someone must have lived there, for adjacent to the hut was a pen full of goats. Lanson thought of knocking on the door to try to purchase milk but wondered what sort of reception he would get so late at night. His second thought was to sneak inside the fence to milk one of the goats, but he had never milked a goat and was not sure how to go about it. Nor did he know how much noise a goat would make at his intrusion.

He began to walk on but had not gone fifty paces when he came upon a small, rude shed. He went to the door and looked inside, and by the moonlight drifting through the cracks in the walls, he made out the silhouettes of two fat cows. He lifted a latch and stepped inside. Finding a pail on the wall, he laid Mossette in an empty manger and set about milking a cow.

Lanson had no more experience milking cows than goats, but at least he had seen milkmaids at work on cows on the farms of Lochlaund. At first no amount of tugging produced any milk, but soon he managed to get a small stream flowing with each pull. It took him longer than he expected, and the pail was no more than a quarter full when Mossette began to stir and whimper. The barn was too close to the hut to risk the noise of a full-blown cry, so Lanson ceased milking and, with fingers trembling in haste, poured the milk into the skin, spilling much of it on the ground. Mossette's wails began to increase in volume, and his sharp whispers to hush only made her cry all the more. He left a copper penny on the milking stool, then turned to pick up Mossette.

But he had forgotten the pail. With a loud clatter he tripped over it and fell headlong to the straw-covered earth. The sudden noise set Mossette to screaming in earnest. Lanson scrambled to his feet, kicking the pail yet again, and scooped up the crying baby. He bumped open the door with his shoulder, and as he stepped out of the barn, he froze in his tracks. Coming directly toward him from the hut was the bobbing light of a lantern.

"Who's there? Stop, I say!" cried a voice from the direction of the light. Panicked, Lanson ducked low and ran from the barn toward the forest. "Halt, I say!" called the voice again. But Lanson kept running. He turned to see the lantern bobbing toward him and ran headlong into the fence enclosing the goats, knocking down a section with a clatter as the rails piled about him. He managed to protect Mossette from harm, but the fall jarred her, and she cried with all the lung power she could muster. The lantern approached to within twenty paces as Lanson scrambled to his feet and ran once more toward the forest. A whisking sound passed his ear, and with a solid *thock* an arrow appeared in the trunk of a tree just in front of him. He began to cut back and forth, keeping the trees between himself and his pursuer as much as he could, but still the lantern kept coming. Suddenly he stepped into a mass of brush, and his foot found no earth beneath it. He skidded and tumbled down the slope of a ravine and landed hard at the bottom.

He managed to curl his body around Mossette, insulating her from the worst of the fall. Immediately he got up and ran along the bottom of the ravine as it curved first to the left, then to the right. He climbed out on the far side and ran through the trees until he felt sure he had lost his pursuer. He dared not stop yet, but he slowed to a brisk walk to catch his breath and let Mossette regain her composure. Unable to sustain a cry throughout the jarring run, she had been making staccato noises as she was jerked and bumped about. Lanson pulled the blanket from her face and looked at her with wonder. She was not crying; she was laughing. He had never heard her laugh aloud, and the delightful sound, coming on the heels of the near disaster, was irresistible. He began to laugh with her until his legs weakened, and he sank down to the roots of a great oak and bellowed like Jove himself until his mirth was spent.

"So you think it hilarious that I nearly got us both killed getting your dinner." Mossette smiled and cooed at the sound of his voice, causing him to wonder at how her happiness so warmed his heart. The gray of dawn began to lighten the forest as he deftly stuffed a twisted rag into the milkskin. "I hope you note and appreciate the high degree of my expertise," he muttered as he placed the milk to her mouth. When she had drunk her fill, he broke his fast on two pieces of the hare he had saved from the day before. Afterward he continued his journey.

It was early afternoon before Lanson stopped again to feed the infant. When she was finished eating, Lanson laid her on her blanket in the shade of a huge, ancient oak. He sat beside her and watched as she waved her arms and kicked her legs, her pink little mouth bubbling and cooing as she gazed at the birds and squirrels that chattered and hopped in the branches above. But in a moment she stopped moving and stared intently. Her mouth began to draw downward, her face turned red, and she began to bawl in utter terror. Lanson looked up in the direction of her gaze. Sitting on a limb just above them was an enormous blackbird, perhaps two feet or more from beak to tail. It stared down on them with eyes pale and yellow as a twilight moon. Lanson chilled at the enormity of the creature and its baleful stare. He understood why Mossette was so frightened. The cold menace in those eyes was unmistakable. Even the child could sense it.

"Get away from here!" he cried as he stood and flung a stone at the bird. Showing no panic, it merely flew to a higher branch. But Lanson wanted the creature nowhere near them and continued a barrage of stones until the bird finally flew off into the forest. He watched it glide southward among the trees until it disappeared. He wished it had flown to the north. He shuddered at the thought that he might encounter it again, for his path lay in the same direction.

He held the squalling Mossette against his shoulder and spoke gently to her, stroking her head and back all the while. When she grew calm again he draped the bag across his shoulder and continued his journey. He had walked less than a quarter mile when he stopped short. He saw the huge bird sitting in the lower branches of a pine some fifty paces ahead. As Lanson approached, the bird left its perch and again flew several yards ahead of him. The dark creature repeated this strange, stalking behavior for another mile or more, which Lanson found more than a little unnerving. However, he walked on and, finally seeing no more of the blackbird, put it out of his mind and began to think on other things.

The sun was low when he came upon another cottage nestled in the woods just off the road. Unlike the previous two, this one was clean and well kept. The roof was freshly thatched, no cracks showed in the mortar of the stone walls, and the shutters were intact and recently whitewashed. Lanson decided to try the cottage as a home for the baby. He knocked, and the door opened to reveal a tall woman. He opened his mouth to speak, but when he saw her face, the words died on his tongue. Her skin was so white it seemed drained of blood, and she was draped from head to foot in black. Her eyes were almost colorless, except for the bare tint of yellow encircling the piercing black pupils. The eyes were exactly those of the blackbird that had hovered before him much of the afternoon.

"What do you want?" said the woman in a voice almost as deep as a man's.

"Do you know of any mother hereabouts who might have lost a child? I found this little girl alone in the woods three days ago."

"I have heard of no such mother," said the woman, "but my husband died not three months back, and I would gladly take the child for company until the mother is found."

The woman spoke the words Lanson had longed to hear for days, but he hesitated. Her whole demeanor disturbed him—the pale eyes, cold as ice, boring through him like a carpenter's awl, the pallid face set hard as stone, and the voice devoid of human emotion. She reached out her left hand to take the child but kept her right arm hidden in the folds of her robe. Still Lanson hesitated. He had heard of unearthly creatures and witches in Braegan Wood. Could this woman be a witch? He hardly believed it, but the look of her . . . how could he take the chance?

"I thank you for your kind offer, but I'll keep the babe until I can find her real mother."

The woman's face hardened even more. Her brows arched, and her eyes widened in anger. "What business do you have keeping her? She's not yours. She belongs with a woman who knows how to take care of her."

"No doubt you are right about that, but I've done well enough with her these three days, and I can keep her for a few more if need be. Good evening to you."

As Lanson turned quickly and walked away, the woman called after him, "How can you keep the child and deprive a grieving woman of something to love?" Lanson did not reply but kept walking. The woman spat at him, and in a voice dripping with venom cried, "For this I place a curse on you, that someday you will slay the person you love most in the world."

Lanson shuddered at the words, but he did not turn or look back. He kept walking into the woods until he had put the house out of sight. As he made his way among the darkening trees the woman's vile threat rang in his mind. Just who was she to put such a curse on him? She was nothing but a freakish, lonely woman trying to frighten him in retaliation for not yielding up the child, he thought. He tried to shake the woman's words from his head as he kept going.

However, he found he could not ignore the disquieting experience. Her curse haunted him, and he began wondering just who she could have been speaking of. Whom did he love most in the world? A few days ago he would clearly have named his father, but his father was now dead, and his mother had been dead almost five years. Perhaps his greatest love should be his fiancée Lamonda, but it was not so. Though he knew it was his duty to make a place for her in his heart, he had not yet managed to do it. He supposed he loved Sir Maconnal more than anyone presently living, but his feelings toward Maconnal certainly did not rise to the level of what one imagined when speaking of the person he loved most in the world. He examined his life and had to admit that he did not possess such a love, and the thought dismayed him. He wanted to love. He needed to love, but there was no one he loved with a passion that filled his being. That fact made the woman's curse meaningless, he decided.

Sunlight now rimmed the west side of the trees in burnished gold, and Lanson found a grassy spot by a stream to stop for the night. He gathered a pile of dead limbs for the evening fire. Then he fed Mossette, laid her near the firewood, and watched as her eyelids grew heavy and finally closed in sleep. Then he curled up in his cape and slept through the night, waking only to feed the fire.

The next morning he fed Mossette and continued his southward march. Before noon he came to the border between Meridan and

Vensaur, but to his consternation, he found armed guards stationed there to bar the road into Vensaur. Aradon was apparently protecting his own border against a possible hostile attack from Brendal.

Lanson could think of no alternative but to turn back and retrace his steps northward through the western edge of Meridan. He searched his mind for some more efficient plan. To turn back would mean a loss of three days at least, maybe four. But he knew there was only one pass through the Dragontooth Mountains into Oranth, and that was the road into Larenton far to the north. He felt certain this pass would not be guarded because of Oranth's treaty with Meridan. His only option was to return and take that pass into Oranth, then follow the southward road from Larenton until he reached Soucroft on the border between Oranth and Vensaur. With a sigh of frustration, he turned and began walking north.

CHAPTER SIXTEEN

The proposal

valonne was working her way among the tables refilling empty mugs from her pitcher of ale when the door opened and a lone man, robed in the gray of the kirk, entered and found an empty table. The cleric sat with his back to her, and she paid scant attention until she approached him to take his order. Though she could see nothing but the back of his head, something about him gave her an immediate sense of uneasiness. After a moment's hesitation, she dismissed the feeling and walked on toward him. But when she was only a table away, she stopped short. It was Gronthus. She was almost sure of it. She turned and hurried back to the kitchen. Since coming to Oranth she had learned, to her dismay, that crossing the Lochlaund border did not put her out of reach of the Kirk of Lochlaund. She could be arrested in any of the Seven Kingdoms for crimes committed in Lochlaund, though only by Lochlaund kirkmen. The power of individual kingdoms to enforce their own laws over their own subjects did not end at the borders.

Evalonne found a rag and bound up her hair, leaving only a few wisps showing. It was fortunate that the inn bustled with twice its normal traffic that evening, and both Gwynnelon and Lurga were helping her serve. She waited until Gwynnelon approached the kirkman before she returned to the dining hall. She watched as the serving girl set before him a mug of ale and he shoved it away. She picked up the mug and walked toward the kitchen, passing Evalonne on the way.

"That kirkman won't drink ale," she said. "Wants water instead. If he knew how much water Dunwig puts in this ale, it wouldn't bother him much."

Evalonne knew the man was Gronthus. Other Lochlaund kirkmen tended to forget the laws of abstinence when traveling in other kingdoms, but not a man like Gronthus. She let Gwynnelon serve the accorder the rest of the night, as well as most of the men within his range of vision. When she found it necessary to venture into that area, she kept her head down and her face turned from him. She was relieved that he seemed to be ignoring her, and her apprehension began to subside. However, when the hands of a drunken soldier groped for her, she pushed him away so forcefully that his chair tipped over, tumbling him to the floor. Bellowing in rage, the man grabbed her ankle.

"Let go of me, you slug!" she shouted, kicking and twisting until her leg came free. In that moment, she looked up and saw the eyes of Gronthus looking straight into hers. Her heart chilled at his baleful gaze, but she gathered herself and went on about her work. Often throughout the rest of the evening she stole a glance toward the kirkman, and half the time she found him looking steadily at her. She knew she had aroused his suspicion.

Later in the evening as Evalonne led a drunken Oranthian herdsman up the stairway to her room, Gronthus followed at a discreet distance and took note of which door they entered. Then he came down and made arrangements with the proprietor for his own room and retired for the night.

When Gronthus first came to the inn, he had paid no particular attention to Evalonne. Beautiful women were snares and temptations to men, and he had long ago trained his eyes to turn away from them—unless it was to search for some sin that would justify their removal from the earth to keep them from luring men into the pitfalls of pleasure. But when he had turned at the crack of the overturned chair and looked straight into the woman's face, he was sure he had seen her before. He could not recall where. He eyed her the rest of the evening and almost decided he was mistaken. He could not remember seeing a woman's face look so hardened and angry. Nevertheless, he would take steps to be sure. It was his duty.

The next morning he arose, dressed, went to the top of the stairway, and looked down into the dining hall. He noted with satisfaction that the girl was already busy serving breakfast to the morning patrons. He backed into the shadows and went to her door. After looking down the corridor both ways, he stole into the room and closed the door behind him.

Inside the room, he looked all about for some clue to her identity. He checked beneath the bed, opened the trunk against the wall, searched behind the lone table and the cracked mirror, and even ran his fingers inside crevasses between the planks of the wall and floor. He found nothing. He turned to leave, but as he put his hand to the door, he heard a scraping sound at the window. He crossed the room and opened the shutters. The noise was merely the limb of an oak tree raking against the sill in the morning breeze. He was about to close the shutter when he saw a tiny glint of light flashing among the leaves. He looked out at the spot where he had seen it, and the flash came again from a branch just below the window sill. He reached into the leaves and his hand closed on a delicate metal chain, which he drew into the room. Attached to the chain was a small, exquisitely carved image of a dove. He remembered seeing a pendant like it on the neck of the woman in Lochlaund who had taken up with Avriel the minstrel. He was almost certain the woman had been with child. Why else would she have left her job and home so suddenly? *Yes, she is surely the same girl,* he thought. He had seen her on the square and at the booth of the fowler in Macrennon. Yet he was not quite sure. The girl in Macrennon was all softness and light, while this girl, though beautiful, had a face hard as stone and eyes chilled with hate.

Whether or not the two were the same, he could do nothing about it at the moment. He was on the bishop's business. He had an appointment with an emissary of Brendal's in Faranburgh this very night to exchange a series of messages between Brendal and Bishop Hugal. But he would return tomorrow evening, at which time he would confirm the girl's identity and take her in chains for trial in

Lochlaund. He left Evalonne's room and descended the stairway to his breakfast. After finishing, he called Dunwig to his table and told him he required a room for the following evening. Then he paid his bill and left the inn.

"Hold a room for tomorrow night," Dunwig called to Golwen across the hall. "The name's Gronthus."

Evalonne froze. Gronthus was coming back. She was in grave danger. She had noticed him eyeing her as she moved about the tables, and he could not help but suspect who she was. In spite of her indenture and her fears of leaving the inn, she had but one thought: she must be gone before he returned.

She pondered the problem throughout the day, but no clear solution came to her. The money she had hidden away was too little to start a new life. The thought of escaping alone through the woods filled her with cold dread. It was an experience she did not want to repeat, but she saw no alternative. And it would have to be tonight. Escape in daylight would be impossible, and tomorrow night would be too late. After the last man had left her room and Dunwig and Golwen were long asleep, she would bundle up her clothes and money, steal a blanket and a wallet of salt pork, slip out of the inn, and travel through the woods until dawn.

As nightfall approached, Evalonne was filling her pitcher with ale from the cask when laughter erupted in the dining hall. She glanced up to see the cause of it. A tall, fine-looking young man had entered, carrying a whimpering baby on his arm. The men at their tables jeered and laughed, calling him such names as nursemaid and fishwife, and asking him where he had left his skirts. The young man ignored the mockery and found his way to an empty table. Evalonne picked up her pitcher and a mug and went to where he sat.

"We've got beef stew and ale tonight," she said. "What do you want?"

The young man looked up at her and his eyes lingered for a moment, clearly reluctant to look away.

"Stew and ale will do," he said, "and please bring a pitcher of warm milk for the babe. As you can see, she's quite hungry."

Evalonne turned away to get his food and wiped her eyes on her apron. Seeing the baby overwhelmed her, and with a rush of emotion, she hastened out of the dining room. The child was so like her lost Luciella. With trembling hands she dipped out a bowl of stew and warmed a ewer of milk, then loaded the items onto a tray. She took a deep breath, reined in her emotions, and told herself she must ignore the child as she walked back to the young man's table.

A man with the looks of this one would surely have turned her head at one time, but no more. Men were now to her like a honey cake she had once been unable to resist and had gorged herself on until she became sicker than she had ever been. For years afterward she could not stand the sight of honey cakes. This man, though boasting a wondrous exterior, was of the sex that used and discarded, wooed and abandoned, promised and deceived, and she would not give him a second glance. Men were like the Venus flytrap, which attracted insects and consumed them: the sweeter the nectar, the more deadly the snare.

Evalonne set the man's food in front of him without a word and went about serving other customers. As usual the men leered at her, picked at her, and made bawdy suggestions as she passed their tables. She mostly ignored them, though when hands pawed at her or tried to lift her dress she slapped them away, spitting sharp retorts and angry curses. The young stranger was struggling to feed the squirming baby and paid no attention to what was going on around him.

Evalonne tried hard not to look at the baby in the man's arms. She ached to hold the little creature and hated herself for it. Hadn't she promised she would never again let anyone near her heart? The child was obviously tired, and the man was having trouble settling her down enough to take the milk-soaked rag he kept trying to force into her mouth. But it was his problem, she told herself, not hers, and she went on about the tables, once again filling empty cups with ale.

A few minutes later the infant began to cry in earnest, and the fumbling man was having no success in getting the milk into her mouth. At the baby's screams, her own maternal longings pierced her heart, despite her efforts to ignore them. Feeling her own milk once again filling her breasts pushed her over the edge, and reason gave way to instinct. She set down her pitcher and marched over to his table.

"Here, let me have her," she said. "I can nurse her for you."

He glanced up, startled. Then with an unmistakable look of gratitude he handed her the squalling infant. She sat at the adjacent table and put the child to her breast. The baby quieted immediately and began to suckle as the grateful man thanked her and turned to eat his stew.

Whistles and catcalls filled the air as the men leered at Evalonne, but she did not even hear them, so totally was she focused on the warm little bundle she clasped in her arms. Her mind whirled with a jumble of emotions. Why was she doing this? She had determined to harden herself against any intrusion past the wall she had erected around her heart. She might regret what she was now doing after the child and her father had gone on their way, leaving her with a renewed memory of the joy that had been wrenched from her. But with the warmth of the baby's soft face against her flesh, she cared not a whit for what she might feel tomorrow. Her heart beat in a euphoric cadence as she gazed into the wide, guileless eyes looking up at her.

Evalonne was so absorbed in the nursing child that she failed to notice the approach of one of the inn's patrons—a huge, burly, half-drunken tanner who carried the reek of his trade with him. He had left his table and was weaving his way to where she sat. She did not know he was beside her until he grabbed her with his rough hands, almost pushing her over. Trying to protect the baby in her arms, she gouged her elbow sharply into his ribs.

"Why, you little harlot!" he growled as he tried to clasp her to him. She struggled to keep the child from being crushed between them, cursing the man roundly as he tightened his grip.

Instantly Lanson was on his feet. "Get away from that woman."

"Oh, so the fishwife wants a fight," he grinned as he released Evalonne and stood towering over her defender. He swung a meat-hook fist at Lanson's head, but Lanson ducked and punched him hard in the chin. The tanner stumbled backward, clattering into the tables behind him. With a snarl he rushed at his opponent, swinging both fists like hammers. Again Lanson simply ducked and drove his fist deep into the big man's ample belly. When the tanner doubled over, gasping for breath, Lanson knocked him back with an uppercut to the jaw, which laid the giant on the floor, bleeding from the mouth. Two diners dragged him out as Lanson returned to his food.

Evalonne continued feeding the baby, surprised when the young man who had sprung to her defense returned to his table without demanding her company. She shrugged and thought no more about it. He had probably acted as much for the child as for her, she realized. Or perhaps he simply wanted to finish his dinner before he got on with what he wanted from her. After all, he was a man, a foul bag of rampant appetites, intent on satisfying one before turning to the next. When the baby had nursed her fill and drifted into asleep, Evalonne reluctantly handed her back to the man and went about her work.

As Lanson finished his meal he overheard diners speaking about Evalonne. "That woman's a rare beauty, but she's a hard one, she is." Another responded, "Aye, and she's been that way since she lost her own babe not ten days ago." Lanson listened with interest. He wondered if she could be the answer to his problem. She could take Mossette and wet-nurse her, and caring for the child would help drive away her grief. Lanson summoned the innkeeper to his table and laid two copper coins before him.

"I want a half-hour with the red-haired girl," he said.

"Of course, my man," leered Dunwig, winking. "And ye'll not be disappointed. I'll send her over."

Moments later Evalonne came to his table and stood before him. The tenderness he had seen in her eyes as she nursed the baby was gone, replaced by a look of cold contempt.

Lanson stood and smiled as he pulled out a chair for her. "Please, sit down."

But Evalonne did not sit. She removed her apron, tossed it on the table, and started toward the stairway. "Why waste time with preliminaries?" she said. "Come on up and I'll give you what you've paid for."

Lanson did not follow but gently insisted that she sit with him at the table. She turned back to him, shrugged, and replied, "Whatever you want. You've bought me for half an hour and you can waste it any way you wish."

When she was seated, Lanson said, "I have heard of the recent loss of your child, and I want to express my deepest sympathy. I know there is no way to compensate—"

"I don't want to talk of it," Evalonne snapped. "Get on with what you have to say or let me get back to work." She folded her arms and gazed at him steadily, her green eyes cold and hard.

"I have a proposal to make you—"

"Of course. Every man does."

"No, it's not what you think. I want you to take this baby I have with me. Feed her, keep her, and care for her. I will pay you well."

"Surely you're not serious!" she spat. "What kind of beast are you to give away your own child as if she were some kind of dog?" She pushed the chair back from the table and stood.

"No, no—you don't understand," Lanson replied hurriedly, inviting her to sit once again. "The child is not mine. I found her abandoned in Braegan Wood, and I could not just leave her there to die. I don't know whose child she is or why she was left there. But she needs someone to keep her, and I am certainly not as well fitted for the task as you are."

His smile was kind, not leering, but she held her emotions in check at his suggestion. "Nevertheless, I will not take her. Someone will surely claim her eventually, and I would be accused of kidnapping."

"Very well, I understand," he replied. "But let me offer you another proposal. I am on a journey that will not wait. Come with me and nurse the baby on the way. After we arrive in Vensaur, I will hire a nurse for the child and you can return here."

Evalonne was silent as she considered the young man's proposal. At first it seemed the answer to her own dilemma, but there were problems. She could not openly leave the inn because of her indenture, and she could not explain to this man that they must leave furtively under cover of night without raising his suspicions. "No, I cannot go with you. I am indentured to the innkeeper here for another several months, and he would never release me without full payment."

"What is the amount of your indenture?"

"I don't know exactly. It seems to keep growing as I work. I'm sure it must be at least ten crowns by now."

"I will pay your indenture if you will come with me," Lanson offered.

Again Evalonne sat silent as she considered his offer. Her first impulse was to take it. But wouldn't she essentially be trading one indenture for another? And why should she trust this man? She knew nothing of him. Though she had hardened her defenses against succumbing to any kind of affection, she had found those defenses vulnerable when she had seen the baby, and they would almost surely crumble with no stone left upon another were she to have the baby in close proximity for weeks. The child would invade her heart and she would become a slave to a bond of affection that would be cruelly broken when the man reached his destination. No, she must not place herself in such a vulnerable position again. She must protect her heart from such an invasion.

As she thought, a plan came to her mind. Obviously, this man had money. She had learned well how to get money from men, and if she could separate him from his purse, she could get free of Dunwig and his ratty inn without great risk and no further commitment. She would decline the man's offer but watch for an opportunity to relieve him of his money pouch when he retired to his room for the night.

"No, I will not go with you," she said with a slight quiver in her voice as she glanced quickly at the baby, then away again.

Lanson looked at her kindly. "I think I understand, and I will press you no further. I cannot expect you to put yourself in a position that will continually remind you of the loss you have suffered. Let me encourage you not to despair. Your pain will diminish in time, and you will find reason for hope in your future."

Evalonne laughed bitterly. "I had hope once," she said, "but now I know better than to hope. Hope is a fantasy, a butterfly forever just out of reach. Hope denies the real truth about life. Life is a foul pit with slimy walls out of which no one can climb. Try and you only sink deeper into the mire. What you offer me is really no different from what I have at this inn. What does it matter whether I am Dunwig's slave or yours? Your words are high sounding, but the truth beneath them is the same as his. You men are all alike—crude, selfish, opportunistic, gluttonous, drunken, foulmouthed, lecherous boors, and we women are doomed to be your slaves, pawns, and playthings. Men provide me with a livelihood but make my life not worth the living. I hate men yet I must have men just to get by, and whether I live another month or another fifty years hardly matters. I may as well live it here. It may be a slime pit, but at least there is a roof over my head."

Evalonne stood to leave. "Our talk is over. You have used up your time."

Lanson drew from his money pouch a gold crown, which he held toward her. She took the coin—more than she had made against her indenture in a month—and tested it with her teeth. Satisfied, she started toward the stairway, but when Lanson made no move to follow, she turned and said, "Are you coming or not?"

"I am not buying anything from you," replied Lanson. "The coin is a gift." Evalonne shrugged and, without so much as a thank-you, went on about her business. But she made careful note of where Lanson kept his money pouch.

CHAPTER SEVENTEEN

escape from hell

anson had intended to sleep at the inn that night, but as darkness fell he had second thoughts. He was uncomfortable with the attention he had inadvertently drawn to himself. His entrance with the baby, his fight with the tanner, and his conversation with Evalonne had made him highly visible to the patrons of the inn, and he wondered if he would be safe when the drunkard got back on his feet. When the drinking grew heavy and the songs loud, he left coins on the table to pay for his meal, slipped out of the inn with Mossette, and made his way down the road in the darkness.

His departure did not escape the eye of Evalonne. She had watched him throughout the evening, and as soon as the door closed behind him, she went to the window to see which direction he took. She could not wait until Dunwig and Golwen were asleep; she had to follow the man now. Golwen was serving ale and mead in the hall, and Dunwig sat drinking and singing with a cluster of boisterous men. Evalonne went into the kitchen and quietly slipped out the back door.

She hurried down the road the young man had taken until the faint moonlight showed him walking far ahead. She slowed her pace to maintain a discreet distance and followed until he turned from the road and entered the woods. She turned at the same place, taking care to step silently on stones and soft grass as she followed the sound of his footsteps into the brush. Shortly he stopped, and she hid behind a distant clump of bushes, where she watched him gather a pile of dried logs, build a fire, and tend to the baby. Finally he cradled her in his arms and lay down to sleep.

For another half-hour she watched without moving until she felt certain he was sleeping. Then with slow, deliberate movements, she rose from her hiding place and made her way stealthily toward him. She stopped to pick up a club-sized log from the stack and watched for a moment to be sure he was indeed asleep. Then she stole forward again. She stood over the man, raised the log high, and brought it down hard on his head. He jerked violently and cried out, immediately putting his hands to his bleeding forehead. He looked at her and said, "So it's you—" But before he could pull his wits together, she hit him again, and his arms fell limp to the ground.

Ignoring the sudden cry of the baby, Evalonne knelt and slipped the money pouch from his belt and began to run into the woods. She felt a stab of remorse as she wondered if she had killed the man, but she told herself she did not care and ran on into the darkness, the bawling of the terrified baby ringing behind her. She tried desperately to ignore the cries as she ran on through the trees. She could still hear them when she reached the road and turned toward the village, and she put her hands to her ears to shut out the sound. After a moment she stopped. She could not leave the baby. Cursing herself, she turned back, scooped up the crying child from beside the inert body of the man, and returned to the village.

By the time Evalonne reached the edge of the town, the motion of her walking had put the infant to sleep again. Many of the cottages were darkened and shuttered as families had bedded down for the night. When she came to one that looked neat and well kept, she ran up to the steps and left the baby. Forcing herself not to look back, she returned to the road and headed toward the inn.

Z

Lanson moaned and clutched his head. Though the forest spun about him so that he could not tell up from west, he struggled to a sitting position and looked around him. Mossette was gone and so was his money. He tried hard to think through the throbbing of his head and dimly recalled seeing the beautiful serving girl from the inn standing over him with a club in her hand. Apparently she had robbed him and taken the baby. He crawled to a nearby tree, pulled himself to his feet, and clutched the trunk until the woods stopped spinning and merely swayed like a boat on a choppy sea. Then he staggered through the trees toward the road, pains shooting through his head as if the hooves of a herd of cattle were stampeding across it. His dizziness increased as he wove his way down the road toward the village, and he fell several times before he reached the edge of it. He must find his way to the inn, he thought, but he could hardly see for the blood that streamed into his eyes.

What was that he heard? He stopped to listen. It was the cry of a baby—Mossette, no doubt—and it came from somewhere just ahead. He staggered forward, trying to focus on the street lantern mounted on a post fifty paces away. But as he approached, the lantern dimmed and went black, as did everything about him. He managed only a few more steps before he fell to the cobblestones.

&v

Impelled by a strong sense of panic after leaving the baby, Evalonne began to run through the empty streets of the village. She rounded a corner not far from the inn and almost collided head-on with the town's watchman, swinging his lantern as he made his nighttime rounds.

"Woman, where are ye goin'?" he asked as she dodged and ran past him.

"I . . . I work at the Red Falcon Inn, and I, uh, just ran an errand for Dunwig. I must get back." She turned and hurried on.

"Stop! Wait a moment," cried the watchman, but Evalonne ran on as if she had not heard.

The watchman, who was also the village constable, watched her as she disappeared around the corner toward the inn, wondering if he should follow. Deciding against it, he shrugged and continued his rounds. He turned the corner from whence Evalonne had come and walked on down the street, looking intently at the cottages on each side as he went. He stopped. He heard a sound. It came again, and he was sure it was the cry of a baby. It came from the doorstep of the shuttered cottage on his left. Holding his lantern high before him, he approached the step and found there an infant of some five or six months, just beginning to cry.

The watchman set down his lantern, picked up the child, and knocked on the door. Soon it cracked open two or three inches, revealing the haggard face and heavy-lidded eyes of a man, blinking and squinting in the light of the lantern. When he recognized the watchman, his eyes widened and he opened the door fully.

"What is wrong?" he asked. "Is the village on fire? Have barbarians attacked us? Is the king dead?"

"Nay, nothin' of the sort," said the watchman. "But ye're not very hospitable to yer guests, makin' them sleep out here on yer step."

"What d'ye mean? What guests?"

"This one right here." The watchman gestured to the baby in his arm. "I found her cryin' here on yer doorstep. Are ye sayin' ye know nothin' of her?"

"I've never seen her before in my life."

"Very well, then. Get on back to yer sleep." The watchman took the baby and walked on. *There's a riddle here,* he thought, and no sooner had he thought it than he saw before him the body of a man sprawled in the street.

"Mercy! It's a night of many mysteries," he said as he knelt beside the prone figure and tried to shake him awake.

Evalonne reached the inn and went directly to Dunwig, who still sat at the table drinking and laughing with his friends, all heavily under the influence of the ale. "What's the balance on my indenture?" she asked.

"Well, I don't rightly have the exact figure in my head."

"Then get it. I want to know."

"I'll do it tomorrow, woman. Ye can see I'm busy now."

"No. You'll do it tonight. Right now," Evalonne demanded.

Dunwig sat scowling at her before he yielded to the determined set of her face. He cursed under his breath, pushed himself up, and staggered to his desk, where he unlocked a drawer and took from it Evalonne's contract. He held it to the lantern and squinted at it. "Looks like ye have somethin' like six crowns t' go before yer free. Should make it in 'bout five more months, I'd say."

"Here's your payment." Evalonne took six crowns from Lanson's pouch and flung them against the table, sending them bouncing and rolling across the floor in six directions. "Now tear up that contract and get this band off my neck."

Dunwig gaped stupefied at the scattering crowns before scrambling to his knees to chase them down. At that moment the door opened, and the constable entered the hall, followed by two deputies he had conscripted. Evalonne stared in horror. In his arms the constable carried the baby she had left on the doorstep. Immediately she ran for the kitchen, but Dunwig, still on the floor gathering the crowns, reached out and caught her foot, sending her sprawling. As he pulled her to her feet and held her arms, Lanson's money pouch clattered to the floor. The constable handed the baby to Golwen, picked up the heavy pouch, and faced Evalonne.

"Where did ye get all this money?" he asked.

"I . . . uh . . . the young man who came to the inn this evening gave it to me. Uh, that is, he paid me for services rendered," she replied.

"The wench is lyin'," Golwen said. "I was watchin' the whole time she was sittin' at the table with the man. He never went up to the room with her."

"What d'ye say to that, woman?" asked the constable.

"That's right," said Evalonne. "After we made the bargain and he paid me, I took him to the woods so Dunwig wouldn't get all the money." She grimaced as Dunwig dug his fingernails into the flesh of her arm. "That's where I was coming from when you saw me in the street tonight."

"And you expect me to believe a man would pay ye all this for one night?"

"I . . . well, no. He paid me only six crowns. Later, while I was coming back, I found his money pouch on the road. He must have dropped it. The hour was late and I didn't want to go into the forest again, so I was bringing it back to you. I know it sounds strange, but that's the way it happened."

"Six crowns is a small fortune. Why would a man pay you that much for one night?"

"He was very wealthy."

"Do ye know anything about this baby?"

"No—well, yes. She belongs to the man we're speaking of."

"And how did she come to be left on a cottage doorstep?"

"How would I know?"

"I think ye do know. Ye were the only person in the street tonight, and not far from where the babe was left. Ye'll get on better if ye tell me the truth, woman."

Evalonne sighed and said, "Very well, I will tell you. Yes, I left the baby on the step. You see, the child does not belong to the man who had her, and he asked me to keep her so he could get on with his journey. That's why he paid me so much money."

"If ye took money to care for the babe, why'd ye leave her on the cottage steps?"

"I was going back to get her. I had to come here and pay out my indenture. Having the child with me would have brought up questions hard to answer. So I left her in a place where I could find her later."

"And didn't ye worry any about leavin' the babe out like that?"

Evalonne said nothing but gazed at her own feet in shame. The constable turned to the men standing behind him and said, "Go bring in the man." The two deputies left the hall and returned moments later, and Evalonne's heart sank as she saw that they carried between them a litter bearing the man she had wounded.

"D'ye recognize this man?" the constable asked Evalonne.

"Yes, he's the man we've been speaking of."

"He's been sorely wounded. It looks as if someone tried to kill him, stole his money, took the baby, and ran," said the constable.

"It may look that way, but when I left this man, he was perfectly healthy and happy. Someone must have come on him afterward and dealt the blow, thinking to rob him."

"Yer story is a strange one, woman. It doesn't have the ring of truth about it. But I'm a fair man, and stranger things have turned out true. So I'll not be sendin' ye up to Widdcroft for trial unless I have a fair case. I'll put ye in a cell for the night, and in the mornin' perhaps this poor soul here will be able to tell his side of things. Dunwig, give me those six crowns."

"But, yer honor, she paid them to me for—"

"Hand them over, Dunwig. I'll put them in safe keepin' until all this is sorted out. If her story turns out true, I'll be givin' them back to ye. Meanwhile, give this man a bed and see that his wounds are dressed."

Reluctantly Dunwig handed the money to the constable and called Gwynnelon to guide his men to a room for the wounded Lanson. "I be runnin' an inn, not a sick house," he muttered.

The constable took Evalonne to the village jail and locked her in a cell. He was sure the girl was not telling the truth. He had seen too much of lying not to know the signs.

By midmorning Lanson was able to walk about, though he was still somewhat unsteady. Shortly before noon, the constable brought him to the town square, where a crowd of villagers who had heard something of the events of the night had gathered out of curiosity. He brought Evalonne from her cell and stood her face-to-face with Lanson.

"The woman here has made a number of claims about last night that ye may not find to be exactly accordin' to the way things happened. She says ye took her into the woods, where she provided for you, ah, certain services, then ye bargained with her to keep yonder babe and paid her six crowns for it all. She says when she left ye to return to the village in the dark of the night ye were well and whole. Some wood dweller must've come along later and bloodied yer head, thinkin' to take yer money. But it seems ye had dropped yer money pouch on the road, and she just happened on it as she was headin' back to the inn. Is this yer money pouch, sir?" The constable handed the heavy bag to Lanson.

"It is mine," he replied.

"I thought as much," said the constable. "I put back in it the six crowns the woman paid to Dunwig. Now, if ye can tell me what really happened last night, I'll hold this woman in my prison until Lochlaund's accorder Gronthus returns tonight. She's a citizen of Lochlaund, I'm told, and he can take her there for trial. What do ye say, man?"

At the name of Gronthus, Evalonne's knees weakened and she began to tremble as despair gripped her. She was caught in her own lie and there was no escape from it. Gronthus would take her to trial before the bishop, and her doom in the Devil's Mouth was inevitable. She would have collapsed to the floor had not the constable's two guards held her arms.

For a moment Lanson said nothing as he gazed at the trembling woman from beneath the linen bandage on his forehead. "Let her go. She has spoken the truth," he said, to the great surprise of everyone on the square.

The constable looked nonplussed. "Are ye sure, man?"

"I am certain," said Lanson. "You have no further reason to hold her. Please bring the child to me."

Gwynnelon handed Mossette to him, and at the constable's signal the men released Evalonne. She stood immobile where they left her, staring in shame at the ground before her feet. She was stunned at the man's reprieve. She did not understand it. This man she had robbed and almost killed had just saved her life. She did not move as he dandled and talked to the laughing baby.

The crowd dispersed, leaving the three of them alone on the square. She could not look up as she heard him walking toward her. *He will insist that I take the baby now,* she thought. *Or he will demand that I go with him and take care of her—and him as well, no doubt.* She saw his boots—still splattered with dried flecks of blood—as he stopped in front of her. She heard the rattling of coins as he opened his money pouch.

"Here, take this," he said.

She looked up and saw his hand extended toward her with seven crowns stacked in it.

"Go ahead, take it," he said. "Buy your freedom. I give it to you with no condition except that you must use it to make for yourself a new life."

Evalonne was stricken. Tears welled up, and she could lift neither her eyes to his face nor her hand to the money. "I cannot take this," she replied, her voice unsteady and choking. "I am an evil woman. I thought I had killed you and I hardly cared. I even tried to leave the child to die in the woods, all to save my own miserable skin, which is not worth saving. And now you, the very man I have wronged, not only save me from a horrible death, you forgive me and purchase my freedom. I'm not worth it. I don't deserve it. Your goodness is a weight I cannot bear. Even now I can hardly think thoughts that are not hard and cold and vengeful. Go from me and leave me to the misery I deserve." She broke down into great sobs and wailed softly as if her heart had broken.

Lanson took her hand and placed the money in it. "There is hope," he said gently as he closed her fingers around the coins.

He turned and walked toward the road, taking the baby with him. Evalonne lifted her head, and with tears still streaming down her cheeks, she watched him until he disappeared around a bend in the street.

She stood staring into the street long after the man with the baby had gone. Clutching the seven crowns, she walked to the Red Falcon and paid Dunwig six of them to cancel her indenture. The innkeeper took the money with greedy fingers and gleaming eyes, the glitter of the gold momentarily blinding him to the business he would lose in the wake of Evalonne's departure. But as he tore up the contract and removed the ring from her neck, his old scowl began to knit his brows and draw down the corners of his mouth.

"Now that ye're out of yer indenture, I'll make ye a deal if ye'll stay on with me," he said. "I'll pay ye a good wage of say, five pence a day; I'll give ye a good room of yer own, ye can stay in and sleep mornin's till noon; and I'll cut ye half of what ye take from yer customers at night. In a year ye'll be a wealthy woman."

"In a year I would be a walking corpse," she retorted as she turned and walked away. After bidding farewell to Gwynnelon and Lurga, she left the Red Falcon Inn, taking nothing with her but the remaining gold crown and the now ragged low-bodiced dress she wore.

She walked out into the sunlight, acutely aware of the fresh breeze on her neck where Dunwig's ring had rested. Now that she was free, what would she do? Where would she go? As she pondered the question, she felt the welling of a strong desire to follow the man who had saved her. She realized that by caring for the infant, she would be risking her unhealed emotions to another heartbreak, but she thought it a risk she must take. Although the man had required nothing of her, she felt almost as if she were indentured to him, but with a profound difference. She was not forced to serve him; she *wanted* to serve him.

The voice of reason raised its alarm. Why trade one kind of slavery for another? Now that she was free, why not throw off all constraints and find her own happiness instead of submitting to the agenda of another? Yet in spite of all reason, the thought of serving this man brought her an inexplicable sense of freedom, of elation— elation that could not be dampened even by the looming shadow of Gronthus, whom she knew would be watching for her on every road and in every inn. It was as if her life were no longer her own. It had been purchased by another, and somehow the thought of giving it back to him did not seem like slavery but freedom.

She left the village by the road south toward Vensaur. She was at least thirty minutes behind the man, but since he had the burden of the baby and she was completely unencumbered, she felt certain she could overtake him by noon. She did not miss her estimate by far. A quarter-hour before the sun reached its zenith, she saw him on the road ahead, just topping a hill. She drew closer, then finding herself feeling a bit shy of approaching, she slackened her pace to keep enough distance between them that he would not see her. What if he did not want her with him now? Indeed, why would he? After all, she had robbed him and almost murdered him. Why would he allow her anywhere near him? Perhaps he had given her the money to insure that she would no longer be a threat to his safety.

Such thoughts slowed her pace until she finally halted as a wave of despair overwhelmed her. Of course he would not want her now. How could she have thought otherwise? She had made herself into the kind of woman she was by her own evil choices, and following a good man to another town would not change her. A squalid life in an inn such as Dunwig's was exactly what she deserved. Dunwig had made her a good offer—the best a woman such as she could expect. Yet she could not go back to him because Gronthus would return and find her there. She could, however, find work in some inn far from Lochlaund, perhaps in the harbor towns in southeastern Meridan. Or she could even board a ship to the southern continent, where she could lose herself in some back-street inn far from the searching eyes of Gronthus. She turned and slowly began to retrace her steps.

But when the man had given her the seven crowns, he had told her that hope must remain alive. He had specifically enjoined her to use the money to start a new life. As she thought on his words, she heard them not merely as perfunctory platitudes, but as a solemn injunction that she must obey as the terms of the gift.

She stopped once more. She was not an animal—a swine bound by an unchangeable nature to return to the sty. She was a person—a daughter of Eve—and she could choose. True, the man might not have her, but she would lose nothing by offering herself to him. How could she live with herself year in and year out until she looked like Gwynnelon, knowing that she did not even have the courage to attempt to climb from the pit? She turned once again and, with resolute steps, began to close the gap between herself and the man who had saved her.

She was almost two hundred paces behind him when she saw him leave the road and disappear into the trees. In a near panic at the thought of losing him, she gathered her skirts and began to run. Panting hard, she reached the place where he had left the road and turned into the woods to follow. She feared he would not be easy to find, but she need not have worried. She had not gone fifty paces before she heard the unhappy wailing of the baby and the man's soothing voice trying to calm her. Soon she saw him. He was sitting on a stone, his back to her, trying to coax the unwilling child to suck on the milk-soaked rag he dangled before her. Without a word Evalonne walked up to him, sat on the stone beside him, took the baby in her arms, and put the child to her breast.

Immediately the babe ceased her crying and nursed with such vigor that one would have thought she had not been fed for days. The man watched without moving, and no words passed between them as

Evalonne, now unaccountably shy in his presence, kept her eyes on the nursing child. After a minute or so she summoned the courage to look up and found him looking at her with a hint of a smile on his face. She needed no words to tell her what his look meant. She was welcome here. He had accepted her. His smile was a scepter extended to give her life as surely as that which the great Persian emperor had extended toward his queen Esther. She could not have stopped the smile that lit up her own face any more than she could have stopped spring from coming. It was her first real smile since her own child had died.

*

That evening Gronthus returned to the Red Falcon Inn. He took his dinner and looked around the hall for Evalonne. When he did not see her, he assumed she was upstairs with one of the men and finished his meal. When she still did not appear, he called Dunwig to his table.

"Where is the green-eyed serving wench?" he asked.

"She's not workin' here anymore, yer grace," replied Dunwig. "But she was not the only bird in my cage. Have ye considered Gwynnelon there? She may not be quite as savory as the green-eyed one, but she knows how to make a man happy, she does."

"Fool! I want no part of your abominable whoremongering. I have other business with the green-eyed one. Where is she?"

"Like I said, she don't work here anymore. She's done paid out her indenture and went on her way—to where, I haven't the foggiest notion."

"She paid out her indenture? Where did a girl like her get the money?"

Dunwig told the accorder the whole story of the events of the night, and the kirkman's face grew redder with each word. When the inn-keeper had finished, Gronthus pounded his fist on the table and growled, "Do you mean to tell me that your stupid, incompetent constable had this harlot in his jail and had the audacity to set her free? The fool will pay dearly for this."

With eyes glaring and a jaw set like stone, Gronthus arose from his seat and hammered his mug loudly on the table, sloshing water all about until all talk ceased and every eye turned toward him. "Listen to me, men. I'm looking for the red-haired maid who until last night served you in this inn. Evalonne by name. Can any of you tell me where she has gone?"

The men exchanged drunken leers, and a few knowing chuckles rumbled from the back of the hall, but no one said a word. Gronthus drew from his pouch a gold coin and held it up for all to see. "Do you see this crown? It belongs to the man who gives me information that leads me to the woman."

"Man," said a lone voice in the back of the room, "if ye be needin' a woman that bad I'll gladly find ye one. But as to where the bosomy wench has gone, well, that's somethin' we'd all like to know."

"Indeed, and we'll pay ye a crown if ye can bring her back to us," called another voice as laughter erupted throughout the hall.

Gronthus reddened and his face hardened like stone. "You whoring idiots!" he cried. "Do you think I want the vile woman for myself? Do you think I would poison my body by commingling with such a bag of pus? You men of Oranth have forgotten that the allure of woman is a trap set to test your commitment to the Master of the Universe. I have come here to remove this snare from you and take her back to her homeland of Lochlaund to be tried."

"We've already tried her—many times and loved every minute of it," called another voice, and again laughter filled the hall.

Gronthus's countenance darkened like clouds gathering for a storm. He raised his arm and pointed a long finger toward the patrons of the inn. "I warn you, men of Oranth. A great doom will descend upon you and your kingdom unless you turn from your evil and learn to resist the pleasures of the flesh. I call each of you to witness that tonight I take a solemn vow before the Master of the Universe. I vow that I will remove this evil woman from your kingdom. I will seek her with all my being, and I will not rest until I have captured her and brought her to trial in Lochlaund." Gronthus took a knife from the table. He pricked his finger and squeezed from it a drop of blood, which he pressed to his forehead as a sign of his pledge, according to ancient tradition. As the men of the inn gaped, he turned and stalked out of the hall and into the night.

CHAPTER EIGHTEEN

THE WILLING INDENTURE

f we're to be traveling together, I need to know what I should call you," Evalonne said as they took their dinner of roasted trout at the end of the day.

Lanson thought for a moment before answering. "I want to be truthful with you. I will not give you my true name for reasons I cannot presently reveal. But you may call me Roburne." He made up the name by combining those of his friends Rogarre and Moburne.

Lanson had mixed feelings about the presence of Evalonne. He still wondered at himself for having said the word that set her free. He knew that in Lochlaund, the truth would have condemned the girl to certain death. Nevertheless, according to the kirk, death was exactly what such a woman deserved. She had brought her doom upon herself. But Maconnal's last lesson had shaken his understanding of the kirk. And the strange Father Clemente in his dreamlike vision had told him that mercy was greater than justice. Though by saving the girl he had gone against everything the kirk had taught him, strangely he felt no pangs of conscience.

He was delighted to have her accompanying him to take care of Mossette, but he could not forget that she had tried to kill him. How could he know whether she had changed? Though he wanted to believe she had, he chose to take precautions. As she bathed upstream, he hid his money pouch beneath a nearby stone and kept his hand on his sword as he lay down to sleep. He slept lightly, awakening often but always finding Evalonne curled up with Mossette in her arms on the other side of the fire.

Over the next few days his wariness diminished, though his precautions continued until one morning he awakened to find his money bag lying beside him—obviously Evalonne's doing. Feeling sheepish for his lack of trust, he abandoned his wariness and slept soundly from that night on.

They continued their southward direction, going ever deeper into Oranth as they journeyed toward Vensaur. Mostly they walked on the road, though when Lanson saw soldiers approaching in the distance, he would usher Evalonne into the woods, or they would angle across a meadow. Although he was ever wary, he was no longer fearful of being seen in villages. He felt virtually unrecognizable in his beard and peasant's clothing, and with Evalonne and Mossette as companions, he thought it even less likely that anyone would guess he was the missing prince of Lochlaund.

When they reached the village of Faranburgh, Lanson bought a new dress for Evalonne from a street vendor. It was a simple peasant's skirt and bodice of undyed homespun, but much more fitting for her pose as the wife of a traveling woodsman, and certainly more modest. He also bought a blanket for her covering at night.

Evalonne was deeply grateful, not only for the dress and blanket, but for all this man had done for her. She longed to find some way to repay him. She was determined not only to care for the baby, but to do anything she could that would lighten his journey. She counted herself no longer her own; she belonged to him. Though he had demanded nothing of her, in her mind he now held her indenture. She knew she was free—indeed, she had never felt freer. It was that very freedom that made her service to this man so sweet.

Yet in spite of this newfound dedication to the man who called himself Roburne, Evalonne could not help but be wary of him at first. It was a reflexive instinct born of her experience with men, and she often found herself tensing or cringing when he came near her. But if he noticed her wariness, he did not show it. He remained always kind and courteous, treating her with a dignity and respect worthy of a great lady. Indeed, his courtly manners and the weight of the gold in his pouch led her to wonder who he really was. Surely he was no commoner.

They continued their journey southward through Oranth, with the prince carrying Mossette and Evalonne walking beside him. They did not make the time he would have wished, for he had to slow his pace to that of Evalonne's and stop at regular intervals for her to feed the baby. If they found themselves near a village when night fell, they would take their dinner at an inn and Lanson would rent a room. He would sleep on the floor as Evalonne and Mossette took the bed. When night caught them on the road, they would find a woods and camp near a stream, or sometimes in a cave or an abandoned hut. Always they slept apart from each other, Evalonne with Mossette in her arms. Sometimes he would hear her weeping softly in the darkness, and he felt a deep pity for her. He knew her heart still ached from the loss of her own child.

Although their pace was slow, Lanson admitted to himself that having Evalonne and Mossette with him brought certain advantages. Not only did they help deflect suspicion that he was a fugitive, their company made the journey more pleasant. The hate and despair he had seen in the woman's eyes were mostly gone now, and in their place was a look of warmth and tenderness that sometimes held his gaze moments longer than his will should have allowed.

Although he had misgivings about the rightness of it, he admitted to himself that he enjoyed the woman's exceptional beauty. It was nothing more than a simple appreciation uncomplicated by illicit intentions. Nevertheless, his lifelong exposure to the doctrine of the kirk intruded on the innocent pleasure, impelling him to force his gaze away from her (though with limited success). He remembered that he was a prince—now an uncrowned king, in fact—and she was a commoner with a decadent past. These facts alone were sufficient to erect a natural barrier that would prevent his heart from inclining toward her. The unwavering courtesy and respect he showed her was nothing more than the way he had been taught to treat all women.

The travelers walked throughout the day, and as the sun began to drop behind the rolling hills, they left the road and went deep into the woods until they came to a stream. Evalonne followed Lanson along the stream until they found a sheltered hollow beneath an over-hanging ledge.

"We will camp here for the night," he said as he handed Mossette to her and began to gather wood for a fire. She placed the baby on the soft grass and set about changing her into dry clothing, cooing and laughing at the child as she worked. Lanson had shot two hares during the day's journey. As he skinned the carcasses and spitted them on stripped pine branches, he gazed with wonder at her way with the baby. Was this warm, laughing girl really the same hardened woman he had met in the inn?

"There, I've got you all warm and dry for the night," she said to Mossette. "See how long you can stay that way." She set the baby near her, took Lanson's flint, and started the fire. After rigging the meat over the flame, she nursed the child while Lanson turned the spits. When Mossette had gorged herself, he took her and played with her as Evalonne completed the cooking and sliced the meat into manage-able helpings for both of them. Throughout the evening he watched her, feeling a growing warmth in his heart at her tenderness with the child and her willing service to him.

It was dusk when they finished their meal and Evalonne wrapped Mossette for the night. Lanson went upstream and bathed. When he returned he stayed with the now sleeping Mossette as Evalonne went to the stream for her own bath. The darkness closed quickly about their camp as the last rays of sunlight abdicated the sky, leaving it to the reign of a great orange moon.

Lanson, weary from the day's walk, lay on the grass and covered himself with his cloak, his back to the stream, where he heard Evalonne splashing about. Concerned for her safety, he intended to remain alert until she had finished bathing, but he must have drifted into slumber's kingdom, for he started instantly awake at the caress of gentle hands on his face and neck. He turned and his eyes widened at the sight that met his eyes. Evalonne knelt over him, her unclad body silhouetted in the caressing rays of the moonlight. He drew a deep, ragged breath. Never in his life had the raw power of temptation assailed him with such force. As her hands wandered down across his shoulders, his heart began to race as his desire strove mightily with his conscience. Then with a herculean act of will, he forced his own hands to grasp hers, and he pushed her away from him. Trying his best not to look directly at her, he grabbed his cape and flung it over her body.

"No, Evalonne," he whispered hoarsely. "We must not do this. Go back to your own bed." Though sweat beaded on his brow from the turbulence in his soul, he got up and knelt by the fire, stirring the embers in agitation as he listened behind him for sounds of her getting back into her dress.

Evalonne sat for a moment as if stunned, then slowly stood, slipped into her dress, and sat on a stone some distance from Lanson and stared into the fire. He glanced over at her and saw on her cheeks a stream of tears glistening in the firelight. She was hurt, he realized. She thought he had rejected her.

"Evalonne," he said in a voice low and gentle. "I have made a vow before the Master of the Universe never to take a woman to my bed until I am married."

"I'm sorry," she replied as she wiped her eyes. "I feel like such a fool. But I owe you so much and I have no other way to pay you."

"I did not free you from one kind of slavery only to bind you with another. You owe me nothing, and you owe the treasure you just offered me to no man but your own husband."

"It is too late for me to hold myself pure for a husband. My innocence has long flown, and it's futile to close the door against it now. I may as well give what remains from the store that has already been plundered."

"What you were does not determine what you are now," replied Lanson. "You need not perpetuate the mistakes of the past."

"If only that were true. But I feel the past clinging to me like a filthy dress that hangs on me for all to see. No one who values purity will ever find any worth in me."

"You can't undo the past, of course, but you can put it behind you and enter the present as a new person ruled by a higher standard. You still bear all the worth the Master of the Universe instilled into you when he made you. And you must hold yourself precious, as he does. You owe me nothing, least of all that which the Master forbids you to give. You already do me a great service by nursing and caring for Mossette."

Without another word the two lay down again, Evalonne a little way from Lanson's feet. She covered herself with her own blanket and closed her eyes, yet the wonder of all she was feeling drove sleep from her. She was amazed at this man who called himself Roburne. Never had a man treated her kindly without hidden motives or given her anything of value without expecting something in return—or more often simply taking what he wanted with no thought of her feelings at all. This Roburne treated her as if she were a jewel of great value to be protected and cherished. A warm sense of well-being flooded her mind and flowed over her body as if powerful arms were enfolding her with care and love. She fell asleep and did not wake until morning.

In the days that followed, what little that remained of the hardened shell that had encrusted Evalonne fell away entirely, and along with it any lingering reservation she felt about trusting Roburne. Indeed, her attitude toward him was one of meekness and humility born of her awe, not only at what he had done for her, but at his continuing chivalry. Even before her troubles began, the Master of the Universe had never been real to her, but this man Roburne was. He had become to her as a god. He filled her being. He was her savior, her lord, the object of her dedication, her purpose for existing, and more and more, her hope for the future.

Evalonne began to realize that her increasingly tender feelings toward Roburne might be love. The thought alarmed her, for she did not want to love a man again. Why make herself vulnerable to more of the kind of pain she had already suffered? Old demons from her months at the Red Falcon—demons she thought she had banished—returned to torment her. Men were men, and in spite of what this one seemed to be on the surface, perhaps after stripping away all the patience, kindness, gentleness, and chivalry, she would find that at the core he was like all the others. But in her heart she knew better. She had seen enough of him in various situations to know that he was at the core exactly what he appeared to be on the surface. None of this mattered a whit, though, because she had no reason to believe that he loved her, and that alone doomed her to repeat the heartbreak she had already endured. Yet in spite of all the warnings reason heaped upon her, she could not help loving this man.

Maybe he will come to love me, she thought. More than once she had caught his gaze lingering a little on her, and she wondered if his courtesy and gentleness might be due in some small part to a touch of tenderness he felt toward her. On the other hand, she knew that in spite of his admonitions to bury the past, her past was certainly an obstacle to her dream. She might change, but the past could not. It was carved in stone. But, unwarranted as it might be, she clung to a thin hope that his affections might yet turn toward her in the future. Knowing her past to be an impediment to such a hope, she thought it best to come clean with him now and hold no secrets that might spring up later to spoil things between them.

As they traveled the next day she told him her entire story—of her good parents and their deaths, of her devastating mistake with the minstrel, of Dunwig's entrapping her into a life of prostitution at the Red Falcon Inn and the shame that came from it, and of the death of her child, though the pain of the telling was almost more than she could bear. She told him of how she lived in constant terror of Gronthus, who was determined to destroy her. Though she had thought little of him the past few days, she would never be able to rest as long as that man pursued her. And she told of her decision to abandon the Master of the Universe.

"Has the Master never given you anything good?" asked Lanson.

"Nothing he did not take away again."

"How do you know it was the Master who took it away?"

"At least he could have prevented its being taken, but he did not. Either he did it or he allowed it. Either he is not as good as we've been told, or he is not as powerful. Either way, a master who allows the kind of pain I've endured is not worth serving."

Lanson saw the old hardness return to her eyes and refrained from further words on the subject. In response to her revelation of her own life, he thought it fitting to tell her a little more about himself.

"I am a trained warrior, also from Lochlaund, and I, too, have suffered a loss. My father was killed, murdered on orders by the treacherous King Aradon of Meridan. I am traveling to the city of Ensovandor in Vensaur, where I will offer my sword to aid Sir Brendal in his quest to keep Aradon from swallowing up the Seven Kingdoms. In exchange for your valuable service to the babe and me on this journey, I will continue my protection of you until we reach the castle where he is residing. After that, I do not know where fate will take me."

As they walked along thus talking, the large blackbird with pale yellow eyes flitted from tree to tree behind them, its keen ears hearing every word. After Lanson finished his brief autobiography, the bird flew from its perch and made its way back to the abbey of the kirk in Oranth.

CHAPTER NINETEEN

SISTER AGANESTA

ronthus sat at the heavy oaken table in his chamber inside the abbey of Brackenshire in the south of Oranth. He kept the room perpetually reserved for his use, and he occupied it often in his travels as Bishop Hugal's emissary between Vensaur and Lochlaund. The day was not cold, but the overcast sky outside his window was as gray as the stone walls about him. A strong wind whistled through the eaves of the abbey. His elbows rested on the table, and he stared at the small dove-shaped pendant he had retrieved from outside Evalonne's window, which he turned over and over in his fingers.

A sudden flapping at the window startled him. He looked toward the sound and blanched at what he saw. Perched on the stone sill was the largest blackbird he had ever seen—well over two feet from beak to tail. He shuddered at the look of the bird's eyes. They were pale yellow, and their gaze pierced him like an arrow.

Unruffled, the bird stared at Gronthus without blinking. Then with a hoarse croak, it flew straight toward him. Gronthus scrambled to his feet and backed away, knocking over his chair and dropping the pendant to the table. The bird plucked up the pendant in its beak and flew out the window into the moaning wind. Gronthus, thoroughly shocked, walked to the window and stared into the gray sky, wondering at the meaning of the strange thing he had just witnessed. As he gazed a knock came at his door and he jumped as if prodded with a sword. He opened the door to a woman, robed from head to foot in black, thin and pale, and taller than he by three or four inches. He looked at her face and started once again. She gazed at him with eyes pale and yellow, exactly like those of the blackbird that had just fled his chamber.

Without waiting for Gronthus to speak, the woman stepped past him and took a chair facing the table. She never showed her right hand but kept her arm hidden within the folds of her black robe.

"Who are you?" asked Gronthus when he had recovered his voice.

"Once I was known as Sister Aganesta." The lie flowed from Morgultha's lips in a voice low and smooth. "But I have long retired from the order. When I found I had the gift of divining the future, I left the convent to live in the mountains as a seer. I commune daily with the Master of the Universe, who reveals to me, his humble vessel, messages of sight and wisdom that I must bear to those who can affect the course of the future."

"So you think yourself a prophetess. And no doubt you have a message of doom to deliver to me." Gronthus had seen such women before—widows, usually, who after years of loneliness often began to hear voices and see visions.

She looked at him sharply, and once again he shuddered. "The Master has given a vision to be delivered to you, Gronthus the accorder. Will you hear it? Or will your doubt hide the truth from you?"

"Speak your message, woman, and I will judge the truth of it."

"It is not your place to judge, but to obey. Yet I will speak the message. Thus has the Master spoken: that not only King Aradon, but the usurper Brendal as well must be thwarted if the Seven Kingdoms are to survive."

"And why do you bring this message to me? Such matters belong in the hands of King Kor."

"Don't play games with me, Gronthus. I know that King Kor is dead, and your superior, Bishop Hugal, perpetuates the illusion that he lives by acting as his voice."

"Such a thing is impossible, and I will not have the bishop slandered thus."

"It is no slander. It is the truth."

"Anyone can make such a claim. Why should I believe you?"

"Where is the silver dove that belonged to the fugitive Evalonne?" she asked.

"How do you know about that?"

"The same way I know how you lost the pendant. Only moments before I came here, a blackbird flew through that window and took it from you. Is this not true?"

"H-how can you possibly know that?" Gronthus stammered.

"Is this the pendant, Gronthus?" With her left hand she held up a delicate chain with the silver dove hanging from the end of it. Her right arm remained hidden within the folds of her robe.

Gronthus merely gaped, utterly dumfounded. "But why do you deliver this message to me instead of to Bishop Hugal? As you said, he is my superior."

"Apparently you did not appreciate the import of the message. I said that not only King Aradon must be thwarted if the Seven Kingdoms are to remain free, but Brendal as well. Your Bishop Hugal is Brendal's man, is he not? The Master's message would be wasted on a man already committed to a cause that the Master opposes. It was sent to one whose mind is not yet captive of either contender for the Seven Kingdoms, one who may have the foresight and the will to dedicate himself to a higher vision. You are that man, Gronthus."

"I am that man? Why should I be chosen?"

"I have seen a vision showing me that Brendal will surely fail to wrench the Seven Kingdoms from Aradon. And if Bishop Hugal of Lochlaund remains a henchman of Brendal's, he will fall when Brendal falls. But you can avoid the snare that Hugal has stepped in. Keep yourself clear of fealty to Brendal and become the hand of the Master, acting on the word that he will reveal through me. Then when Brendal falls, and Bishop Hugal with him, who but you is likely to become the next Bishop of Lochlaund?"

Gronthus felt his blood quicken at the woman's words, and he hoped his face did not betray him by reddening. He had often thought he would make a better bishop than Hugal, but he had steadfastly refused to play the court games and indulge in the flatteries and manipulations necessary to secure higher office. Justice would be well served if the office he had desired but never sought came to him simply because of his sheer dedication and uprightness. He liked what he heard, but there were difficulties.

"Even if I did entertain your suggestion, I do not have the kind of power needed to thwart Brendal and Aradon, who both have armies at their disposal."

"It is not always armies that bring down kingdoms," she answered. "Skill and cunning on the part of a few, supported by invisible powers that the Master will provide, will be enough. As an official of the kirk, you have the power to commandeer acolytes for assistance from any abbey in the Seven Kingdoms, and the Master has placed at my beckoning beings with power you cannot imagine, ready to add their immense strength to the fray once you show initial signs of success. And such success is not as remote as you imagine."

Gronthus tried to focus on the woman's words, but his mind had already galloped to the great chair in the abbey, where he saw himself sitting in red robes and a mitred cap. "What does the Master want of me?" he asked.

"The Master has revealed to me that a young man is now wandering through the edges of Braegan Wood. With him is a beautiful woman with red hair and green eyes whom I think you know."

Gronthus sat up in his chair. "The harlot Evalonne!"

"Yes. This wanderer has taken up with the woman you have vowed to capture. But there is more. They carry a child with them— a baby not yet six months old, who is certainly the missing daughter of King Aradon."

"Aradon's daughter? How has such a thing come about?"

"Brendal arranged the kidnapping, but something went awry and the kidnappers abandoned the baby in the woods. This wanderer found the child, and now he and Evalonne are taking her to Brendal in Vensaur. I don't have to tell you what will happen when Brendal gets that baby. He will have Aradon in the palm of his hand, and a good chance of bringing the Seven Kingdoms under his own control. But, Gronthus, what if you got the child instead of Brendal? You would have your hand on the tiller of the ship of the Seven Kingdoms. You could steer this island in any direction you chose."

"Indeed I could," said Gronthus. "But how will I find this couple and the child?"

"It has been revealed to me that they are not far from here at this moment. In three days they will approach the village of Soucroft, the last town in Oranth before crossing into Vensaur. You can easily arrest them there on charges of unlawful cohabitation. And Evalonne, at least, is a citizen of Lochlaund, thus subject to you as the accorder of the kirk in that kingdom."

Morgultha could see by the gleam in Gronthus's eye that she had found the right spark to ignite his ambitions. She had fed his sense of pride so that it swelled and smothered his first tendencies to distrust her, and she now had him hooked like a trout in a moat. As long as she held before him the promise of the glory he secretly coveted and convinced him that her instructions issued from the mind of the Master, she could lead him like a mule following a carrot to do anything she wanted.

"My work here is finished for now. But tell me, does the bishop still have a taste for Rhondilar red wine?"

"Of course not! Kirkmen of Lochlaund never touch fermented drink."

"Of course not," replied Morthultha. "However, they do use wine in certain holy rituals, I believe." A sneering smile slowly contorted her face, and again Gronthus felt his spine chill. She reached into her robes and drew out a bottle of translucent red liquid. "Take this gift to your bishop. It should serve to endear yourself to him."

"Thank you, Sister Aganesta. I will give it to him when I return to Macrennon."

Morgultha arose from her chair and moved toward the door. Gronthus stood as well and thought somehow she seemed even taller than when she came in.

"We will meet again soon. At that time you can report to me your success and I will recount to you any further revelations from the Master."

"It will be as you say, Aganesta." Gronthus opened the door and bowed deeply as she left his chamber. He watched as she walked into the gray wind, her black robes flapping and billowing behind her. For a moment he thought the cape took on the shape of great black wings, much like those of the ominous bird that had invaded his chambers earlier, but he dismissed the vision as the work of his over-stimulated imagination and closed the door. Immediately he called to have his horse saddled and provisions packed. In an hour he was on the road to Soucroft.

CHAPTER TWENTY

PURSUIT

t was midafternoon when the man Evalonne knew as Roburne, with Mossette on his arm and Evalonne walking beside him, topped a hill and looked toward the blue mountain ridge that formed the horizon ahead of them. Between them and the mountains were patches of sown fields dotted with ponds that sparkled like diamonds in the sun. The sunlight gleamed golden on the thatched roofs of farmers' cottages nestled in groves of trees among the fields. He stopped in the road and pointed. "See the cluster of buildings and cottages at the base of the mountain? That must be Soucroft, the last village in Oranth. It's on the River Rennet that runs to the south sea. When we go through Soucroft and cross the river we will be in Vensaur, and not more than three days from Ensovandor, where we will meet Brendal."

"Three days?" said Evalonne. "Last night you said it would take at least five."

"And so it would if we continued walking, but I think it safe now to hire a driver to take us to Ensovandor in a carriage. We've encountered no pursuit in the villages, and no one seems to have eyed us with suspicion. Once in Vensaur, we can travel openly on the road without danger. And if we're to be on the road anyway, we'll make better time riding than walking."

Evalonne was less certain that it was safe yet to abandon caution, but she could not answer his reasoning, so she said nothing of it. "How do we cross those mountains?" she asked.

"I'm told there is an easy pass between the ridges. Just beyond Soucroft we cross the bridge on the Rennet and keep to the road south."

They had begun to descend the hill into the fertile valley when they heard the drumming of a horse's hooves behind them. "Quick, off the road," said Evalonne. "We can hide in that grove of trees over there."

He saw no need for such caution so far south of Lochlaund, but acceding to her persistent urging, they left the road and hid in the thicket until the lone horseman passed. Evalonne watched the rider diminish in the distance. Though she could not recognize him, she knew by the gray robe and cowl that he was a kirkman, and her heart felt as if a cold hand were gripping it.

"Must we go through Soucroft?" she asked.

"Of course," Lanson replied. "We have nothing to fear so far south of Lochlaund, and we need to replenish our provisions. Why are you so skittish about Soucroft?"

"I don't know, but I have this strange feeling that we'll meet danger there."

"Nonsense! All the dangers are behind us. Besides, I'm ready for a proper meal, and I've heard there's an inn in Soucroft that serves the best mutton in the Seven Kingdoms. Come on." He took the reluctant Evalonne by the hand and once again they returned to the road.

In Soucroft they found the inn, and the ravenous prince got the meal he had longed for. Evalonne nursed Mossette as she ate, and afterward they went into the street to purchase dried meats, which they packed into their pouches for the journey ahead. Evalonne remained uneasy as they made their way through the cobbled avenues narrowed by vendors' stands and crowded with milling shoppers. The image of the mounted kirkman would not leave her mind, and she continually scanned the jostling crowd and looked often behind her.

The prince found the vendor he wanted and bought several strips of salt pork. He was packing them into his bag when Evalonne suddenly clutched his arm and said, "Roburne, it's him! We've got to get out of here before he sees us."

Just as Lanson turned to look, Gronthus, less than fifty paces away, caught sight of them over the heads of the crowd. Immediately the kirkman gave a signal as he pointed to the pair, and five conscripted acolytes, also robed in gray, began to push through the shoppers toward the couple.

"He's got men with him," Lanson said as he took Evalonne's hand and forced an opening into the throng of pedestrians. After several paces she looked behind them and saw Gronthus and his henchmen pushing men and women out of their way right and left.

"They're gaining on us," she cried.

"Bend down so they can't see us," Lanson urged. They ran with their heads lowered until they came to an intersection. He pulled Evalonne to the left, and they turned into a lane a little less crowded, where they were able to free themselves enough to run. When Gronthus and his men came to the intersection, the accorder stopped and looked in all directions. He sent two men to the right and two to the left, as he and the remaining man continued straight on.

"Stop those two!"

Lanson and Evalonne heard the shout and looked back to see two gray robes running toward them, some fifty paces behind.

The fleeing couple turned the next corner and ran until they came to an alley. They ducked into it, dodging piles of refuse and scattering dozens of cats, and ran until they emerged into the next street. The street was crowded, and they were forced to slow their pace as they wove their way through the wagons and pedestrians. They turned again into the next alley, doubling back in hopes of confounding the pursuers. The alley led them to a narrower and less-traveled lane. They ran the full length of it until they reached the last building in town, a large barn, beyond which stretched a field of fresh stubble.

Lanson looked back to see a gray-clad kirkman running full pace toward them. He led Evalonne around the corner of the barn, found a door, and slipped inside. The lower floor was filled with empty animal stalls. *Too obvious for a hiding place,* he thought.

"Up there," he said, nodding toward the loft. They climbed the ladder and stepped onto the upper floor, half filled with hay. "Quick, under here," he ordered, handing her the baby and scooping away at a heap of straw. At that moment the door below them opened and they froze in their tracks. The couple peered through the slats in the floor and saw their pursuer enter the barn and move stealthily toward the stalls. Lanson edged toward the only window in the loft and looked out. Below sat a wain piled high with hay. The wagon was hitched to a team of oxen, ready to be driven away. A driver sat on the board waiting for a stableboy to open the gate.

Lanson motioned for Evalonne to remain silent as he ruffled up a pile of hay, making it appear that someone might be under it. Then he took Mossette from her and led her to the window. "Jump," he whispered. Evalonne looked at him as if he had gone mad. "Hurry! Jump!" he repeated, and after a moment's hesitation, she leapt out the window and into the hay below. "You're next, little one," he said as he pitched Mossette out the window. She landed beside Evalonne and burst into a fit of laughter. Lanson came quickly afterward and immediately dug into the hay and covered them all.

The gray-robed pursuer heard the sound above and climbed to the barn loft. Seeing the obviously disturbed hay in the corner, he found a pitchfork, tiptoed to the pile, and with a yell of triumph, plunged the prongs deep into the hay. When the points hit the floor, he jerked up the tool and thrust it again and again, then swept the hay aside in a frenzy until, with an unkirkmanlike curse, he realized no one was there.

He went to the window and looked out just as the gate screeched open and the driver of the hay wain cracked his whip over the oxen. The wagon pulled away, and as the pursuer turned back into the hayloft, the ebullient sound of a baby laughing emerged from the wagon. He scurried down the ladder and ran from the barn, shouting for the driver to stop. But the wagon was too far ahead for the driver to hear him. The kirkman ran after the wagon, trying to keep sight of it, even though he could not keep pace.

Lanson peered between the slats in the side of the hay wain and saw that they were moving at a pace that would outdistance any pursuer on foot. The wagon made its way down the road with the town to the right and open fields to the left. Just as it was about to reach open country, it lurched to a stop. The driver uttered a string of emphatic curses, and from his vantage point Lanson could see why. A sizable herd of sheep blocked the road ahead, and it would be several minutes before the wagon could move again—plenty of time for the gray-robed man to catch up with them.

"Quick, out of the wagon," said Lanson. He emerged from the hay, leapt from the back of the wagon, and reached up to help Mossette and Evalonne to the ground. The driver, still bellowing at the shepherds, took no notice of them. Lanson took Evalonne's hand and they dashed into the nearest street and ran until it fed them into another. They turned south, and since only a few people were in sight—mostly making for the alehouses and inns by now—they alternately ran and walked until the lane ended at a wharf on the River Rennet. Lanson looked in both directions for an outlet but found none.

The wharf stretched a hundred fifty feet along the water's edge with three piers extending into the river. All the piers were empty but one, at which was tied a small boat, its single sail furled and its deck loaded with brown sacks tied at the top. A bin on the dock beside the boat was half filled with potatoes. Apparently workers had gotten the craft partially loaded before the sun touching the treetops signaled the end of the workday. The docks were abandoned.

Lanson, carrying Mossette, led Evalonne to the boat. He handed her the baby and began to untie the first of the two lines that secured the vessel to the dock, looking up often toward the street. He had just undone the first rope and was working with the second when he saw the shadowed form of the robed kirkman emerging from a side street. He jerked the line loose, gave the boat a hard shove, and jumped aboard.

Taking up the pole from the deck, Lanson pushed the craft away from the dock. When the acolyte saw the boat move away, he began to run toward it. He gained speed as he approached, and when he reached the end of the pier, he made a mighty leap toward the stern. For a moment it seemed that he would reach the boat, but while he was in the air the distance increased just enough that his fingers raked across the transom as he splashed into the river. He began to swim toward the receding stern but, hampered by his robe, soon gave up the chase. He returned to the dock and ran dripping back into the village, shouting the name of Gronthus.

Lanson thrust the pole deep against the bottom of the river, pushing the boat toward the far shore. The Rennet flowed wide as it passed by Soucroft, and Lanson had been poling for over a quarter-hour before they neared the south bank. Evalonne sat cradling Mossette as she looked downriver at the stone bridge two hundred yards distant, now silhouetted against the setting sun.

"Roburne, look!" she cried, pointing toward the bridge. Five robed men, all mounted and riding hard, galloped across it. "It's Gronthus and his men. They see us!"

Lanson put all his strength into each thrust of the pole, and moments later the bow of the boat pressed into the underbrush. He leapt to the bank and tied the boat to a tree, then helped Evalonne disembark and took Mossette from her. Evalonne began to run upstream, away from the bridge, but Lanson grabbed her arm and pointed up toward the mountain.

"This way," he said.

"Up that mountain?" Evalonne was incredulous.

"It's our only choice," he replied as he took her arm and led her up the grassy slope.

In moments the grass ended at the base of a rocky tumble of boulders, and the angle of ascent increased sharply. Lanson found a path through the clefts and juttings of the mountain's crags, and soon the climbers were forced to grapple with their hands and search for footholds with each step. They heard the drumming of hooves along the river and looked down to see five riders reining in their horses directly below them. A moment later an arrow whirred past Lanson's ear and hit a stone just inches from his head. More arrows followed, one of them snagging in the loose folds of Evalonne's dress.

"There's a ledge directly above us," said Lanson. "We should be safer there."

He stretched his arm upward, grasped the lip of the flat surface, and pulled himself upon it. He set Mossette far back from the edge and reached downward to pull up Evalonne. Another volley of arrows flew about them as he brought her to safety. He set her next to Mossette against the mountain wall and collapsed beside them to catch his breath.

"We should be safe here until dark," he said. "I see a path that may lead us on up the mountain and over the top, but we would be hopelessly exposed if we tried to take it now."

The arrows continued for a few more minutes, then ceased. Lanson crept toward the edge and peered over it at the five kirkmen below. They had put away their bows, and now stood near their mounts speaking with each other, occasionally pointing along the river and gesturing as if giving directions, often glancing up at the ledge where the couple had found temporary refuge. Though the men were too far below for Lanson to hear their words, it was clear that they were discussing their next move. Judging by the gestures, he guessed they were planning to circle the base of the mountain and cut off escape on the other side. He watched until the gray robes mounted their horses and galloped westward toward the bridge.

Lanson backed away from the edge and again sat next to Evalonne, who was now nursing Mossette. "No doubt Gronthus will ride around this mountain and wait for us to come down on the other side," he said. "However, he cannot do it quickly. It's not a small mountain, and even from here you can see that the road veers far to the west before it curves back to the south. And from what I've heard, the pass takes a southwesterly direction, meaning he's got a fair journey ahead of him tonight before he can cut back to the east and reach the south side of this mountain."

"What can we do?" Evalonne asked. "He's got us trapped here as surely as if we were in a castle under siege."

"Maybe not. Perhaps we can get down the backside of this mountain before he reaches it," Lanson replied. "When our little lady laughaloud finishes her dinner, we must continue our climb."

"But it will soon be dark," said Evalonne.

"No matter. We've got to do it. If we hurry, we might make the peak before the night turns black."

As the orange ball of the sun drowned itself in the river, Evalonne shuddered to think of the coming darkness and clasped Mossette tightly to her. "I hate this time of day," she said, her voice tense with apprehension. "It's the in-between time when things are changing, when nothing is what it seems to be. It's neither day nor night, dark nor light, black nor white. It's like the darkness is a thing itself—a creeping evil swallowing up everything around us."

When Mossette had had her fill, Lanson put Evalonne on the upward-winding natural path and followed behind with the baby in his arms. The rocky surface of the mountain was rugged enough that footholds and handholds were numerous, and the climb was easier than he had expected.

In a quarter-hour they reached another ledge some six feet deep and twelve wide where they stopped to catch their breath. They looked out over the city of Soucroft, now sparkling with lights from cottage windows and taverns. The sky still glowed orange in the west, where only the top third of the sun remained above the horizon. Evalonne pointed east toward the huge rising moon and said, "Look at that flock of birds. What kind could they be, flying so late in the evening?"

Lanson looked where she pointed and saw fifteen or twenty flying creatures approaching, their black wings flapping ponderously in the darkening sky. He sensed something strange about these birds and watched them intently as they came closer. Soon he could make out the shapes of their wings and see the enormity of them.

"Those are not birds—they are bats," he said. "Huge ones! And they appear to be coming toward us."

Indeed the creatures did not waver in their direction but loomed larger and larger as they flew directly toward the ledge where Lanson and Evalonne watched. The creatures' bodies were the size of cats, some even larger, with wings spanning five feet or more. A high-pitched screech pierced the air as the bats drew close enough for the two on the ledge to see their hideous faces with mouths opened wide, eyes glowing red, and yellow fangs bared.

Lanson drew his sword and put Evalonne with the baby behind him. He planted his feet as the bat in the lead swooped toward him, and with a sure sweep of his weapon, hacked through the creature's neck, sending it tumbling downward through the air, its wings flapping uselessly. Two creatures swooped down in the wake of the first, and Lanson hacked a wing off one as the other dived toward his neck. He knocked it away with his free hand, then brought it down with his backstroke. Evalonne crouched behind him, bending over Mossette to shield the child with her own body.

Now the bats filled the air all about the ridge, circling and attacking as Lanson fended them off with desperate sweeps of his sword, sometimes connecting, sometimes missing as the creatures swooped and darted about him. Soon his arms and legs were bleeding from bites, but he noticed neither the blood nor the pain as he cut at the screeching creatures in a frenzy. But he could not fight them all at once. As he met an attack from his right, three bats swept in behind him and clamped their needlelike fangs on Evalonne's skirt and, with black wings beating furiously, began pulling her toward the edge. Clasping Mossette in her right arm, she clutched at the stony floor of the ledge with her left hand, but her fingers raked across the surface as the creatures dragged her along. She let go of Mossette momentarily to grip the stone with both hands, and in that instant the claws of two more bats clutched the clothing of the child, lifting her into the air and away from the ledge.

"Roburne!" screamed Evalonne.

Lanson turned and, with a frenzy of kicks and thrusts of his sword, knocked the two creatures from Evalonne's dress. With his free hand he grabbed a wing of one of the two carrying Mossette, who now dangled perilously beyond the safety of the ledge, bawling at the top of her lungs. Two bats attached themselves to Lanson's back and began biting viciously as he tugged at the wing, trying to pull Mossette back to where the ledge would catch her fall. But already off balance when he caught the wing, he had little of the ledge left in front of him and could not get the leverage he needed. He began to tip precariously forward.

With a cry of rage, Evalonne got to her feet and, with clenched fists, beat at the two bats on Lanson's back until they let go and circled out into the air to regroup. She hooked both hands into his belt and pulled with all her might, and slowly at first, then with increasing momentum, they moved backward until the ledge was again beneath Mossette. Lanson plunged his sword into the creature's side and it released its burden. The remaining bat could not carry the child alone, and the baby dropped to the stony surface, where Evalonne immediately scooped her up and covered her again with her own body.

Immediately two bats were upon her, and one sank its teeth into her back before Lanson's sword ripped away its side and he slashed hard at the other, breaking its wing. He kicked both over the edge and stood ready for the next attack. But no attack came. Only two bats were left, and after circling toward his ready sword two or three times, they gave up the fight and disappeared into the near darkness.

Lanson stood panting as Evalonne remained huddled over the screaming Mossette. "They're gone," he said. As he spoke he heard a rustling from the rocks below and looked down to see a black shadow fly away from the mountain and into the night. Thinking it another bat, he watched as it flew across the rising moon, which silhouetted its black wings clearly. It was not a bat. It was a huge blackbird.

When Mossette had calmed down and Lanson had caught his breath, he walked to where Evalonne sat with the baby in her arms and knelt before her.

"Thank you, Evalonne," he said, laying his hand gently on her shoulder. Immediately he jerked it away as if from a hot coal. The brief touch shot an unexpected thrill of warmth through his arm that quickened the beat of his heart. He looked at her and could not turn his eyes away. At that moment she had the appearance of a goddess. Everything about her seemed perfect—the evening glow like fire on the rim of her hair, the exquisite contours of her face, the glistening moistness of her full lips, the clear eyes sparkling like translucent emeralds under long, dark lashes. Every detail that made up the being before him filled his mind with wonder. Here was an incredible work of art, a masterpiece of creation bearing the weight of immense significance.

He remembered the other time the woman had drawn him with such force—the night she had offered herself to him in the moonlight.

But tonight the spell was altogether different—he was drawn not by the power of the female but by the power of the feminine. Not the rutting grip of raw lust, but an enchantment, magical and impelling, that seemed to penetrate to the core of his being. For a moment it seemed that a veil had been lifted, showing him beauty as the truth of all creation—beauty as a beam from the glory of the Master himself reflected in the nature of everything he had made.

The warnings of the kirk arose instantly in his mind, smothering the pleasure of the touch and the vision of the beauty beneath a wave of guilt. What had he been thinking? He must not be taken in by the temptation of beauty. Its glory was an illusion, its power a snare. He must not enjoy that which was forbidden by the Master. How quickly the lure of woman could draw one against his better judgment into a headlong chasing after the wind of pleasure! Maconnal was surely mistaken in thinking this force that so assaulted man's will was of the Master. He blinked to free himself from the trance and forced his eyes to look away.

"We must get on up the mountain," he said as he stood.

The sun set shortly after they resumed their climb, and the rising moon gave them just enough light to find their way to the peak. Standing on the high ridge, Lanson looked southward over Vensaur. Immediately beneath the mountain huddled a thick woods, and he could see in the distance the glint of moonlight on a stream that disappeared into the trees five miles or so from the base of the mountain. He was certain that Gronthus had not given up. No doubt the accorder thought he had them trapped like a cat in a tree. If he could cut off escape, he could hold them on the mountain until they had to come down for food and water.

However, from his vantage point Lanson could see that he had been right in thinking it would take the accorder considerable time to climb the pass, which angled to the west and doubled back to the peak where Lanson and Evalonne now stood. Gronthus would not expect them to descend the mountain at night. If they could get down into the woods and make it to the stream before sunrise, they could hide there through the day and take up their journey again at nightfall. He pointed to the stream and said, "We can't rest yet. We must get down this mountain tonight, work our way through those woods, and try to make that river before dawn."

Descending the mountain took longer than he had expected, mostly because they were on the shadowed side and finding solid footholds was more precarious in the darkness. But they reached the grassy slope at the bottom without mishap and entered the blackness of the woods, where they found a narrow deer path, faintly visible in the moonlight. Following the path was not as tiring as it might have been, for the ground sloped gradually downward as they plodded on toward the river.

When morning came they still had not reached the river, and Lanson could see that Evalonne was near exhaustion. They stopped to rest, and as she nursed Mossette, he picked enough wild berries to feed both of them. They drank from one of the many brooks in the forest, then moved on down the deer path, refreshed but still weary. Morning brought the colors of the forest to life, and though the trees grew fewer, wildflowers swayed to the dance of butterflies, and birds chirped as they scratched in the leaves and dirt about the roots of the boles. Mossette, now awake and happy after her feeding, gazed about wide-eyed, cooing and jabbering as they walked along.

"I thought we would have reached the river by now," said Lanson.

"How will we cross it?" asked Evalonne.

"Can you swim?"

"Yes, but what about Mossette?"

"I can carry her and keep her head above water."

"What's that noise?" Evalonne asked, suddenly tense.

They kept still and listened. Though distant, the sound was unmistakable. Hoofbeats.

"There's no place to hide here," Lanson said. "We must run to the river."

They ran until Evalonne had to stop for breath. The beat of hooves drummed on behind them, clearly louder than before. Once again they ran, and Lanson looked back and saw a flash of movement among the trees, still some distance away. But it would not be long before the horses closed the gap. He looked ahead and saw to his dismay that they were coming to the edge of the forest. With no trees to hide them, they would be exposed and vulnerable. Evalonne ran just ahead of him, and as she reached the end of the trees, she came to an abrupt stop and screamed. Lanson drew up beside her and looked down into a chasm some fifty feet deep, at the bottom of which flowed the river he had been searching for.

"We must jump," he said. "Swim as fast as you can to the other side, angling downstream. Try to reach that wooded area over there." He pointed to a thick grove of trees on the far side of the river.

But Evalonne froze and could not move.

"You said you can swim, didn't you?"

"Yes, but I . . . I can't jump." Without another word Lanson put his hand to her back and pushed her over the edge. He cradled Mossette firmly in his arms, turned his back to the river, and fell, his arms and legs curled around the child. To his surprise, Mossette laughed with delight as they fell through the air. They plunged into the river, and he feared she would choke and gag when they emerged from their dive, but with a baby's instinct for not breathing under water, she did not even cough or sputter. When they surfaced he saw Evalonne just ahead and heard angry shouts high on the ledge behind. The next moment an arrow hit the water some eight feet to his left, and an instant later another splashed not three feet from his head.

"Evalonne, hurry!" he cried as he redoubled the power of his strokes.

A moment later he saw her splashing through the shallows and heading for the woods. More arrows fell around him as he reached the bank and followed. Once hidden in the trees, they stopped and gasped for breath.

They were safe for now. Lanson knew by what he had seen of the land from the peak that Gronthus had no quick way to cross the river. It was too deep to be forded, and by the time he followed it to a village with a bridge, he and Evalonne could be miles away and essentially lost to the accorder.

Near exhaustion, the two of them plodded along until they found a camping place in a wooded area by a brook, where they stopped and rested for the day. At night they walked on until they came to a road angling southeast. When morning came they arrived at the village of Norfeld, where they found an inn and breakfasted. After their meal, they went to the town square, where Lanson in-quired around until he found a merchant with a cart loaded with wool and cider for delivery to Ensovandor. He bargained for two seats on the cart, and by noon he and Evalonne were on their way toward Brendal, seated with their backs to the driver on a pile of sacks filled with wool. They arrived in Ensovandor three days later.

PART III

ENSOVANDOR

CHAPTER TWENTY-ONE

A CALL TO WAR

he sun had not been up more than a half-hour as an ox-drawn farmer's cart lumbered into the outskirts of Meridan's capital city of Corenham. The sides of the cart bulged with fruits, lentils, cucumbers, corn, melons, and cabbage. On the board sat two men, the one holding the reins looking resolutely ahead with sharp, clear eyes, while the other swayed and nodded, his eyes heavy to the point of closing.

"We had a good year here in Meridan," said the grizzled farmer. "From what I been hearin', farms all over the kingdom have yielded about double since Aradon became king."

The man beside him realized he had been spoken to and opened his eyes, trying hard to concentrate on what the farmer had said so he could hold up his end of the conversation. "Do you really think the crowning of Aradon had anything to do with good crops?" he asked in a voice weak but clear with precise diction. The man's courtly speech belied his appearance. He seemed around forty-five years of age. His hair was long and unkempt, his beard untrimmed, and his clothing stained and tattered.

"All I can tell you is what I been seein'. And it's not only the crops. I swear there's more fish in the streams and more game in the forest. And they're sayin' that since Aradon's bairn came along, more babes have been born in Meridan than since the days of Perivale, though how anyone knows how many were born in his day, I can't rightly say."

"Well, surely Aradon is not responsible for that," said the rider dryly.

"Say what you will, I've heard that a good king blesses the whole land. And it appears that Meridan's got herself a king like none since Perivale himself. Garn, you should have seen the man in the great tournament a year and a half back!"

"I've heard the tale of it," said the rider, fighting to keep his eyes open.

The cart rolled through the streets of Corenham, which were beginning to fill as merchants and tradesmen opened their shops. The farmer drove straight toward the center of the town, clearly marked by the enormous statue of the great Perivale looming high above the buildings and cottages. Beneath the statue Meridan's trade center, Cheaping Square, already bustled with vendors and buyers, though the hour was early. As they reached the square, the farmer brought the cart to a halt, almost tumbling his weary passenger from his seat.

"This is as far as I be goin'," said the farmer.

"I thank you for the ride," the man replied as he dismounted, slowly and stiffly. "Forgive me that I have nothing to offer you for your services."

"It was my pleasure havin' you along. Be sure a time will come when you can be doin' a like favor for another. May the Master be with you."

The passenger left the farmer on the square and, with unsteady steps, walked up the broad street toward Morningstone Castle, enormous and magnificent on its high marble hill with the morning sun gleaming on its stone towers. His tread slowed as he trudged up the road to the castle gate. He stood before the guards, panting hard and swaying with weakness.

"State your name and your business," said the sentry.

"I am Sir Werthen of Vensaur. I am here to see King Aradon."

The guard looked hard at the man. His beard, wild hair, and ruined clothing belied his claim, though the precision of his speech gave it credence. While the guard was trained to exercise caution, he had also been warned not to take appearances at face value. "You hardly have the look of a knight. What credentials can you give me?"

"I can give you none. As to my appearance, I am a fugitive, not from justice but from injustice, forced to flee and hide in the wilderness. I had to make my way here by my wits with what help I could get. But it is imperative that I speak with King Aradon. I have news of events in Vensaur that he would profit to know. As you see I am weaponless and no threat to the king." Even the effort of speaking seemed to weaken the man, and his knees began to tremble until he sank to the cobblestones, where he remained.

The guard summoned a page and sent him to the king's secretary with the traveler's message. Then he turned back to the man and said, "If I read aright, you've not been well fed on your journey. I will have you taken to the kitchen for a good meal while we await the king's word."

"I thank you for your kindness," said Werthen, "but I'll not dine until I see your king."

The guard took the man by his arm, helped him to a bench just inside the castle gate, and summoned a page to bring him a drink from the well. A quarter-hour later another guard came to usher him into the great throne hall of Morningstone Castle and into the presence of King Aradon, who was sitting on the high throne at the far end of the hall. With unsteady steps, the man approached the throne and bowed.

"Your majesty, I am Sir Werthen of Vensaur, and I know the fate of my king Umberland, who vanished from the eyes of his subjects some two months back. And I wish to tell you that . . ." Werthen could not finish his thought but collapsed to the polished flagstone floor. King Aradon stood and descended the dais.

"What is wrong with him?" he asked the guard.

"I'm told he made the journey from Ensovandor in hiding, mostly by foot, and has eaten little, sire."

Aradon had Sir Werthen brought to Little Hall, where a full meal was prepared for him. Aradon sat opposite him at the table and drank a cup of mead as the knight fell to the first proper meal he had eaten in weeks. When Werthen had regained some of his strength, he wiped his mouth on a napkin, looked at Meridan's young king with gratitude, and spoke in a voice much stronger. "I am most grateful for your thoughtfulness, your majesty. Please forgive my appearance, for I have traveled far and under difficult circumstances. If you will hear me now, I will speak what I came to tell you, to wit the fate of King Umberland of Vensaur."

"I will certainly hear you," said Aradon. "Say your piece."

"Thank you, your majesty. I am a knight in King Umberland's court and, for some fifteen years, a close friend of the king. Perhaps you have heard that Umberland never returned from a hunt two months ago. I was with the king on that fateful hunt. He and I had ridden ahead of the others, for the dogs were baying and we were hard on the trail of a wild boar. Umberland and I veered aside to follow our dogs, who were hot on the scent, but the rest of the hunters missed our turn and went straight on. Intent on the hunt, we did not even notice that we were alone.

Suddenly from out of a copse of trees, a group of six riders, all mounted and armed, abducted both the king and me and took us away through the woods, far from our hunting companions. They brought us to a long-abandoned manor deep in the forest and took us inside, where we found ourselves standing in the presence of Brendal Seven Fingers. Brendal sat at a table with Lord Caldemone, one of King Umberland's high-ranking knights. Brendal did not bother to explain why he had abducted the king, what he was doing in the manor, or why Caldemone was with him. Though Umberland could see that his throne, and even his life, was in danger, he stood tall and straight before the two traitors, neither asking, nor begging, nor pleading for mercy or information. It was a fine thing to watch, sire." Sir Werthen's voice swelled with pride, and he dabbed at the corners of his eyes with his napkin.

"Why they did not kill us we were never sure—perhaps to hold us as hostages if needed. At any rate, they threw us into a prison beneath the manor and, as we heard later, placed Caldemone on Umberland's throne. King Umberland and I occupied separate but adjacent cells, and I soon found that mine had two loose bars in one of the windows. Night after night I worked these bars, prying, twisting, and scraping away bits of cracked mortar with my fingers." He turned his palms upward toward the king to show the hard calluses on his fingertips.

"Eventually, I managed to remove two of the bars and escape. I could not free Umberland because of the guards. And his health worried me. He had begun to cough deeply and became daily thinner and weaker. I knew he would not be able to travel even if he did escape, especially on foot, as we would be.

"I knew better than to return to Ensovandor. Brendal would not have taken the king had he not been ready to take the castle. I knew I would be hunted, so I stayed away from the roads and made my way through wilderness and woods as I traveled to you. I have lost count of the days it has taken me to get here, but I know we have no time to lose if we are to save King Umberland. King Aradon, I urge you to assemble your army now. March into Vensaur and rescue your friend Umberland. Before his abduction he was committed to aligning Vensaur with the Seven Kingdoms, which is certainly the reason Brendal deposed him. It is well known that Brendal is plotting to prevent the confederation. Umberland is your friend and ally, and a key to the success of the reformed empire. And unless he is rescued soon, he will surely die, if he has not already." The knight turned up his cup and finished the last of his mead, dabbed his napkin at the corners of his mouth, and looked at Aradon with eyebrows raised in expectation.

"I commend you for your courage and loyalty to your king," said Aradon. "As for me, I am strongly inclined to aid King Umberland. But a matter of this magnitude must be laid before the Hall of Knights. I will present your case before them myself as soon as we can convene a meeting."

He had pages prepare a bath and chambers for the exhausted knight and ordered a suit of clothing for him. Aradon then returned to his throne, where he sat with his chin resting on his laced fingers as he thought how conveniently Werthen's report played into his own needs. Almost from the moment of his baby daughter's disappearance, he had strongly suspected Brendal as the perpetrator. He had no proof but logic. Because of Brendal's military inferiority, he needed a hostage as leverage to stop the uniting of the Seven Kingdoms.

But why had no message come listing his demands? Without such a message, Aradon could not confirm his suspicions and had no warrant to attack Brendal. But now that he knew this seven-fingered outlaw had deposed and imprisoned King Umberland, he had all the excuse he needed. He could call Sir Denmore and have the army assembled immediately.

But how could he be sure of his own mind? His heart had been severely wounded, and he was in no condition to be objective in making such a decision. Was his concern for the kingdom or his daughter? How could he call Meridan's farmers and tradesmen to leave their farms and shops and their own wives and children if his true motive for putting their lives in jeopardy was to save his own child? If he placed his subjects at such risk to meet his own needs, what kind of king would he be?

But if he did not do all within his power to save his own child, what kind of *man* would he be? That was the dilemma that faced him—whether to be a king or a man. Whether to risk the lives of others for a possible rescue of his own daughter, or to sit passively and do nothing when he had in his hand the power to destroy an army on the mere possibility that such a war could save her. Now, on the basis of Werthen's story, he did not have to make such a decision. He could simply assemble his army and march to Ensovandor with unassailable justification. But he could not escape the question that still dogged his mind. Was his eagerness to drive out Brendal and free Umberland really an excuse to find his daughter?

Aradon rang for a page, and one came to him immediately. "Have the Lord Chamberlain call a meeting of the Hall of Knights to be held this very evening," he said. He marched from the throne hall and ascended the stairway to his chambers.

Five hours later all of Meridan's forty-two knights, along with Chancellor Aldemar, sat facing the dais where Aradon sat on his throne. The only woman in the hall was Lady Kalley, who accompanied her husband, Sir Olstan the Silent, ready to read his hand signs and speak for him should he wish to participate in the debate. Sir Werthen, freshly bathed with beard and hair neatly trimmed and wearing a new suit of clothing, sat in a chair just to the right of the dais. King Aradon stood and addressed the assembly.

"Honorable knights of the Hall of Meridan, we have information that calls for a decision. Sitting beside me is Sir Werthen, a knight of the court of Vensaur, whom some of you know already. This morning Sir Werthen came to me bearing the grim news that King Umberland has been deposed, and a puppet now sits on his throne, controlled by the outlaw Brendal."

Murmurs of outrage rumbled through the hall as Aradon continued. "The question we must address is whether to gather our armies and lay siege to Ensovandor and root out this usurper. I will relate to you all that Sir Werthen told me, after which you may question him as we open the floor for debate. Following the debate, I will call for a polling of the Hall, the results of which will give me the basis for my decision."

Aradon told the Hall the entire story of Umberland's capture and imprisonment, of Werthen's heroic escape and journey to Corenham, and of Brendal's taking the reins of government behind the puppet Lord Caldemone. His passion rose in the telling, and before he finished, fire flashed in his eyes and anger in his voice. After calling for debate, he wiped his brow and sat again on his throne.

Immediately Sir Prestamont stood. "Do you know how many men Brendal commands within his castle?"

"Ensovandor Castle accommodates well over five hundred men on all ramparts," answered Sir Werthen. "I'm sure that Brendal will conscript at least twice that many and hold the reserves within the castle as replacements."

"Does Brendal have so many men?" asked Sir Halliston.

"Not of his own," replied Werthen, "but undoubtedly he will bribe or coerce at least a few of Umberland's knights, and force farmers and tradesmen of Ensovandor to take up arms as well. He could meet you with an army of two thousand or more."

"Will Umberland's subjects be so easily coerced to follow his usurper?" asked Sir Karramore.

"King Umberland is a good king and the people of Vensaur love him. And conversely, they have little love for Brendal. But who knows what kind of deception he may have used to sway them? You can be sure that the people of Vensaur do not know that Brendal has Umberland in chains. Brendal is a devious man."

Sir Llewenthane listened to the debate as long as he could, his face slowly reddening and his frown deepening. Finally he could contain himself no longer. He came to his feet and in a voice tense with passion said, "Knights of Meridan, why are we wasting words? This seven-fingered mole who calls himself a man has disrupted the Seven Kingdoms long enough. He has spread havoc everywhere he has been, first in Valomar, where he plotted with his father to depose King Tallis, then in Meridan, where he joined Morgultha and Lomar and took over villages on our kingdom's borders. And now he has taken Vensaur, has imprisoned a good king, and threatens to disrupt the unifying of the Seven Kingdoms. How can we choose any course but to assemble an army immediately and root this slime-dweller out of his lair and restore Umberland to his throne?"

"I agree with Sir Llewenthane," said Sir Halliston, rising from his chair.

"As do I." Sir Prestamont rose.

"And I," shouted Sir Karramore, also standing.

Immediately the remaining knights were on their feet, along with Lord Aldemar and Sir Denmore, all shouting their affirmation of Llewenthane's call to arms. Llewenthane looked around him, his mouth gaping in utter shock at this unaccustomed endorsement of his call to action. Aradon sat unmoving on his throne, then stood and motioned for the knights to take their seats again.

"I strongly support the action just expressed by the Hall. But before I give you my decision, I must bring before you another factor. Since the disappearance of my baby daughter, Vallia, many of us have thought it likely that Brendal was behind the abduction. I must frankly tell you that I cannot clearly read my own motives in this matter. The head is muddled by the heart. I confess to you my fear that I am at least as motivated by my hunger to find my daughter as by any concern for King Umberland and the unity of the Seven Kingdoms. I cannot be certain that I am not calling knights and citizens of Meridan from their manors and cots as much for my own needs as for those of the kingdom. If any of you wish to recant your call to arms on the basis of my divided mind, I hereby give you the right."

The Hall sat in silence for only a moment before Sir Olstan arose with Lady Kalley beside him. His hands traced a series of fluid signs, which his wife spoke into words. "Your majesty, my husband, Sir Olstan the Silent, says that were the rescue of your daughter the only reason for this expedition, he still would affirm it and endorse it with all his heart."

Immediately every knight in the hall stood and with one emphatic voice echoed Sir Olstan's declaration. Aradon stood silent, momentarily unable to speak as his eyes welled with moisture at this magnificent expression of the love his court bore him. He motioned for the knights to take their seats and rendered his decision. He would call together Meridan's army and, in three days, march into Vensaur to rescue King Umberland and root Brendal out of Ensovandor. At Lord Aldemar's urging, Aradon sent a letter to King Bronwilde of Oranth asking him to raise his own army and join Meridan's in Vensaur to assist in the attack on Brendal's occupied castle.

That night Aradon told Queen Volanna of his decision, and she was glad of it.

"I will go with you," she said.

Aradon would not hear of it. "The battlefield is no place for a woman. I will not risk losing you to the straying of some chance arrow."

But she was adamant. "How can I stay here wondering whether you have found our daughter and whether she is safe? And if you do find her, can I wait here five days while you journey homeward? No, I will be there to hold her the moment she is found."

Aradon argued that her hopes were rising beyond what was wise. He had no proof that Brendal had Vallia. She could be setting herself up for a heartbreaking disappointment. But Volanna did not budge. In the end Aradon agreed to have her accompany the army to Vensaur in a carriage, but he imposed certain terms upon her. She would wait out the battle far behind Meridan's troops and would not stray from her post without Aradon's leave. Volanna agreed and Aradon gave orders for the needed preparations.

Three days later the army of Meridan began the march toward Vensaur.

CHAPTER TWENTY-TWO

The Offer of the Sword

he evening sun hovered an hour above the horizon when the cart carrying Lanson and Evalonne topped the crest of a hill overlooking a wide valley. "Look yonder and ye can just make out the outlines of Ensovandor Castle," said the driver. "We should be there by noon tomorrow."

Evalonne looked but said nothing. When they arrived at that castle, the new world she had found would be lost forever. This man who called himself Roburne would join Brendal's army and find a home for Mossette. His protection of her would cease, as would her usefulness to him. She would be cut adrift to find a new life for herself. But she did not want a new life. She had come to realize that she loved this man, and she knew that he had warmed toward her as well. She often caught him looking at her with a light in his eyes that had not been lit when their journey began. With her woman's insight into the meaning of such things, she felt certain that he had begun to care for her, at least a little.

She had fallen in love not only with Roburne but with Mossette as well, and she realized that for the first time since the death of her own baby girl, she was truly happy. If her life would continue just as it was now, she could ask for nothing more. She had begun to harbor a hope that in spite of her past, Roburne would somehow come to love her enough to marry her, that no one would claim the child, and that the three of them could settle into a cottage somewhere and live out their lives in bliss.

At first she had kept this hope at bay as a mere fantasy with no root in reality. She had not forgotten that Roburne was undoubtedly a nobleman, and a wealthy one, while she was merely a commoner. Nevertheless, in spite of the social gulf between them, the new gleam in his eye had elevated her fantasies into possibilities. But now as Ensovandor Castle loomed on the horizon, such notions collapsed in a rubble of foolishness. Roburne was on a mission, and though she had been a help to him and a diversion that pleased his eye for the moment, he would now get on with his vengeance against King Aradon and she would become a mere memory.

As the day ended, the driver of the wagon left the road and drove among the trees, where he found a sheltered place by a stream, and they made their last camp. Roburne roasted a partridge and a hare he had shot in the afternoon as Evalonne nursed and bathed Mossette. After they had eaten, all lay down to sleep, the driver in his wagon, Evalonne with Mossette, and Roburne a little apart from them.

Lanson did not sleep immediately. He too felt regret that the journey was ending. With Evalonne accompanying him, it had been pleasant—indeed, more than pleasant. The barrier he had erected against her was no longer solid. The kirk's abhorrence of women hardly entered his mind anymore, seeming now so contradictory to his delight in her as to be unthinkable. The distance in their stations and, even more, the fact that so many men had used her had been a hurdle over which his inclinations would not dare leap. But now these obstacles seemed much smaller. As he had told her himself, the truth about the woman was not in the past but in the present. She had shed her past as a butterfly sheds its cocoon and emerged as a creature of ever-unfolding beauty. This Evalonne was not the same woman he had met at the Red Falcon.

Yet much of his old reluctance remained, and at times the pendulum of his thought would swing and the kirk's voice would intrude, telling him he could not so summarily dismiss its righteous judgments. Should he, the rightful king of a nation, even consider taking a woman as queen whose past was so tainted? Especially a woman whom the kirk condemned and was even now hunting down to place on trial? But on the other hand, as Maconnal had suggested, was it possible that the kirk reached beyond its rights in exacting strict justice on one who had repented? He knew he was challenging the kirk's authority by helping Evalonne escape Gronthus, and he wondered if in opposing the kirk, was he also opposing the Master of the Universe? Lanson lay on his back listening to the gurgle of the stream and the crackle of the fire, gazing up into the glittering heavens as such thoughts churned in his mind until sleep overtook him.

They arose at dawn and got back on the road. Shortly after noon the wagon entered Vensaur's capital city. The driver drove directly to the trading square, where Lanson and Evalonne parted from him and began walking toward the castle at the south edge of the city.

As in most cities, the streets of Ensovandor teemed with citizens and tourists going about their trading, selling, baking, crafting, and herding. But the city was unlike others of the Seven Kingdoms in that the people spoke little and kept their eyes either on the cobblestones or focused straight ahead. The few who looked at Lanson and Evalonne at all eyed them with suspicion or merely glanced and quickly looked away.

The couple continued along a narrow street until they came to an inn bearing above the door a wooden sign so chipped and peeling they could barely make out the words, *The Raven's Egg.* The inn was more than half filled with diners huddled over their tables and talking in low tones. When Lanson and Evalonne entered, all talk ceased, and the patrons turned and stared at them before turning back to their ale. Lanson thought it strange that an inn so full should be so quiet. But he found a table and Evalonne began to nurse Mossette. Some of the patrons continued to give them sidelong glances, and others leered openly at Evalonne. After several minutes, a serving girl with stringy mats of hair and a face bathed in sweat came to their table and stood with her hands on her hips.

"What d'ye want?" she said.

"We would like—"

"Today we got beef stew and ale."

"As I was about to say, we would like beef stew and ale," said Lanson lightly.

Without responding the girl hurried away and in moments returned with a tray containing two bowls and two cups, which she plopped on their table without a word, and went on about her business. There was no banter or laughter in the hall, and no boisterous behavior. The talk that in most inns reverberated from the rafters was here merely a low rumble, and the look of the patrons, leaning over their tables with their heads together, gave the inn a conspiratorial atmosphere. Lanson could feel the eyes of the diners upon them as they ate their stew. He took Mossette from Evalonne and said in a low voice, "Something is wrong here, though I have no idea what."

"I can tell ye what's wrong." The serving girl had just come up behind him. "Our kingdom 'as been invaded, that's what. Just yesterday we 'eard that King Aradon 'as crossed into Vensaur with over twelve 'undred men, and Bronwilde of Oranth is with 'im five 'undred strong. That's what's wrong, man."

"Aradon is in Vensaur? Can this be true?" asked Lanson.

"It's true all right," growled a man at the next table. "Three guards from the Vensaur-Meridan border came gallopin' in yesterday with their 'orses 'alf dead, shoutin' the news in the streets as they 'eaded for Ensovandor Castle."

"Surely Brendal is prepared to defend Ensovandor," said Lanson.

No one replied but all stared at him in silence until a voice from another table spoke up. "Brendal is conscriptin' men and—"

"Don't be tellin' this stranger what Brendal is doin'," said a warrior, rising from his seat on the far side of the room. The ring of swords being drawn from their sheaths filled the air as five warriors at the same table rose with him and advanced toward Lanson. "You can tell by the man's speech 'e's not from around 'ere," the soldier continued. "He could be Aradon's own man for all we know, posin' with this woman and child as a travelin' family while gatherin' information for Aradon 'imself."

"I am not Aradon's man," said Lanson.

"We say you are a spy," the warrior insisted as they moved toward him.

"Quick, to the door!" Lanson whispered to Evalonne as he handed Mossette to her. He drew his sword and followed her, backing all the way to keep his face toward the advancing warriors. They reached the door, and Evalonne escaped just as the first of the warriors slashed at Lanson. He caught the thrust with his own blade and, with a quick backstroke, gashed the man's forearm, causing him to scream and drop his weapon. Lanson engaged the man behind the first as he kicked over a chair, tripping an attacker from his right. A series of lightning strokes drove his opponent several steps back, and a feint and a thrust ripped through the chain mail and gashed the man's shoulder. Blood came pouring through as the warrior fell across a table and to the floor. The three remaining warriors thrust tables aside and advanced simultaneously toward Lanson. He backed toward the door and was only a few feet from it when a patron extended a leg in his path, and Lanson went sprawling to the floor. Immediately three sword points were at his neck, chest, and belly.

"Drop your sword if you don't want to die," said the warrior standing above him. Lanson relinquished his weapon and got to his feet. Two of the men manacled his wrists while two others went out and found Evalonne, who was clutching Mossette tightly, and brought her inside.

"What is your name and from whence do you come?" the warrior demanded of Lanson.

"I'll give my name to none but Brendal."

The warrior drew back his hand and smote Lanson hard on the side of his face. "I said, what is your name and from whence do you come?"

"I will tell only Brendal," repeated Lanson, blood trickling from the corner of his mouth.

The warrior drew back and hit him again and would have hit him a third time, but his companion stopped him. "Let's get 'im to Brendal."

The soldiers clustered around the pair and escorted them through the streets to Ensovandor Castle, which towered above the city on its eastern side. Evalonne still clutched Mossette as if she thought the child was about to be wrenched from her. The soldiers explained their mission to guards at three checkpoints between the castle gate and the keep, and each time they were passed through. Finally they came to the great doors of the throne hall, guarded on either side by armed sentries, who heard the soldiers' story and sent a message inside. A quarter-hour later the sentry got word to usher them into the hall for an audience with Brendal Seven Fingers.

Lanson was surprised at the lack of decorum in the hall. More than a score of men were standing or sitting here and there about the room in clusters of threes or fours, all engaged in their own pursuits as if they were in a bathhouse or barracks. One group sat on the floor, huddled in a tight circle, playing some kind of dice game. Two men leaned against a pillar, talking to a young woman and laughing raucously. Others sat about in chairs or on benches, some drinking, others engaged in lazy conversation. One man was sprawled on a bench snoring with gruntings like those of a burrowing hog.

After the soldiers had brought Lanson and Evalonne a few paces into the room, all activity stopped and the room went silent as a crypt, except for the snoring, and all eyes turned toward the couple. On seeing Evalonne, several of the men whispered and sniggered to each other behind cupped hands. This affront brought heat to Lanson's face, and he strained at the manacles on his wrist until they marked his skin. The captives were brought to the foot of the throne, where they stood silent as Brendal gazed over the party. When his eyes settled on Evalonne, he took on an expression not unlike greed. Again Lanson reddened and tugged at his manacles.

"Who is this you have brought before me?" Brendal asked the soldiers.

"We do not know, sire. He refused to tell us."

"We will see that his tongue is loosened before he leaves here today," said Brendal, his face as cold and hard as the iron in his voice. "Why have you brought them to me?"

"We found them at the Raven's Egg, and they were askin' questions about Aradon's army and what you were doin' to defend against 'im. We could tell by their speech they are not from Vensaur, and we thought they might be spies. When we tried to bring them to you, the man 'ere resisted and wounded three of us before we captured 'im."

"A single man fought the six of you and wounded three? I can see that with defenders like you I needn't worry about Aradon." Brendal glared at the soldiers with undisguised contempt before he turned to Lanson. "I have three questions for you, my hot young roebuck. And you'd best loosen your tongue to answer them straightaway, or I will have it cut out. Who are you? From whence do you come? And what are you doing in Vensaur?"

"I am not an enemy to you, Sir Brendal. Indeed, I have traveled far but for one purpose only, and that is to offer you my sword to help defeat the tyrant Aradon."

"You have traveled from where?" asked Brendal.

Lanson's mind whirled as he groped for the safest answer. Already in this brief meeting with Brendal, he found that he neither liked nor trusted the man and felt it unwise to divulge too much information about himself or Evalonne. And, having seen the hunger in Brendal's eye as he looked at her, he felt a strong need to keep her close to him while they were under this man's banner. "My name is Roburne. I come from southern Lochlaund, sir, near the kingdom's border with Meridan. Aradon's butchers murdered my father in a raid there and I will not rest until I am avenged against him."

"And the woman with you?"

"She is my wife, sir, Evalonne by name. And the child is our daughter."

"Evalonne. What a beautiful name, and thus an appropriate one," said Brendal, with a smile and a softening of his voice. "What is your child's name and how old is she?"

"Her name is Mossette, sir, and she is six months old."

Brendal stared silently at the two of them before he spoke. "Roburne and Evalonne, will you dine with me this evening? I will arrange for a nurse to care for your child."

"I thank you, Sir Brendal, and we gladly accept," said Lanson. "But if you please, we will keep the child with us. Travel has made her fretful when left with others."

"As you wish. A page will show you to your chambers."

The soldier nearest Lanson unlocked his bonds, and a page appeared instantly to lead the couple to a room on the ground floor of the keep. Additional pages brought a tub and buckets of water to the room. Evalonne bathed herself and Mossette as Lanson found the trough on the practice lawn near the castle armory, where he bathed and trimmed his beard. When he returned to the room, he found Evalonne dressing Mossette, who lay on the bed cooing and playing with her toes.

"Brendal is not the sort of man I expected," he said.

"If his eyes are windows to his thoughts, I dare not get within ten feet of him," she replied. "I felt like a caged mouse in the presence of a hungry cat. We mustn't stay here. We must find a way to escape before tonight."

"You are right. I don't trust him at all. But for the moment we are bound by a common enemy. I would make a pact with a snake if I thought it would help me defeat Aradon."

"Didn't you see how he stared at us before inviting us to dinner?" said Evalonne. "I'm sure he suspects already that we are not quite who we say we are. It's only a matter of time before he learns the truth."

"I think we are safe for the moment. With Aradon marching against him, he needs every warrior who will stand with him."

"Very well," replied Evalonne. "But tonight we must speak of ourselves as little as possible. We must reveal nothing of our past or our travels together."

"I agree. We must be on our guard tonight."

Soon after they had rehearsed what they could say and what they could not, a page knocked on their door and ushered them to the dining hall, where Brendal waited alone but for two guards stationed against the wall behind the table where he sat.

Servants brought in the food, a more meager fare than Lanson had expected, consisting of little more than baked chicken and cheese with slightly stale black bread and heavily watered wine. As they ate, Brendal said little but asked pointed questions to keep the pair talking as he watched them closely. Lanson had no liking for the way he continued to eye Evalonne.

After finishing his meal, Brendal leaned back in his chair and belched loudly. "I, too, have reasons for hating Aradon, and not only

Aradon, but his wife, Volanna, as well." He held up his right hand, which was missing the thumb and two adjacent fingers. "Aradon cost me more than half my right hand—the chance stroke of a fortunate bumbler. And Volanna cost me my welcome in my own homeland as well as my father's life. I will see them both in the grave, but not until I have punished them by thwarting their dreams and wrecking their happiness. Apparently you hold similar grudges?"

"My own quest is twofold," said Lanson. "First, as I have already told you, to avenge the cowardly murder of my father. And second, to expose Aradon's knavery to the Seven Kingdoms and undeceive them in their belief that he is worthy to be high king of this island."

"What was your father's name?" asked Brendal.

"K-Karlon, sire, holder of an estate granted to our family by King Kor's great-grandfather Gunderlon during the reign of Perivale."

"And how did you acquire your battle skills?"

"I was in training to become a knight in King Kor's Hall. I was to have been presented for acceptance into the Hall and the vigil of induction when my father was murdered."

"Most unfortunate," said Brendal. "And have you been trained in archery as well as swordsmanship?"

"Indeed I have, sir."

Brendal did not reply immediately but studied the face of his guest as Lanson grew first uneasy, then alarmed. Such scrutiny affirmed Evalonne's suspicion that the man suspected something about him. As the evening wore on, the impression deepened until he wondered if he should heed her advice to flee for the safety of the three of them. He decided he would stay until Aradon was defeated, but no longer.

"Roburne, I have a proposal for you," said Brendal. "As you know, even as we speak Aradon is on Vensaur soil and advancing toward Ensovandor. He could arrive here as early as tomorrow evening or the day after at the latest. Join me in defending this castle and you will receive a twofold reward. First, you will achieve your expressed desire—to avenge your father against Aradon's treachery. And second, I will give you an estate in Vensaur along with knighthood in my own court. How do you answer?"

"I accept your generous offer, sir," said Lanson. Brendal arose and the two men shook hands, Brendal with his left. After he dismissed them, Lanson and Evalonne, with the sleeping Mossette in her arms, left the hall and returned to their quarters.

CHAPTER TWENTY-THREE

The Siege of Ensovandor

rendal rose early the next day and, flanked by two guards, walked through the halls and yards of the castle on a tour of inspection. From the moment he had heard that Aradon's army was marching toward Vensaur, he had begun to stock his larders and fortify the ramparts. He had planned his strategy three days back, choosing not to meet Aradon in open battle. He knew he did not have the loyalty of the citizens of Vensaur, and he doubted that he could conscript an adequate army for a face-to-face war. He could have coerced the men of the town to fight, but he doubted they would muster up sufficient commitment to his cause to defend it with their lives. He decided his best defense was to gather into the castle as many men as he could coerce or buy and prepare for a siege. He had managed to assemble just under seven hundred archers and swordsmen, with whom he felt certain he could defend the castle against a force four times that number. And from reports he had received, Aradon was marching with a little under two thousand men.

Using himself as the standard by which he judged all men, Brendal was sure that when Aradon found the town of Ensovandor undefended, he would rout it before attacking the castle itself. While the men of the town would not rally to Brendal's cause, they would defend their own homes, and thus Aradon's forces would be diminished before he attacked the castle—all at no cost to Brendal in lives, funds, or weapons.

By late afternoon Brendal stood at a window and looked down on the courtyard. A steady line of ox-drawn carts, laden with produce, cheeses, hay for the cattle, and barrels of ale and mead, rolled through the gate. Interspersed among the wagons, farmers herded a dozen small groups of cattle and goats.

The armorer had reported to Brendal that the store of arrows was far from adequate to defend against a lengthy siege. Brendal had ordered the man pilloried for the oversight and demanded that smiths and fletchers work long into the nights to replenish the supply. He intended to stock the castle with enough food and weapons for at least three months. If the siege lasted so long, his defenders could hold out and decimate Aradon's numbers daily until he gave it up and withdrew to Meridan. On the other hand, if Aradon was foolish enough to storm the castle, Brendal's men could pick them off from the turrets like fishers spiking trout in a stream.

As Brendal gazed at the castle gate with its raised portcullis, the furrows in his brow deepened. The only crack in his confidence of success grew from a tidbit of news he had received two days ago just as Aradon was crossing into Vensaur. His border scouts had reported that Aradon was bringing a catapult. That news alone would not have shaken him. Besieging armies commonly used catapults to lob firepots and stones over castle walls, demoralizing the residents with ever present random danger. But spies in Meridan who had seen the catapult under construction reported it to be of a size like no other ever built.

"They call it a trebuchet," said one of them. "The arm of the thing is a whole pine tree, and the net is the size of a wine vat. They can lob a cow with this machine. When they were testin' the thing, I saw it fling a boulder the size of a 'og as if it was nothin' more than a pebble."

Without blinking or changing expressions, Brendal had suddenly lashed out with his good hand and smote the man hard across the mouth. "Why do you spread such tales?" he growled. "There is not a machine in existence that can hurl a stone of that size. You will say no more of this either to me or to others. Do you understand?"

"Indeed, sir," the man muttered through bloodied lips.

Brendal had waved the men away and thought on what they had reported. Though they might have stretched the tale somewhat, he knew there must be some substance to it and began scouring his brain for a defense against such a machine. As of yet he had found none.

But the coming of the man who called himself Roburne put a new idea into his head. If he could not defend against Aradon's trebuchet, perhaps he could find a way to use the destruction it would wreak to solve a dilemma he had found on his hands. The dilemma was Roburne himself. From the moment the man had been presented to him, Brendal had felt that he should know him. As he studied his guest at dinner last night, he had become virtually convinced that Roburne must be the missing son of King Kor of Lochlaund. He had once met Kor, and this man's resemblance to the king was too strong to deny. If he were indeed Kor's son, Brendal knew that in spite of his attempt to hide his identity, he spoke the truth about having a vendetta against Aradon. And that would be sufficient to ensure the man's loyalty, at least until Aradon was defeated.

If Roburne was indeed the son of King Kor, he was the rightful King of Lochlaund. He would be a danger to Brendal when he came to the throne of Lochlaund because Kor, before his death, was committed to aligning with Aradon. And while Roburne was solidly with Brendal now because he thought Aradon had murdered his father, when he eventually learned the truth he was certain to turn against him and become Aradon's ally.

Brendal thought the safest course was to have Roburne put to death. It would be easy. He could simply accuse him of being a spy and hang him. But with the impending siege facing him, he needed good warriors, especially archers, and that very morning Brendal had tested the man's archery and found it as good as his claim. He could put an arrow through a barrel hoop at a hundred paces and split an apple five times out of seven at fifty. Brendal's dilemma was that he both needed Roburne and needed to do away with him.

Brendal turned from the window and strode out upon the top of the wall until he reached the ramparts directly above the castle gate. He looked out over the green flats beyond the moat to the clumps of wood and brush from which Aradon would likely launch his attack.

He judged where he thought Aradon would anchor his trebuchet. As he gazed and pondered, the idea came to him that this giant catapult could solve his problem. He would assign to this so-called Roburne command of a contingent of his best archers stationed on the gatehouse ramparts just above the castle drawbridge. The task of these men would be to rain arrows on any of Aradon's men who tried to bridge the moat and batter down the gate. No doubt Aradon's trebuchet would be aimed at these very ramparts to knock out the archers. It would be the most deadly position on the entire wall, and likely as not, Roburne and his men would perish there. Thus Roburne would for a time serve an important defensive purpose, then he would be dispatched before the truth made him a danger to Brendal's schemes. Furthermore, with Roburne out of the way, he could take the beautiful Evalonne as his own. Brendal smiled to himself at the cleverness of it all as he walked back to the keep and ordered food and wine brought to his chambers. After finishing the meal, he retired to his bed.

No rooster had yet crowed when Brendal, sleeping like the dead, felt a hand shaking him in the darkness.

"Brendal. Brendal. Wake up, sir. There is news," came the tentative voice of his valet.

The back of Brendal's hand found the man's cheek even in the darkness and sent the man sprawling across the floor. "What do you mean waking me in the middle of the night?" Brendal grumbled as he lit a candle with his flint.

"Sir, Aradon's army is approaching the gate. We could see them arriving at the oak grove just moments ago."

"You lie!" Brendal shouted as he hit the man again. "Aradon has not had time to attack Ensovandor and march here."

"He did not attack Ensovandor, sir. He has come directly to us."

"He's a fool. He could have had the town for almost nothing. It was undefended." Brendal frowned darkly as he ran his good hand through his rumpled hair. "Well, why are you just standing there? Sound the alarm, idiot!"

The valet bowed deeply and hurried from the room.

✍

It was still an hour before sunup when the blare of the horn startled Lanson instantly awake. He arose from his blanket on the floor as Evalonne, sleeping on the only bed in the room, stirred and tried to calm Mossette, who was also awakened by the horn. They both knew the meaning of the sound: it was the signal calling the men of the castle to arms. Aradon had arrived.

Evalonne helped Lanson into the armor Brendal had provided and bristled at the poor quality of it. The breastplate was not even of metal but of enameled leather, and somewhat brittle leather at that. As she eased the rusted helmet onto his head her face reddened and her eyes flashed fire.

"Is this the best armor he could give you?" she spat. "You might as well be naked as to wear this flimsy stuff."

"It will have to do. The armorer said this was all he could find."

"All he could find indeed! Has it occurred to you that Brendal must want you dead? Why else would he put you at the most dangerous post in the castle and give you armor no better than parchment? Don't go, Roburne. You don't have to do this. We can still escape."

"I must do this, Evalonne. I must avenge my father."

She turned abruptly away and folded her arms as hot tears ran down her cheeks. Like every woman who sees her man off to battle, she knew she might never see him again. But she kept such thoughts to herself. She had to remember that she was not his woman. Aside from her intuitive awareness that at least a measure of her love had been passed like the flame of a candle from her heart to his, she had no reason to believe that it burned in him as anything more than a flicker. Therefore her surprise was great when she felt his hands on her shoulders, turning her to face him again. With a touch like a caress, his finger brushed away the tears from her cheeks. Again he took her shoulders gently in his hands, as if she were the most precious jewel they had ever held, and placed a tender kiss where the tears had been. Then without a word, he turned and walked out the door. Evalonne, standing open-mouthed and tremulous, put her fingers to the place where his lips had touched and held them there until Mossette, now hungry, began to whimper. Evalonne fed her, aware all the while of an exquisite burning as from a caressing flame that lingered on her cheek.

As Lanson stepped into the hallway he had little time to think on the thrill of the kiss or of why in that moment he had chosen to silence the warnings of the kirk that whispered continually in his mind. He found the castle corridors filled with men running or walking rapidly to their battle posts. He climbed briskly to the top of the gatehouse and took his own position on the ramparts, and soon his twenty archers were assembled with him. Ganwold, a stocky, black-bearded man who had been captain of the archers before Lanson arrived, leaned against a turret with his arms crossed, scowling at his new commander. Several small barrels of arrows had been rolled up to the ramparts. And between every other archer sat two buckets, one filled with gummy tar and the other with oil.

Lanson walked along the rampart inspecting the readiness of his men. "Where are the rest of our arrows?" he asked Ganwold.

"What do you mean, 'the rest'?"

"When we have emptied these barrels, where do we find additional supplies? I need to know. In the heat of battle it may be impossible to have them brought to us."

"There'll be no more brought to us. These arrows are all we 'ave."

"That can't be so. A siege can last for months. We haven't enough arrows here to last a week."

"Like I said, these are all we 'ave." Ganwold turned and walked away.

Lanson could not believe him, but he did not have the leisure to pursue the matter. He ordered the archers to their positions and instructed them to save their arrows until Aradon's men reached a certain point, which he marked by pointing out a stone some seventy yards distant.

As the gray of dawn gave shape to the field before them, the ready defenders of Ensovandor Castle could make out in the distance a dim movement, which they knew to be Aradon's army. Shortly afterward they could hear a faint rumble, the sound of marching footmen and mounted knights advancing toward the castle. As light from the east pushed back the darkness, they could make out definite forms in the first line of marchers and the silhouettes of the mounted warriors directly behind them. And behind these warriors rolled more than a score of wagons laden with food, weapons, and the dismantled siege machines.

Sunlight began to illumine the grassy field before the castle as the front line of Aradon's footmen reached a point some fifty yards behind Lanson's landmark stone. A commander's voice shouted a halt. Lanson could now make out considerable detail in the army before him. The commander was an armored knight mounted on a sorrel horse, and beside him rode another knight on a white mount, whose armor gleamed golden in the morning sunlight.

"The man in the golden armor will be King Aradon," said Lanson to his men. "And the knight beside him calling commands to the army is certainly his general, Sir Denmore. If either comes within range of your arrows, strike him down immediately."

In the gathering light of the morning, the castle's defenders watched the army move about, some unloading the carts while others began to assemble the siege machines. Most of the activity focused on three centers. The first unit began assembling a "cat," which was essentially a mobile, tunnel-shaped house constructed of wood, having a peaked roof covered with animal skins. The house was ten feet wide and thirty feet in length, with the apex of the roof reaching a height of about fifteen feet. The cat was mounted on low wooden wheels, lifting the bottom of its walls only a few inches above the ground.

The second group began to assemble the battering ram. It was a large one, Lanson noted, a pine trunk at least three feet in diameter at the base. The log would be suspended horizontally by ropes within its own wooden housing, also roofed with animal skins. Like the cat, the whole structure was made mobile by wooden wheels attached along the two sides.

Lanson could not make out what Aradon's men were building in the third cluster of activity. By noon he could see a vertical tower constructed of six or eight beams twenty-five or thirty feet high, leaning toward each other, pyramid-like, as they rose into the air. Later in the day he could see that the machine was a catapult, for a horizontal axle had been mounted at the top of the pyramid and an arm consisting of a pine trunk over forty feet long pivoted on the axle, which ran through a hole in the trunk drilled about one third the distance from its heavy end. At the longer, lighter end of the log was attached a rope netting, and from the heavy end hung a counterweight consisting of a wooden bin filled with boulders. The entire apparatus was mounted on wooden wheels almost the height of a man. Lanson marveled at its size. It was twice as large as any catapult he had ever seen. Nor had he seen one operating on the principle of the counterweight as this one did.

As the day drew toward its close, Aradon's three siege machines stood ready, and the soldiers turned their attention to unloading portable mantlets—wooden shields the height of a man, mounted on brackets that made them self-standing for the protection of the front line of archers. By the time the sun set, Lanson had counted over a hundred mantlets, and more were coming as dusk darkened into night.

When the darkness was complete, Brendal's men saw the campfires of the enemy dotting the blackness like fallen stars. The castle defenders slept at their posts, alternating in four watches. But no one slept well. Sounds of creaking, scraping, rumbling, and the clanking of logs came from the field in front of the castle throughout the night. Lanson and his men could see the movements of the army only faintly as indistinct shadows in the moonless darkness. Nevertheless, when the sounds and shadows told him of enemy activity right at the edge of the moat in front of the castle gate, he roused his men and rained several volleys of arrows into the shadows, but to no apparent effect. Except for a few shouts and curses, the sounds of movement remained unchanged, neither diminishing nor ceasing.

At the break of dawn Lanson looked out over the parapets. Facing the gate of the castle at a distance of some seventy yards stood a triple line of three hundred mantlets, each with an archer standing in readiness behind it. He looked both to the left and to the right and saw men stationed at much wider intervals about the castle as far as he could see. Apparently Aradon intended to concentrate his attack on the castle gate, posting just enough men around its perimeter to ensure that no one escaped or entered by the postern gate or over the wall.

Lanson looked directly in front of him. The cat had been brought to the very edge of the moat, directly facing the gate. Already the moat in front of the gate was a quarter filled with logs and stones, and more were stacked behind the cat, ready to be carried through it and dumped into the water to make a crude bridge to the gate. And behind the cat stood the battering ram, the sides of its housing covered with overlapping layers of cowhides to protect the soldiers inside from arrows. Directly behind the three rows of archers loomed the trebuchet, its derrick towering some thirty feet into the air, its net loaded with a stone the size of a sheep, and its mighty arm restrained by ropes, awaiting the order to arch forward and hurl the huge missile toward the castle wall.

On each side of the trebuchet stood several scores of footmen, available either to take up arms or man the war machines, and behind them stood two hundred or more mounted and armored warriors, including Sir Denmore and King Aradon.

When the first gleam of sunlight shone on the top of the castle wall, Brendal mounted the gatehouse parapet and stood beside Lanson as he gazed at the army amassed before him.

"How do you read what you see, Roburne?" he asked.

"Aradon is concentrating his entire attack on the front of the castle," replied Lanson. "We must double our archers on the front walls to meet him—put a pair at every crenel. One can shoot while the other nocks his arrow. We need to rain arrows on them relentlessly. We don't need so many archers around the rest of the castle, at least for now."

"And while we're all defending the gate, he will have men scaling the back and side walls with ladders."

"They have no ladders. They're putting all their hope on their archers and their war machines."

"Surely your archers can hold them at bay."

"Not for long unless we get more arrows," Lanson said. "Aradon's men are extremely well defended with their mantlets, the cat, and good shields. Even their battering ram is housed. We get very little target, and that only at intervals when their archers shoot from the sides of their mantlets or when we can catch a man momentarily unshielded."

"Then your vaunted marksmanship must rise to the fore."

"We will do our best, sir. But we must have more arrows than what has been allotted to us if we are to have any chance of holding them back. Where are the arrows, Sir Brendal?"

Brendal turned to Lanson and a snarl twisted his face. "You have all the arrows you need, Roburne. See that you do not waste a single bolt."

Lanson started to reply, but at that moment a trumpet blared from the field as Aradon and Denmore rode up into the open space between the mantlets and the cat and faced the gatehouse parapet where Brendal and Lanson stood. Remembering Lanson's orders, the archers on the wall immediately nocked their arrows and took aim on the king and his general.

"No!" shouted Lanson. "This is a parley. We must not harm them now."

Brendal gave Lanson a look of utter contempt as all the archers lowered their arrows except for Ganwold, though he did relax his bowstring.

"Brendal, do you hear me?" Aradon's voice rang out clearly.

"I hear you," snarled Brendal. "What is the meaning of this unlawful invasion of a sovereign kingdom? Has your ambition got the best of your vaunted honor?"

"I am here to free King Umberland and place him upon his rightful throne. Lay down your arms, open your gates, let us enter peacefully, and there will be no loss of life. You will receive a fair trial. If you refuse to surrender, I will take the castle by force and deal with you and your men by the terms of war. Which will it be, Brendal?"

"I know your scheme, Aradon. Free Umberland and he will be in your debt, will he not? You can force him to enslave the independent Kingdom of Vensaur under your whip. No, I will not surrender. I will defend Vensaur's independence against your impudent invasion. You cannot penetrate this castle. Go back to your anvil, blacksmith."

"I have no other purpose than to place the rightful King of Vensaur upon his own throne, and I will not turn aside from that task. Open your gates and lay down your arms, Brendal. Spare Vensaur from the stain of blood upon her soil."

Brendal half turned toward Ganwold, gave an almost imperceptible nod, and immediately Ganwold bent his longbow and an arrow flew through the air toward Aradon. It glanced off the side of his helmet.

"That is my answer, blacksmith," shouted Brendal as he turned and strode from the parapet. Aradon and Denmore wheeled their steeds about and returned to their stations near the trebuchet, where Denmore shouted the order for the archers to begin the battle.

Immediately the air was thick with arrows flying in both directions. A long line of Aradon's soldiers, working in pairs, brought logs and stones into the back end of the cat and dropped them into the moat at the front end. The men walked behind mobile mantlets outfitted with small wooden wheels, which shielded them entirely from the view of Lanson's archers. Lanson marveled at the efficiency of the operation. His archers could hit no target but the mantlets, the shields, and the roof of the cat. After four or five volleys, he did not think a single arrow had yet marked the flesh of any of Aradon's soldiers.

"Flame an arrow and shoot it into the roof of the cat," Lanson ordered the archer next to him. The man dipped an arrow in tar, then plunged it into the bucket of burning oil. It flamed immediately, and the archer nocked it and let it fly toward the cat. The moment it penetrated the skin roof, the flame snuffed into a wisp of gray smoke. Lanson ordered a dozen more shots into the cat before telling the archer to cease. "It's no use," he said. "They have soaked the skins."

From the field Sir Denmore shouted the order to launch the trebuchet. The men released the ropes restraining the long end of the huge pole, allowing the counterweight at the short end to drop, arching the long end high in the air with ever increasing speed until, with a jerk that shook the entire structure, it stopped short near the apex, releasing the stone from its net.

From the castle wall Lanson and his men watched as the boulder came tumbling through the air toward them. It hit with a jarring thud against the castle just to the left of the gate. Aradon's soldiers reloaded the trebuchet. They added several stones to the counterweight and, with ropes attached to horses, pulled the front of the machine a scant few inches to the left. They rolled another sheep-sized stone into the net and again released the arm. This time the stone flew ten feet above Lanson's head and crashed into a fence inside the wall below him, releasing two dozen goats, which bolted, bleating loudly in panic as they bounded all about the courtyard. The soldiers on the trebuchet removed half the ballast they had added, loaded the net again, and launched a third stone. This time they found their range. The stone crashed into the turret manned by Ganwold, shattering it and hurling the man and his alternate to the ground two stories below.

The battle progressed throughout the day with little change in the pattern of attack. So well protected were Aradon's men that Lanson and his archers managed to pick off fewer than a dozen of them, and those were replaced immediately. Their arrows reached a few more of the shielded soldiers as they marched into the tunnel of the cat, but not enough to impair the progress of Aradon's operation.

Meanwhile the methodical stone barrage from the trebuchet began to destroy the turrets above the gatehouse, leaving Lanson's men fewer crenels from which to shoot. By midafternoon Lanson had already lost eighteen of his forty men, and with seven turrets destroyed, he had no protection for their replacements. He was surprised at the order and preparation of Aradon's forces compared to the lack of preparation on the part of Brendal's. He looked down the wall and saw that the moat was now three-quarters dammed, and the cat rested entirely on the logs and stones Aradon's men had piled into the water.

Typically in a siege, the defending army had all the advantages—the protection of walls, a high vantage point, and little exposure to arrows. But Lanson could see that this siege would last nowhere near three months. Indeed, as the day wore on he began to wonder if it would last the night. If the soldiers manning the cat continued at their present pace, the moat would be bridged before morning, which meant Denmore could bring up the battering ram at daylight and begin pounding at the gate. Perhaps Brendal had been right, he thought ruefully. It seemed they would need no more arrows because the war would not outlast their meager supply.

CHAPTER TWENTY-FOUR

VENGEANCE

hroughout the night the men on the wall heard the clanking, heaving, and splashing of Aradon's men piling stones and logs into the moat to fill the remaining gap to the castle gate. Lanson noted that Aradon had chosen his time of attack wisely. In the moonless night the castle defenders could see nothing but dim shadows, which made poor targets for archers with no arrows to spare. Twice he ordered a volley of arrows into the shadows but to little effect. When the sounds told him the soldiers had almost reached the castle gate, he had stones brought up to the ramparts and tipped over the wall onto the men beneath them. The first stone brought a cry and a string of curses from the darkness below, but as additional stones followed the first, hearty cries of approval and laughter made Lanson realize he was doing the attackers' work for them. His stones were becoming part of their dam.

He then ordered barrels of boiling oil brought to the ramparts and dumped onto the soldiers below. But he could hear no sign that the tactic was slowing their work or doing any damage. By now the workers were no longer careless about stepping from under the protection of the roofed cat and merely pitched their stones and logs out the opening and into the moat.

As dawn approached, a command rang out of the darkness to back the cat away from the gate, and the creaking, groaning, and rumble of wheels on planks told the defenders on the wall that the dam was finished. As dawn began to break, they watched helplessly as the battering ram in its skin-covered housing rolled up the road toward the castle gate like a great caterpillar. The tall housing seemed alive, moving by its own power, manned as it was by forty hidden men pushing it forward from the inside.

"How can we possibly defend against such an attack?" Lanson muttered to the archer standing nearby. "Not a man is visible. No doubt the roofing skins are soaked with water and nothing we can drop on them will have any effect."

Nevertheless, he ordered a volley of flaming arrows shot at the roof of the battering ram's housing, but as he suspected, the shafts buried themselves in the many layers of water-soaked skins and were snuffed out immediately. The ram did not waver in its inexorable march toward the gate. It reached the dam and began to roll forward onto it.

"It is futile to stand here and watch the gate go down," Lanson fumed. "We must change our tactics immediately. I must see Brendal. Keep watch and put an arrow in any skull that pokes out."

But at that moment a hail of arrows from the mantlets across the moat caused all Lanson's men to duck behind their turrets. Three archers fell from the wall, each with an arrow protruding from his body. Lanson and his men nocked their bows, but as they rose to shoot, another wave of arrows met them, and two more of his archers fell to their deaths. Once more they stepped into the crenels to shoot, and a third wave of bolts drove them yet again behind their turrets. Aradon's men were shooting in alternating waves, giving Lanson's archers little or no time between volleys to launch their own arrows. He thought if he could get the rhythm of their timing, he could give the order to shoot between the third volley and the first, but even that would mean he could launch only one arrow to Aradon's three. No sooner had he thought it than a crash on the wall beside him took away the turret and the two men standing next to him. The trebuchet had awakened. *This is futile,* he thought again. *I must find Brendal.*

Between volleys of arrows and stones Lanson watched the inner courtyard for any sign of Brendal. When he saw him standing with two of his aides on the rampart of the keep, he leapt down the steps and ran across the courtyard and into the keep, then bounded up the spiral stairway to the roof where Brendal stood.

"Sir Brendal," he said, "we cannot penetrate Aradon's protection, nor stop his war machines. He has bridged the moat and his battering ram is at your gate. Our arrows cannot find targets. The turrets on the gatehouse ramparts are almost gone and the walkway is beginning to crumble. The gate will be down before noon and we can do nothing to stop them."

"And just what do you suggest?" asked Brendal.

"Open the gate and let them in," replied Lanson.

"Let them in! Are you daft, man?"

"They will soon come in whether we will it or not. You can save your gate and your portcullis if you let them in. And you can control the timing of their entrance to when you are ready for them."

"Better not to let them enter at all."

"But we cannot stop them."

"What have you been doing with your arrows—picking your teeth?" Brendal bellowed. "I thought I had archers on my walls. If you can't hit them outside the castle, what makes you think you can do better when they come in?"

"We have a better chance inside the castle than out," Lanson explained. "We can drop boulders and hot oil on them as they come through the gate. We can place archers all around the gate and pick them off as they enter. The rest of the archers can stay on the battlements and rain arrows on them as they get into the courtyard. They'll not have the protection of their mantlets and sheepskins."

"You're forgetting they outnumber us three to one."

"But from the walls we will have the advantage of height. They will be vulnerable and exposed as they cross the courtyard."

"You have the advantage of height now and your arrows can't seem to hit anything but the ground. Why do you think you will do better with the enemy inside our walls?"

"They will be unprotected and—"

"I've listened to enough of your battle genius, Roburne. If the best strategy you can think of is to let the enemy inside the castle you are charged to defend, you'd best get back to your post. Your advice is no better than your marksmanship."

The two aides with Brendal chuckled as Lanson reddened at the insult. But he held his tongue, bowed curtly, and returned to his place on the gatehouse battlements.

Nothing had improved in his brief absence. He arrived just as a hail of arrows forced his archers to duck behind the remaining turrets. The second wave came as the first ended, and the third followed moments after the second. The defending archers were getting desperate.

Meanwhile, boulder after boulder from the trebuchet pounded the ramparts at now regular intervals and with ever increasing accuracy. Soon two more turrets shattered and another four archers hurtled into the courtyard. The top of the wall became riddled with cracks, and stones began to crumble and fall to the ground. As the bombardment continued, five more of Lanson's archers took arrows in their bodies and fell from the ramparts.

A dull thud shook the wall, followed seconds later by another like it, and another and another as the forty men inside the battering ram's housing swung the great tree forward on its suspending ropes, bringing its full weight hard against the wooden gate. After each impact they allowed the tree to swing freely backward, then pushed it forward again until it met the thick beams of the gate. Soon they set up a steady rhythm and the heavy thudding could be felt throughout the castle like a ponderous heartbeat.

Lanson knew it was now merely a matter of time. "Save your arrows," he shouted. "You will need them when the gate comes down."

No sooner had he spoken than a great stone from the trebuchet crashed into the top of the already weakened wall. A shower of stones tumbled into the courtyard below, leaving a twelve-foot breach in the wall and destroying an equivalent section of the rampart floor. Looking across the gap, Lanson could see three of his men huddled behind the two remaining turrets. They were stranded. The only stairway down to the courtyard was on Lanson's side of the breach, and when the trebuchet took out the two ramparts that protected these men, they would face certain death.

"Bring me a rope," cried Lanson. He flung it across the gap where one of the stranded men caught it and tied it to the remaining stump of a turret. Lanson tied his end to an intact turret, and the first of the three men began to hand-over-hand his way across the chasm. Arrows flew about him as he hung suspended in the center of the gap, one piercing his calf. As he neared the edge, Lanson and another archer reached out and pulled him to safety as the second man took to the rope. But he did not fare as well. As he approached the center, a volley of arrows flew through the gap, one piercing his shoulder and another plunging deep into his back. He screamed in agony as his hands released the rope and he plunged to his death.

The third man grasped the rope and stepped off the broken ledge. He swayed back and forth over the chasm as he worked his way along the rope, arrows flying all around him. He was two-thirds across when a stone from the trebuchet crashed into the remaining stump of the turret to which the rope was tied, sending an avalanche of stones to the courtyard and freeing the far end of the rope. The archer managed to retain his grip on the rope as it swung suddenly downward from horizontal to vertical, where he dangled precariously over the jagged stones of the crumbled wall.

"Hold on to my belt," Lanson shouted to the archer behind him. He stepped up to the edge of the breach, took the rope in his hands, and began to pull the dangling man upward. As soon as Aradon's archers spotted him, arrows flew all about him, two wedging in his armor while two others bounced off his helmet and one grazed his arm. But in moments Lanson had the archer hauled to safety, and he sat panting behind a turret while the steady, thunderous boom of the battering ram continued.

As Lanson would learn later that morning, his saving of the doomed archer earned him the fierce loyalty of the men placed under him. Since the coming of Sir Brendal, they were not accustomed to their superiors having any care for their lives.

Lanson ordered all but five of his men to abandon the gatehouse and take up positions on the ramparts of the front wall.

"Save your arrows," he told them. "Shoot only at sure targets, and when the gate comes down, turn on the Meridan soldiers as they enter the courtyard."

The relentless thud of the great log against the castle gate reverberated in Lanson's mind so that he did not think he would ever forget the sound. He and the five archers remained on the gatehouse,
letting few of their own arrows fly as they watched through the
crenels for an occasional hapless archer to stick his head from behind
his mantlet. Fewer enemy arrows came their way now as the archers
on the ground realized the defenders at the top of the gatehouse were
no longer a threat to the ram. While Lanson and his men watched,
another huge stone hit the wall below them, jarring the parapet and
deepening the growing breach in the top of the gatehouse. They continued their selective archery until the man next to Lanson suddenly
laid hold of him and jerked him roughly toward him.

"What do you think you're—"

At that moment a stone from the trebuchet crashed into the turret where he had stood, shattering it and taking out the rampart floor
behind it.

"I thank you, man," said Lanson.

The rhythmic pounding against the gate went on and on until
the sound began to take on a different texture—not quite so solid,
and punctuated with an afterbeat of sorts. Lanson knew the meaning
of it. The door had loosened enough to slap against the framing
behind it. The battering went on for another hour as he and his men
continued their pinpoint archery into the line of mantlets below. The
sound of the battering ram changed abruptly as a beam of the gate
splintered and gave way, followed shortly by another and another. A
quarter-hour later the gate was down and in another half-hour, the
portcullis as well. A great shout went up from Meridan's army as their
mounted knights galloped across the dammed moat and into the
castle.

Brendal pulled all archers off the perimeter walls of the castle and
armed many of them with swords and axes to meet the invaders as
they entered the bailey. He placed others on turrets at the top of the
keep and at the arrow loops inside its walls. Over a hundred of
Brendal's mounted knights stood ready as the gates went down and
Aradon's knights poured into the castle. The two waves surged toward each other and met with a ringing cacophony of steel as foot

soldiers poured in behind them. Lanson and his archers rained down several volleys of arrows, but soon the two armies were so mingled in hand-to-hand combat that the archers could no longer shoot without hitting their own men. At that moment Lanson saw King Aradon in his golden armor ride into the castle astride his white charger.

"Lay down your bows and take your swords, men," cried Lanson as he drew his own blade and bounded down the steps into the fray, slashing right and left with great strokes as he made his way toward the king he hated.

&v

Inside the keep a terrified young woman had watched the battle from a window on the second floor. She put her hands to her face and gaped in horror as the castle gate fell and Aradon's soldiers swarmed into the bailey. She did not watch long before she realized that Brendal's men were no match for Meridan's army, which would soon storm the keep. In panic she left the window and ran through the corridors looking for a place to hide. She pulled at every latch and pounded on every chamber door, screaming for entrance at each. Finally one opened to her, and she stood face-to-face with the frightened Evalonne, who was clutching the baby Mossette tightly to her bosom. The woman froze for a moment as a flash of recognition shot through her panic. She knew the baby was Aradon's daughter, for she was Glynnora, its kidnapper.

Her panic vanished instantly. She realized she had found the key to certain victory. She backed away and mumbled an apology for knocking on the wrong door, then ran boldly up the stairway toward Brendal's chambers. Though Glynnora was Morgultha's servant held at Ensovandor against her will, she knew that all was lost for her mistress, as well as for her captor, if Aradon got his daughter back. She would give Brendal the key to victory, then let Morgultha deal with him in her own time.

The guard at Brendal's door denied her entrance, but she would not be turned away. She soon convinced him that he would be held responsible if he kept Brendal from hearing what she had just learned.

"Ye'd better not be makin' a fool of me," said the guard.

"Oh, no," she replied. "You can't hold me responsible for that."

The guard opened the door and led her through the corridors toward Brendal's room. Long before they saw him they heard his voice shouting in fury.

"You're all a gaggle of incompetent, cowardly idiots! I stocked and armed this castle for a siege of three months, and in less than two days you let that peasant blacksmith inside our walls. I've never heard of a castle being taken in so short a time. You should be hanged, and I may do it yet."

"But, sir, he was better prepared than any army we've ever met. He came with mantlets for almost every man. His cat and battering ram were impenetrable, and no one counted on such a machine as the trebuchet—"

"I'm sick of your excuses," Brendal sputtered. "You've seen war machines before and should know how to defend against them. Now you have the audacity to come groveling to me saying the battle is lost. What battle? Aradon had no resistance. You cowards never gave him a fight."

"The battle is not lost, sir," came Glynnora's voice from the doorway.

Brendal turned and glared at her. "Who let that wench in here?"

"I have news that will win you the victory—today," she said.

"It will snow in hell before I need battle advice from a woman. Get her out of here."

"No! Wait!" she cried as the guard took her by the arm and pulled her toward the doorway. "You must listen to me. You can still win the war."

The guard opened the door and struggled to put her out.

"Aradon's baby daughter is right here in this castle," she shouted.

Brendal's head suddenly snapped toward her. "Release her," he said to the guard. "Speak, woman. What do you mean?"

"Just moments ago I accidentally opened the wrong chamber door and inside it stood a woman holding a baby. It was the same baby I myself took from the crib in Morningstone Castle little more than a month back."

"And the woman holding the baby—what did she look like?"

"She was what you men would call savory—well formed with a full head of fine dark red hair and green eyes."

Brendal began to understand a little of the mystery of Roburne and Evalonne, and a terrible smile twisted his face as he nodded to the captains standing nearby. "Bring the babe to me. Now!"

Glynnora led the three men to Evalonne's chamber, where they smashed the bar and kicked open the door. Evalonne huddled in a corner, clasping the crying Mossette tightly in her arms.

"Give me the babe, woman," said one of the men.

Evalonne stared wide-eyed, saying nothing. The men went to her and began to pry the child from her arms.

"No!" she screamed. "Leave her alone!" She sank her teeth into a forearm in front of her face, and a rough hand slapped her across the cheek. It took two of the men to pull her arms away as the third took Mossette, now squalling at the top of her lungs. Evalonne leapt up in a frenzy, clawing, kicking, biting, scratching, and screaming like a wildcat. She inflicted several lacerations, gouged a finger into an eye, and tore the top of an ear before one of the men caught her hands. He held her fast as the other dealt several blows to her face until blood poured from her mouth and nose and she fell to her knees. They kicked her into the corner and rushed from the room, taking the screaming Mossette with them.

Evalonne watched the men leave through a pulsing storm of vivid spots. She forced herself to her feet and, putting her hands to the walls for balance, stumbled out of the room and followed the echo of the running feet down the corridor.

Brendal took the still-crying baby and strode from the room. He climbed a stairway to a turreted balcony overlooking the courtyard, where the din of clashing steel and bellowing men rose up from the battle below. He scanned the turmoil until he saw Aradon, still mounted on his white charger, his sword cutting down men left and right. Brendal stepped to the front of the balcony where all could see him.

"Aradon!" he bellowed as the child screamed with all her might. "Aradon. Stop the battle and hear me now."

Aradon lifted his hand and shouted for the battle to halt. Lanson, standing near the stairway to the balcony, ceased his pursuit of the king and looked up at Brendal. The only sound was that of the bawling Mossette as all eyes turned toward the balcony.

"Aradon, do you recognize this brat?" Grasping the child by one leg, he held her up for all to see, like a fowler displaying a prize chicken.

Aradon blanched and drew a sharp breath.

"Aradon," Brendal called again, "if you want this child to live, you will do as I say. Command your army to lay down their arms. Surrender yourself to me, and the Kingdom of Meridan to my authority. Refuse and I will slay this child here and now before your very eyes." Aradon sat tense and speechless. He could not surrender the nation he had been charged to lead and protect just to save his own daughter, but neither could he speak the order to resume the attack that would bring about her death. The crying child was the only sound as all eyes looked from Brendal to Aradon, Aradon to Brendal, waiting to hear what word King Aradon would speak.

The moment Brendal had finished speaking and held up the baby, Lanson understood the truth about who Mossette was. But as much as he hated Aradon, he could not stand the thought of killing this child he had nurtured and protected for days. It was not she who had murdered his father. She was not to blame for being Aradon's daughter. Brendal's threat to her life outraged him. Glowering with anger, he leapt up the stairway toward the commander, pushing and weaving through the men standing on the balcony.

"What is your word, blacksmith?" Brendal shouted.

He lowered the child and placed her across the turret in front of him. She lay there, stomach down, precariously balanced with her feet kicking toward him and her head hanging over the courtyard three stories below as he drew his sword with his left hand. He lifted it high above the child with the point aimed directly at her back.

Aradon, his face contorted in agony, opened his mouth to speak, but before a word came out, another voice bellowed from the parapet. "Don't do it, Brendal!" Lanson ran toward him, pushing soldiers aside right and left. "Stop! Stop this now!"

Brendal paused and looked toward Lanson, who was fast approaching with his sword in hand. He raised his own sword and brought it down hard toward the baby. Lanson lunged, his sword stretched desperately in front of him. He felt the metal of Brendal's sword scrape against his own as it deflected to the side of the child. Lanson tumbled against Brendal's knees, knocking him a few paces back, and his own sword clattered to the stone floor. He got to his knees and scrambled toward it. But Brendal began to kick at him viciously, forcing him to roll across the stone floor far from his weapon. Brendal turned back to the turret where Mossette lay and again raised his sword to strike the child. In desperation, Lanson fumbled for the knife at his belt, drew it, and lunged toward Brendal. He drove the blade upward through the man's ribs. Brendal's sword clattered to the floor as he sank to the stones, choking and gasping his final breath.

As Brendal fell, Lanson looked up from the floor to see Mossette's kicking feet disappear from view over the edge of the turret. He leapt toward her, reached over the turret and barely managed to clutch her leg before she fell beyond his reach, and pulled her back to safety.

Immediately Brendal's aides, now recovered from the shock of their leader's death, rushed toward Lanson, who took Mossette and ran along the parapet to the stairway. He descended to the courtyard below, where he darted in and out among the clusters of soldiers who had resumed their fighting. Brendal's captains followed close behind, gaining on him with each step. With the child in his arms, Lanson could neither turn to defend himself nor run fast enough to outstrip them. Ahead of him he heard a shout and looked up to see a woman running toward him, her face caked with splotches of blood and one eye swollen almost shut.

"Give me the baby," she cried as they drew closer, and Lanson realized with a shock that the battered woman was Evalonne.

He handed her the child, and she ran from the battlefield as Lanson picked up the sword of a fallen warrior and turned to face his attackers. Brendal's three captains engaged him immediately, and though his skill was great and he held his own with a defense they could not breach, he soon began to retreat as he tired from the effort of keeping three swords at bay. He knew he could not last long before a blade found its way past his own. He had begun to look for a way of escape when another swordsman emerged from the surrounding battle and took up the fight at his side. It was all the help Lanson needed. He stopped his retreat and held his ground, and in moments the two had the three stepping backward with every stroke. Lanson soon downed one, and an instant later his companion downed another. The third turned and ran to save his life.

With the duel ended, Lanson stood, breathing hard, and noticed that the battle around him had ceased. At Brendal's death, many of his men had lost heart and given up the battle. The few who had fought on had soon realized the futility of their cause and surrendered as well. Lanson turned to thank the man who had come to his aid, but when he looked his savior in the face, his teeth clenched and his eyes narrowed. The man was none other than Aradon himself, the man he hated most in the world. He did not sheathe his sword but stood facing the King of Meridian, his eyes glaring with cold hate.

"I have just saved your daughter; you have just saved my life," said Lanson. "On that score the scale is balanced. But there is one more account to be settled—the cowardly murder of my father, a man who admired you and was on the verge of coming into your federation. He now lies dead, killed at your hand. Stand and defend yourself!"

Before Aradon could ask the name of his opponent or his father, Lanson raised his blade and attacked. The king could do nothing but raise his own sword to defend himself. As the duel began, soldiers gathered about the fighting pair to form an arena.

At first the combatants tested each other, thrusting and parrying tentatively until each began to feel the weight of the other's blows. To the onlookers the opponents appeared to be evenly matched. Neither seemed able to penetrate the other's defense. Aradon was reluctant to press any advantage because he knew they were fighting under mistaken premises. The man had lost his father and the deed was apparently being laid to his charge. He did not want to compound the tragedy by killing an innocent man he did not even know. The young king held his own, often retreating as he studied his opponent's tendencies and looked for a way to end the fight without harm.

After several minutes of intense swordplay, the two men broke apart and stood panting as they gazed at each other.

"You are a most worthy opponent," said Aradon, "but surely neither of us has committed a crime worthy of death. Explain your charge against me that I may defend it."

"You know full well what you have done," replied Lanson through gritted teeth, "and I will waste no time repeating it now."

"At least tell me your name."

"My name is Lanson, son of Kor."

"Ah, King Kor of Lochlaund. I did not kill your father, Prince Lanson. Let us stop this battle and talk before we create another tragedy."

In reply Lanson ran toward Aradon and rained on him a shower of blows that sent the king reeling backward before he regained his footing. They fought on for another ten minutes. Then Aradon detected the flaw he had been seeking in his opponent's style. At the turn of his stroke from left to right, Lanson allowed a slight pivoting of his wrist that swung the sword sharply, causing a momentary change in the contour of his grip. Aradon timed his own stroke carefully and caught Lanson's sword at the turn when his grip was vulnerable and sent it flying from his hands. Quick as thought, Lanson darted to pick it up, but Aradon's foot was already on it. Lanson slowly looked up at Aradon, waiting for the thrust that would end his life.

"Now we shall talk," said Aradon as he sheathed his sword. Slowly, Lanson stood and faced the king. Aradon stooped, picked up Lanson's sword, and handed it to him, hilt first. Lanson took it and slid it into its sheath.

"I did not kill your father, Prince Lanson. The delegation I sent to Macrennon to sign the treaty with King Kor was murdered en route, and it was days before I knew of it. Indeed, it was long before Meridan knew of Kor's death, as we received a letter from him declaring the treaty void, claiming as his justification our failure to appear at the signing ceremony. We learned later that the letter was a forgery and that your father was dead."

"Why should I believe you?" said Lanson.

"Why should I have murdered King Kor, an ally ready to join the Seven Kingdom federation?"

"Lust for power. You coveted his lands."

"Nonsense! Can't you see what happened? Whoever murdered your father also murdered the delegation I sent to sign the treaty. They took the treaty and the clothing from my men, posed as my delegation, and murdered your father to keep him from signing the treaty."

"What proof do you have for such a story?"

"Did you recognize any of my men on the night of the murder?"

"Of course not. You sent butchers, not diplomats. I saw the signs but failed to heed them."

At that moment a commotion arose from among the men watching, followed by a string of curses. Lanson and Aradon turned toward the sound to see Sir Denmore and Sir Olstan bringing up a man whom they held between them.

"Here is the proof you need," said Denmore as he threw at Aradon's feet a shield bearing the blazon of the rampant griffin. "Sir Olstan found this man among Brendal's defeated swordsmen and recognized the crest of King Kor on the shield." Sir Olstan jerked on the shackles that bound the man's wrists. "Tell the king what you have already confessed to us," commanded Denmore.

In a quavering voice, the captured warrior told Aradon and Lanson that he was part of a band assembled by Brendal to murder both the delegation of Sir Eanor and King Kor. As he finished speaking, Lanson sank to his knees before Aradon.

"I beg your forgiveness, King Aradon. I have wrongfully accused you and spent weeks hating you and seeking your death. Please accept my heartfelt contrition."

Aradon took Lanson by the arm and raised him up. "Certainly I forgive you. Please accept my deep sorrow at the death of your father. He was a great king."

At that moment the crowd surrounding the two men parted, revealing a young woman standing in the doorway to the keep. Evalonne, her hair glowing like fire in the sunlight, clasped Vallia in her arms as if she were her most prized possession. Tears gathered in her bruised eyes as she slowly descended the steps and walked toward King Aradon. Aradon, his own eyes moist with longing, saw his daughter's face for the first time in weeks. He walked toward Evalonne until they stood facing each other. Then, with trembling hands, he reached toward Vallia. When the child saw her father, a huge, gurgling grin lit her face, and she reached and strained toward him. Aradon received his daughter and clasped her to his bosom as he buried his face in her blanket.

"Bring my horse," he said huskily. He mounted and, with Vallia held firmly in his arm, rode through the crowd of watching soldiers. Once out of the castle gate, he spurred his charger to a gallop and took his daughter to her mother, who was waiting in the grove not far beyond the walls of the castle.

CHAPTER TWENTY-FIVE

The end of the dream

valonne stood watching King Aradon as he rode out the gate of Ensovandor Castle holding Mossette tightly. Her heart was a maelstrom of whirling emotions. She knew it was good that the babe was in the arms of her true father, but she was not sure she could stand the emptiness of her own arms without her. Absently she wiped the moisture from her eyes and stroked her arms as if comforting them in their loss. She turned and saw Roburne gazing at her, in his eyes a look hard to read—concern or pity or perhaps something even greater. He began to walk toward her, but after a few steps three or four men gathered around him and drew him away. He turned and looked at her once more before disappearing into a crowd of men.

She stood wondering at the meaning of his look until the moans and cries of the wounded men strewn about her drew her from her reverie. She went to the man lying on the ground nearest her, knelt over him, and gently removed his hands from his bleeding forehead. She tore a strip from the hem of her dress and began to bind his wound.

Other women came out of the keep to attend the wounded as well. Sometimes they worked alone, and sometimes in groups of three or four when a soldier had to be moved or held down while an arrow was drawn or a broken bone set. At first these ministering angels went about their work with faces grim in silent outrage at the destructive futility of war, attending the most grievously wounded first. As they turned to the lesser wounded their mood lightened and their tongues loosened. Evalonne bound the broken fingers of a swordsman sitting against the outer wall, listening to the chatter and laughter of three young women cleansing the lacerated leg of a man nearby. She paid little attention until she twice heard them utter the name Roburne. She strained to hear more.

"And so it turns out that 'is name's not Roburne after all. It's Lanson, and King Aradon called him a prince," said one of them.

"Prince of what kingdom?" said another.

Evalonne could not hear the answer, but her breath caught as she felt an instant tightness around her heart. Of course. She should have guessed. Her Roburne was the missing Prince Lanson of Lochlaund. Her heart sank within her and the sunlight turned bleak and thin.

"Did you see his eyes?" the girls continued.

"Oh, yes! Blue as a summer sky."

"With a body like Hercules himself."

"I wonder if he's married."

"No, but I hear he is betrothed to a high lady in Lochlaund."

Evalonne's hands trembled and her eyes blurred so that she could hardly see the strips of linen she wrapped around her patient's hand.

"Owww!" the soldier moaned as he jerked his hand away.

"I'm so sorry," said Evalonne as she wiped her eyes and loosened the bandage she had wound much too tightly.

She was crushed. Her world had just collapsed. She now knew that not only was Mossette lost to her, but Roburne—Prince Lanson—as well. Or more accurately, he had never been hers to lose. She was sure he had begun to love her a little in spite of her past, but now she could see that her hopes of his wedding her had been a fantasy created from the empty air of her own longing. Now she could understand why he had encouraged neither her love for him nor his own budding feelings toward her. He was betrothed, and he would do nothing to dishonor his chosen bride.

Her bright hopes plummeted like twin stars falling from the sky. Lanson had come to the end of his quest, and dear little Mossette had found her rightful parents. She had been nothing to either of them but a servant to meet their momentary needs, and they needed her no longer. They would return to their lives of love and happiness, and she, after tasting the sweet fruit of hope, would return to her life of lonely despair. In spite of Lanson's insistence that she could rise above the mistakes of her past, it was clear that she could not. Nothing would change for her. She had sinned grievously and would find no peace until she came to terms with the fact that the Master of the Universe could not be mocked. One's sins would cling like leeches until they sucked all life from the soul and left one a shell like Gwynnelon, dead to all possibility of joy or love.

One thing she knew to be utterly true, and no past sin or present despair could change it. She loved Lanson. She loved him dearly. She loved him with all her heart and soul, more than she loved her own life. But the hard truth was that she was a fallen, tainted woman, not fit to be the wife even of an honest farmer, much less the prince of a kingdom. She knew what she must do. If she truly loved Lanson, she must get out of his life. She would leave today and no longer confound his heart and conscience with her presence.

Midafternoon had passed before all the wounded were tended and carried from the courtyard. Unnoticed in the continuing bustle of cleanup and repair, she went to her room, gathered her few things, wrapped them in her blanket, and walked out of the castle. She continued straightaway on the northern road past the abandoned mantlets and the trebuchet and through the grove on the slope of the hill. As she climbed the road up the hillside, a horse nickered in the grove to her right, and she turned to see a dozen or more of Meridan's soldiers among the trees, and in the center of them King Aradon's white stallion. Aradon himself stood near the horse, his arms around the most beautiful woman Evalonne had ever seen. The woman held Mossette (the only name Evalonne knew for the child), and she was laughing and talking to the baby as the king's smiling face beamed down upon them. Evalonne turned away and continued walking, her cheeks yet again wet with tears.

⚘

Lanson looked up from his trencher, loaded to capacity with veal, lentils, cheese, nuts, and leeks, and gazed absently across the hall full of diners. Next to him sat Meridan's Queen Volanna, holding Vallia on her lap. She had adamantly refused to leave the child to attendants. Sitting next to the queen was her husband, King Aradon, and next to him King Umberland, newly released from imprisonment and ebullient in his freedom. On the far side of Umberland sat his queen, and next to her Sir Werthen. Soft music from a small band of lutes and timbrels sweetened the air, providing a sea of bright melodies upon which floated the chatter and laughter of the guests. The return of King Umberland had steadied the ground under the people of Vensaur, giving them cause to celebrate.

Often Queen Volanna and King Aradon engaged Lanson in conversation, and Princess Vallia thought nothing of climbing out of her mother's lap into his. While he accepted these attentions with grace and humor, Lanson slipped back into a melancholy reverie the moment they turned away. The burden of his thought was singular. *Why did Evalonne leave without explanation or farewell? Where could she have gone?* In the aftermath of the war, which had ended two days back, he had immediately been asked to organize and direct men of both armies to clean up the courtyard and repair breaches in the wall and other damage inflicted by the trebuchet and battering ram. At the time he was too occupied to speak to Evalonne, though he had seen her more than once attending the wounded in the courtyard. Later in the day he had looked for her in the bailey and in the hallways of the castle, but he had seen no sign of her. Finally as his day ended an hour after sunset, he went to his room and found that her clothing and blanket were missing. At first he refused to believe that she had gone, but he could think of no other explanation.

Why did it matter to him that she was gone? Theirs was a chance encounter in which they merely served each other, meeting the needs of the moment. Naturally she would leave now that their journey was over and the mission completed. He meant nothing to her, and she would get on about her business, probably returning to some inn to resume her life as a serving maid. And she should mean nothing to him. She was a commoner, a tainted woman, and much too beautiful to be trusted. The voice of the kirk, which of late he had been tempted to ignore, raised its stern voice again. It was good that she was gone.

Nevertheless, early the next morning he had gone to the gate-house and asked the guards if they had seen her leave. One of them did remember seeing a girl of her description walk away from the castle in the late afternoon.

"I remember 'er red 'air, sir. It was lit up like fire in the evenin' sun."

"Did she have anything with her?" asked Lanson.

"As I recall she was carryin' somethin' like a bag or a blanket, sir."

"Which way did she go?"

"Straight up the road. As you know, she was a beauteous lass, sir—though 'er face was bruised up a bit—and I watched 'er till she went over the 'ill yonder."

Lanson had thanked the man and ridden up the road, but as he crested the hill he knew it was futile to give chase. He had no idea which way she might have gone. Or why he should want to follow if he did know.

A tug on his arm brought his thoughts back to the present. He looked down to see Vallia beaming on him her toothless grin, pulling at his sleeve and trying to climb into his lap.

"She loves you," said Volanna, smiling as he took the child in his arms, "and so do my husband and myself. You saved our daughter's life and gave her back to us. We will be forever grateful to you."

"I will always treasure your gratitude, and even more your for-giveness. It makes my blood run cold to think I could have ruined all by killing her father."

At that moment King Umberland stood and signaled his herald to rap the hall to silence. "Ladies, gentlemen, knights, and guests," he began, "I thank you for your presence tonight. We have much to cele-brate, and this feast has been a mere token of my appreciation to those of you who have made this celebration possible.

"First, I thank the many of you who refused to join Brendal in his war against King Aradon's attempt to liberate this kingdom. And I thank you knights and captains of the army of Meridan—Sir Denmore, Sir Llewenthane, and others who led Meridan's army to a quick victory over Brendal. And I thank my dear, brave, and loyal friend Sir Werthen, who escaped from Lord Caldemone's estate, where we were imprisoned, and made his way afoot and in hiding to Aradon in Meridan.

"And lastly I owe thanks to King Aradon for many reasons. As I lay for long days in Caldemone's dungeon, hope of rescue began to dim. I will never forget yesterday morning when I awakened as I had done every day for many weeks, dreading with a sickness of heart another day in that cramped, darkened cell. I had been awake only for minutes when angry shouts and the ring of steel met my ears, followed soon by the tread of feet in the corridor. You can imagine my surprise when King Aradon, Sir Denmore, Sir Llewenthane, and Sir Olstan appeared like phantoms at my cell door, unlocked it, and brought me out of my prison and here to my throne.

"And you can imagine my elation when I heard that Brendal and Caldemone had already been overthrown, and I could claim my crown again, a gift from all the men I am honoring tonight. I thank you, one and all. I shall never forget what you have done for me and the Kingdom of Vensaur.

"I have but one more thing to tell you, then the evening is yours. Tonight I am pleased to announce my intention to bring the Kingdom of Vensaur into the Seven Kingdom federation."

Immediately the hall erupted in applause and cheers as King Umberland motioned for King Aradon to stand with him. After the noise subsided, Aradon spoke to the crowd.

"Most noble King Umberland, citizens of Vensaur, and guests. The confidence and goodwill you have expressed to me and my men tonight is most gratifying and humbling. May this joining of hands between our kingdoms be long and fruitful, and may the Seven Kingdoms stand as long as they serve to bring honor to the Master of the Universe.

"I wish now to introduce to all of you the third king in our midst tonight," Aradon continued. "Prince Lanson, will you stand please." Lanson stood. "This man is not really *Prince* Lanson; he is rightfully *King* Lanson, designated ascendant to the throne of Lochlaund on the death of his father, King Kor." Many in the hall gasped at the news. Few had heard that King Kor was dead.

"The Kingdom of Lochlaund is presently suffering under the

rule of a usurper who has hidden the fact that Kor is dead and is ruling in his name. Since Kor was overthrown by an internal palace coup, I believe this usurper can be deposed without the force of an army. Lanson can return and claim his throne because the army of Lochlaund will not fight against its own prince, though he will need protection against the plotters within the palace. King Lanson, if you will ride to Macrennon Castle, I offer to you without condition and without any reciprocal requirement, two hundred men at your command to secure your throne in Lochlaund. As to whether Lochlaund should join the federation of the Seven Kingdoms, you are free to make that decision with no pressure from me."

Again the crowd applauded as King Aradon took his chair and Lanson rose to speak to the hall.

"I thank you, King Aradon, for your generous offer. I do accept it with deep gratitude. As to the question of whether I will align Lochlaund with the Seven Kingdoms, it is my strong inclination to honor the intention of my father and vow fealty to you as our high king. However, Lochlaund has been deceived into believing that you were my father's murderer, and I would not outrage them with confederation before I clear the misunderstanding. I must first set things right in my own kingdom."

"I commend you for your wisdom and bid you Godspeed," replied Aradon.

Two days later Meridan's army had the trebuchet, the cat, and the battering ram dismantled and loaded onto wagons. Aradon and Volanna bade farewell to Umberland and Lanson, then left with their army and returned to Meridan.

Lanson, riding with the two hundred mounted warriors who had volunteered from Aradon's army, set out for the north on the same day. As he rode through the gates of Ensovandor Castle and up the road where Evalonne was last seen, his heart grew heavy. He tried to shut out all thoughts of her, but they stormed his will and flooded his mind—the lilting songs she would sing as she stirred the campfire, the shimmering glory of her hair falling softly on her neck and shoulders, the breathtaking loveliness of her face and form, the glow in her eyes as she nursed Mossette, her trilling laughter echoing like golden bells among the trees, as well as the softness of her gaze when she looked at him. He chided himself for missing the girl so much and resolved to strengthen his will against such thoughts. The kirk was right. The loveliness of women was a snare—a temptation too strong for a man's will to resist. It was a blessing that she was gone. Now he could forget her and turn his thoughts back toward his dedication to the Master of the Universe.

CHAPTER TWENTY-SIX

RETURN TO LOCHLAUND

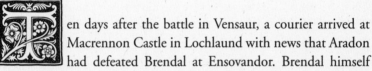en days after the battle in Vensaur, a courier arrived at Macrennon Castle in Lochlaund with news that Aradon had defeated Brendal at Ensovandor. Brendal himself was dead, and Prince Lanson was riding toward Lochlaund with two hundred of Aradon's soldiers at his back. Bishop Hugal did all he could to quell the panic this news ignited among the conspirators. He told them they could gather Lochlaund's army and hold Macrennon against Lanson, but his words went unheeded. Since the death of King Kor—and Hugal's attempt to foster the belief that the king was alive but gravely ill—many of the prominent merchants and tradesmen in the town had become distrustful of the "protectors" in their king's castle. One could see it in the stony glare, the down curl of a lip, and the leaden silence that greeted any new edict announced from the castle. The conspirators doubted that they could raise a large army or a loyal one, and the morning after the courier arrived, Hugal found that every one of them had fled in the night, leaving him alone to face the return of Prince Lanson.

Thus no battle awaited Lanson as he and Aradon's men rode into Macrennon. The drawbridge of the castle was down, and the guards at the gatehouse waved him inside. He dismounted in the courtyard and, with twenty of Aradon's men, walked into the keep, where servants bowed to him and Bishop Hugal waited for him at the door of the throne hall, robed in gray with his cowl over his head, hiding his face in shadows.

"Welcome home, my prince," said the bishop, bowing low. "Your safe return is the Master's answer to many a heartfelt petition. Long have we sought for news of your whereabouts, and many have been sent in search of you. Your return will bring joy to the people of Lochlaund."

"I thank you, Bishop Hugal," replied Lanson. "Where are those who murdered my father? I expected a welcome of steel and arrows."

"And so it would have been had they not received news that your return was accompanied by Aradon's warriors. They fled in the night, may the Master be praised."

"And you, Bishop Hugal, why have they spared you?"

"It seems that even the most hardened of heathens often fear to bring harm to a kirkman. And by fortune or providence, on that infamous night of the murder, I had temporarily left the hall, and the insidious attack occurred before I returned. Rather than kill me, they made me a prisoner right here in this castle and used my knowledge of the kingdom and its affairs to good effect as they took over the government."

"You mean that you actually helped them in their takeover?"

"You might say that in a sense, I did, your highness. At first I had no choice. They forced me at sword point to aid them. But I soon found that I was able to temper many of their judgments and preserve much of your father's ways. And as I gained their confidence, I continually looked for any opportunity to turn the usurpers out of the castle."

"The usurpers apparently perpetuated the lie that my father was still alive," Lanson said. "Once in the Kingdom of Oranth I overheard soldiers looking for me, ostensibly to return me to my father."

"Yes. May the prince forgive me, for that little deception was of my own devising. I thought it best for the kingdom that all should think their king yet alive. I did not want Lochlaund's enemies to see any opportunity in the turmoil of our inner devastation."

Lanson noticed that Bishop Hugal leaned heavily on a walking cane and was beginning to tremble. The kirkman's voice seemed weaker than the prince remembered and had a bit of a rasp to it.

"Are you well, Bishop Hugal? And if I may be so bold as to ask, why do you wear your cowl over your head?"

"I cover my head in deference to a vow I have taken, the substance of which must remain between myself and the Master of the Universe. I will remove the hood when the terms of the vow are fulfilled. As to my wellness, I admit that I am a little tired, my prince. I fear that the death of your father and the ordeal of the past weeks have taken their toll on my stamina. If we could merely sit, I would tell you all that has happened since your departure."

"Thank you, Bishop Hugal. I will avail you of that service at a later time. I need to get Aradon's men quartered and settle into my chambers."

"Very well, your highness. And we must see to your coronation at the earliest opportunity. The people will rejoice to see you on your father's throne." Bishop Hugal bowed and started to depart when Lanson called after him.

"What can you tell me of Sir Maconnal?"

"We have neither seen nor heard anything of him since he departed on a mission for your late father shortly before his murder."

"Very well. Thank you, Bishop Hugal."

The bishop bowed a little awkwardly, leaning heavily on his cane, and Lanson watched him as he walked away stiffly and slowly, as if each movement brought pain. Lanson wondered vaguely if all the answers Hugal had given him squared solidly with reality, but the issues were complex, and at the moment too many things pressed his mind to pursue the thought. He wondered about Maconnal. Had he received Lanson's message and stayed clear of Macrennon? Or had he missed the message, returned unaware of the danger, and perished at the hands of the usurpers?

❧

The coronation was held one week later, and Bishop Hugal placed the crown of Lochlaund upon the new king's head. As King Lanson's reign began, the bishop appeared often in the throne hall, always cowled and leaning heavily on his cane, to advise and guide the young monarch to render judgments and uphold standards for conduct approved by the kirk.

Yet when the new king had freedom to render judgments on

matters not constrained by the kirk, it soon became clear to the citizens of Lochlaund that he had a heart for the people. One of his first judgments was of a case in which a candlemaker had been imprisoned because he could not pay the tax levied during the reign of the usurpers. King Lanson judged the tax to be double what it should have been and not only halved it but gave the man ninety more days to pay. This case prompted him to investigate the prisons of the city, in which he found many whom the usurpers had locked into filthy cells for failure to pay exorbitant tax levies. He reduced the taxes to reasonable levels, forgave the tax entirely for many who had become impoverished by their incarceration, and gave the others reasonable time to pay. When news of poverty came to him, he had food drawn and distributed from the royal granaries. He allowed limited hunting and fishing in the royal forests and streams where it had been prohibited by the usurpers. And to the great delight and relief of the poorest of Lochlaund, he passed a law in the Hall of Knights that strictly limited the terms of indenture, increased the minimum payment for indentured servitude, and placed restrictive and humane rules on the treatment of indentured servants.

Such decisions drew reproof from Bishop Hugal. Though they did not violate specifically any doctrine or ordinance of the kirk, he warned of the danger of making the lives of the people too easy. "Without stones in their paths, they can develop no spiritual muscles," he had said. But Lanson in his exile had trod those paths himself and pointed out that they were already strewn with enough stones that most peasants could build their mansions in heaven with them. There was no need to add more. When Lanson said such things, Hugal would withdraw into silence, or he would tell Lanson in a voice tense with restrained anger that he was not following the path of his father, who would never make decisions that incurred the disapproval of the kirk. Such criticism stung the young king at first, for he had no intention of defying the kirk or dishonoring his father. But his course was set. His time among the people had stamped their struggles indelibly on his mind, and he would devote his reign to relieving them of what burdens he could. Once the people of Lochlaund saw that the new king had their good at heart, they warmed to him, and their anxiety about the future began to dissipate.

But in judgments involving the kirk's moral restrictions, King Lanson followed the law to the letter. One afternoon as he sat on his throne, a gray-robed kirkman brought into the hall a young chargirl. She stumbled forward, her hands chained in front of her. Lanson asked for the charge, and the kirkman said the woman had been caught in a stable at noontime holding and kissing a stable hand. The evidence was conclusive and unassailable. After eating a quick lunch, the woman had entered the shed where the young man was working. The kirkman had followed and found the couple in the kiss. He had caught the woman, but the man had escaped.

"They have engaged in unfitting behavior, your majesty," said the kirkman. "They have violated the kirk's ordinance against public displays of affection between men and women. The woman should be put in stocks for a day as a public example of what happens when people flout the law of the kirk." Lanson, having experienced the powerful lure of a woman himself, did not need the advice of Hugal to sentence the girl. He ordered her to be placed in the stocks until sundown. He would do all he could to prevent his kingdom from sliding down the slope of moral corruption into utter alienation from the Master.

King Lanson had been on Lochlaund's throne no more than a month before he began to hear hints from his knights and aides, and even from some of the merchants and tradesmen who had dealings with him, that he should find a queen and get about the task of siring an heir. "We don't want a war over succession," they would say, or, "When the king is fruitful, the land prospers," or, "Have you noticed the Lady Maguaine? She would make a fine queen for Lochlaund, don't you think?" And there was no shortage of counts and earls eager to introduce their daughters to him. Lanson turned all such hints aside. Though he tried hard to shut it out, the image of Evalonne so haunted his nights that he could muster no interest in other women.

Bishop Hugal, with his nose to the air catching the scent of every sentiment emanating from the minds of the people, knew that pressure was building for the king to marry. On a summer morning six weeks after Lanson's coronation, he came to the young king and reminded him of his father's desire that his son would marry the bishop's niece Lamonda. Lanson was in general becoming immune to Hugal's admonitions to follow the path of his father. He could see that such appeals were largely the bishop's attempts to manipulate him into imposing his own policies on the kingdom. But as he listened to the bishop, he remembered that the match with Lamonda was one of the last wishes his father had expressed to him. Indeed, the contract would have been signed already had the king not been murdered.

In deference to his late father, Lanson acceded to Hugal's urging and resumed his relationship with Lady Lamonda. Or rather, he allowed her to resume her relationship with him. But he found that his heart would not open to admit the countess, for it was filled continually with the fair image of Evalonne, a comparison from which Lamonda suffered like a wasp to a butterfly. For her part, Lamonda was eager to become queen of the kingdom and began to push Lanson hard to set a date for the wedding. But he could not bring himself to do it, finding one excuse after another that made every time she proposed impossible.

Early one morning Lanson finished his breakfast and went to the library, intending to review some of the laws of the kirk that Bishop Hugal had invoked the day before. As he entered the library door his jaw dropped and his eyes widened like saucers. At the table with a book opened in front of him sat Sir Maconnal, looking ready to begin the morning's lesson just as in the days of Lanson's education.

"Maconnal! What . . . what are you doing here? Where have you been?"

Instead of answering, Maconnal rose to his feet and walked to where the king stood dumfounded. He opened his arms and the two friends embraced.

"I owe you my life, King Lanson. When I—"

"Please, Maconnal, you are my dearest friend. Drop the title and call me Lanson."

"Thank you, sire. I will obey except when public protocol demands the respect of formality. Now, let's take our old chairs, and for today's lesson I will tell you my story, though it's a simple one. But first, let me express my deep regret at the death of your father. He was a good king and a good friend. I know you miss him sorely."

"Thank you, Maconnal. Yes, I do miss him."

"As I began to say, I owe you my life. While returning from your late father's mission to the southern continent, I stopped at the Hathfield Inn in Stoneledge of Meridan, as is my wont. The innkeeper gave me your note warning me not to return to Lochlaund, so instead I turned into Oranth and journeyed to the estate of my old friend Lord Kenmarl, an earl of Oranth. I had been his guest for a fortnight when news came that Aradon had defeated Brendal and reinstated Umberland as King of Vensaur. We heard nothing more until a week ago when a messenger came with the news that Lochlaund's usurpers had fled and Kor's son Lanson had been crowned king. Immediately I left Kenmarl and came here.

"I arrived last night some two hours after sundown. You had retired to your chambers. The lord chamberlain wanted to inform you of my arrival immediately, but I insisted that he not. I needed the night's rest before seeing you. Though the tables had long been cleaned of dinner, the serving woman Alenia insisted on feeding me, and as I ate she gave me all the news I had missed. She told me of how you saved Aradon's daughter and by your own sword ended the tyranny of Brendal. You have done the Seven Kingdoms a great service."

Lanson glowed inwardly at the praise. His teacher's approval meant much to him.

"At my request," continued Maconnal, "Alenia awoke me early this morning and got my breakfast. I had planned to come to you in the throne hall, but wanting to display her newfound ability to read, she checked today's docket and found that you were to be in the library. This Alenia is a remarkable servant, by the way. Before I left I had just begun to teach her to read, and during the weeks of my absence, she has made remarkable progress entirely on her own. The woman has a good mind and a good heart. She may be worthy of serving you in some more responsible position."

"I am so happy that you are back, Maconnal. With all the turmoil and upheaval in the Seven Kingdoms, I was afraid you might have perished. I need you as my advisor."

"I am honored, sire. And I will be delighted to serve you in any way I can."

From that day forward, Lanson and Maconnal met every morning for breakfast, after which Lanson would practice an hour with the swords while Maconnal instructed Alenia in the library. Afterward they would meet in the throne hall, where Lanson would take up his duties as king with Maconnal as his primary advisor.

One morning about a fortnight after Maconnal's return, while the two men were at their breakfast, Maconnal turned to Lanson and said, "From what Alenia has told me, you have not been consistent in some of the judgments you rendered before I came."

"What judgments are you speaking of?"

"Didn't you place a young woman in stocks for kissing a boy?"

"Yes, I did. Such behavior violates the law of the kirk."

"Didn't I advise you to kiss a girl yourself?"

"You did, but I learned by my own experience that it was poor advice."

"By your own experience? What on earth are you talking about?"

Lanson became silent, looking at his hands folded on the table. Then he sighed deeply and said, "I met a young woman while escaping to Vensaur. I agreed to conduct her safely to Ensovandor in exchange for her help with Aradon's daughter. We traveled together for almost two weeks. Twice on this journey I found myself strongly attracted to this woman. Indeed, to my shame, I almost succumbed to her charm, and even now it takes all my will to force her image from my mind. Against an allure so strong as that of women, one must never give in to the most seemingly innocent dalliance. No kiss or touch is safe."

"What were your feelings toward this woman?"

"I pitied her. Though she is perhaps a year or two younger than

I, she has seen more tragedy and ill-use than most of us see in a lifetime, the worst of which was the loss of her own child, a loss which almost brought her down. I felt sorry for her and did all I could to give her comfort on our journey."

"Lanson, did you love her?" Maconnal asked, looking hard into his friend's eyes.

Unable to meet his friend's steady gaze, the young king toyed with a sliver of beef on his plate. "I could not allow myself to love her, though had I not been a prince, and had she not been . . . well . . . unmarried when she had the child and, uh, ill-used by so many men, I could have come to love her."

"I do believe you are a snob, King Lanson."

"A snob? I think not!" Lanson looked up and spoke a little huffily.

"You are the high and pure king of a nation, while she is merely a lowly peasant, and one with an unseemly past. Therefore she is far beneath the exalted atmosphere of your ethereal existence and unworthy of your royal attention. Isn't that it?"

"Of course not! I cannot choose a bride solely for my own selfish pleasure. I must consider what is appropriate to the nation of Lochlaund and what the kirk will approve."

"And what the kirk will approve? Perhaps you should consider the standards of a higher court. What will the Master of the Universe approve? Are some persons of more value to him than others? How much more is a king worth to him than a peasant?"

Lanson stared out the window. "Of course you are right. The Master makes no distinction of worth between king or peasant, saint or harlot. But I cannot simply ignore the edict of the kirk. I have tested those waters enough lately with minor judgments to know what a storm I will stir if I oppose the bishop in a matter of this magnitude."

"I'm not asking you how difficult it might be—I'm asking you what is right."

"On the subject of women, the kirk is right. Their danger to men is real. Their appeal is almost more than the strongest will can resist."

"Lanson, I do believe you are hiding behind the laws of the kirk. You are in love with this girl."

"Not so. As I told you, I did not allow myself to love her."

"Then why can't you forget her? Why do you let the mere thought of her erect a barrier between you and your betrothed?"

"How did you . . . ? What do you mean? What barrier?"

"The barrier that keeps you from setting a wedding date with Lady Lamonda."

Lanson got up from the table, walked to the window, and ran his hand through his hair in agitation. "I don't know. Perhaps I do love Evalonne. But if so, it is to my discredit. And there are reasons other than her past or social strata. As my father pointed out to me, Lamonda is an upright woman with all the attributes of a good queen. The fact that I cannot warm toward her does not mean that she would not be the best wife for me. My heart turned toward Evalonne simply because being with her brought such joy. And I know this is wrong. To desire a thing simply because it pleases me is surely self-serving. I must root out of my mind all thoughts of Evalonne. It would not be right to wed Lamonda while I secretly harbor an illicit desire for another woman."

"So the desire for joy is illicit and self-serving?" A touch of exasperation tightened Maconnal's voice.

"You know the answer to that better than I." Lanson began to pace back and forth as he spoke. "The Master of the Universe has put a fence around pleasure. Pleasure tends to lead men and women away from him, so he has placed all things pleasurable inside the fence and forbade us to seek them, lest we succumb to the tug of pleasure and get drawn to our destruction."

"Lanson, the kirk has done a great disservice by distorting what the Master of the Universe intends for us. Yes, since the Fall weakened man's will, pleasure has become a danger. It is fenced not because it is wrong, but because it is *strong*. The fence is not erected to forbid but to protect. It has a gate through which we may legitimately enter. Think of pleasure as a spirited stallion too strong for man's weakened will to control. It must be tamed or it will carry us for a ride we cannot stop, throwing us in the end. But we do not forbid the riding of horses because there is danger in it. We learn to control the animal's power. And when we learn such control, the riding of horses is both beneficial and exhilarating."

"But as you say, we are fallen. Our weakened wills could use some protection."

"Yes, but in its efforts to protect us, the kirk has gone much too far. It strives to keep us safe by forbidding everything that has any hint of danger in it. Drunkenness is wrong, so they forbid drinking. Gluttony is wrong, so they forbid the eating of anything savory. They fear the power of music, so they consign the kirk to singing tuneless, doleful chants without lutes or harps or flutes. Adultery and fornication are wrong, so they forbid the acknowledgment of any pleasure in the way of a man with a maid. As a result, our image of the Master is horribly distorted. We see him with a frown on his face, dangling virtually irresistible pleasure and beauty before us and glaring down with disapproval when we are drawn to them like honeybees to cherry blossoms. Lanson, it is not the Master but the kirk that denies us the experience of pleasure. Pleasure and beauty are gifts from him, given for our delight. He wants his creation to be joyful, to live in love and beauty, to be ecstatic with the life he has given. He urges caution, not denial."

"How can you dismiss the doctrines of the kirk so easily?" asked Lanson.

"I don't dismiss them easily. In my early days, I intended to become a cleric. I even entered a monastery near my home in Rhondilar, where I spent every spare hour in the library delving into the old scrolls. I would read the scrolls in the abbey library here in Macrennon if Hugal would allow it."

"Why won't Hugal allow it?"

"When I came to Lochlaund after being expelled from the monastery in Rhondilar, news of it was sent ahead to Bishop Hugal."

"You've never told me of this. I did not even know that you had a religious bent, much less a religious education. Why were you expelled?"

"It was a result of my time in the monastery library. I found that many of the kirk's doctrines were not supported by the scrolls—mainly that the kirk prohibited many practices that the scrolls did not. In those scrolls I found that every teaching, every law, every warning of the Master had but one purpose—to bring man into joy.

I began to question many of the kirk's rules and laws, asking why they ventured so far from the intent of the scrolls. But instead of answering, they got rid of me."

"I don't understand," said Lanson. "I have read most of the old scrolls myself—Sentacian, Branamour, Perendiel, and Rullendia—and as far as I can tell, the kirk upholds every detail of every law in them."

"These men wrote much later than you have been taught. You have not read the original scrolls; you have read only scrolls about the scrolls—scrolls written deliberately to obscure and shift the meaning of the originals. The originals have all the earmarks of having been written by men guided by the Master of the Universe himself."

"Maconnal, this is incredible. If I did not know you, I would think you were either a liar or a lunatic. Why would the kirk hide the original scrolls and write laws that do not square with them?"

"The reason is to protect us from a truth too dangerous to acknowledge. And given the kirk's mind-set, the reason is plausible, even noble. One of the monks in the abbey of Rhondilar, a kind and wise man, and the only one to defend me in my examination for expulsion, came to my cell the night I was packing my things to leave. He sat me down and told me that what I had found in the old scrolls was true, but it was a truth that must be kept from the people for their own good. The central truth of the original scrolls is that the Master has given man an immense amount of freedom. That truth must be kept from fallen man because he is not able to bear it, he said. Man is too depraved to be trusted with the kind of freedom the Master allows. It would destroy him. The taste of a little would lead him to crave more. Lured by beauty, he would plunge into pleasure, lose all sense of restraint, turn away from the Master, and descend into utter destruction."

"But isn't that true?" asked Lanson.

"Yes, it is. Freedom is the very doom that has destroyed the civilizations of the past. So the kirk deemed that the only way to save the Seven Kingdoms was to severely restrict freedom. Denounce all beauty, fence off all pleasure, and make it an untouchable evil. Better a bland, humdrum, gray, constricted life of stability than one rampant with the mindless, unrestrained pursuit of joy that leads to certain disaster. The kirk saw no middle ground. The least slip would plunge one over the edge. Therefore all pleasure and beauty were painted as temptations designed to test man's fidelity to the Master.

"There is truth in what the man told me. Remove freedom and you do stabilize society, because freedom has always been the bane of man. But freedom is also the blessing of man. His capacity to choose gives him significance and makes him something more than a mere spoke in the wheel of the universe. The Master took a great risk in giving man the freedom that could bring him to either glory or destruction. But he thought it worth the risk. He does not require that we live safely but boldly—to take the risk and grasp the good he offers."

"So he did not create beauty and pleasure as lures to test our fidelity?"

"Not at all. Beauty and pleasure are reflections of the Master himself. He is the ultimate beauty—the source of all joy and delight—and in the beauty and pleasure he gave us, we experience something of him. Beauty and pleasure are not temptations; they are beams from his own glory. We are not to deny these rays of his light that glow all around us, but let our hearts travel up them until we delight in the ultimate source of all delight."

"Why have you never told me these things?" Lanson was incredulous.

"At first I had a duty to your father. I could not violate his confidence in me by undermining beliefs he held to be true. But when he began to question some of the kirk's hard policies himself, I fed him more and more of what I had learned. And I had just begun to feed you from the same trencher before fate intervened."

"The sum of all you say is that I should marry for love and not for duty."

"It is not my place to tell you whom to marry. Nor is it anyone else's."

"Well, it hardly matters, does it?" sighed Lanson. "For one thing, I do not know where Evalonne is. And what is more serious, she is a felon. The kirk is pursuing her not for a mere dalliance but for committing an offense worthy of death. Should I as king defy the kirk and commute that sentence?"

"One of the primary teachings of the old scrolls is mercy. The

Master himself pardoned a woman caught in the very act of adultery."

"But we've been taught that mercy is a danger. If we do not enforce the penalty for disobedience, what incentive do people have to obey?"

"You've put your finger on the big question. Mercy seems to undermine obedience, yet the old scrolls show that the Master chose to extend mercy. The kirk, on the other hand, has chosen to punish disobedience without exception. You, the new king, are in a unique position to decide by which of these principles you will rule your nation. And I have a premonition that you will be called upon to make that decision soon." Maconnal looked at Lanson cryptically.

"What do you mean? Are you a prophet as well as a theologian?"

"A premonition is not a prophecy. I mean nothing specific. But I can see the cloud hovering on the horizon and it's blowing in your direction. May I request a boon from you, my king?"

Lanson struck a theatrical pose and spoke in stentorian tones. "Ask and it shall be granted, my good man, even up to the half of my kingdom."

"Since you are so generous, I will double my request. First, I beseech you to continue to put off your wedding date. Second, I ask that you send me on a quest."

"Denied. I cannot do without you."

"Would you please hear me out before giving your answer? Send me on a quest to find this Evalonne who dominates your mind. If I do not find her within two months, I will return and you can proceed to wed Lamonda. If I do find her—well, you will have some hard decisions to make. What do you say, your majesty?"

Lanson gazed out the window the span of a dozen breaths before he turned to Maconnal. "Your request is granted, and I will comply with the terms. I will not settle any wedding plans with Lamonda for two months, or until you return with Evalonne, whichever comes first."

The next day Maconnal made certain discreet inquiries and made it known quietly in certain quarters that he was looking for a beautiful, red-haired, green-eyed woman. Two days later he left for the Kingdom of Oranth.

CHAPTER TWENTY-SEVEN

THE GAME

Lamonda sat in her chambers. Her eyes stared without seeing at the open book on her lap as her fingers fidgeted with the pages. The book was a commentary on the kirk fathers' regulations governing courtship and marriage, its heavy boards bound in leather and gilded with gold leaf on the embossed title. Her uncle Hugal had brought the book to her from the abbey library. On the table at the end of the room, a supper was set with chairs and place settings for two. Traces of steam drifted from the covered dish in the center.

Suddenly she stood and hurled the book across the room. Its leaves flapped in the air until it thudded against the wall and fell to the floor, its pages crumpled and bent. She began to pace about the room, her face hard as stone and her hands balled into fists. *What is wrong with that man? Why won't he let me set a date for the wedding?* She had asked him again that very morning, offering two dates three months from now. But again, Lanson had found some lame excuse—something about attending a tournament in Valomar—and she had turned on her heel and stalked out of the room. Had he been any man but the King of Lochlaund, she would not have put up with such elusiveness. But she was careful not to push his patience so far as to risk his breaking off the engagement. She would endure the humiliation for now, but when she became queen, he would be the one who did the enduring. She would see to it. And where was Griselda? She should have arrived ten minutes ago.

At that moment a knock came at the door and she heard her friend's voice calling from the other side.

"Where have you been?" demanded Lamonda as she unbolted the door and Griselda hefted her considerable bulk into the room. "Don't you know that punctuality is one of the Master's—"

"Oh, get off your lectern," said Griselda with a wave of her hand. "You should have been a man so you could be a monk or a bishop yourself."

"It's hard to distinguish your insults from your compliments. But no matter. What do you have to tell that's so important you had to see me tonight?"

"Like I said in my note, I think I know why King Lanson will not set a wedding date. But it can wait. I'm starving. I'll tell you as we eat." Griselda made straight for the table. Her news was too big simply to drop without whetting Lamonda's desire to hear it.

But Lamonda knew how to play Griselda's game. She would puncture the girl's smug self-satisfaction by showing no particular interest in this news of hers. Griselda could be insufferable, and her pride needed to be brought low. As the two women sat and began their meal, Griselda spouted all the requisite small talk and made all the proper polite inquiries into family welfare, hoping to see her friend beg or demand that she get on with the telling of her secret. But Lamonda outplayed Griselda at the game, and finally it was Griselda who could not wait to spill her story.

"You know that I have an uncle in Meridan, I think."

"I've heard you mention him," Lamonda replied.

"Well, we just learned that he was a warrior in King Aradon's army at the siege of Ensovandor. You see, my father just came home from a trip to Meridan, and you will not believe what my uncle told him." Griselda took a huge bite of goose and chewed deliberately as she waited for Lamonda to prod her on. But Lamonda merely picked at her own plate, betraying no interest at all.

"King Lanson was at Ensovandor too, you know," Griselda went on. "Except he wasn't king yet. At least, not officially. Anyway, my uncle was there when Lanson killed Brendal to save King Aradon's baby daughter. And as Lanson took the child and ran from Brendal's men, he saw a beautiful flame-haired woman come to him—a woman Lanson obviously knew very well—and he handed the babe to her so he could draw his sword and defend himself." Again Griselda loaded her mouth with a generous helping of goose, and again Lamonda forced herself to remain silent. But Griselda glanced up at her friend and exulted in what she saw. Lamonda's eyes were wide and her lips slightly parted in obvious shock. Griselda swallowed, took a sip of mead, wiped her mouth, and continued.

"Then on the next day, my uncle was at the guardhouse when who but Prince Lanson himself came out and asked the guards if they had seen the red-haired girl leave the castle. He described her in great detail. And when the guard told him he had seen just such a girl leave the gatehouse the day before, the prince seemed quite distraught and asked all manner of questions about which direction she went, who she was with, and what time she left." Griselda inserted a whole leg of the goose in her mouth and slipped the meat from the bone with her teeth, chewing deliberately while Lamonda looked as if she were standing on the edge of a cliff.

"Well, go on!" said Lamonda.

Griselda had won the upper hand. She swallowed and took another sip of mead before she continued. "Naturally, by then my uncle was quite curious about the girl, so he made a few inquiries of his own and you will never guess what he found out." She paused and began to take another bite, but Lamonda put a restraining hand on her arm.

"What did he find out?" she demanded.

"I hate to tell you this, Lamonda, and ordinarily I wouldn't, but it's something I feel you really need to know. He found that Lanson had traveled with this girl from the north of Oranth all the way to Vensaur. They were alone, together, for over a fortnight. Can you believe it? And rumor has it that he has fallen in love with her, which could be true, given the way he was asking after her."

"Just how did your uncle learn all this?"

"He asked guards, soldiers, servants in the castle, whoever he could. But the worst news is yet to come. I'm not supposed to tell you this, but you have a right to know. I've been told by someone who should know that King Lanson has just ordered Sir Maconnal to begin a search for a peasant girl with red hair and green eyes named Evalonne. And furthermore that—"

"Where did you hear such a thing?"

"I'm sorry, I really can't say. But as I told you, it's from someone who should know."

"Rumors! Lies! The whole thing is preposterous. Why would the King of Lochlaund pursue a peasant girl?"

"Why would you think?" Griselda arched her eyebrows. "They say she is a rare beauty."

"As if that should matter to an upright king."

"Well, I wouldn't know about all that. But you have to admit, it does much to explain why he won't set a wedding date."

Lamonda glared at Griselda as she nonchalantly stuffed her mouth with yet another bite of goose. As Lamonda thought on it, her friend's story seemed all too plausible. It fit closely with many things she had seen and heard in the past few weeks since Lanson's return. And considering his outrageous behavior toward her on the balcony the night of King Kor's murder, it was not hard to believe his head could be turned by a pretty country wench. How could Lanson do this to her?

For the rest of the evening Lamonda said little while her friend chatted on in smug satisfaction, knowing her news had stirred Lamonda to the core. The game had begun poorly for her, but she had won it after all. She left early in the evening after cheerfully admonishing her stricken friend not to worry. All would come out well in the end.

As soon as the door closed on Griselda, a guttural cry tore from Lamonda's throat as she kicked the book on the floor and sent it tumbling across the room, its pages flapping about like the wings of a wounded bird. She yelled for her servant to come and remove the remains of the meal, then threw herself into her chair and glared at the one candle still burning in the room. What was the idiot Lanson thinking? If he thought he could slip this voluptuous wench into his life and see her on the side without consequences, he was a fool as well as a felon. She would find it out and never let him forget it. It would be her key to utter control over him for the rest of their life together. But what if he was thinking of wedding this girl instead of her? No! The idea was absurd. Yet he consistently refused to set a wedding date, and such procrastination would be needless if he wanted the harlot merely as a mistress.

In the morning I will tell Uncle Hugal of this, she thought as she got up from her chair and dressed for bed. But sleep eluded her. She writhed and twisted as she thought of a thousand ways she would make Lanson do penance for this deed after they were wed. But finally her anger burned to exhaustion and she slipped into the realm of dreams. She found herself sitting beside Lanson on the throne of Lochlaund when a prophet from the mountains entered the great hall. He was dressed in rags, his hair and beard were foul and unkempt, and his eyes glared with the anger of a god. The hall went silent and all eyes followed him as he marched toward the dais. Slowly he raised a bony arm toward the throne and Lamonda blanched with fear.

"You!" the prophet thundered as his skeletal fingers pointed toward Lanson beside her. "You are not fit to be king, for you have committed the abomination of adultery against your kingdom and against your queen."

Lamonda's fear vanished as Lanson sank deep into the cushions of his throne, his eyes wide and his hands shaking in terror.

"Seize him!" boomed the prophet.

Immediately guards converged on Lanson, bound him, and led him away. His terrified eyes turned toward Lamonda, and he wailed loud, sniveling pleas for mercy and forgiveness. But Lamonda sat unmoved with her chin thrust forward, gazing down at him in cold contempt.

"What would you have us do with the man?" asked the prophet.

"Bring me his head in a basket," replied Lamonda.

The prophet bowed and gave the order, and moments later a guard brought in the basket, blood seeping through its woven reeds and dripping on the stone floor. He held the grisly thing toward her, and she leaned forward to look inside. She shuddered with disgust at the stare of the cold dead eyes in the severed head.

"Take it away," she said and breathed a long sigh of relief.

Moments later Lanson's crown was brought in, and the prophet, who somehow was now her uncle Hugal, robed and cowled, took the crown and placed it on her head. A great cry of exultation broke from the people in the hall as they shouted over and over, "Long live Queen Lamonda!"

L

When Lamonda awoke in the morning, the satisfaction of the dream lingered with her as she dressed and prepared to visit her uncle Hugal and tell him what she had learned from Griselda.

Bishop Hugal sat behind the desk in the gloomy shadows of his chambers, the cowl of his gray robe covering his head and shadowing his face in blackness. Lamonda sat on the other side of the table facing him. Thick gray curtains covered the windows, and the only light in the room came from the single taper on his desk. Hugal listened silently and without moving, his hands folded into the robe on his lap as Lamonda repeated the story Griselda had told her.

"You say the girl's name is Evalonne?" he said when she finished. "Very strange, very strange indeed. The name seems familiar to me. Ah, yes, I remember. I believe I have heard the accorder Gronthus speak of such a girl. He is in the abbey at this moment. I shall call him in and hear what he has to say of her."

Gronthus was summoned, and at the name of Evalonne a heavy scowl soured his gaunt features. "Yes, I know of such a woman. She is a fornicator and a harlot. For months she has been a fugitive from the kirk's justice, escaping through Oranth into Vensaur with the help of a wandering swordsman. We lost her trail at the edge of Vensaur, but I now have eyes in Vensaur and Oranth who will report to me anything they hear of this devil's spawn. She will not elude me forever."

As Lamonda listened to Gronthus, she had no doubts about the identity of the wandering swordsman he spoke of, and anger reddened her face like an ember. Griselda had spoken the truth, it seemed.

"Furthermore, the woman is a heretic," continued Gronthus as his hand reached inside his robe. He held up a delicate silver neck chain from which hung a silver pendant in the shape of a flying dove.

"I found this outside her window at an inn in Oranth, apparently ripped from her neck and thrown out."

"Let me have the trinket, if you please." Bishop Hugal held his opened hand toward Gronthus. "I will keep it safe until you need it for evidence at the woman's trial. I thank you for coming in, Gronthus. You may go now."

The accorder hesitated as if reluctant to part with the pendant, but he dropped it into the bishop's hand. He bowed slightly and took his leave.

When the door closed behind him, Lamonda looked into the blackness of Bishop Hugal's hood. "We must do something, Uncle. If Lanson finds this wretched wench who has heated his blood, he may be idiot enough to make her Lochlaund's queen instead of me."

"You have nothing to fear, dear niece. You heard Gronthus: the woman is a fugitive who has committed a capital offense. There is no way the king can defy the kirk and wed such a woman. On that score alone your throne is safe even if we do nothing. But I see a great opportunity here. By taking the right action we can rid the kingdom of this vile creature and put King Lanson under our control for the rest of his life."

"I had already thought of something like that," said Lamonda. "We could let Sir Maconnal find her and bring her to Lochlaund, locate where Lanson keeps her, catch him with her some night, and hold him hostage to our will in exchange for our silence."

"Or there may be a better way," said Hugal. "What if we were to find her before Maconnal does? We could bring her to trial before Lanson himself and he would be forced to condemn her to death by the laws of the kingdom. We would be rid of her and the king would become a virtual puppet of the kirk."

"I like what I hear, dear Uncle. But how can you find her?"

A deep sigh issued from the blackness of the bishop's hood. "I will have to think on that, girl. Forgive me, but I am a bit tired this evening. Please take no offense that I must now ask you to leave me to my rest. I will summon you after I have formed a plan."

"Uncle, I am concerned about your health. I don't think you are well."

"I am well enough—just working and studying too much. Our new king seems intent on flexing his power. He has been going his own way on so many matters it keeps me jumping to review old laws and restrictions I had come to take for granted. But I am well—just tired."

"I'm not sure you are telling me all. Your walk is slower, you often use a cane, you move stiffly, you breathe harder, and I have not seen your face since—"

"I told you I have taken a vow." Hugal's voice rose in irritation.

"And your voice has become a little coarse. Something is wrong that you will not tell me. I shall summon a physician in the morning and—"

"No! You will not summon a physician. You are not listening to me, girl. I am well, and I will thank you to speak no more of it. Now go and let me rest."

"Very well, Uncle. Good night." Lamonda spoke sharply as she rose from her chair and huffed from the room, closing the door hard behind her.

Hugal was not well, and he knew it. He had not been well since he had drunk from the bottle of Rhondilar wine Gronthus had brought him—a gift from a sister in Oranth. Though he had recovered from the initial sickness in a matter of days, the effects had lingered and worsened since. Often in pain, he spent many sleepless hours each evening before his nightly drought of wine took effect.

In the nights following his meeting with Lamonda, he spent those hours thinking on the matter of the fugitive Evalonne. He knew that since Gronthus was seeking the woman—indeed, that finding her had become an obsession with him—there was little need to duplicate the accorder's search. Gronthus's single-minded efficiency at bringing sinners to justice was legendary. He thought his best course was to thwart Maconnal's search lest he find the girl before Gronthus did. But how? For two days he spent his evening hours in thought, sitting in his chair, his hands folded beneath his chin as he stared into the darkened room. Occasionally he idly fingered the silver dove and chain on his desk.

Finally the solution came to him. All he needed was to deceive

Maconnal into thinking Evalonne dead, and he would call off his search. The next morning Hugal sent for a man with whom he had often dealt when needing a task done secretly or outside the bounds of strict legality. The man came to Hugal's chambers the same afternoon. He was a big man, tall with a chest like a barrel and a black patch over his left eye. Bishop Hugal explained what he wanted of him and gave him Evalonne's pendant. The two haggled over price for a few minutes, then Hugal paid the settled amount and sent him on his way.

That evening he dined with Lamonda and told her what he had done.

CHAPTER TWENTY-EIGHT

ThE FUGITIVE

hree days after his promise to King Lanson, Maconnal took leave of his duties and rode south into Oranth. He knew the roads and towns well, having traveled the route often on his way to the port of Vensaur on diplomatic missions for King Kor. His inquiries had produced a lead. A friend had overheard a traveler from Meridan describe a red-haired, green-eyed woman he had seen while returning from the siege of Ensovandor. The friend brought the man to Maconnal, where he had repeated his story.

"Where was this woman when you saw her?" asked Maconnal.

"She was walkin' with a group of travelers goin' north out of Levonwicke. That's the first town north of Ensovandor," the man replied.

"How did you happen to notice her?" asked Maconnal.

"Hardly anyone could forbear lookin' at her, sir. Though her face was bruised up a bit, everyone could see that she was uncommonly beauteous."

"Why was she with the group of travelers? Were they her family or friends?"

"Nay, sir. In fact I was in the group myself. We were all goin' the same direction, and it seemed good to travel together for company and safety."

"Did you talk to the girl? Did she say anything about herself— who she was, where she had been, where she was going?"

"I tried to talk with her. Would like to have got to know her a bit better, if you know what I mean. But she wouldn't say much. Wouldn't keep a conversation goin' with me or anyone else. She was courteous enough, but her eyes had a look like they were seein' things inside her head instead of out in front. After a while we all gave up and left her to herself. As to where she was goin', she never said. The first town we came to after Levonwicke was Dunnestan. I suppose she must have stayed there, because when we gathered to continue our journey the next morning, she wasn't with us."

"Did she give you her name?"

"Yes, she did. I asked her, you know. What was it, now . . . oh, yes. Somethin' like Evalorre, or Evaloren. I can't quite remember exactly, sir."

The man had told Maconnal enough to justify a journey into Oranth. He had thanked the man, given him a silver coin for his trouble, and left for Oranth the next day. He had been on the road for nine days, and from the crest of the last hill he had seen the cottages and buildings of Dunnestan cuddled among the trees and rises in the valley below. He came into the town just before sunset, found the inn, and secured lodging for the night.

The next morning he was on the square asking questions of merchants and vendors as they set up their stands and canopies for the day. He found no dearth of people who remembered seeing a girl of Evalonne's description pass through some weeks ago. "Hers was a face and form a man's not likely to forget," explained one cheeseseller. No one was sure where the woman went, but all agreed that she did not stay in Dunnestan. Two men thought they had seen her walking toward Lorganvale. Maconnal left Dunnestan before noon and rode on to Lorganvale. For the next three days, he followed such clues northward through four villages and out of the Kingdom of Vensaur to Soucroft in Oranth. At Soucroft he got news at an inn of a red-haired woman who had left two days before heading northwest toward Brancester.

He arrived at Brancester in the middle of the day and went directly to the square to begin his questioning. Several vendors remembered a red-haired beauty who had come to the town about three weeks ago looking for work. Some said they had seen the girl on the square since then, and one man insisted he had seen her as recently as three days ago. Maconnal's hopes rose that she could yet be in the city, and he redoubled his efforts to find someone who knew where she might be working.

One man, a seller of apples and pears, claimed to have seen her speaking with the town baker, who had just bought a sack full of apples from him.

"She was wantin' work in his bakery," said the man. "She was tellin' him she could bake with the best of them, and from what I could tell, he seemed interested."

"Which way is the bakery?" asked Maconnal.

"Go down the lane yonder," said the man, pointing as he spoke, "until ye come to the shop of Blaymer the cobbler. Turn right and ye'll find the bakery about five or six doors on yer left. Ye can't miss it."

Maconnal thanked the man, paid for an apple with a copper penny, and headed for the bakery. He did not notice the girl of about twelve who had made a purchase from the appleseller just before Maconnal arrived. She had been standing nearby, listening to every word the two men had spoken. Her name was Mariella, and she was the daughter of the very baker the men had been discussing, sent to the square to purchase another bag of apples. The moment Maconnal turned away, she took a back street and ran the entire distance to her father's shop.

Mariella had immediately liked Evalonne when her father had hired her two weeks ago. But she realized with a child's insight that the young woman hid in her heart a great sadness. And she knew by the way Evalonne often looked behind her that she was in constant fear of being followed. Mariella knew nothing of Evalonne's past, but she could not believe any evil of her and could not imagine that whoever was pursuing her meant her any good. Thus when she arrived at the bakery, she rushed to Evalonne and tried to speak while catching her breath from her run.

"Evalonne, there is some stranger in town lookin' for you. He has asked about you in every shop and stall on the square. And he's on his way to the bakery right now. He'll be here at any moment."

Evalonne's heart froze. "Gronthus!" she said as she tore away her apron and threw it on the board. "Mariella, I must leave this moment. If that man finds me, my life is over."

With fingers flying, she gathered her few things from a corner shelf, bundling them into a parcel as she started for the anteroom. But she stopped cold before she reached the door. She heard voices coming from the room. The baker was speaking with a man whom she did not recognize, but she was sure he must be one of Gronthus's men. Quietly she backed away from the door, pressed herself against the wall, and listened. The baker was telling the man that the woman he was looking for did indeed work for him. She was in the kitchen even now. He would take him to her.

In a panic, Evalonne scrambled up to the loft as Mariella rattled a pile of pans to cover the sound of her feet on the ladder. The men came into the kitchen and looked all about.

"Mariella, where is Evalonne?" the baker asked.

"Um, I think she went out to the storeroom to get a bag of flour."

Maconnal followed the baker out of the kitchen toward the storeroom, and the instant the door closed Evalonne flew down the ladder and ran out the front of the shop into the street. She pushed and dodged her way through the crowd, running until she was out of breath, then walking until she could run again. She turned into side streets and ducked into alleyways until she came to the edge of town. Before she stepped into the road, she took a scarf from her pack and bound it around her hair, then fell in between two clusters of walking travelers as they left the gates of the city.

The farther she got from Brancester, the more the traffic thinned as the varying speed of the walkers tended to break up the clusters. A few yards ahead of her walked a young couple at about the same pace as herself. The man, obviously a farmer, carried in his arms a baby a little older than Mossette. The man often put his arm about the waist of the young woman, and she often took his arm and placed her cheek against it. Once the woman got a pebble in her shoe, and her husband handed the baby to her, knelt and removed the shoe, shook out the pebble, and slipped the shoe on her foot again. After a brief kiss, they resumed their journey. As evening approached, the couple left the road and followed a short trail to their own cottage, nestled in a grove of oaks and pines surrounded by pens and fences—not unlike the cottage of Evalonne's dreams. With bitterness rising in her heart, she forced her eyes away from this display of domestic bliss that she was denied.

She continued on the road alone and arrived at the village of Engleham just before nightfall, where she secured lodging at the inn. The next morning she continued walking northward. Though the road was far from crowded, just enough travelers moved along it to make her feel secure from bandits or predators. She walked through the day, stopping only to eat the food she had packed at the inn and rest her weary feet. As night approached she reached a woods where she left the road and wandered deep among the trees, looking for a safe place to bed down for the night. It was almost dark when she found a hollow beneath a ledge where she built a small fire and curled up to sleep.

But sleep did not come easy. As she huddled lonely and shivering beneath the ledge, the gallery of her mind began to fill with pictures of the domestic bliss she had witnessed—the devoted farm couple on the road, their happiness spilling over into laughter and caresses; the magnificent tableau of Aradon and Volanna after the battle of Ensovandor, a look of utter adoration on his face as his wife hugged their daughter to her breast; her own mother and father, gazing at each other and talking quietly in the firelight glowing from the hearth, a perfect picture of deep contentment. In spite of her resolve to bar Lanson from her mind, she tried to warm herself by fondling the fantasy that it was he who walked with her on the road, laughing and loving. It was he who adored her as she held their own child. It was he who gazed at her in the evening firelight. But instead of warming her, such thoughts only aggravated the ache in her heart. Lanson was gone. He was not hers. He belonged to someone else whom he would adore, touch tenderly, and gaze at in the firelight. Her future as far as she could see it was no different from the present. She was a fugitive and would ever be running and hiding, ever without a home, ever unloved and alone. She drew up her knees, hugged herself tightly, and wept until finally she fell asleep.

Evalonne was still sleeping when the gray of dawn stole into the woods, followed shortly by the barest glint of sunlight touching the tops of the trees. She came awake suddenly, aware of some kind of presence nearby. She could hear the wheezy breath of some creature hovering above her. Though her heart began to beat like the wings of a thrush, she dared not open her eyes. She began to tremble and, fighting a terrible dread of what she might see, opened one eye a mere slit. Looming directly above her was the black hulk of some huge thing—a man, a troll, a monster out of some fable—she could not tell.

She screamed, suddenly and loudly.

A deep, guttural growl came from the creature's throat, and it stepped back a pace in apparent confusion. The movement helped Evalonne's eyes define the shape of the thing, and she could see that it was a man, though a huge one.

"Who are you? What do you want?" she cried.

"I . . . I be Dwag." The words came slow and halting. "And I don't mean to hurtin' you. Uh, I be with the master's sheep out there, you know. And, uh, I smell wood that was been burnin', so I camed to see 'bout it. I don't mean to hurtin' you for sure. No, not at all."

By now Evalonne could make out something of the features of the man. He was very tall and bulky, brown bearded and slack jawed, with deep-set eyes that blinked frequently. He was dressed in simple worker's garb. She knew immediately from his speech and the confused intensity of his gawking stare that Dwag was slow-witted, and her panic subsided. She stood, brushed the leaves from her skirt and bodice, and ran her fingers through her hair.

"Who is your master, Dwag?"

"He be, uhhh, Branwydd."

"Branwydd owns the farm and you work for him?"

"Nooo, Branwydd don't own the farm." Dwag gave out a guttural guffaw as if such an idea were preposterous. "He don't own the farm. Lord Kenmarl own the farm. Branwydd don't own no farm, for sure. Hah-huh-huh!"

"And who is Lord Kenmarl?"

"Ahhhh . . . he is . . . uhhh . . . he is Lord Kenmarl. He own the farm. Branwydd don't own no farm." Dwag grinned as if the idea was the funniest thing he had ever heard.

"I see. Dwag, do you think you could take me to Branwydd?"

"Suurre. I take you to Branwydd. He don't own no farm, but he be a good man, for sure. He give me walnuts, and I cracks them with my hand, like this, see." Dwag took a walnut from his pouch and smashed it between his palms as if it had been a bird's egg. He held the crushed fragments of shell and pulp toward her in his opened hand. "Do ye be hungry?"

Indeed Evalonne was hungry. She had not eaten since noon yesterday. Besides, she thought it best not to offend the man with a refusal. "Thank you, Dwag," she smiled as she picked the pulverized pieces of nut from his palm.

Dwag grinned with delight. His generosity was not often so appreciated. "Here, I make you more." He crushed three more nuts simultaneously—all he had left—which she ate with gratitude, both for the nuts as well as for the fact that there were no more.

"Now I take you to Branwydd, for sure," he said as he turned and lumbered along the base of the ledge.

Immediately they came to a field where perhaps two hundred sheep were grazing, the droplets of dew on their thick beige coats sparkling in the morning sun against the backdrop of a luminous green hillside. She followed Dwag across the field, often running a few steps to keep pace, and tried to comb her tangled hair as they walked. Soon they came to a large barn, and Dwag went directly inside the opened door where two men were bent over a yearling sheep, applying an ointment to a wound on the animal's neck.

"Braaanwydd," drawled Dwag, "this woman ask to see you. It's all right. She won't hurt no one, for sure. She think you own the farm." Again he burst into his braying guffaw.

One of the men stood and looked toward Evalonne. "Thank you, Dwag. You did the right thing. Now you may return to your sheep." Dwag turned and lumbered away.

The man was of middle age, but strong and lean, with a short graying beard and a kindly face that featured a set of clear blue eyes with deep crinkles at the corners. "Who are you, woman? And what brings you here?" he asked.

"My name is Evalonne, and I am in need of work," she replied.

"How did you come to seek it here? This farm is far enough from the road."

"I came here accidentally. I was on the road from Brancester, heading for the next town north. I slept in the woods last night and Dwag found me there this morning."

Branwydd looked at her as if he surmised there was more to her story than she was telling. Evalonne could not meet his steady gaze and soon cast her eyes to the ground. But he chose not to pick at any wounds on her heart with more questions.

"Well, since Dwag says 'you won't hurt no one, for sure,' that's good enough for me." A smile played at the corners of his mouth. "Can you herd cattle?"

"I never did, sir. But I can learn."

"How about goats or sheep?"

"No, sir."

"Well, as you say, you can learn. There's plenty of work here if you don't mind doing various chores. I'll have you filling in wherever you're needed. At times you'll be a chargirl, a milkmaid, a house servant, a baker, or a shepherdess. Do you think you can handle it?"

"I know I can, sir."

"Good. I'll put you to work shortly. But first, see the table under the shelter beneath the elms yonder where the women are bustling about? That's where the workers take their breakfast each morning. They've just finished, and there's plenty left over. Go take your fill, then return to me and I'll give you your first task."

The breakfast, set before her by a chattering, matronly woman who insisted on refilling Evalonne's plate over and over, was the freshest, finest meal she had eaten since leaving Lochlaund. Afterward Branwydd put her to work in a nearby field picking beans with a half-dozen other women. She worked the entire day, stopping only for a brief lunch and occasional drinks from a nearby well.

When the shadows of the pines lengthened across the field, another hearty meal was readied for the workers, and some of the women led Evalonne to the table. It seemed to her that every person on the farm took care to make her feel welcome and a part of the chatter and merriment that rose from the gathering. After the meal, the women took her to a secluded pond, hidden from view of the men within a cluster of oaks, where they undressed and bathed, laughing and chattering all the while.

Afterward they showed her to the women's quarters where she would spend her nights. It was a daub-and-wattle house consisting of a single large room containing twenty beds, rough hewn but sturdy, each fitted with a straw-filled mattress, a down pillow, and a blanket. She was amazed at how clean and tidy everything was. A bed was designated as hers, and she undressed down to a loose shift and lay on the mattress to sleep.

Her back and arms were sore from the unaccustomed bending posture of bean gathering, but she was grateful for all the day had brought her—good company, good food, and good lodgings in an out-of-the-way place where Gronthus might never venture. Perhaps she would not be a fugitive the rest of her days after all. Perhaps she had found a place where she could stay and restore some measure of order to her shattered life.

Sleep came more quickly than on the night before, but as her body and mind relaxed, so did her resolve to bar Lanson from her thoughts. His fine face and strong form stepped into her dreams and would not be banished. Nor could she escape him during the days. At every maid's mention of some handsome stable hand or woodcutter swain, the image of Lanson would invade her mind again, reviving the ache in her heart.

On the next day Branwydd sent Evalonne into the field with Dwag to tend the sheep. Though simple, Dwag cared for his flock as if they were his children and knew by experience or instinct more about nurturing and protecting sheep than anyone on the farm— "more than anyone in the county," Branwydd had said. In the next two days Evalonne learned much from him. On the third day Branwydd got word that one of the kitchenmaids had fallen ill and sent Evalonne into Lord Kenmarl's manor to replace her.

☙

Maconnal left the baker's shop frustrated that Evalonne apparently had gotten wind of his coming and escaped just before he arrived.

He guessed the truth—that the girl had thought him to be one of Gronthus's men and had run for her life. He questioned vendors and merchants along the lane and on the square, but no one had seen a woman of Evalonne's description.

Maconnal reasoned that she might not have traveled farther north for fear of moving closer to Lochlaund and Gronthus. He left Brancester and rode west, and in the evening arrived at the village of Greenmeade. He spent the night at an inn, and the next morning questioned every merchant and tradesman in the village. Again, no one had seen the girl, so he returned to Brancester that evening and the next day took the eastern route until he came to the village of Gorth, but with the same result. No one had seen such a girl. He returned to Brancester tired and baffled after four days of futility. *The girl must have gone north after all,* he thought. Tomorrow he would ride toward Engleham.

He arose early and rode north, arriving in Engleham not long after noon. He went directly to the square and began questioning the merchants, vendors, tradesmen, and even a few of the buyers. This time some of the answers gave him a glimmer of hope. A meatseller, a farmer, and a woodcarver all remembered seeing a woman who matched Evalonne's description coming through the town four or five days ago. But no one had seen her since.

Thus encouraged, Maconnal took his questions from booth to booth on the square until he arrived at an open shop belonging to a weaver and his wife, displaying blankets, shawls, towels, and cloaks in a rainbow of colors. The weaver, a small, thin man with a balding head, was holding one end of a shawl he was showing to a woman, pointing out the quality of the threads and the strength of the weave. His wife, a woman of vast hip and bosom and a set of double chins, held the other end. Maconnal waited until the customer walked away and the weaver's wife scowled and spat after her before he began his inquiry.

"I'm searching for a young woman, about nineteen years old, with red hair, green eyes, a fair face, and a fine figure. Have you seen such a girl?"

The man hesitated, then glanced furtively at his wife, who stood with her hands on her hips, glaring at him. "Well, I can't rightly say that I noticed—"

"Oh, he seen her all right," said his wife. "His eyes got round as saucers and his jaw dropped 'most to his knees. Stared at her the whole time she was walkin' down the street. It's a wonder the Master didn't strike him blind right on the spot."

"Which way was she walking?" asked Maconnal.

"North," replied the woman. "She was on the street right here, headin' out of town, I surmise, 'cause we never saw her again. And believe me, if she had come by here again, this ooglin' fool of a husban' would've seen her for sure."

"And you never saw her again?" Maconnal addressed the husband.

"Never again," replied the weaver.

"I thank you for your help," said Maconnal as he bowed to the couple and moved on.

He had not walked more than a half-dozen steps when he heard a heavy voice behind him. "Excuse me, sir."

Maconnal stopped and turned around. Before him stood a large, stocky man, black bearded with a black patch over his left eye. Standing on either side of him were two other men. "Excuse me, sir, but I couldn't help overhearin' you question the weaver pair. We know somethin' of the woman you're askin' about, and we can tell you why she's not been seen here for the past few days."

"I will appreciate any information you can give," said Maconnal.

"First, I should ask if you are next of kin to the poor woman."

"No, but what do you mean 'poor woman'?" A vague sense of dread began to tighten Maconnal's belly.

"Well, sir, I don't like to be the one bearin' evil tidin's, but the truth is, the woman has drowned. It happened four days ago."

Maconnal's heart sank within him, and he could hardly draw breath to speak. "How do you know this?"

"The three of us saw it with our own eyes." The man's companions nodded and muttered their affirmation. "We were walkin' by the river, which has been up since the rains in the highlands, you know, and we saw in the distance a woman bathin' above Stony Falls. We reckoned she must've been a wanderer unknowin' of the ways of the river or she'd've never bathed there. She was swimmin' out in the middle, and though we was still a good distance away, we could see that she was driftin' toward the falls. We called to her, but she couldn't hear for the sound of the water, so we started to run to where she was. But we was on a high ledge, and by the time we found our way down, she had done gone over the falls. In fact, we heard her screamin' as she went down. I'll never forget the sound. Hear it in my sleep every night since. Anyway, it took us even longer to get to the bottom of the falls, and though we searched the river downstream until sunset, we never found her body. And no one has seen her since."

"How can you be sure it was the same woman?" asked Maconnal.

"Even from our distance, you couldn't miss that red hair, sir. Oh, and one more thing. The next mornin' we went back to the river with the constable and searched again. Found nothin' but her clothes still layin' on the bank. And with her clothes we found this." He reached into his wallet and took out a delicate silver chain with a dove-shaped pendant hanging from it. "Maybe you recognize it, sir?"

Maconnal numbly took the pendant and examined it. Carved into the metal on the back of the dove he could make out the name "Evalonne." He sighed deeply and thanked the men for their information. With heavy tread he walked back to the inn and called for his horse. His search was over.

Had Maconnal turned to look back, he would have seen the one-eyed man grinning at his companions at the success of their deception as he placed a silver coin in the hand of each of them.

Maconnal rode north out from Engleham shortly after noon, his mind drawn toward Lanson and how he would receive news of Evalonne's death. The sun had dropped to just above the tops of the trees before he came to himself and realized he would not make Faranburgh before nightfall. No matter, he thought. He was near the estate of Lord Kenmarl. Though it was a little out of the way, he would veer aside and avail himself of the hospitality of his longtime friend. Dusk darkened the forest before Maconnal reached Kenmarl's manor, but it hardly mattered, since he had been there often before and knew the road well enough.

Lord and Lady Kenmarl had just been called to dinner when the doorman announced the arrival of Sir Maconnal. Kenmarl embraced his friend warmly, ushered him to the dining hall, and had the servants set a place for him at their table.

"What brings you to Oranth?" asked Kenmarl as the three ate their meal.

"A mission for King Lanson," replied Maconnal. "It's all done now, and I'm on my way home." Maconnal told his friends nothing of Evalonne. He thought it a private matter of the king's that he was not at liberty to discuss.

"And how does the new king fit his throne?"

"Quite well, I think," replied Maconnal. "Indeed, I am encouraged by the decisions he has made so far. I think he may be just what Lochlaund needs to break the yoke of the kirk from the neck of the kingdom."

"What are the prospects of Lochlaund getting a queen soon?" asked Lady Kenmarl. "It's ill luck for a kingdom not to have a queen beside her king, you know."

"So I've heard," said Maconnal with a sigh. "It seems that we will get our queen soon enough. King Lanson will be wedding Lady Lamonda in a matter of weeks. You both will receive invitations, of course."

"Lady Lamonda?" she replied. "Isn't she the bishop's niece? If she's the woman I remember, I wonder if King Lanson won't find the yoke of the kirk a bit heavier than he thinks."

&v

The serving maid who had just refilled the diners' goblets burst into the kitchen eager to tell the other maids what she had just heard.

"Listen to this," she said. "Do you remember Prince Lanson of Lochlaund, who stayed overnight here about eight months ago?"

"How could we forget?" said the girl at the dish tub as the others in the room sighed and made swooning noises. Evalonne, sitting on a stool slicing potatoes, stopped breathing for a moment as her heart skipped a beat.

"Well, Lord Kenmarl's guest is a man from Lochlaund who knows the prince, and guess what? He's the king now, and he's gettin' married in just a few weeks."

The girls all groaned and expressed deep disappointment that this delectable morsel of prime manhood had been taken off the market. Evalonne dropped the plate she held and it shattered on the floor. She was surprised at the grief and despair the news rekindled. She had known already that Lanson was betrothed, but word of the imminent wedding stunned her anew. What she had held at bay as a distant possibility that fate might somehow change now loomed as a certainty. Though she had neither right nor reason to expect anything else, the thought of Lanson wedding another woman pierced her to the core. But she had no choice other than to come to terms with it.

"I'm sorry," she said as the chief cook came toward her.

"Ah, it's only a plate," he said. "Just take the broom to it and use a bit more care."

She remained stoic as she got the broom from the corner, but as she stooped to sweep up the shards, she pressed her apron to her eyes to staunch a sudden flow of unbidden tears.

The two serving maids had all they could handle in taking the next course into the dining hall, and the chief cook sent Evalonne with them to replenish the diners' drinks. She entered the hall behind the servers and quietly set about the task of pouring mead into cups and goblets. Though her hands still trembled from the shock of the news she had heard, she did well enough with the cups of Lord and Lady Kenmarl. But as she poured the mead into Maconnal's cup, a few drops missed their mark and splashed onto his hand.

"Oh, I'm so sorry," she said as she took a small towel and wiped the liquid away.

"No harm done," he replied.

In the past few days, Maconnal had missed no opportunity to look carefully at every girl he encountered, thinking any one of them could be the object of his quest. But now the quest was over and he felt no need to continue such scrutiny. Furthermore, he was tired and preoccupied with the weight of the news he must bear to his king, and he did not even look up at Evalonne as she took her pitcher and left the hall.

Early the next morning Maconnal took leave of Lord Kenmarl and departed for Lochlaund.

CHAPTER TWENTY-NINE

NIGHT OF DESPAIR

t was not long past midafternoon and Lanson had just entered his own chambers when his chamberlain announced that Sir Maconnal had returned and was waiting to see him. His heart leapt with hope. His friend had returned long before the end of the sixty days, which surely meant he had found Evalonne. But Maconnal entered, and the moment Lanson saw his face, a cold chill ran through his body. Something dreadful had happened. The man was haggard and drawn. There was no laughter in his eyes, no hint of joy, no promise of good news. In that moment Lanson tried to steel himself against any blow that fate could deal. But he failed.

"Lanson, I have terrible news. Evalonne has drowned."

At the sound of the impossible words, Lanson's soul shrank within him. For almost a minute he stood staring, motionless and unthinking, his will resisting the intrusion of this ravaging news. But in moments, the outrageous fact pushed through and overwhelmed him so that he fell heavily into his chair.

"No, you are mistaken," he said, his voice a hoarse whisper. "She cannot be dead. I have seen her, and she is the most alive creature I have ever known."

Maconnal spoke softly. "I understand how you feel, Lanson."

"How could you?" Lanson blurted with unintended viciousness. "How could you know what it is like to lose someone who has grown to be a part of you? It's like losing an arm or a leg. It hurts. It hurts more than I could possibly have imagined."

"I know. I lost a wife." Maconnal sank into a chair beside his friend. "We were young. I met her not long after my banishment from the abbey of Rhondilar. Ah, I remember as if it were but a few days ago. She was to me like wine, like sunshine, like spring air alive with the scent of apple blossoms, the part of myself that I had been missing and didn't even know it. Our time together was short, but it was a lifetime, and one of never-ending joy." Maconnal paused and sighed deeply. "She died a year after we were wed. In childbirth. The baby died too."

"I'm so sorry, Maconnal. How did you go on?"

"It was the hardest thing I ever did. But it was also the simplest. I just went on. Each day you simply do what needs to be done."

Maconnal stayed with Lanson for another hour, talking little, trying to get him to take food, and offering his deep-felt sympathy. When the sun's rays reached from the window almost to the opposite wall, Lanson persuaded Maconnal to leave. He needed to be alone. Maconnal complied, but he secured a room for the night just down the hallway.

"I will be close by," he said as he left. "You call for me anytime tonight, for any reason."

While Maconnal was with him, it seemed to Lanson that the grief was bearable, as if his friend were carrying half the load of it. But moments after the man's departure, the full weight of his loss descended on him with crushing force. His eyes darted about the room in panic as if looking for some way out of this stifling prison of despair that was closing in on him like the walls of a shrinking cell. He felt as if a cold hand were squeezing the life from his heart. Finally, he put his head in his hands and great sobs wrenched his body.

The sun tipped the rim of the distant hills when he arose and, hardly knowing what he did, stalked into the corridor with uneven steps and made his way out to the stables, where he ordered his favorite horse to be saddled. He mounted and galloped out of the castle, across the drawbridge, and on down the road until he came to Kelterwood Forest. He turned the horse from the road and slackened the reins, letting the animal wander at will among the great, solemn trees as he slumped in the saddle, his chin on his chest, heedless of his direction. When the horse finally stopped, he slipped off and sank to the earth against the trunk of an ancient oak.

Lanson rested his head on his arms as his horse grazed on the grass nearby. He did not move for almost a half-hour and gave no heed to the fact that the forest about him was darkening rapidly. Already the trees had faded to dark gray with nothing but black shadows showing between them. He knew he should have left the woods before the darkness was complete, but he did not care. One thought seared his mind, and he could no more shut it out than a burning coal could shut out the fire within it. Evalonne was dead.

"No! No! Nooooooooo!" he screamed into the darkness. But the sound fell flat around him. Again he wept, then threw himself down between the snaky roots of the tree to sleep or die; he hardly cared which.

He slept fitfully, dreaming of his happy journey to Ensovandor with Evalonne walking and laughing by his side, her green eyes sparkling and her red hair glistening. In his dream, night fell and she slept on the grass close by him. Suddenly her scream pierced the darkness, and he awakened to see the hideous creature with the face of a gargoyle and the body of a lizard pulling her into the blackness of the woods. He tried to spring up and draw his sword but found that he could not move his limbs or even cry out to her. He watched helpless as the creature dragged her away, and as she disappeared into the forest, he heard a voice as rich as the ringing of a great bell calling his name. He awoke with a start and sat up. On a stone ten feet away sat the man he had seen in his dreamlike vision in Braegan Wood the night he had found Mossette. His white hair and long robe were lit from above by some moonlike light, though there was no moon shining that night.

"Father Clemente?"

"Lanson, what are you doing in these woods?" asked Clemente. "Don't you know that Maconnal and everyone in the castle are looking for you?"

"I had to get away," replied Lanson.

"And did you get away?"

"No. The horror I was running from is with me still."

"And what were you running from?"

"A hurt worse than any I have yet felt, a hurt that I cannot understand. I met a young woman, Evalonne by name, whom the accorder Gronthus has dogged like a foxhound for months, determined to condemn her to death. And now he has done it. He forced her to stay in hiding, living in the forests and by the streams, making her way as best she could without the comfort of home, the company of people, or the protection of love. She drowned in a river, being a stranger to its banks and unaware of its dangers until it was too late."

"But did not the kirk have an accusation against her?"

"It did. And she had committed wrongs. But she had turned from that life and begun to live a new one. Gronthus and the kirk are blind to all but her guilt. They can see nothing but her past wrongs and find no place for mercy even in a life that has renewed itself. I tell you, Father, I will see that Gronthus comes to the same kind of justice he has inflicted upon Evalonne. And when I have that little mouse in my grasp, I hope he pleads for mercy. I will give him mercy—the same kind of mercy he showed to Evalonne."

"I see," said Clemente. "You want mercy for Evalonne but justice for Gronthus."

"Her sins grew out of love and circumstance, and she has repented of them. The heart of this Gronthus is inflamed with death and destruction, a flame kindled and blown to a blaze by a kirk obsessed with imposing a standard of purity that no one can meet."

"Can you be so sure of what is inside the heart of Gronthus? It may be burning with such a single-minded dedication to righteousness that mercy is consumed in the flame. But his need for it is as great as Evalonne's. Indeed, all men and women have the same need of mercy, and all are equally undeserving—those who know they need it as well as those who do not."

Father Clemente's words tasted bitter to Lanson, and he said nothing in reply.

"Lanson, you have duties to perform and others to whom you are responsible. Even now many are anxious for your safety. Isn't it time to return to the castle and get on with your life?"

Lanson sighed deeply and agreed. He took the reins of his horse and walked beside Father Clemente, who led him out of the forest. As they approached Macrennon Castle, the first rays of the morning sun painted an orange rim on the eastern side of it. Lanson gazed at the ancient structure, looming massive and immutable in the distance as if it had been there since the earth's first morning and would be there still after all suns died.

"How short our lives are compared to the things we build," Lanson mused. "Yonder castle has known my father, his father before him, and his father before him. And before them it knew the invaders from across the southern sea. After I am gone it will know my children and their children after them for generations to come. Men and women are merely flashes across its threshold, their lives coming and going like mayflies while it endures through the ages. The things men make outlive their makers many times over."

"You are mistaken, young King Lanson. The truth is the opposite of the seeming. Castles, the civilizations that build them, and even the stones they are built of are as mere breaths compared to the life of a man or woman, which is created to be eternal. When all the stones in all the castles ever built have crumbled to dust and blown across the field, your life will yet be in the wee hours of its never-ending morning."

They walked on, Lanson staring hard at the castle as he pondered Father Clemente's strange words. Moments later he turned to reply, but Clemente was not there. Lanson looked all around, but the man was nowhere to be seen. He mounted his horse, rode on to the castle, and took up his life as king of his people.

Lanson refused to wear his grief like an outer garment for all to see, but closed it inside and never spoke of it except to Maconnal, and seldom even to him. His decisions were deemed to be wise and his attention to the needs of his people focused and complete. He was courteous to all—lords, ladies, and commoners alike. The only difference anyone ever noted was that at moments when his attention was not absorbed by matters of state or the petitions of his subjects, he would sit and stare with glistening eyes into the distance.

A week after Maconnal's return Lanson fulfilled the terms of his agreement and called on the Lady Lamonda. He told her that he would honor the intended betrothal arranged by his father and her uncle, and she could set the wedding date for whenever she wished.

She set it for one month from that day.

CHAPTER THIRTY

The flower in the stone

enmarl's overseer Branwydd was impressed with the new girl on the estate. Though he had moved her almost daily from one chore to another—filling in for an ill herder on one day, rushing her to help load hay into a barn before a rain on the next, helping the women weed the fields on another, or milking the cows in the gray dawn—she threw herself wholly into every task. She never complained about the heat, the length of the day, or the weight of the pails or bags or sheaves. She always expressed gratitude for anything done for her, whether it was a drink of water, help in lifting an overloaded basket, or even the daily meals for all the workers spread at the end of the day on the long tables beneath the elms.

Evalonne was happy, or if not truly happy, at least content. The work was hard but to her liking, for it varied from day to day, and the freshness of each task helped shut her mind against the intrusion of thoughts heavy with hopeless longing and bitter despair. But often at night such thoughts still assaulted her with a fury against which she had no defense.

She had been on the estate little more than a month when such a night came upon her. The air outside the windows was warm and quiet, the full moon coating the tops of the barns and fields with a silver sheen. The other women in the room slept soundly, but Evalonne was held captive by the ghosts of her past. One by one, faces drifted across the stage of her mind, hovering there in spite of her efforts to close the curtain and escape into sleep. The face of her dear infant daughter laughed and cooed, her wide blue eyes gazing into her mother's with utter trust. Silent tears soaked Evalonne's pillow as her arms ached to hold the warmth and softness of the little round treasure that had left her so soon.

Then Lanson appeared, tall, broad shouldered, and straight as a lance, his strong face glowing with the light in his blue eyes and his even teeth flashing white through his smile. He was every inch a king, she thought. For more than an hour she turned and twisted in anguish, longing for the delights she had beheld but could never taste.

A soft whisper drifted through the shadows of the room. Evalonne lay still and listened. It came again, and the form of it was unmistakable. "Evalonne . . ." A voice somewhere in the room was whispering her name. She sat up and looked about at the other beds. All the women were asleep. *One of them must be dreaming,* she thought as she lay down again.

"Evalonne." The whisper seemed to fill the room, and once more she sat up and looked all about. Suddenly she tensed and almost screamed. Standing in the open doorway was the silhouette of a man, robed in a long coat of forest colors, his white hair and beard rimmed silver in the moonlight. As she watched, he reached forth his hand and motioned for her to rise and follow him. Then he turned and walked from the house.

Why she chose to follow she could never explain. She had reason enough to be wary of strangers looking for her. But at that moment she knew somehow that she should follow the man and did not even think of resisting. He led her across the field to the line of trees that marked the course of a stream flowing through the estate. When they reached the stream he led her toward two stones in the moonlit grass beside it, and they sat upon them. Though his hair was white and his face grave as if it held the secrets of the ages, Evalonne could see that the man was anything but old. His flesh glowed with the health of youth, and his eyes were clear as a cloudless sky. His smile put her completely at ease. She felt that she knew this man, though she was sure she had never seen anything like him in her life. His eyes, his smile, something about the way he looked at her reminded her of . . .

of whom? *Lanson*, she thought. *He reminds me of Lanson. No, he looks nothing at all like Lanson. He reminds me of my own father. But no, not really. Perhaps Branwydd, or strangely, even Dwag . . .* She stopped the hopeless guessing game and simply asked him the question, "Who are you, sir?"

"I have many names," he replied in a voice like liquid silver, "but to you I am Father Vitale."

"Something about you is vaguely familiar, but if I had seen you before I would surely have remembered."

"You have seen something of me in the face of everyone who loves you."

A warm thrill ran through her at his words. "And why have you called me out, Father Vitale?"

"Your grief has called to me, Evalonne. I have heard the groanings of your heart and the fall of your tears. I have come not to take away the grief but to ease the burden of it. Tonight if you will release to me the secrets you have locked in your heart, they will no longer torment your nights."

After only a moment of reticence, Evalonne unburdened her soul to this being with the face of a youth and the wisdom of the ages. She told him of the blows she had endured, of the death of her parents, the betrayal of Avriel, her plunge into poverty, the pursuit of Gronthus, her descent into harlotry, the death of her daughter, the loss of Mossette and Lanson. She explained that in her bitterness she had renounced the Master of the Universe for abandoning her and allowing so many storms to ravage her life.

"If I mattered to him, he would not have let all these woes fall on me," she said.

"The blows you have suffered are severe," said Father Vitale, "and they are more than many people endure in a lifetime. You know already that many of your tragedies grew out of your own choices, which does not for a moment diminish the weight of them. But the very fact that you can make choices—that right and good is not forced on you against your will—is the gift of dignity and meaning that the Master gave you when he made you. Your choices give you a part in the cosmic drama. You affect the shape of eternity itself with every decision you make. The freedom to make these choices means you can choose wrongly as well as rightly, and the result of them can be evil as well as good."

Evalonne's fingers idly picked at a loose thread in a seam of her shift. "You are right, of course," she replied. "I know that my own bad choices brought much of my misery on me. But not all of it. Why did the Master take my baby girl from me? She was the one bright ray in my dark existence. She was all I had. She was my only happiness, and he took her from me. Why?" Her voice quivered with the memory of the pain, and she snapped the thread from the seam and balled it in her fist.

"I cannot tell you exactly why your child died, but I can tell you it was not the Master's doing. When humanity's first parents made that pivotal choice that banished the Master from their lives, enormous evil forces that had been held at bay moved on the earth and wreaked chaos on the order of nature so that disease, canker, destruction, and death infected all creation, inflicting on all mankind seemingly random tragedies not of anyone's making. All are victims at one time or another."

"The Master may not have caused her death, but surely he could have prevented it," Evalonne insisted.

"Yes, he could have prevented it." Vitale's hair shimmered in the silver moonlight as he nodded in affirmation. "He has the power. But he also has the power to see into the future, even into the future that would have been had your daughter lived. We do not know what kind of pain, disease, loss, or other horrors might have filled the child's life. The Master may have allowed her death as a mercy to spare sufferings with consequences far beyond those that you now suffer at her loss. She might even have grown up and made choices of her own that would have placed her outside the reach of the Master, which would have been the ultimate tragedy. Instead, the Master let her come to his arms now, where she lives in delirious joy."

"I can only be happy to know that she lives in joy, and I would not deny her that. Yet it hurts so much not to have her with me that I can hardly bear it."

The strange man laid his hand gently on Evalonne's. "Remember when you were a child and you begged your father for the tiny oaken doll you had seen in the woodcarver's shop? You were heartbroken when he would not buy it and moped about for days. Then on your birthday a week later your parents gave you a magnificent lifelike doll they had made themselves. Your father had carved and smoothed the face and hands and painted them so they looked almost alive. Your mother had sewn a little dress of white linen trimmed in blue ribbon and given the doll a head of hair made of flaxen threads. Your doll made the woodcarver's look crude and paltry."

She nodded and smiled at the memory as Father Vitale went on. "The Master of the Universe loves you like your father, Evalonne. He withholds only to give better. The loss of your child was necessary to bring you into an infinite joy you cannot yet imagine."

"But the pain is so great . . ."

"I know. I am very sorry. And the only answer I can give you is that the Master is not a stranger to pain. He suffered too, you know."

Evalonne looked into Father Vitale's eyes and saw them shimmering with moisture. "I know," she said. "And there is comfort in knowing. Yet I can't help but think sometimes that the pain we endure is too great for us. I wonder if our freedom is worth the pain."

"The Master thought it was. And you will think the same when time has healed the wound in your heart. His only alternative was a manipulated universe, a toy for him to play with, men and women being nothing more than puppets or chess pieces for him to move about and pretend their actions had meaning. Neither he nor you would find joy in such a world."

"But how will I find joy in any world? It is as you said: my own choices brought ruin on me, and in my anger I foolishly renounced him. I am an outcast to him and an enemy to his kirk—a fugitive under the sentence of death who will find no peace but in the grave."

"All men and women, if they only think of it, are under the sentence of death. The grave eventually swallows each, and no one knows when his doom will come. Yet peace is possible for everyone, including you, Evalonne."

"How is it possible, seeing I have renounced him?"

"Return home, child." Vitale turned and opened his arms toward her. "Return to him. He is waiting for you to come home to him so he can hold you safe in his own arms. Storms may blow and crack about you, your world may shatter, your body may be ravaged, but you—your heart, the core of your central self—cannot be touched as long as you stay in the safety of his arms. Even if the kirk brings you to your death, you will find yourself safe within his arms—the same arms that even now enfold your infant daughter, the arms of him who loves both of you like a father."

"It has never occurred to me that the Master of the Universe actually loves me. I thought he was my judge, not my father." A wave of longing washed over her as hot tears flooded her eyes. "I am so ashamed of shutting him out. I want to come home, Father Vitale. I want to come home to him."

Vitale's hand reached about her and clasped her shoulder. At that very moment all fear and grief left her as if evaporating into the air. She felt warm and secure, certain that nothing could ever really hurt her as long as she remained within the clasp of his comforting embrace. She wiped her hand across her eyes to clear away the tears and turned to Father Vitale to speak. He was not there. She still felt the warmth of his hand on her shoulder, but he was gone. With a mind full of wonder, she returned to the house and lay once more on her bed. In moments she was asleep and did not awaken until morning.

Branwydd came to Evalonne as she was eating breakfast with the other workers and told her that today she would take a flock of sheep to the west pasture for grazing. He had sent Dwag into Engleham for supplies.

An hour later she was sitting on a white stone looking out over the sheep, listening to the soft, ripping sounds as the animals pulled tufts of grass from the moist earth. The day was warm. A fresh breeze caressed her face and teased her hair, rippling through the grass like waves on a lake. Clouds tumbled across the sky; flowers of all colors waved in the breeze as butterflies flitted over them. Birds in the trees about her chirped and sang and fluttered down from their perches to

hover about the sheep, harvesting the grasshoppers and beetles fleeing from their foraging teeth.

Beauty flourished everywhere. And as Evalonne basked in the
sunlight and exulted in the greenness of the grass and trees and hills,
she had no thought of her tragic losses and dashed hopes. She remembered something Lanson had once told her: "There is nothing created
that is not good. Evil has no real existence. It is merely a turning away
from, a misuse of, a parasite on, or a corruption of good. For evil to
exist at all, it must destroy. Canker, rot, scum, and rust owe their survival to the good upon which they prey. Were evil to triumph over
good, it would bring about its own annihilation, for in destroying all
good it would have nothing more to feed on. Good can exist without
evil, but evil cannot exist without good. Evil must destroy, but only
the good is creative." She had not understood him then, but now the
meaning became clear.

In spite of her many tragedies, good kept pushing at her as it
pushes up the grass from the ground, the butterflies from their co-
coons, the birds from their eggs, and the lambs from their mothers'
wombs. Lost in her reverie, she moved her hand absently across the
stone on which she sat, and her fingers brushed the feathery softness
of a tiny white daisy. She looked at the little flower, which had pushed
its way through the stone and now shone pure and bright and delicate. Good was relentless. Even when trapped in hard, unyielding
barrenness, it found its way through and blossomed into beauty. Evil
could crush and ravish, but it could not repress the rampant good
that permeated the earth. Only the good was real and worthy of her
allegiance.

Why not embrace the good? Evalonne thought. The good was calling to her, entreating her to lay aside her grief, step into the sunlight,
and join the dance. Why should she refuse? Why let the past smother
her longing for joy? She looked about her. It was obvious that the
world was created for ecstasy. Beauty did not have to exist. The world
could have been created gray as the moon and soundless as a stone,
without aromas or textures or songs to delight the senses. It could
have been created simply to function efficiently, empty of laughter
and beauty and love. But it was not. It was created for delight.

Yet Evalonne paused before the invitation. She wondered at herself. How dare she even think of reaching out for joy after all she had suffered? Her tragedies paraded through her mind, demanding their due of grief. Was it right to think of happiness with so much calamity filling her past? Yet she looked out at the hills, at the stream winding through the meadow. She listened to the rustling of the leaves, the singing of the birds, the distant call of an amorous herdsman to a milkmaid, and wondered, *Why not?* Did the fact that she had been buffeted make the good any less good? Was it evil to participate in the joy that now invited her instead of clinging to the ashes of the past? Why remain brooding in the shadow of delight? Why not plunge back into the creative flow? Why not place herself back in the hands of the Master of the Universe and accept whatever he had in store for her?

"Why not, indeed?" she uttered aloud, surprising herself as well as the grazing ewe nearby, which paused to look up at her in stupid wonder. Evalonne laughed. She would come back to the Master. She would place her life in his hand and release her grip on her grief. She would accept the joy he thrust at her.

She could not sit still. She arose from the stone and took the hem of her skirt in her fingers while her graceful feet stepped through the crossing paces of a country dance she had learned as a child. She wheeled and pranced across the grass with happy abandon, her face turned upward, presenting to the heavens a smile of exultation as she lifted her hands to embrace the love she felt flowing from the heart that beats above the universe.

ℒ

The blacksmith heaved the heavy plowshare onto the back of the cart, then stood back and wiped his huge, roughened hands on his leather apron. Dwag, standing beside him, handed him a much-folded parchment.

"Would ye look at Branwydd's list here and tell me if I got everything on the cart?"

"Of course, Dwag." The blacksmith unfolded the parchment and began walking around the cart, glancing often at the paper and jabbing his finger toward the barrels of salt and flour on the wagon bed as he counted them. "It's all here," he said as he handed the list back to Dwag.

Dwag grinned broadly as he mounted the board and reached for the reins. Branwydd would be pleased with him. He had finished the list much earlier than he expected and would get back to Kenmarl well before sundown. As he picked up the reins, a kirkman robed in gray approached and called to the blacksmith.

"Ah, excuse me, my good man. Could I have a word with you?"

The blacksmith stopped and turned. "What can I do for you, Father?"

"I am looking for someone—a woman, under twenty years old, fair of face and form, with red hair and green eyes. She may have come to this village some weeks ago."

"I've not seen such a woman," replied the blacksmith.

"Very well. I'm sorry to have bothered you." The kirkman turned to go.

"I seen her," called Dwag from atop the cart. It did not occur to the innocent that a kirkman would have anything but good intent toward Evalonne. "I see her just yesterday."

"Where did you see her?" asked the kirkman.

"Why, she work on Kenmarl Estate. She work good, for sure."

"Do you know the woman's name?" asked the kirkman.

"For sure. Her name Ev'lonne. Ever'body know her name."

"That is the one. How can I find her?"

"I goin' there now. Get on. I take you."

The kirkman climbed onto the cart and sat beside Dwag. Dwag popped the reins and the two dappled draft horses pulled the cart, creaking and groaning with the weight, out into the lane and toward Kenmarl Estate.

CHAPTER THIRTY-ONE

The Trap of Conscience

he shadows of the trees behind Evalonne lengthened until they almost reached the woods that grew up the slope of the far side of the meadow. She sat on her stone and looked out over the sheep, most of them still as statues except for the slight bobbing of their down-turned heads as they cropped the thick grass. She stood up, stretched, and turned to walk up the ridge behind her. Her replacement should arrive shortly. When she reached the top, she gazed down into the valley below. Kenmarl's manor—a small castle, really—nestled in the trees at the foot of the hills on the far side of the valley, stood solid and stately in the evening sunlight. In the center of the valley, between the ridge where she stood and the manor, she could see the barns and the smaller buildings around them. She saw the women in the bean field, now beginning to pour their sacks into baskets, which the men would carry to the barn. A few men milled about the barn, putting up tools and pitching hay for the horses. A cluster of women gathered at the tables, preparing another evening feast for the workers. But no one was coming to replace her yet.

Beyond the barn a cart moved slowly up the lane behind two muscular, dappled draft horses. Evalonne could make out Dwag's unmistakable hulk on the board and someone sitting beside him. Moments later the cart stopped in front of the barn and the two men dismounted, Dwag on one side and the man, wearing a long gray robe, on the other. Evalonne's heart froze. He was a kirkman. He even had the look of Gronthus, though she could not be sure at this distance. Instinctively she drew herself behind a tree and continued to watch. Dwag came around the cart and pointed to the place on the rise where Evalonne had just been standing, and immediately the two men began walking toward the ridge. Now she could see the face of the man with Dwag.

It was Gronthus.

Evalonne ran as fast as she could back down from the ridge toward the sheep. She crossed the pasture through the midst of them and disappeared in the woods on the other side. She had a momentary pang about leaving the sheep, but the thought of Dwag coming eased her conscience. She had no choice but to flee. She made her way into the deep woods, running as best she could through the brush and brambles that snagged her skirt and scratched her ankles. Soon she came upon a narrow trail and made better time.

Suddenly a chasm some six feet in diameter yawned in the earth before her. She barely stopped in time to keep from plunging into it. It was a trap, one of the many that Kenmarl's hunters had dug in the forest. In the bottom of the pit, some eight or nine feet deep, an angered boar growled and pawed at the sides of the hole. Evalonne drew back, her heart pounding, and stepped around the pit. She ran on, weaving along the narrow trail. Each time she came to a fork, she took the one that led her northward. She had been in the forest before and knew something of the trails. She and three other women had covered the pits with branches and grass after Kenmarl's hunters had dug them, and she had learned that the forest was narrow to the east and west but extended several miles to the north. She ran on until she left the parts of the woods she knew. The hunters no longer attended the few pits they had dug this far north, having reaped sufficient game from their more accessible traps. They had recently made an expedition into the forest to fill in the more distant ones.

After running for a half-hour or more, Evalonne suddenly stopped again. Directly in front of her she recognized another of the animal traps, this one with the covering branches and leaves still intact, awaiting its victim. Apparently it was one the hunters' dismantling expedition had missed. She stepped around the pit and kept running.

Her sides ached and her breath came hard and fast, but she dared not stop. She ran on, stumbling often as her legs began to lose their strength. Finally she reached a stream and collapsed on the bank beside it, gasping and wheezing for breath. When she regained control of her breathing, she sat up on her knees. She looked behind her and listened. Hearing nothing but the chirping of the birds and the faint rustle of the breeze in the tops of the trees, she stretched out on the bank with her head over the water, pushed back her hair, and drank deeply. No drink had ever tasted so good. She raised her head to get her breath, then plunged her mouth to the water again. But she realized that in that moment she had seen something amiss—something odd about the reflection in the water. She raised her eyes and looked again at the surface of the pool. Within the ripples she made out the reflection of something dark and vertical. She lifted her eyes to the far bank and saw on a stone just above the reflection a pair of booted feet, and above the feet a gray robe, and above the robe a face staring cold and hard at her. Gronthus!

As quick as thought she was on her feet running back down the trail that had brought her. Gronthus splashed across the stream and followed like a hound on the scent of a fox. How had he managed to get in front of her? She had expected him to follow her into the woods, but all the time she had been running toward him. Apparently he had anticipated her direction and had run alongside the woods, where without the impediment of underbrush and snaking trails, he could make much better time than she. He had simply entered the woods at a place ahead of her and waited for her to arrive.

As she ran she looked back over her shoulder. He was gaining on her. Her rest had been too brief to renew her strength, and soon she was gasping for breath and stumbling again. He was not more than thirty feet behind her now and would soon catch her unless . . . unless she could lead him to the abandoned trap. She took the trail toward the covered pit. If she could reach it before he reached her, she might escape yet. She glanced behind her again. He was no more than ten feet back and gaining with every step. Her legs were weakening and her sides burned as if hot coals were searing them. Where was that pit?

She rounded a curve in the trail and he followed, now only a pace behind, so close she could hear his breathing and the flapping of his robe. A moment later his breath was almost in her ear, and she felt his hand upon her shoulder. She lunged forward, and his fingers raked across her back but came away empty. He reached again. At that moment she saw the branches and leaves of the pit immediately ahead and leapt forward with all her strength. She fell to the solid ground on the far side as she heard his surprised cry and the snapping and rustling of branches and twigs as he tumbled into the pit.

She glanced quickly into the hole. Gronthus's arms flailed about among the tangle of branches, and a moment later his face appeared from behind a cluster of dried leaves, wide-eyed and open-mouthed, looking up at her in dazed surprise. Immediately she got up, stepped around the edges of the pit, and ran on northward into the woods. Her wobbly legs soon gave way and she tumbled to the earth. She got up, her breath coming in hoarse wheezes, and forced herself to slow to a walk. She need not run anymore, for Gronthus could not climb out of the pit. And since it had been abandoned as a trap, no one from Kenmarl would be checking it. He would starve there. She was free of Gronthus forever.

In spite of the darkening shadows about her, Evalonne walked along the trail buoyed by a lightness she had not felt in many months. A heavy burden had been lifted. Gronthus was gone forever. She was free. No more running, no more hiding, no more looking over her shoulder for the gray shadow of pursuit. She no longer felt tired. She walked on with a lighter step and a new firmness of stride as her exhaustion fell from her like barrels rolling off a cart.

But soon a sense of unease began to unsettle her thoughts. It had been there all along, hovering in the shadow of her exultation. The image of Gronthus loomed in her mind, looking surprised and bewildered as she had last seen him in the shadows of the pit. A wave of guilt swept over her for leaving him to certain death. But what choice did she have? Had he caught her, he would have taken her to her doom. How could anyone expect her to act differently? She shut him out of her mind and kept walking.

Moments later the face of Gronthus again crept into her mind, looking up at her from the pit, and again she shut it out. Perhaps someone would happen along the trail and pull him out. But she knew it was unlikely. Kenmarl's hunters would not venture that deeply into the woods until winter, when all fields were harvested and game was scarce. How long did it take one to starve? Weeks, she thought, though she had heard that one could not live without water for more than three or four days. The thought of being the cause of such cruel torture made her heart sink. But it was no less than he deserved. His relentless pursuit had tortured her for months. She walked on, the weight of her thoughts slowing her pace to little more than a stroll.

Perhaps she could find a way to save him without putting herself at risk. When she reached the next village north she could tell someone of his plight or send a message to Kenmarl to have him rescued. But such a plan was laden with dangers. She could be questioned too closely. Gronthus's own men could be waiting for her in the village. And rescue tomorrow might be too late if wolves found him tonight. At least such a death would be quicker than thirst or starvation, though hardly painless. Again she saw his face staring bewildered from the darkness of the pit as if from the grave itself. If she left him to die, would that face ever cease to haunt her?

Evalonne stopped walking. She sighed deeply, turned, and began to retrace her steps. When she reached the trap, the darkness of the woods was almost complete, and she could see nothing in the inky blackness of the pit. Her first thought was that he had found some way out and could be lurking somewhere in the shadows about her.

"Gronthus," she called.

"I am here."

"Gronthus, I have a proposal." She paused but he did not answer. "I have no wish to see you die. All I want is my life and my freedom. Renounce forever your pursuit of me and I will help you out."

"I cannot do that," replied Gronthus.

"Why not? If I leave you here, you will almost surely die."

"That seems likely."

"And if I get you out, I will almost surely die."

"That is a certainty."

"Then why should I let you out?" The pangs of conscience that had tormented her were fast dissipating.

"I do not expect you to let me out."

"I don't understand. Don't you want out?"

"Of course I want out. I would not expect you to understand—you who have no sense of obedience to law or duty. I am totally committed to a higher power, to my duty, and to my vow to bring you to justice. I will give my life rather than forsake that duty."

"Oh, Gronthus, Gronthus!" she cried in exasperation. "I want to save you, but you leave me no choice."

"You always have a choice—the simple choice of every daughter of Eve in any situation. Either you do what you know to be right, or you do what seems best for yourself at the moment."

There was no sound in the forest but the chirping of the crickets and the croak of the frogs in the distant stream as Evalonne stood silent, wrestling with the wrenching alternatives that seemed so simple to Gronthus. Finally she stirred and looked about her. In the deepening darkness she could see some six feet to the side of the pit the dim form of a fallen tree, about twelve feet long and eight inches in diameter. With considerable tugging and slipping, she managed to drag the heavy end of the log to the edge of the pit.

"Watch out," she said as she pushed it over the lip of the hole until it tilted downward and Gronthus caught it in his hands. He set the end of it on the floor of the pit and tried to climb, using the knots and stumps of broken branches as footholds. But as he placed his weight on the log, it twisted to the side and he slipped off. She wanted desperately to run, but she waited as he tried again and again until it was clear that he could not climb out unless she held the log steady for him. With a sigh she took hold of two protruding branches at the top and held tightly as he made his way up. The moment he set his foot on the trail, she let go and turned to run. But she was not quick enough. He clutched her firmly by the arm, drew a length of rope from his robe, and bound her hands together behind her back. After wiping the palms of his hands on his robe, he pointed down the darkened trail.

"Start walking."

Gronthus remained behind Evalonne, marching her westward until they came to a stream. He paused long enough to give his hands a thorough washing. Minutes later they came out of the forest and found that dusk had not yet yielded to night. There was easily enough light to find their way to the road, where Gronthus turned them southward, away from Kenmarl and toward the village of Engleham.

They reached Engleham shortly before midnight and went to the Moonstone Inn, where Gronthus had stabled his horse. He took from his saddlebag a light three-foot length of chain with manacles on each end. He clamped one end to Evalonne's wrist and the other to his own. Instead of securing a room for the remainder of the night, he bargained with the innkeeper to let them sleep in the common room, where he and Evalonne each took a bench. The next morning they breakfasted, both silent as stones, then he secured an additional horse and manacled both of Evalonne's hands in front of her. They rode northward toward Lochlaund.

Throughout the journey they spoke little and, for hours at a time, not at all. Evalonne noticed that he would hardly even look at her, and when he did it was with an expression of contempt bordering on disgust, as if she were some kind of fetid abomination reeking of dung. She had never before seen such a look on a man's face. On the sixth day, just after they had crossed the Sunderlon into Lochlaund, she grew weary of the long silences. She turned to him and said, "You utterly hate me, don't you, Gronthus?"

"I hate evil," he answered.

"And you see me as evil. You hate me because of my sin-tainted past. Isn't it so?"

"I hate sin in all its forms. Sin is an affront to the Master of the Universe. Your sin clings to you and makes you abominable in the eyes of the Master. I, as his servant, can do no less than look at you through his eyes and hate what he hates."

"Is there no way for one to be absolved of sin?"

"One can be absolved of some sins through penance, pain, and discipline. But other sins are so despicable that nothing will cure them but death."

"Cannot I be absolved of my sins?"

"No. Your sins are unto death. Besides, you are a woman, and you have inherited the evil nature of your mother Eve, who plunged humanity into all the woes and ills that make this world a vale of tears. Woman's very nature is evil. Eve seduced her husband, Adam, and her daughters still seduce men with their infernal beauty into turning away from the Master toward evil, carnal desires. Women are the scourge of the race. The farther men stay from the contamination of women, the purer they remain."

"Is that why you always wash your hands each time you touch me?"

Gronthus said nothing but Evalonne persisted. "How is it that woman is evil? Didn't the Master of the Universe himself create both male and female?"

"He did. The creation of woman is the one act that he has repented of."

"The Master of the Universe repented? Are you saying the Master erred?"

"He did not err. He made the woman perfect and pure in body and spirit—much more like the man than she is now both in form and temperament. But she departed from his way and became the most evil of all creatures, acquiring beauty from her new master the devil and using it to lure men to destruction. It was not the creation of the woman but her departure from him that caused the master to repent."

"Do you mean to say that beauty is an evil?" she asked. But Gronthus did not answer. He had wasted more words on this woman than was his wont with those of her sex. He would cast no more of his pearls before such a swine. She fell silent as well, and no more words passed between them that day.

Three days later Gronthus and Evalonne arrived in Macrennon. Gronthus took her directly to the abbey on the east side of the town. He ushered her down three flights of stone steps and into the dim corridors of the dungeon, where he removed her manacles and locked her inside a windowless cell. Her only furniture was a six-foot wooden rack hung by chains from the wall. The only light came from the dim glow of a torch fifty feet down the corridor.

"Gronthus, I saved you from a pit not worse than this hellhole. Surely you don't intend to leave me here."

He looked hard at Evalonne as he inserted the key and locked the cell. Her eyes were wide and pleading, her lips parted with incredulity. But without a word he dropped the key into his pocket, turned away, and walked down the corridor. He climbed the dungeon stairway, went out to the well in the courtyard, and scrubbed his hands as his father had taught him to do each time he touched a woman. He sat for a moment on the edge of the well as he dried his hands.

He barely remembered his father and did not remember his mother at all. When he had grown old enough to realize that other children had mothers, he had asked his father why he did not have one. His father's face had grown hard and cold as he knelt before his son and clutched both shoulders in his hands. Gronthus winced as he remembered the pain of the man's fingers digging into his flesh. "Ye're blessed not to have a mother," he had said. "Stay away from women, Son. Never look on them; never touch them. They're the bane of Adam's race. Thank the Master each day when ye rise and each night when ye lie down that ye have no woman in your life. They be fickle and heartless, and they bring ye nothin' but pain." That was all the answer Gronthus ever got, and days later his father had taken him to the Abbey of Lochlaund and left him there. He had been raised by monks until he took his orders and had never known another home.

Gronthus left the well and reentered the abbey. He climbed the stairway to the second floor and knocked on Bishop Hugal's chamber door. He knocked again and waited another minute before he heard the scrape and clank of the bolt being drawn and the door creaked open.

Bishop Hugal stood in the doorway, his gray cowl hiding his face in its dark folds. Gronthus greeted his master and bowed low before him. Hugal bade him enter, and Gronthus noticed as the bishop turned toward his chair that he walked much slower, more stiffly, and with the shuffling gait of an old man. He spoke with a hollow, rasping sound in the back of his throat. He reached his chair and, using his cane for support, eased himself painfully into the cushions.

Gronthus wondered about his master's keeping his head covered at all times. He had asked Hugal of it before and had been told he was fulfilling the terms of a secret vow. Yet Gronthus wondered. A monk attending the bishop had told him that their master had fallen sick immediately after drinking of the wine that Gronthus had brought from Sister Aganesta.

"You are not well, my master," said Gronthus.

"I am well enough," the bishop replied shortly. "What brings you here, Gronthus? The hour is late and the king's wedding is tomorrow."

"I have captured the harlot Evalonne, your grace. And I have ample evidence and sufficient witnesses to take her before King Lanson for immediate trial."

"That is the last thing we want to do," replied Hugal. "This is the very woman King Lanson has been searching for. The fool thought he was in love with the vile creature, and now he believes she is dead. If we bring her before him now, we risk him calling off his marriage to Lamonda."

"But she must be brought to trial, your grace. The law demands it."

"Of course, of course. But the trial need not be immediate. We can hold her secretly until the king is safely wedded to Lamonda. After a few days we can bring her before him and force him to condemn her to death according to kirk law. Thus we will rid ourselves of this threat to the purity of Lochlaund's throne, and it will be by Lanson's own sentence." Hugal began to chuckle at the irony of it all until a spasm of coughing seized him.

After he recovered his composure, he said to Gronthus, "You have done well, my son. You must be tired from your long journey, and I will not keep you any longer. Go with my gratitude."

Gronthus bowed low. "Thank you, your grace."

He turned to go, and as he reached the door, Hugal called to him. "One thing more, Gronthus. Where are you holding the strumpet?"

"In the abbey prison, your grace."

"In what cell?"

"Cell number sixteen."

"Good. You may go now."

Gronthus left and went to his own quarters.

CHAPTER THIRTY-TWO

The prisoner of the Law

hile Gronthus was speaking with Bishop Hugal, another meeting was in progress in an anteroom of Macrennon Castle. Lanson sat in a chair opposite Lamonda with his chin on his hand as she went over a long list written on a parchment roll, reading off each item as Lanson responded. Off in the shadows of the room sat Lady Dulessa, acting as chaperone for the pair at Lamonda's insistence.

"Are you certain you know exactly where to stand after you march to the dais?" asked Lamonda.

"I step to my right in front of the bishop," replied Lanson, stifling a yawn. The ordeal had begun over two hours ago.

"Yes . . . go on."

"Go on where?"

"What do you do after you stand on the dais?" Lamonda made no attempt to hide her exasperation.

"Well . . . I, uh . . . I wait for you?"

"No! No! No! You turn and look out over the audience toward the door in the rear of the hall where I will enter." Lamonda emphasized each word as if speaking to an idiot child, her fist pounding the arm of the chair as she spoke. Lady Dulessa shook her head.

"Of course. I knew that," replied Lanson. "It's much too small a detail to be concerned about."

"No detail is too small to be concerned about. Especially since you will not pay attention." Dulessa's emphatic nod affirmed Lamonda's accusation.

"We have rehearsed the sequence, the dress, the moves, the pace of the marches, where we will stand, and what we will say until I could do it all in my sleep," said Lanson. "And speaking of sleep, the hour is late and the day has been long. We'd best get some rest tonight or we may indeed find ourselves sleepwalking tomorrow."

"I am appalled at you, Lanson. Here it is the night before your wedding and you can't even take the time to be sure of your own part in it."

"But I am sure of it. I know every—"

"You don't even care about all I've done to make this wedding an occasion for Lochlaund to remember. All you have to be concerned about is your own little part. I have to handle everything—the wardrobes, the banquet, the seating of the guests, the music, the candles, the attendants—which reminds me, are you sure Maconnal has had a new suit made? I wouldn't want him embarrassing me with that old faded, threadbare rag he always wears."

"Yes, Maconnal has bought a new suit," sighed Lanson.

"I do wish you had chosen someone else as your groomsman. My uncle says that Maconnal is—"

"Maconnal is my friend. He will be my groomsman. We've been over this enough. It is futile for you to raise the issue again." Lanson arose and walked toward the door.

"Sit down, Lanson. We've not gone over your speech at the banquet."

"I have already prepared my speech for the banquet."

"I have not yet heard it. Recite it so I can tell you what I think of it."

"You shall hear it at the banquet. Good night, Lamonda. Good night, Lady Dulessa." Lanson bowed formally and left the room.

As Lanson walked the corridors to his own chambers, he wondered, as he had wondered many times, if he was not placing too much importance on following his father's will in the wedding of this woman. But rightly or wrongly, he did feel the hand of his father upon him. He had wondered aloud to Maconnal if the Master of the

Universe did not sometimes pair mates for reasons other than love. Perhaps unlikely men and women were thrust together so the friction generated by their differences would smooth out the rough edges, polishing and reshaping both into vessels with a greater capacity for glory. Perhaps Lanson would melt Lamonda's coldness, and perhaps she would correct defects in him he did not even know he had.

Maconnal had replied that the best of marriages generated quite enough of such corrective abrasion. One need not seek it in greater abundance. Nevertheless, with no better alternatives, and with the nobles of the kingdom pressing him to wed, Lanson resigned himself to follow the will of his father. He would marry Lamonda on the morrow. Of course, if Evalonne had lived . . . Lanson's throat grew tight and his eyes blurred at the magnitude of his loss. He reached his chambers, undressed for bed, and slept fitfully through the night.

Lanson was not the only sleeper having trouble with his rest that night. Gronthus, in his spare but spotless abbey cell, lay wide awake glaring at the wooden slats of his ceiling. He was angry. The face of Evalonne filled his mind and he could not force it out. He could not forget how she had looked at him when he had last seen her, her eyes wide and bewildered, her lips parted in dismay as he locked the cell and turned his back on her. He gritted his teeth in consternation and would have muttered a curse, but no curse had ever crossed his lips and he would not allow one to contaminate them now.

What right had this creature to invade his mind? She was a woman—a vile, unclean, evil woman. Surely he had been right to pursue her even after she had saved him from sure death. It was his duty, and mere personal sentiment should not deter him. Besides, he had warned her that even if she got him out of the pit, he would not relent in his pursuit. Yet she had chosen to rescue him of her own free will. It was not of his doing. He was innocent of any wrong. So why couldn't he close his eyes and sleep? Law was law and that woman had flouted it. Law was law and he had a duty to it. An ironclad duty. He had no choice but to bring her to justice. It was unjust that her face would not leave him in peace.

Gronthus had never suffered such proddings of conscience before and did not recognize the alien activity that now fevered his brain. His conscience was a stranger to him, for he had never given it cause to present itself, though it should have done so many times before. Had the training of the kirk furnished his mind with more of the warmth of empathy and less of the coldness of law, his conscience might have found a home there. It would not have shocked him now with this late introduction. Being a stranger to conscience, Gronthus did not welcome it or consider its claims to be valid and tried repeatedly to shut it out and send it on its way. But it would not leave, and throughout the night it presented to his troubled mind the pleading face of the woman who had saved him so he could condemn her to death. Who had, in fact, given her life to save his.

☙

There was yet a third person who could not sleep that night. Like Gronthus, Bishop Hugal could not get the image of Evalonne out of his mind. But unlike Gronthus, it was not conscience that afflicted him. Long ago he had trained that intrusive voice not to meddle in his pursuits. When it did interfere, he had so often shut it into a dark chamber that it no longer even raised a whisper. Indeed, he did not even know whether it was still alive and never gave the question any thought.

After King Kor's death, when Hugal still occupied the king's chambers, he had imprisoned several women in the tower to do penance and had gone to them through the passageway he had found to offer them a way to buy their freedom. Lanson's return had evicted him from the castle and denied him this occasional diversion. His thoughts now descended to the cell in the dungeon two levels below his chambers where Evalonne was imprisoned. Hugal pulled his cowl over his head, took his cane, and made his way down the steps to the dungeon. A lone monk was sitting at guard in front of the gate to the cells.

"Open the gate for me," Hugal said. "I could not sleep tonight, for I felt the hand of the Master upon me, urging me to pray with the new prisoner. Please give me the key to cell number sixteen."

The monk bowed and complied. Hugal took the key and walked

painfully into the prison. The only sound in the dark passageway was the tapping of his cane and the shuffling of his sandals against the stone floor as he made his way to the end of the corridor and turned the lock to Evalonne's cell. By the dim light of the torch on the wall, he could see her supple body in the straw on the floor. His eyes devoured every detail. She was sleeping on her side with her hands folded beneath her cheek. Her lustrous hair fell softly about her face, and his eager eyes traced the smooth contours of her form as she lay stretched out on the floor.

Hugal reached out to stroke the velvet of her cheek. Some sound, some sense of presence, some dark shadow that crossed Evalonne's mind brought her awake. She opened her eyes and saw the hand hovering above her face and sat up suddenly, backing away with a rustle of straw.

"Who are you?" she demanded, sitting on her heels with her hands on the floor like a crouched animal ready to spring.

"Quiet, my child. I am one who has come to do you good."

"The only good you can do me is to get me out of this cell."

"That is exactly what I am prepared to do. But first, you must cooperate with me."

"What do you want?"

Bishop Hugal told her.

Mustering every ounce of strength she had, Evalonne sprang at the dark figure before her. She felt the crack of a rib and heard his sudden expulsion of air as her shoulder plowed into his abdomen. He took two or three steps backward before falling against the door, knocking it open. As Hugal lay on the stones doubled over, wheezing for breath, Evalonne lunged forward, intending to run out of the cell and into the hall, but she stopped short. The outer gate would be locked, and she would never make it past the guard posted there. Instead, she rolled the hooded figure out of the cell and closed the door between them. Moments later, Hugal got to his feet and staggered toward the cell.

"I'll teach you to strike me!" he rasped as he grasped the bars and tried to pull the door open. But Evalonne pulled from the inside, and he could not budge it. She realized with wonder that she was stronger than he. After a minute or so of futile tugging, Bishop Hugal, wheezing with a sound like the hiss of a snake, locked the cell door, cursing Evalonne all the while, and shuffled his way down the corridor. She heard the tapping of his cane long after the darkness swallowed him.

ᔕ᷎

Morning came, and Lanson arose early, feeling a weight of dread heavy in his belly. Though he had little appetite, he went down for breakfast and found the castle servants already bustling with preparations for the wedding, to be held at the third hour of the afternoon. Maconnal was at the table waiting for him.

"You still don't have to do this, you know," said his friend. The look Lanson shot him in response told him that the matter was settled and he need not bring it up again. But Maconnal persisted. "You may not realize it, Lanson, but your father, King Kor, was changing. Yes, he did agree with Hugal on your marriage to Lamonda, but I'm not so sure that if he had lived he would have insisted that you go through with it. Indeed, I perceived that the more he thought on it, the less certain of it he became."

"But he thought the match was a good one for the kingdom," replied Lanson.

"That he did, for it would show solidarity between the kingdom and the kirk. But you might be surprised at the turmoil in your father's mind concerning the kirk. He was beginning to question many of the kirk's stances and judgments."

"But he did uphold them."

"He did, but not without strong misgivings. My fear today is that this marriage may pull you back into the kirk's web."

"I will not allow my wife to determine the kingdom's policy," Lanson said.

"A noble sentiment. A brave assertion. But it's balderdash. This woman will find a way to shape the kingdom's policy or you will find that this castle is not wide enough to escape the misery she will contrive to inflict upon you."

"Maconnal, I'm so grateful to you for brightening the morning of my wedding day with your genial companionship."

"Very well, I shall clamp my teeth upon my tongue. Finish your breakfast. You have a long day ahead of you, not to mention a long life—or at least one that's sure to seem long."

The two ate quickly, talking little, then went directly to the throne hall. All suits and business of the kingdom had been suspended for the day, allowing the king to greet the many guests who would arrive for the ceremony, as well as to make his own preparations for the wedding.

Lanson took the throne as Maconnal found a seat at the side of the hall where he could watch the events of the morning and greet any of the guests whom he knew. The lord chamberlain informed King Lanson that several earls, barons, knights, and other nobles already waited outside the hall. The king ordered the doors opened, and the herald began to announce the guests as they entered and the king received them. The hall filled as those who had been received began to mill about, using the occasion to seek out old friends and finesse diplomatic liaisons. Bishop Hugal, moving even more painfully than usual, and Gronthus, looking particularly haggard, also entered the hall.

"Baron and Lady Kenmarl of Oranth," announced the herald, and Maconnal looked up to see his old friend come through the door with his wife and approach King Lanson. Behind them followed two Oranthian knights and three servants, including the slow-witted Dwag, who bore decorated coffers containing gifts for the royal couple-to-be. After the king had received the lord and his lady and uttered his thanks for the gifts, Kenmarl and his party bowed and moved into the crowd.

Maconnal wove his way through the guests and welcomed Kenmarl and his wife to Macrennon. As the three of them began to visit, the servant Dwag spotted Gronthus strolling through the crowd nearby.

"Father Gronthus," he called in a voice that could be heard in the rafters. Gronthus stopped, looked up, and without responding moved quickly away. But Dwag was not so easily deterred. "Father Gronthus," he called again as he caught up with the kirkman and grabbed him by the arm. "You find lost girl?"

"You mistake me for someone else," growled Gronthus and made haste to move away, looking all about to see who might have heard the exchange.

"Nooo, it was you for sure, 'member? You come to pasture lookin' for red-haired girl. But we not findin' her. You said you go into woods to find her. You 'member?"

Maconnal had been only half attending Dwag's query of Gronthus, but the mention of a red-haired girl suddenly caught his attention. He did not hear Kenmarl's report of the fine crop year they were having in Oranth; his ear was carefully tuned to Dwag and Gronthus.

"Let go of me this instant," demanded Gronthus.

"I sorry," said Dwag as he released his grip. "Just want to know if you find her. Been sore worried 'bout her, for sure. Not see her after you come."

"You are an idiot," Gronthus spat as he turned away and slipped into the crowd.

Maconnal excused himself from Lord Kenmarl and took Dwag aside into an anteroom.

"Dwag, who was the girl you were speaking of to Gronthus?"

"Her name Ev'lonne."

Maconnal's heart leapt. "How did you know this Evalonne?"

"She work at Kenmarl. Sometime she work in field, sometime herd sheep, sometime in manor. But you know. You there. You saw her, for sure."

"I saw her? What do you mean?"

"You eat dinner with lord and lady. Ev'lonne serve wine to you."

"I don't think so. I would have noticed."

"She did. She did. I 'member. She spill on you hand. She 'pologize. But you not upset. You good man. Not talk bad to poor Ev'lonne. You good, for sure."

Maconnal thought back on the dinner that night and vaguely recalled the incident. He had just that day learned of Evalonne's death and was so preoccupied that he had not even bothered to look up at the girl serving him. But apparently Evalonne had not been dead after all. Someone had deliberately misled him into believing she was. Who? And why? Maconnal could guess the answers.

"Thank you, Dwag," he said as he opened the door and led the man from the room. "Today you may have saved a kingdom from sinking into darkness."

As Maconnal walked swiftly into the hall, Dwag stared after him, his mouth gaping open and his brows knitted in painful concentration as he scratched his head. "I never save no kingdom. I save a sheep sometime, but I never save no kingdom, for sure."

Maconnal peered over the crowd and spotted Gronthus on the far side of the hall, speaking with the hooded Bishop Hugal. Maconnal worked his way toward him. But Gronthus saw him coming and, after bending toward Hugal and whispering, turned and wove his way toward the door at the end of the hall. Maconnal began to push and shove, jolting and bumping against startled knights and ladies, apologizing as he went. He reached Gronthus just as he went out the door and caught him by the arm in the corridor.

"It seems to be the day for clutching kirkmen by the arm," said Gronthus.

"Where is Evalonne?" demanded Maconnal.

"Why should I even know of whom you speak?"

"Don't play with me, Gronthus. You do know. Dwag insists that she was alive and working on Kenmarl's estate weeks after a man in Oranth assured me she was dead."

"Who are you going to believe, an idiot or a kirkman?"

"That choice is simple. According to Dwag, who lacks the guile to lie, you came looking for Evalonne at Kenmarl after I was there. Now I have two questions for you, and by answering them truthfully, you can repair my broken confidence in the veracity of kirkmen. Did you find Evalonne, and where is she?"

"First, let me tell you that I never lie. And second, that I never reveal privileged information to a heretic."

"And just why is the whereabouts of a common tradesman's daughter privileged information of such great importance to the Kirk of Lochlaund?"

Gronthus said nothing.

"You know where this woman is."

Gronthus merely stared impassively at Maconnal, who realized

he would get nothing more from the kirkman. But the man's refusal
to answer gave him strong reason to suspect that Gronthus had found
Evalonne and had her hidden away, waiting for the kirk to find some
way to use her against Lanson, should he be so bold as to depart from
kirk doctrine. He had to find her. And quickly. He turned from
Gronthus and ran down the corridor to the steps that led to his room.
Gronthus watched him until he disappeared into the stairwell, then
slipped into an alcove and waited.

Maconnal leapt up the steps three at a time and sped down the
corridor to his chambers. He opened the trunk in the corner and dug
through the clothing until he found the clerical robes he had worn
when he was an acolyte in Rhondilar. He removed his doublet,
slipped the robe over the rest of his clothing, and bounded down the
stairway and out of the castle.

Watching from his alcove, Gronthus saw him rushing from the
castle to the stables and followed at enough distance to avoid notice.

As Maconnal galloped toward the abbey, he hoped he was not on
a fool's errand. He had no idea where Evalonne might be hidden—
nor even if she had been caught, really, though he strongly suspected
by Dwag's testimony and Gronthus's reaction that she had. If they
had captured her, they might simply have confined her to the abbey
dungeon. It was safe enough from outside eyes, as none but kirkmen
were allowed to enter it.

He rode up to the abbey gate, dismounted, and pulled his cowl
over his head. He rang the bell, waited two or three minutes, then
rang it again, giving the rope a few additional tugs. Moments later a
robed monk appeared, stumbling and rubbing his eyes. Obviously
the bell had interrupted his nap. Maconnal explained that he had
traveled from Rhondilar with a certain nobleman to honor King
Lanson at his wedding. However, not being invited to dinner at
Macrennon Castle, he begged to dine at the abbey table. The monk
yawned and opened the gate to him with no questions.

"Come this way," he mumbled as he shuffled across the courtyard. Maconnal tied his horse and followed, biting his tongue to keep
from hurrying the man along. They entered the door of the abbey
into a room of gray stone, furnished only with a bench at one end and

a large chair at the other. The dark walls were bare. From the center of the wall facing the door, a long, arched corridor opened to the interior of the abbey.

The monk pointed to the bench and said, "You may wait here. At the belling of noon I will take you to the meal hall."

Forcing his tense muscles to feign nonchalance, Maconnal sat on the bench as the monk took the chair. Not wanting to encourage conversation, Maconnal clasped his hands on the lap of his robe and bent his head downward as if he were in his devotions. But he need not have worried. Soon he heard the unmistakable rattle of human snoring and glanced over to see his host slumped forward in sleep. Maconnal waited until the rhythm of the snores became regular, then he rose carefully from the bench. But not carefully enough. Something clanged and scraped on the board beneath him, and he realized to his dismay that he had forgotten he had his short sword still buckled beneath his robes. The monk sputtered and blinked, and Maconnal quickly sat down again. But soon the snoring resumed and settled into a regular cadence. Again Maconnal rose, holding his sword against his thigh, and walked softly around the sleeper into the corridor.

He breathed a sigh of thanksgiving that the corridor was deserted and walked slowly along it, looking into each of the arched doorways as he passed them. The first was closed. The second opened onto a stairway leading upward. The third opened into a large hall, where he saw several robed figures seated on benches and standing in groups of two or three. He hurried on past.

The next door opened onto a stone stairway leading downward, which Maconnal thought likely was the way to the dungeon. He turned toward it when three monks, talking together in lowered voices, came into the hall from the far end and began walking toward him. He checked his turn and moved toward them instead, his head bowed and his hands clasped as if in deep meditation. They did not so much as greet him as they passed, and when they turned into the dining hall behind him, he wheeled around and walked quickly back to the door that opened onto the descending stairway.

Maconnal crept down the steps and in moments reached the

stone floor. The air was rank with the odor of mildew, rancid straw, and human excrement. He reached a turn in the corridor, and ahead he could see by the light of a torch on the wall a robed figure sitting in front of a gate of barred iron. The monk was silent, his hands loose in his lap and his head bowed forward. Maconnal approached silently and stopped six feet in front of him. The deep breathing and slight wheeze told him that this monk, too, was asleep.

A ring of keys hung on a spike driven into the mortar just above the sleeping kirkman. Maconnal knew he might retrieve the keys without waking the man, but he would never be able to open the lock without considerable clanging and scraping. He put his hand on the man's shoulder and shook it gently.

The monk sputtered and came half awake. "What . . . oh . . . is it time?"

"I'm here to relieve you a few minutes early, brother," said Maconnal. "They're gathering for lunch upstairs."

The man mumbled his thanks and plodded off toward the stairway. Maconnal watched until he rounded the corner, then took the keys from the spike and began to try them in the lock. On the fifth key it clanked and swung open. He entered the dark corridor, peering into each cell as he passed. Several of the prisoners were female, but none fit the description of Evalonne until he reached the last cell at the end of the corridor. In the dim torchlight he could make out the figure of a woman sleeping on the straw in the back of the cell, the light barely picking up a few strands of red in her hair.

"Evalonne?" whispered Maconnal. She did not answer.

"Evalonne," he repeated in lowered tones. "Say nothing. I have come to take you out of here. But there are dangers. We must take care." He took his keys and, after several attempts, found the right one and opened the lock. "Come quickly. We must hurry."

Still she did not respond. He dared not raise his voice but entered the cell, leaving the key in the lock, and bent down to shake her gently awake. She looked up, eyes wide, and opened her mouth to scream, but he quickly clapped his hand over it. "Say nothing," he whispered. "I am a friend come to take you out of here. But there are dangers and we must move carefully." She thought her attacker of the night had returned and began to fight him off. But she looked at his face and recognized him as Kenmarl's dinner guest upon whom she had spilled wine. She quit fighting, and he removed his hand from her mouth.

"Are you able to walk?" he asked.

She nodded and said, "How did you find me?"

"No time for questions now," said Maconnal as he helped her up from the straw. "We must hurry."

At that moment the door of the cell slammed shut, followed by the click of the lock. They turned in surprise. Glaring at them from outside of the bars was the smug, hard face of Gronthus.

No words were spoken. No words were needed. Maconnal knew that no amount of pleading would penetrate the hard crust of law that imprisoned Gronthus's humanity. He knew that Gronthus was convinced he was acting justly. He had trapped a heretic in the act of thwarting the process of justice.

The accorder stood immobile, staring with satisfaction at the shock on Maconnal's face. He looked at the face of Evalonne, her sad eyes wide and her lips parted in dismay, exactly as she had looked at him when he had captured her, exactly as she had looked at him every night since, hovering in his mind against his will, keeping him from sleep. How long the three stared at each other, they did not know. It seemed but a moment; it seemed an eternity.

It began to dawn on Gronthus that a momentous choice lay before him. If he chose what he had known to be right from the time he was an acolyte under Hugal's tutelage, that face would continue to haunt him every night as he writhed upon his bed. If he chose the opposite, he would turn his back on all he had learned and believed and lived by, but that face would disappear and his mind would be free. He continued to stare. He could not choose. His mind refused to make the impossible decision between the very structure of his life on the one hand and his conscience on the other, and it released his hands to act on their own. Without changing expression, without taking his eyes off his stricken prisoners, he lifted the key to the lock, hesitated for a moment, inserted it, turned the key, opened wide the door, and stood beside it.

Maconnal and Evalonne stared in disbelief. Gronthus said nothing but waited beside the open door like a butler. Maconnal came to his senses and took Evalonne by the hand.

"Come, Evalonne," he said, never taking his eyes from the immobile Gronthus.

Gronthus did not move as the two prisoners passed through the door, but as they started down the corridor he called to them. "Wait."

Evalonne tried to run on, but Maconnal pulled her to a halt and turned to see Gronthus removing his robe. "You will need this," he said. "Put it on the girl or you will have no chance of getting out of the abbey. Maconnal took the robe, wrapped it around Evalonne, tied the sash loosely about her waist, and covered her head with the cowl. He turned to Gronthus and said, "The Master of the Universe will bless you for this." Then he took Evalonne's hand and they hurried down the corridor.

Gronthus, standing immobile in his brown undershift, said nothing but remained still and impassive as he watched the two disappear into the darkness of the corridor. When they were out of sight, he stepped into Evalonne's cell. The clang of the cell door echoed through the dungeon as he shut it behind him. He took the key, reached through the bars and turned it in the lock, then pitched it into the corridor.

PART IV

SACRIFICE

CHAPTER THIRTY-THREE

Ṫ🜚є Ṫʀɪᴀʟ

here is Maconnal? Lanson wondered. His groomsman had disappeared in the middle of the morning and had not shown up for the midday meal. Shortly after eating, Lanson had sent pages throughout the castle to find him, but they returned and assured the young king that his friend was nowhere within its walls. Now the afternoon was drawing on, the wedding was an hour away, and the man was still missing. Lanson retired to his chambers with his valet to begin final preparations. But first he drafted a note to Lamonda, who had spent the day preparing in rooms within the castle, and gave it to a page for delivery. The note told her that his groomsman Maconnal was missing. He suggested delaying the wedding until his groomsman could be found.

A quarter-hour later the page returned with a note in Lamonda's emphatic hand insisting the wedding must go on as planned. The delay would humiliate her more than Maconnal's absence, though one would have thought the man would have more respect for her than to wander off on the day of her wedding. Lanson could easily find another groomsman from among the many noblemen in attendance. And he had best do it quickly.

Lanson reddened as he scanned the note, then he crumpled it and tossed it into the fireplace. He knew that Lamonda hated Maconnal and was undoubtedly gloating over his absence. He thought briefly of drafting a note of refusal, but with a sigh of resignation, he relented and submitted himself to his valet to complete his ceremonial plumage.

But he would not conscript a substitute groomsman. He would meet his fate alone.

Ten minutes before the appointed hour, King Lanson, dressed in silk tights and an embroidered doublet with gilded trim and slitted sleeves, and trailing a heavy cape the color of wine, strode out of his chambers under the ceremonial escort of six guards and marched through the corridors to the great hall. He stopped at the heavy oaken doors and drew a deep breath as his valet gave him a final inspection, smoothing and pulling and adjusting until he nodded to the door-man and the doors swung wide.

The herald announced the entrance of the king, and the seated guests all arose as he marched to the dais, where Bishop Hugal—strangely, still cowled—stood waiting. Lanson mounted the steps, took his place just to the side of the bishop, and looked out over the guests toward the door where Lamonda would enter, exactly as he had been instructed.

The lute and harp began to play, the doors swung slowly open, and everyone in the hall turned toward them to witness the entrance of the bride. But to the surprise of every eye, two kirkmen entered the hall instead. They were robed in gray with their cowls covering their heads, and they walked side by side as they approached the dais, where Lanson and the bishop stood. Lanson blinked in surprise as he ran Lamonda's instructions through his mind once more. He should have paid better attention. He did not remember two monks being on the program. He looked past the two figures to the back of the hall and saw Lamonda standing in the open door, gowned in white, her fists clenched at her side, a look of consternation clouding her face. Something was going wrong.

The monks stopped at the foot of the dais, and one of them reached up and pushed his cowl back from his head.

"Maconnal!" said Lanson. "Where have you been? What in thunder are you doing?"

"King Lanson," said Maconnal, "there is a case on your docket scheduled for trial three days from today. I have good reason to think it urgent that your majesty hear this case now and make your judgment immediately."

"Hear it now?" Lanson was incredulous. "Have you gone insane? Have you forgotten that a wedding is about to commence in which you are supposed to be the groomsman? The case can wait until its proper time."

Without a word Maconnal turned and pushed the cowl back from the head of the figure beside him, and waves of lustrous russet hair billowed from their confinement.

"Evalonne!" Lanson whispered. "Evalonne, you are alive!" He stood stunned, his emotions a chaotic turmoil of shock, disbelief, and wild elation. Oblivious to all in the room but her, his eyes devoured every detail of the face he had thought he would never see again.

Abashed by his unwavering gaze, Evalonne blushed and sank to the steps in a deep curtsy, where she remained.

"Sir Maconnal," the voice of Bishop Hugal rasped through the hall. "Would you explain the meaning of this outrage? Tell us how and why you managed to free this woman from the abbey dungeon."

"And you can tell us how and why she came to be reported dead," retorted Maconnal.

"Whether she was thought dead is not at issue here. The issue is that this woman has been indicted for a capital offense, and you have removed her from prison. I demand to know what the king will do about this outrage."

"Her reported death is indeed an issue," replied Maconnal. "It was a deception, and I think I know exactly who—"

"Enough!" said Lanson. "If you men are determined to shout accusations at each other, we'd best follow Maconnal's recommendation and have the woman's trial right now." He turned to the stunned audience. "I do hope my honored guests will forgive this sudden change of plans. You came for a wedding and instead it seems that we are about to conduct a trial. Any of you who wish to leave are free to go."

No one left.

"Very well then, we shall proceed with the trial." King Lanson took his throne. Bishop Hugal took the chair to the right of the dais and Maconnal the one to the left. A chair for Evalonne was placed in the center of the hall at the foot of the dais facing the king, where she sat with her head bowed and her hands folded on her lap. Lanson turned to the bishop. "You are the accuser, Bishop Hugal. Proceed with the charges."

"If it please your majesty, I request that the accorder Gronthus be called to serve as my aide."

King Lanson nodded to the herald, who issued the call for Gronthus. He repeated it twice, but when no answer came, Lanson commanded Bishop Hugal to proceed without him.

"Very well, your majesty. The accorder has given me a thorough catalog of the woman's crimes, and I can conduct the prosecution myself. I had thought to wait until after the wedding to keep from marring this festive occasion, but if you insist, now will do very well."

Bishop Hugal stood and, leaning on his cane, shuffled forward until he loomed over Evalonne. "The Kirk of Lochlaund lodges the following charges against the woman you see before you, Evalonne by name, daughter of Langus, before his death a wheelwright in the city of Macrennon. First, the kirk accuses the woman Evalonne of engaging in an illicit carnal relationship with the wandering minstrel Avriel. Second, the kirk accuses the woman Evalonne of giving birth to a child without the legitimacy of wedlock. Third, the kirk accuses the woman Evalonne of employ as a harlot at the Red Falcon Inn in the village of Larenton in Oranth. Fourth, the kirk accuses the woman Evalonne of failing to face her sins and give herself over for discipline, choosing rather to flee the kirk's corrective judgment, leaving Lochlaund and hiding at various locations in Oranth and Vensaur. Fifth, the kirk accuses the woman Evalonne of living for as many as nine days with an unidentified wandering swordsman while escaping the justice of the kirk. Obviously this woman is thoroughly wanton and has lived a life of habitual immorality."

The Bishop turned from Evalonne and faced the king. "Your majesty, I have witnesses within this hall who have come to Lochlaund to confirm the truth of these charges, whom I shall call at the appropriate time. Before I take my seat, I take the liberty to point out to the king that each of these crimes save one—her escape from justice—is punishable by death in the Devil's Mouth." Hugal hobbled to his chair and sat.

"How does the woman Evalonne plead?" asked King Lanson.

Evalonne did not look up but spoke in a voice clear and steady. "I am guilty of all the charges save one, your majesty. I deny that there was anything illicit in my relationship with the wandering swordsman with whom I spent nine days. I merely traveled under his protection."

"Do you really expect the king to believe that a man traveled with such as you for nine days and remained chaste?" demanded the bishop. Then turning toward King Lanson, he said, "I'm sure the king will find such a denial incredible."

"I attest to the truth of what she claims," said King Lanson, "for I was that wandering swordsman. We fell in together while I was escaping assassination."

A ripple of surprise swept through the audience, and Lamonda, still standing in the darkness of the hall doorway, clenched her fists as her face went livid with anger.

"Well, we certainly cannot impugn the word of the king himself, can we?" said Hugal. "Nevertheless, by her own confession, she stands guilty of the other four charges. Therefore no witnesses will be necessary and there is no need for the trial to continue. The king will now do his duty and condemn this woman to death in the Devil's Mouth."

Maconnal stood and said, "Your majesty, before you pronounce sentence, may I say a word?"

Bishop Hugal objected. "Your majesty, there is no defense against a confession. This trial is over."

"You may speak, Sir Maconnal," said the king.

Maconnal stepped toward Evalonne, who looked up at him as he spoke. "Evalonne, without coercion or duress, you have been so free to admit the sins with which you have been charged that I must ask you this: are you proud of these sins?"

Evalonne looked down at her hands in her lap. "No, sir. I am deeply ashamed."

"As you committed these sins, did you realize you were sinning?"

"I did, sir."

"Are you telling the court that you cared nothing for the law of the Master of the Universe? That you defied it and flouted it as being of no consequence?"

"No, sir, it wasn't like that. I knew the law, but I was weak. I placed my own wants in front of the law and somehow pushed aside what I knew to be right."

"And how did you feel afterward?"

"Terrible, sir. I knew I had done wrong, and I hated it. I hated myself for doing it."

"When you descended into prostitution at the Red Falcon Inn in Oranth, was that by choice?" asked Maconnal.

"Yes."

"Yes? What do you mean, Evalonne? Didn't the innkeeper deceive you with the contract of indenture, then threaten you with breach of it when you refused service to his customers?"

"He did, sir. But still, it was my choice. I could have refused, and I should have, in spite of the threats."

"But you were with child. Refusal would have meant being turned out, perhaps imprisoned for debt, perhaps meaning death to you and your unborn baby."

"That is true, sir. Nevertheless, I should have refused. Some things are worse than death."

"What would you do if the same choices were presented to you again?"

"Here in this court before all these witnesses, with my life at stake, and with the benefit of hindsight, I find it easy to assert what my heart tells me is true—that I would never make those choices again. Indeed, that is what I have resolved. But, sir, in spite of my resolve, in spite of the merciless punishment my conscience has inflicted on me, I know that I am a weak woman. I cannot be sure I would never fall again, though if I did, I'm not sure I could live with myself."

Maconnal turned to the king. "Your majesty, I think I have never heard confession and repentance more honestly expressed. This woman has sinned. But not in defiance of the Master, not because she refused to accept his law as her standard." Maconnal turned to the audience. "I wonder how many among you would not have made the same choice as the accused when threatened with imprisonment or poverty or death? And how many of you would be as honest with yourself and the court as this woman has been? Though a promise never to fall again might save her from death, she admits that her weakness might overcome her resolve." He turned back to the king. "Your majesty, Evalonne has fallen, and her sins are real and grievous. But she has repented. In spite of her weakness, which we all share, she holds the law of the Master of the Universe as her standard. I beg mercy for her and urge you to grant her a pardon."

Bishop Hugal stood, sputtering. "Outrageous! This is outrageous. Your majesty must not listen to this heretic. Unlike barbarian kingdoms, Lochlaund is ruled by law, not by the whims of a king. You cannot override the law and grant clemency for a capital offense."

"Your majesty," replied Maconnal, "mercy and forgiveness have always been at the heart of what the Master is about with mankind. The oldest scrolls show us clearly that in its beginnings the kirk encouraged forgiveness and mercy alongside obedience to law. Law defines the behavior of perfect humans, but since all are fallen and none perfect, forgiveness and mercy have become the only way to life."

"Mercy is the way to death," retorted Hugal. "It is law that holds the kingdom together and prevents anarchy. Mercy breeds disregard of law. Disobedience must be punished or law will be flouted in favor of individual desires and the kingdom will disintegrate."

Sir Maconnal responded, "But without mercy the kingdom will become a desolate, unpopulated wilderness because no citizen will survive the penalty of law. We are all guilty of breaking the law, Bishop Hugal. Justice condemns us all, and only by mercy can we survive."

"The very existence of the Kingdom of Lochlaund proves you wrong," replied Hugal. "The kirk has always insisted on strict enforcement of law, yet the kingdom survives."

"You misstate the truth," accused Maconnal, glaring at his adversary. "Forgiveness and mercy were prevalent in the courts of the Seven Kingdoms until the death of Perivale. In his day and before, sentences such as you are demanding today were often commuted, and the kirk did not have the right to override the king's decision. It was only after

Perivale's death that the kirk claimed this right, and it was never written into law."

"The kirk gained this right in order to save the Seven Kingdoms from moral disintegration," said Hugal. "At the death of Perivale the empire plunged into near anarchy, and none of the nations would have survived even as separate kingdoms had not the kirk stepped in and insisted on strict enforcement of moral law."

"That is true," replied Maconnal, "and it was a commendable thing the kirk did. In a time of extraordinary crisis the kirk stepped into the gap and took extraordinary measures. But when the battle was won, the Kirk of Lochlaund should have laid down the sword, as did the kirks of the other six kingdoms. When the government of Lochlaund stabilized, the kirk should have relinquished its power over the judgments of the king."

"What?" cried Hugal. "And let this kingdom lapse back into moral anarchy—as we see happening even now in kingdoms like Meridan and Valomar? No, Sir Maconnal, the kirk could not abandon its responsibility then, and it cannot abandon it now. Though the kirk's power to veto is an unwritten code, one hundred twenty years' acceptance of it has made it just as binding as if it were written into the book of law."

"But the Kirk of Lochlaund has lost its balance," Maconnal replied, "as all autocratic powers do. It has imposed on the kingdom a moral code more restrictive than that of the Master himself. And it is by fear that you coerce the people into obedience. You deny mercy and force them to live under the ever present threat of death for any slip into moral sin."

"You are right, Maconnal. Fear commands obedience and maintains order when nothing else will. It is right to fear the Master of the Universe, for he is just. His laws are immutable. His commands are to be obeyed."

"Bishop Hugal, there is an incident recorded in the old scrolls that says much about how the Master of the Universe deals with sinners. I'm sure you will recognize it, and perhaps you can explain to us why this story never appears in our current texts. When the Master assumed human form, a woman was brought to him, caught in the very act of adultery, much like the woman you forced the late King Kor to condemn not long before his death. The mob that caught her was ready to stone her to death. Do you remember what the Master did with this woman? After giving her an injunction to sin no more, he released her."

Maconnal turned from Hugal and spread his hands as he addressed King Lanson. "Mercy and forgiveness are what the Master is about with us, your majesty. This is at the core. On the basis of this woman's confession, I am sure the Master has forgiven her. And you, as king, must do no less. I urge you to grant her a pardon." Maconnal returned to his chair.

The bishop turned toward the throne, lifted his arm, and pointed at the king, his finger quivering with rage. "King Lanson, I give you fair warning. If you defy the will of the kirk and pardon this woman, you are in danger of having charges of heresy brought against you. You know that in the Seven Kingdoms the kirk has power to amass an army from any six kingdoms to depose a heretical monarch. It was done once against the King of Rhondilar in the time of your great-grandfather, and it will surely be done to you if you defy the kirk and grant leniency to this sinful woman."

Bishop Hugal turned and hobbled to his chair. Silence loomed for a long moment as all eyes except those of Evalonne turned toward the king, who sat immobile, his elbows resting on the arms of the throne and his hands interlocked in front of his chin. Evalonne sat unmoving, her head down, her eyes closed, and her hands folded on her lap. Lamonda, still peering through the slight opening in the great doors to the hall, stood with her ladies, waiting to hear what verdict Lanson would render.

King Lanson stood. He stepped forward, his stride firm and his face resolute. "Citizens of Lochlaund and honored guests, I agree with Sir Maconnal that mercy is at the heart of the Master of the Universe. I also agree with Bishop Hugal that no kingdom will stand without a firm adherence to the principle of law. Now hear my decision. I hereby reclaim the lawful right of kings in the Seven Kingdoms not only to issue sentences in capital cases but to issue pardons as deemed appropriate. In light of her declaration of repentance witnessed by all here, along with my own witness to her return to upright behavior, I choose not to condemn the woman Evalonne. I hereby proclaim her fully pardoned of all offense and grant her freedom."

Over half the guests in the hall responded immediately with cheers and applause while the rest sat in stunned silence. Bishop Hugal stood and, without a word, hobbled out of the hall by a side door. Lamonda left her post at the great door and hurried to her rooms, her face beet red in anger and humiliation. Maconnal's throat tightened with pride at the courage of his student king, and he silently shook Lanson's hand. Evalonne sat without moving, her eyes downcast and her hands folded in her lap. All knew the king had made a momentous decision that could cause a major upheaval in the kingdom, perhaps even a war.

Lanson, with Maconnal close behind him, stepped down from the dais and approached Evalonne, still seated with her head bowed in silence. He knelt before her, took her hands in his own, and said, "Evalonne, you are free now, and you may go if you wish. But frankly, I still fear for your safety. Those whom I have defied with my decision likely will not accept it. They may pursue you yet in spite of your pardon. Let me offer you my protection. I propose to place you under guard in the north tower until this conflict is resolved or we at least comprehend the shape of it."

Evalonne looked up at the king. "Once again I accept your protection, your majesty."

"Excellent!" replied Lanson, standing and drawing her to her feet. "The north tower is well appointed, well lighted, and warm. You will be comfortable there." He turned to his friend. "Maconnal, summon Alenia and a pair of pages to have a bath drawn for Evalonne, as well as clothing secured, a meal prepared, and a guard posted at the door of the north tower room."

Again he turned to Evalonne. "I have much to say to you, but it must wait a little while. Have no fear. I must attend to a bit of business, then I will come to you shortly." He took her hand and pressed it to his lips, then turned again to Maconnal and said in a voice husky with emotion, "Thank you, my friend." He turned on his heel and strode toward the great doors.

He made his way through the crowd, many of whom gushed their congratulations and support of his decision, as many others drew away from him or looked at him with fearful eyes. Many of the lords and knights in the assembly who feared the power of the kirk found each other and began to speak in low tones about the implications of what the king had just done. Lanson hurried as best he could toward the great door where he had last seen Lamonda peering into the hall. But when he reached the door, she was nowhere to be found. With long, quick strides, he walked down the corridor. Passing a window, he noticed the sky darkening with a churning bank of ominous clouds. He reached her chambers and knocked on the door.

"Who is it?" came a voice from inside.

Without answering, Lanson swung open the door. Lamonda sat in a chair with Ladies Dulessa and Griselda sitting nearby. Griselda cooled herself with a goose-feather fan. Lamonda gasped as Lanson entered and rose to her feet. "What do you mean, barging in here like this!"

"I must speak with you," said Lanson.

"If you've come to tell me the trial is over and we can go on with the wedding, you have some gall. I can't believe you delayed our wedding on the whim of that heretic Maconnal. And I can't believe you pardoned that vile, filthy strumpet. Not only have you humiliated me, you have set yourself against all I hold dear—the kirk and my uncle. Do you think I will just ignore all that and wed you as if nothing has happened? What appalling arrogance!"

Dulessa nodded emphatically and Griselda's fan oscillated like a dog's tail.

"I agree," said Lanson. "That is what I've come to speak of. We must call off the wedding."

A wave of alarm swept over Lamonda. She saw the queenship of Lochlaund slipping from her grasp. "I did not say I would not marry you. I said you have humiliated me. But I'm willing to rise above this affront and do my duty to the kingdom."

"No, Lamonda. We must call off the wedding. You and I do not love each other. We've both been acting from a misplaced sense of duty. Before the events of today we might have found a way to live in a perpetual state of truce, but not in love. Now with your uncle opposing me, even a truce seems unlikely. Our life together would be a continual battle. Besides, I am in love with someone else."

Lamonda's eyes narrowed and she glared at Lanson. "It's that strumpet, isn't it? That vile wanton, that harlot!"

Dulessa nodded and Griselda fanned.

"How can you, a king, wed a common woman, especially one whose own mouth has condemned her?" Seeing Lanson unmoved by her tirade, she changed tactics and began to cry. "How can you do this to me? Elaborate preparations have been made. We have spent a fortune on clothing, decorations, food, drink, and special servants. Prominent kirkmen, kinsmen, and friends have come from all over the Seven Kingdoms. I will be shamed and humiliated," she wailed as great tears soaked her kerchief.

"Yes," Lanson said, "I am sorry that we have inconvenienced so many of our guests. But we must not correct that error by committing a greater one. We must call off the wedding."

Seeing Lanson still unmoved, Lamonda's anger flared again. "You have forgotten that my uncle is a powerful man, capable even of toppling kings. Cross him and your very crown is in jeopardy. You may lose your throne unless you share it with me." Dulessa nodded emphatically, and Griselda's feathers accelerated into a blur.

"I am sorry, Lamonda. My decision is final. Good day." Lanson bowed and left the room. As he closed the door behind him an angry shriek came from the other side and a vase shattered against it. He walked back down the corridor toward the throne hall, hearing the distant rumble of thunder rolling through the darkening sky. He smiled grimly. If Lamonda's wrath could spawn such a storm, perhaps she was closer to the Master than he had thought.

He reached the hall to find the guests milling about, talking among themselves and wondering what would happen next. Lanson found Maconnal and drew him aside. "Please tell the guests that there will be no wedding. Give them my thanks for their presence and my apologies for their inconvenience, and honor all offers of hospitality we have extended. When you are finished, come to me in my quarters. We must speak of what has been done today while I give

Evalonne time to clean up and dine. Then I will go to her and see if she will consent to become the next Queen of Lochlaund."

From the throne hall Lanson went straight to the castle's wardrobe room and from the racks of suits and dresses selected a rich purple gown trimmed with threads of gold. He summoned a page to take it to the tower room, then went to his chambers to await Maconnal.

CHAPTER THIRTY-FOUR

TÞE SUBSTITUTE

valonne walked behind Alenia and an armed guard as they climbed the winding stairway to the tower room. The guard unlocked the door and the women entered. The chamber was all Lanson had promised and more—a large room with embroidered curtains, a thick rug on the floor, an elaborately carved bedstead, and a round oaken table with four chairs set around it. Several candles in brass candlesticks tinged the air with reddish gold. Alenia lit a fire in the hearth, and soon a half-dozen pages arrived with a large bathing tub and several buckets of water, along with towels, combs, brushes, and other items for Evalonne's toilette.

When the pages left, Evalonne undressed and slipped into her bath. As she scrubbed and soaked, Alenia bustled about the room dusting the furniture and checking the condition of the bedclothes and curtains. When the bath was finished, Alenia wrapped a large towel around her, sat her in a chair, and began to brush her hair. "Apparently King Lanson failed to think that you would need clothes to wear. Isn't that just like a man?"

"Nevertheless, I am grateful to him. Indeed, I owe my life to him. I could see by the debate between Bishop Hugal and Sir Maconnal that freeing me was an act of courage on the part of Lans—I mean, the king."

"It was an act of great courage," replied Alenia. "He has placed his throne in jeopardy."

"I am so sorry to be the cause of it."

"You have not caused the king to do anything he did not choose to do."

"I can't understand why a man such as he would risk his kingdom for a woman such as I."

"Well, I suspect the king has reasons that reach deeper than reason itself. But in another sense, it had nothing to do with you at all. He was risking himself not merely for a single person but for the principle that the Master cherishes his creatures and does not want to condemn us but to save us, even from our own folly."

"How did King Lanson learn this in a kingdom where it is not practiced?"

"From Sir Maconnal. Maconnal has shaped Lanson into the sort of king who would make the decision he made this afternoon. Maconnal has been Lanson's tutor since the prince was a boy, and he is now his closest advisor. He had the courage to point Prince Lanson out of the darkness in which the kirk has immersed this kingdom. Sir Maconnal is the finest man I have ever known."

Evalonne could not help but notice the tremor of pride in the woman's voice, but she said nothing of it. "I, too, have reason to be grateful to Sir Maconnal. Without him I would still be in the abbey prison. But what has made Sir Maconnal the kind of man he is?"

"The Master of the Universe himself. Maconnal learned the true nature of the Master from the old scrolls and dedicated himself to becoming more like him. As Maconnal became more like the Master, Lanson, exposed daily to Maconnal, became more and more like Maconnal and thus more like the Master himself."

"Oh, I understand just what you are saying, Alenia," said Evalonne. "This passing on of the likeness of the Master has continued even through Lanson. In the days when we were fleeing together, I sensed something in him that I wanted to emulate. I wanted to become more like him. I wanted to be what he was."

"And from the turn your life has taken, I can see that you have succeeded, Evalonne."

At that moment a knock came at the door and the guard opened it to admit a page, bearing in his arms a dress of fine purple linen trimmed in burnished gold. "The king has selected this garment for the woman Evalonne," he said.

"Sometimes these men surprise us," said Alenia as she took the dress and dismissed the page. She ran her fingers across the rich fabric. "This is something King Lanson did not learn from Maconnal. He would not have thought of sending clothing at all, and if he did, he would never have the sense to select anything like this. He wouldn't know a peasant's shift from a queen's robe."

"Do you and Sir Maconnal . . . uh . . . are you . . ."

"Maconnal lives in his own world of books and ideas. He did teach me to read, but he has taught many others as well. Aside from that he hardly knows I exist, except as an occasional buzzing fly, which he swats at or shoos away."

Alenia finished Evalonne's hair and helped her into the dress. After considerable tightening, lacing, smoothing, and brushing, she stood back to assess the results. "Evalonne, I have never seen a woman more beautiful. You look like a queen."

"Thank you, Alenia. But I have no idea why the king is treating me so well. Nor why he is coming up to see me. Surely he has better things to do on his wedding night. Do you know what might be on his mind?"

"Well, I do have an idea, but it's only intuition. With men you never know. He could be wanting to discuss the weight and balance of broadswords, falconry, or the best forests in the Seven Kingdoms for hunting boar. But I'd guess that tonight something else is on his mind."

Again a knock came at the door and the guard admitted two pages, one bearing a tray of food and the other a jug of wine. They spread the meal on the table, poured the wine, bowed to the women, and left. Evalonne had never seen a finer meal—roasted hen, several cheeses, leeks, a savory soup, carrots, radishes, and a large bowl of nuts. Evalonne urged Alenia to eat with her, insisting there was more than enough for two, but Alenia would not.

"I must leave so you can eat and rest. You want to be at your best when the king comes. Have no fear, Evalonne, all will be well. He wills you only good. And you are safe here in his castle. The guard is standing outside your door, and if you need anything, tell him and he will get it." She gave Evalonne a reassuring pat on the shoulder and left the tower.

Evalonne finished her meal. She snuffed out all the candles but one and lay on the bed—careful to keep her dress and hair from disarray. The wind and thunder sounded from the high window, and thoughts of the many things she did not understand churned in her mind. Why was King Lanson keeping her here? Why was he coming to see her, especially on this night? No doubt after sending her to the tower room, they had resumed the wedding and he was married by now. Perhaps his protection of her sprang from a sense of guilt at having to turn away from her after the bond that had grown between them during their travels together.

Oh, if only we could have wed! The persistent longing intruded once again into Evalonne's mind. But it had been impossible from the beginning. He was the king. She was a commoner and a fallen woman. Yes, she had been lifted from the pit and forgiven, but her past was still hers, and he could never have wed her. She knew that. But it was a hard truth that she had not yet come to terms with. She was not sure she could bear his coming tonight. How could she endure the sight of this fruit she was forbidden to taste? Yet perhaps even a momentary beholding of him would provide her a kind of nourishment, and she would find a way to survive on such a meager ration, storing his image in her heart against the famine of her future.

The thunder continued to rumble and roll, and a draft of air blew out the only candle still burning. As she felt her way toward the candle, she stiffened, suddenly alert. She had heard a noise, and now she sensed some presence in the room. "Lanson?" she called.

A firm hand clapped over her mouth while others clasped her arms, and she heard the rattle of chains and felt the cold iron of manacles clamped to her wrists. She tried to wrench free and kicked at her captors with all the force she could muster, but to no avail. They carried her twisting and struggling across the darkened room and through an opening in the wall, where they forced her downward into a winding, cobwebby stairwell.

ℒ♥

Darkness had fallen before King Lanson finished his meeting with Sir Maconnal and attended to several other issues generated by his pardon of Evalonne. He had called into the meeting seven other knights whom he was certain would remain loyal to him, and with them had assessed the loyalty of the rest of the Hall. If it came to war, which knights were likely to support the king and which would support the bishop? They thought they could count on about fifteen of the forty knights of the Hall, while another twelve were likely to align with the bishop. On the remaining thirteen, opinion was divided. But Lanson could see that if it came to war, especially if the bishop called for troops from the six other kingdoms, his reign would be in jeopardy. On the other hand, he was sure that Umberland of Vensaur would come to his aid, as well as Aradon of Meridan and Tallis of Valomar. He left the meeting with fair confidence that he could retain his throne, but he needed to find a way to avoid a civil war.

Such thoughts fled Lanson's mind as he climbed the circular stairway to the tower room. He wondered why he felt such a fluttering in his stomach as he approached the chamber. He had never been ill-at-ease in Evalonne's presence before. What if she did not love him? What if she declined his invitation to marry him? With such thoughts rattling in his mind, he approached the guarded door.

"Is she alone?" he asked the guard.

"She is, sire," the man answered.

Lanson rapped lightly upon the door. When no response came, he knocked again, louder. Again, there was no response. Perhaps she could not hear because of the wind and thunder raging outside. Using the hilt of his sword he knocked a third time, and when no answer came he commanded the guard to unlock the door. To his surprise the room was dark, but he could see by the frequent lightning flashes from the high windows that it was also empty.

"Bring a torch," he said.

The guard removed a torch from a hallway sconce, and holding the light aloft, the two men entered the darkness and looked all about. The room was clearly empty.

"How do you explain this?" demanded King Lanson.

"I . . . I cannot explain it at all, sire."

It was obvious to Lanson that the guard was as shocked as he.

"I swear to you, sire, that the woman never left the room. Least-wise, she never came out the door where I was standing."

"Who entered the room while she was in here?" Lanson walked all about the room as he spoke, looking for anything amiss.

"Only the maid Alenia and six pages, sire."

"Summon Alenia immediately. No—wait. What's this?"

Lanson stood next to the wall, running his fingers along a verti-cal line where the stones did not abut concisely. The stones to the left of the line jutted outward from the plane of the wall some four or five inches. Lanson gripped the abutment as best he could and pulled. It moved. He and the guard pulled together, and it swung open to re-veal a hidden door.

Without hesitation Lanson entered the darkened passageway, the guard following closely behind. A stone stairway led them downward, and soon they came to a landing fronting a wooden door, which they tried to open. But when they found it would not budge, they con-tinued on down the stairway until they came to another door, which was ajar. They entered carefully, looking all about as if expecting an attack. Then Lanson relaxed.

"These are my own chambers," he said. "I think I see what has happened. Someone who knew of this secret passageway has entered it through my rooms and abducted Evalonne. No doubt the door we could not open was their way of escape. They locked it behind them to prevent pursuit. I have little doubt as to who is behind all this.

"Quickly, summon a page. Tell him to have my horse and Sir Maconnal's readied immediately. I will find Maconnal myself. You go and summon at least a dozen soldiers—a score if you can get them—and have them ready to ride with us in ten minutes."

A quarter-hour later seventeen mounted riders galloped out of the castle and turned onto the road that led to Lochlaund Abbey. The wind howled and popped their capes as peals of thunder echoed across the black sky. Flashes of lightning lit the road, and the smell of damp soil filled the air, though no rain fell yet. After five minutes of hard riding, they came to a crossroad, where Sir Maconnal suddenly drew up and called the company to a halt.

"What are you doing, Maconnal?" demanded Lanson, his mount stamping and wheeling, impatient to resume the pace.

"I have been thinking. I'm sure we will waste our time riding to the abbey. We had best make all haste to the Devil's Mouth."

Lanson's heart froze at Maconnal's words, but after only a moment of hesitation, he bellowed the command, "To the Devil's Mouth!" He wheeled his charger about and galloped down the eastern road toward Black Mountain.

✍

Evalonne stood just inside the teeth of the Devil's Mouth and, by the light of a lantern hanging from the roof, stared into the blackness of the pit before her. Her shackles had been removed, but her arms were firmly in the grip of two abbey guards. A hissing sound, deep and hollow, emitted from the pit as billows of steam rushed upward from it and swirled around their feet. Directly across the pit stood Bishop Hugal, black as a shadow against the flashes of lightning bursting in the jagged clouds behind him. The wind moaned like voices of the damned among the crags and crevasses of Black Mountain.

"No one ever escapes the justice of the Master of the Universe." The words, uttered in a guttural, rasping voice, issued from the blackness of the bishop's cowl. "Your attempt was futile. The Master has triumphed, as he always will, and you will now pay the price for opposing him."

To Hugal's chagrin, the woman neither quailed nor cried out. But that would change. He would see to it. "Do you see the black pit before you? It is indeed the mouth of the devil, the entrance into a hell of horrors the likes of which you have never imagined. Let me tell you what awaits you in this pit. You will wander in the darkness of a labyrinth for days. You will stumble on the bones of victims before you. You will hear the growls and cries of creatures unspeakably horrible who are waiting to tear the evil flesh from your limbs. Your accursed beauty will reap its just reward."

Still Evalonne gave no sign of fear, neither quaking nor crying out, but stood calm and immobile with her eyes closed.

"And do you know what you will find at the center of the maze?"

Hugal pointed a pasty finger at Evalonne, and his voice rose as his throat tightened with anger. "You will meet the hideous face of the master of all evil, the face no one may behold and retain sanity, the face of the master you have served with your wanton life. And your face will take on the likeness of that face. You are about to discover the truth behind beauty, the reality to which beauty is the mask, the horror to which beauty lures men. And you will become that horror. What do you think of that, woman?"

The bishop watched to see the effect of his words, but Evalonne did not move. Her expression did not change, and she said nothing. Hugal began to tremble with rage. The woman should be wailing and begging by now. She had no right to meet her fate without terror. It was part of the punishment. "Cast her into the pit," he cried.

The guards brought Evalonne to the edge of the abyss and prepared to push her into it. At that moment the sound of hoofbeats on the road beneath them rose above the howling of the wind. A voice rang out, loud and strong, echoing off the sides of the mountain.

"Hugal, stop! Stop at once!"

"Wait a moment," said Hugal, holding his hand toward the guards as he looked out over the ledge. "It's King Lanson. I want him to see this. Hold the woman and await my word."

Lanson dismounted and made his way up the stones to the mouth of the skull, Maconnal and the soldiers following close behind.

"King Lanson," said the bishop. "What a fortunate surprise. You are just in time to witness the justice you have denied your kingdom." Hugal raised his hand. "Guards—"

"No, Hugal! Don't do this. There is no need. It serves no purpose."

"I will do it, King Lanson, and there is nothing you can do to stop me."

"Yes, there is, Hugal. There is one thing that I think will make you reconsider."

"And what could that be, your majesty?"

"Take me. Take me instead. Release this woman and take me in her place."

The bishop paused for a moment, his hand still poised to give the signal of death. He hated this king. He hated the direction his reign was taking. He hated the fact that the kirk could not control him. Before him now was a golden opportunity to rid the country of this heretic monarch without going through the cumbersome process of political maneuvering and petitions for war. He slowly lowered his hand to his side. "I accept your offer, King Lanson."

"No!" cried Evalonne, twisting hard to wrench herself from the grasp of the guards and fling herself into the pit. She freed one arm and jumped over the edge, where she hung precariously, held only by the grasp of one guard's hand on her forearm. Lanson sprang forward beside the guards, and the three of them pulled her back to the surface, while she writhed and kicked to free herself and plunge into the pit. But Lanson and the two guards prevailed. When they had Evalonne again standing safely in their grasp, Lanson called Maconnal and handed the now weeping girl to him.

"Take care of her for me, Maconnal. Remember, she is a free woman now." He took the crown from his head and handed it to his friend. "If I do not return, the Hall of Knights must choose a new king."

"Seize him!" cried Hugal. "Seize him now!"

The guards moved toward the king, but he drew his sword and backed them away. Then he stepped up and stood atop the ridge of stone teeth and, with sword in hand, jumped into the blackness of the pit.

CHAPTER THIRTY-FIVE

Τhe Amateur Petitions

ir Maconnal and Evalonne stood just inside the teeth of the Devil's Mouth, shocked beyond belief as they gaped into the black maw that had swallowed King Lanson. Bishop Hugal and his two guards stood a little away from them, completely immobile. At that moment it began to rain in torrents.

Maconnal tried his best to follow King Lanson's instructions and conduct Evalonne back to Macrennon Castle, but she refused to go.

"How could I leave?" she said. "I will hold vigil for his return."

"No one has ever returned from the Devil's Mouth," replied Maconnal, sick at heart as he gazed at the crown in his hands.

"But according to the legend, return is possible," she replied.

"Yes, according to the legend, return is possible." Maconnal sighed. "I will hold vigil with you."

Maconnal dismissed the fifteen castle guards and commanded them to return to their posts at Macrennon Castle. He helped Evalonne down the rocky slope to a flat ledge just below the skull and found stones for both to sit upon. Bishop Hugal and the two temple guards followed soon afterward. Evalonne and Maconnal watched the flickering torch approach as Hugal, accompanied by his two guards, crossed the flat stone to where the couple sat. He faced Maconnal with his two guards standing behind him.

"You have Lochlaund's crown, Maconnal. Shouldn't you return it to the chancellor for safekeeping until the Hall meets?"

"I will do exactly that, Bishop Hugal. But not until Evalonne and I have completed the ritual vigil."

"Surely you don't believe the king will return."

"I will complete the vigil," repeated Maconnal.

"Very well. Do as you will. But give me the crown and I will take it back to Macrennon tonight."

"I would sooner trust a lamb to a crocodile."

"You accuse me of the evil you harbor in your own heart," said the bishop, pointing his stubby finger at Maconnal. "You crave the crown yourself. I have long suspected it. Guards, seize this man and take the crown from him."

The guards advanced toward Maconnal, who was immediately on his feet with his sword point at the throat of the nearest guard. They backed away.

"Again you defy me," said Hugal. "Very well. But as long as you possess the crown, I will not let you out of my sight." He found a stone some ten paces away, where he sat facing Maconnal and Evalonne, the blackness of his hood gaping like a miniature of the Devil's Mouth, which loomed above him. His two guards stood behind him, one bearing the lighted torch.

For the next two hours, Maconnal and Evalonne said little, sitting immobile on the stones as the rain soaked them thoroughly. But Evalonne paid no heed to the rain. Her eyes were focused intently on the stone skull rising dark behind the bishop. Water dripped from her hair and streamed over her face, running in little rivulets off her nose and chin.

After a while the rain slackened to a drizzle, but her eyes never wavered from the stone face. Suddenly the bishop arose and hobbled toward them, his guards following close behind. Evalonne stiffened and Maconnal stood and again drew his sword. The bishop took no notice but continued to approach. Maconnal tensed, ready for battle, but Hugal walked right past him to the edge of the plateau and looked out over the plains beneath the mountain. Maconnal followed the bishop's gaze and saw what had caught his attention. On the road beneath them flickered scores of torches, all moving toward the mountain. From the valley beyond came dozens more, and as Maconnal's eyes grew accustomed to the distance, he could see a steady stream of lights dotting the winding road all the way from Macrennon.

"What is the meaning of this?" rasped Hugal.

"It appears that Evalonne and I will not be alone in our vigil," replied Maconnal. "Apparently word of tonight's events has got out, and the people love their king enough to care about his fate."

A guttural cry of impotent fury tore from the bishop's throat as he raised his cane and struck it hard against the ground. Then he turned and hobbled back across the plateau and, with the help of his guards, climbed back up the stony slope to the Devil's Mouth, where he stood watching the procession of torches winding its way up the mountainside.

Maconnal watched too as the first torches appeared on the plateau. As they came closer he recognized the ruddy face of Colwydd, a baker in Macrennon, accompanied by his wife. Following him were a half-dozen tradesmen, many of whom Maconnal had seen in the town. Soon he saw the faces of three fellow knights of the Hall, Sir Fenalane, Sir Wickram, and Sir Drengal. The march continued until the plateau was filled with a mix of tradesmen, knights, lords, farmers, and merchants, many of whom Maconnal knew and others he did not. Looking beneath the plateau he saw a sea of torches, no longer moving, filling the road up the slope and the grassy plains at the base of the mountain. A few more torches moved yet on the distant road as the last of the marchers approached the assembly.

Sir Maconnal estimated over five hundred watchers gathered on the plateau and the plain below, with another hundred or more still coming. His eyes grew moist and a lump swelled in his throat. He had told Bishop Hugal the truth: the people loved their new king. The kirk may have gripped their lives but not their hearts. Far from being outraged by the king's pardon of a fallen woman and his defiance of the kirk, the people were heartened by his challenge to the cold orthodoxy that had so long oppressed them.

Maconnal looked out over the assembled citizens. Knights stood beside farmers, lords beside tradesmen, fishwives beside ladies, all oblivious to the drizzling rain. Every eye was turned toward the stone skull, hoping against all reason to see the figure of their king emerge from the blackness of the eye socket. A wave of emotion engulfed Maconnal, and almost without volition he lifted his hands high and spoke.

"Master of the Universe, you see us citizens of Lochlaund gathered tonight, and you know why we are here. We love this king you have given us, and we want him returned to us. It is that simple. We want our king back. His reign has been short, but he has ruled us well. And he loves us. We know he does by the sacrifice he made tonight for a woman who had no other hope of life. We know that no one has yet returned from the Devil's Mouth, but we know that if you guide him, he can return. Master, take his hand. Lead him through the maze, out of the pit, and back to us. We want him back, Master. We want our king back." Maconnal's voice broke and he stopped speaking. He lowered his arms and dropped his head as tears flowed from his eyes.

Most of the watchers who knew Sir Maconnal (or knew of him) listened with wonder to his petition. Long familiar with his disdain for the ways of the kirk, they were baffled to find him praying at all. None but kirkmen were allowed to offer public prayers. And they were even more amazed to find his prayer earnest and heartfelt and, in words common and direct, devoid of the ritualistic expressions they had been taught made up a proper prayer. "He sounded just like he was talkin' to a friend," said a cartwright who described it later.

Though the experience of a layman praying in public was a new one, all the watchers felt their hearts lifted by the prayer, and moments after Maconnal ceased, another voice rose from the crowd as a potter from Macrennon took up the petition. "I say Sir Maconnal spoke it right, Master. King Lanson be a good king, and we was hopin' to have him around for years to come. We plead with ye, sir, don't take him yet. Bring 'im back to us." When the potter ceased, a knight took up the prayer, and after him a farmer, and after the farmer a shepherdess. "Master, sir—sire, I be nothin' but a keeper of sheep, but I knows a good shepherd when I sees one. And our king was a good—"

Suddenly an angry voice from above the crowd cut her short. "Stop! Stop this outrage now!" All the watchers looked up to see

Bishop Hugal standing on the ledge in front of the Devil's Mouth, his hands hidden inside his wide sleeves. "Do you think the Master hears such paltry petitions as yours? Do you think he is one of you that you dare address him in the common tongue? Do you think just any of you can step out of your shop or field or barn and approach the Master of the Universe? Don't you know it takes a lifetime of purging the soul and dedication to his service to become worthy to address him? I tell you he is outraged by your audacity tonight—not only by your coarse words and impertinent presumption, but by the nature of your petition as well. How dare you plead for the life of a king who has defied the kirk and betrayed the Master? King Lanson's death is the Master's will, and you heap abomination upon your heads to plead his cause. Cease from this folly. Stop these amateur petitions for an unjust cause and return to your homes. I myself will plead with the Master to turn from his wrath and diminish your punishment."

For a moment after the bishop's speech ended, the watchers were silent. Then the voice of the shepherdess continued as if she had never been interrupted. "Our king was a good shepherd to us, Master, and we be needin' a good shepherd. We been too long in the dark. In this shepherd you given us, we were seein' a glimmer of light. And unless ye give 'im back to us, we don't know where to find light. Give 'im back to us, sire. We be wantin' 'im back."

One after the other the petitions continued. From time to time Maconnal added his own voice to them, and occasionally he glanced at Evalonne, whose eyes were still locked on the great stone mask above them.

Bishop Hugal stood above the watchers trembling with rage as the rain ceased, though the thunder continued to roll in the distance.

THE CAVERNS OF
THE NEPHILIM

anson could see nothing as he hurled downward into the pit. His fall was vertical, and the fearful speed at which he plunged, along with the steam rising about him, took his breath away. He heard a distant hissing sound from somewhere far below. Soon he began to feel the rough wall of the pit, first merely brushing against his left side, then scraping him with considerable pressure, and he realized the pit was no longer vertical but had begun to curve. It curved more as he fell until he was sliding at a forty-five degree angle on a scree of loose clods. He tried desperately to come to a stop. He had no idea how the slide might end. He might be dashed to pieces against a stone or plunge to his death over a ledge. He grasped at the scree with his fingers and dug in his heels, but to no effect.

The hissing below him became much louder as he descended, and the steam wetter and thicker. The angle of the slope continued to lessen until he finally managed to stop his slide. The hissing had grown to a roar, which seemed to issue from some point immediately in front of him. A torrent of wet, warm steam rushed up against him as he sat assessing his condition and surroundings.

Soon he could barely make out through the steam a dim reddish glow on the edges of what appeared to be stones and boulders piled all about him. Cautiously he felt his way forward and found that he was on a high ledge. He crawled to the edge of it and looked down into a fearfully deep abyss from which the steam billowed. At first he could see nothing for the rising clouds, but soon he could make out far below a jagged streak of reddish orange as bright as lightning. He could see movement within the streak and realized he was looking into a river of molten stone. Looking down to his right he could see through occasional gaps in the clouds of steam a massive, subterranean waterfall spewing out of the wall below him and tumbling into the abyss. It was the water from this cataract cascading into the river of molten stone that produced the deafening hiss and the billowing steam.

Lanson crawled carefully along the ledge until he came to a wall of stone. He stood up and, using both hands, felt his way along the wall until something brushed the back of his shoulder. Startled, he tried to turn about and found that he could not. What he had felt was another stone wall. He realized he had entered a funnel-like passageway, which had narrowed as he continued until it was barely wide enough to admit him. Though he wanted desperately to get away from the relentless noise of the steam, he hesitated to continue into the narrow space. He had an irrational fear of being confined in close places. But seeing little choice, he moved forward into the passage. Strangely, he found the tunnel lit by a dim, almost imperceptible reddish orange light. He could not identify the source, though he could see that it came from somewhere far ahead of him.

He began to sweat and feel a rising panic as he inched sideways along the narrow passageway. But in moments the passage abruptly doubled in width and turned to the left at an angle of about ten degrees. Lanson noticed that the increased width of the passage was all to his right, as if the right wall had been pushed outward about two feet. Though the walls were rough and uneven, the tunnel maintained a fairly consistent width until after thirty or forty feet, when it abruptly widened again, this time to the left, and at the same time angled slightly to the right.

When the sudden widening and slight turning occurred a third time, Lanson felt a rising sense of something uncanny about these widenings and turns. He walked forward a few more feet, then turned to look behind him. In the dim, unexplained light, he saw the dark openings to two passages—the one he had just come out of and a like one just beside it. It was as if he were standing inside the base stem of a *Y,* looking toward the fork of the two arms. It took him a moment to grasp the significance of what he saw. Then he realized he was in a maze trap of insidious design, a maze that would lead its victim ever to its center while cutting off all possibility of finding his way back.

The maze was like a two-dimensional version of a tree with the twigs feeding into branches, branches feeding into limbs, and limbs feeding into the trunk. He was like an ant that had begun its journey in the outermost twigs at the end of the branches and was making its way toward the trunk. The design of the maze made reaching the trunk inevitable. It was like descending into a series of *Y*s from the top. Descending from the fork into the stem required no choice. The choice came when one traveled in the opposite direction and ascended from the stem into the fork. As twig met branch, branch met the limb, and after many such junctures a limb finally met the trunk, it would be impossible to look back and identify which of the many limbs, which of the limb's many branches, which of the branch's many twigs had been his entry point. He could not go back. He had little choice but to follow the maze to its center and meet whatever fate awaited him there.

As he moved forward into the passageway, now some six feet wide, he noticed that the light had increased slightly, though its hue was still a lurid reddish orange. Suddenly he stopped cold and his heart froze. Ahead of him sat a woman, her back to the wall of the tunnel, her legs drawn up in front, and her head resting on her arms, which were folded across her knees. Her hair was long and hung lank about her face and shoulders. In the dim reddish light, he could make out no other details. Wary and filled with dread, he moved closer to the figure. Apparently she did not hear Lanson's approach, for she neither moved nor made any sound. When he was within a step of her, he stopped.

"Woman, are you well?" he asked.

She did not respond.

"Do you need help?"

Still she did not respond, and Lanson reached out his hand and shook her gently. To his horror, when he removed his hand, she slowly fell over on her side, maintaining her drawn-up pose all the while. He jumped back in horror. She was dead and had been dead for a long time. The stiff hair fell back and revealed skeletal fingers only partly covered with a thin layer of parchmentlike skin, and a face that was little more than bare bone.

As he watched in horror, some black creature crawled out of the empty eye socket and dropped to the floor. Again he jumped back. It was a scorpion the size of his hand, with its pincers working ahead of it and its tail curled above its bloated body. As he watched the hideous creature crawl away, he noticed several more like it moving about the floor.

Lanson shuddered and went on, careful not to tread on the scorpions. He tried not to think how the woman must have died, wandering in the hopeless maze until hunger, thirst, isolation, and fear had driven her to such despair that she simply sat down and wept herself to death.

He had not walked far until he came upon another body sprawled across his path. This one had been dead much longer, for no skin was left at all, and only a few tatters of clothing hung here and there on the mottled bones. He could not tell whether the person had been a man or woman, but the red skull grinned up at him as if sharing some fiendish joke that only the two of them could appreciate.

As he continued he found other skeletons and bodies. Most of them were women where he could tell at all, and most had been dead for a long time, though he saw the body of one woman who could have died as recently as several months back.

For a while the only signs of life were the scorpions, but they were joined later by lizards longer than his foot and great scaly toads larger than his two fists, looking at him through baleful eyes with pupils like vertical slits. As he passed they would hop or crawl away, disappearing into holes or slipping into the stagnant puddles that began to appear in the path.

Soon the rugged tunnel widened yet again, and Lanson continued on. He saw lying on the ground ahead of him some object that looked vaguely like a basket or a cage for a small animal. As he came closer he saw that it was neither. It was a human rib cage. This discovery startled him even more than the intact skeletons, because he knew that for a body to be thusly destroyed, something or someone had done the destroying. He walked on, even more wary and with a quicker pulse.

Soon he found a broken femur, and a little farther on a pelvis with the other femur and shin still attached. Twenty paces farther he found the skull, lying face up on the stone floor with two jagged holes punched into it, one in the forehead and the other near the ear, as if two giant fangs had bitten into the poor victim's head. Lanson wondered what sort of beast could have left such marks, and his only answer was, a huge one. In fact, as he thought on it, such a creature's size would explain why he had seen no signs of damaged skeletons in the narrower passages. He drew his sword and walked on.

After a while the passage widened yet again, and he continued in silence for what seemed hours, though he had lost all real sense of time. The red-tinged darkness all about him began to seep into his mind, dulling his thoughts and dimming his hope. He tried to think of the bright world of Lochlaund far above him with its green hills, blue ridges, and sparkling lakes. He tried to think of the sun glowing on the velvet contours of Evalonne's face, but the picture would not form. No image of beauty or light could rise above the weight of the lurid darkness through which he now plodded.

Just when he began to think the passage was endless, it widened once more, now some thirty feet across and almost as high. Shortly afterward he could see ahead of him a dramatic increase in the orange light. He quickened his pace, and within minutes he reached the end of the tunnel where it opened into an enormous room—so large that he could see neither roof nor walls ahead or to the sides. The tunnel in which he stood opened high on the wall of the room so that the floor of it was several stories below him.

He walked up to the edge where the tunnel ended and looked out over the view before him—a vast, ruined landscape with enormous stone monoliths jutting upward between gaping fissures and orifices that disfigured the ground like great boils and lacerations. Many of these earth wounds festered with pools of fire, glowing red and sometimes running like an infection over the edges of the gashes that spawned them. Some belched black smoke while others were dormant and crusted where the molten stone had cooled and coagulated into black scabs.

Here and there among these holes lay gray-greenish pools of stagnant water, some bubbling, others emitting clouds of steam. The giant vertical stones jutting upward from these pits and pools glowed red in the light about them. Many stood as tall as houses and small buildings, and several ran up to a height far above the level where Lanson stood, penetrating the gray smoke that veiled the roof above. These stones were pitted with erratic holes of irregular shape and varying sizes, looking like eroding windows, some black and opaque while through others he could see into the distance beyond. He saw no grass, no trees, no bushes or flowers of any kind. The odor was like that of rotting eggs.

He looked for a way to descend into the vast room and found the remains of a trail that wound its way from the lip of the tunnel down the steep ledge toward the floor. He worked his way down the trail until he was standing on the floor of the gigantic cavern. The trail became something of a road before him, and he began to follow its winding turns through the pits of fire and towering stones, expecting soon to see the wall of the far side of the cavern.

He did not know how long he walked, but instead of reaching the end of the cave, each turn opened before him a new vista of larger and taller stones. Some soared upward like spires or obelisks, with occasional spans of straight edges and squared corners showing among the crumbled sides and pocked surfaces, giving him the uneasy feeling that these towers were not natural, but artifacts shaped by the hands of intelligent beings.

Further on this impression of intelligent design became even more evident. Many of the structures were clearly buildings, though taller than he had ever imagined possible. He came across the obvious remains of columns, some standing though broken off like lopped tree stumps, others sprawled crumbled and broken on the earth. Here and there he saw arched doorways in the sides of buildings, and just ahead a towering arch within a high wall. The top edge of the wall was jagged and crumbled. He began to sense some sort of order in the placement of the buildings.

He moved toward the great arch. As he reached it and looked inside, he gasped and stiffened. Looming before him was a monstrous reptilian creature, over three times his own height, and shaped much like the dragon of his nightmares. An instant later he realized the creature was merely of stone, but it was several minutes before his heart stopped racing. On the other side of the lane stood a mirror image of the same beast, identical but for the head, which had crumbled away.

The lane inside the gate curved no more but lay straight before him, rising slightly until it disappeared in a drifting fog of steam and smoke. As Lanson continued up the road, it was clear that he was walking among the ruins of a fallen civilization. The ravaged buildings that lined the road, some with pillars, friezes, and arches still intact, suggested a genius rivaling that which he had heard existed in the nations of the southern sea. He continued to encounter huge statues of monstrous and hideous creatures, crouched on cracked and crumbling pedestals, some like lizards with gargoyle faces, others essentially humanoid with goatlike horned heads and hooves, all displaying fiendish snarls. Though mostly decayed, many of these creatures retained enough form to be eerily lifelike. His spine chilled as he passed them.

Lanson knew he was inside what had been an enormous city that celebrated or worshiped these hellish beings. He continued to walk ever upward on the sloping avenue until he could see through the veil of gray smoke the vague outlines of an enormous columned building. It was less damaged than any of the structures he had yet seen. Even the roof was still intact, supported by rows of towering stone columns, pitted and cracked, but still plumb and apparently solid. A reddish glow emanated from within the columns. He felt certain the structure must have been a temple and the center of worship for the people or beings who had built the city.

He reached the flight of at least forty steps at the base of the temple and began literally to climb them, for they were much too large for him merely to step from one to the next. They were carved from great stone blocks, now cracked and chipped, each almost waist-high to Lanson. And it took him two strides to step across one of them. *The creatures who lived here must have been huge,* he thought. Finally he topped the final step and leaned against one of the stone columns to catch his breath, marveling at the sheer enormity of the structure. He was sure it would take at least eight men with their arms outstretched fingertip to fingertip to reach around one of the columns.

He turned toward the interior of the temple, and deep within the darkness he saw the cause of the red glow. A fire burned in a brazier set on a pedestal in the center of the vast floor. Cautiously, Lanson walked toward the light, and as he approached he could see towering behind it against the far wall a sculpture of a huge beast with the upper body of a man and the loins and legs of a reptile. The face was exactly that of the beast of Lanson's nightmares, bestial and reptilian with cold, glaring eyes that slanted downward beneath heavy brows toward a snoutlike nose that covered a wide mouth lined with long, irregular fangs. The statue was more lifelike and better preserved than any Lanson had yet seen, and he shuddered at the sight it.

Suddenly a voice echoed throughout the temple. "Welcome to my world, King Lanson."

Lanson stopped short. Standing behind the fire was a single figure, tall and still and robed from head to foot in draping black. From the hood of the robe gazed the face of a woman, glowing red in the light of the brazier. Lanson's heart froze when he looked into those eyes, which were pale almost to the point of being colorless and appeared hard as stone beneath their heavy lids.

"Who are you?" asked Lanson.

"My name is Morgultha," replied the woman.

Lanson's blood ran cold. He knew the name. Standing before him was a creature of legend, born hundreds of years ago, preserved from natural death by spells and unholy alliances, driven by a ruthless ambition for power and conquest that had made her the bane of the Seven Kingdoms since before the reign of Perivale. In spite of the thrill of horror he felt, the thought flashed in his mind that he had seen those eyes before. But before he could follow that trail, the woman spoke.

"I have anticipated this meeting for a long time, King Lanson."

"How could you have known I would ever enter this underground world?"

"Oh, it was inevitable. Ever since you chose to set yourself against the will of the Bishop of Lochlaund, your descent into my world has been virtually assured."

"Your world? What is this hellish place, and why do you call it yours?" he asked.

"It is mine by inheritance. This subterranean city was once a kingdom of great glory and power, and even the greatest of the ancient civilizations on the surface of the earth have never equaled it. But this kingdom fell long before any civilization our history records, and I discovered it—or more accurately, was led to it—in the latter days of my youth. I have spent much time here since."

"Why do you desire a meeting with me?" asked Lanson.

"I need a boon from you, King Lanson. And I am prepared to offer you a gift of immense value in return."

"I know who you are, Morgultha. And I know that any boon you crave of me will be used to wreak some great evil on the Seven Kingdoms. I will grant no boons or make any bargains with such as you."

"Not even to get out of this pit?"

"Least of all that. I came here of my own free will, and I do not sell my life so cheaply."

"When you hear my offer, you will find yourself more interested than you think. Listen to me, King Lanson. I am about to reveal to you secrets I have never revealed to anyone alive. Then I will tell you why I am favoring you with this knowledge. As you may know, we are deep within the roots of the isle of the Seven Kingdoms, far beneath the ocean floor. Black Mountain, of which the Devil's Mouth is part, was once a fountain of fire drawn from the very heart of the earth itself. That fountain ceased eons ago when a civilization older than the most ancient recorded plugged up the conduit of the fire and built the underground city you see here."

"Who were these people?" Lanson was fascinated in spite of himself.

"The things you see here were built long before the great flood by creatures who were half men and half gods—born from the unions of rebellious angelic beings with the beautiful daughters of men. Many of them were seers, and others had access to knowledge available only to the messengers of the Master of the Universe, by which they long knew the flood was coming. They built this civilization far underground, tightly sealed off from the overworld, thinking to escape the coming waters. These vast caverns were formed when they drained the molten stone from them and shut off the fountain of fire." Morgultha stood still as stone. The only movement was in her lips, and the light from the brazier flashed orange on her long teeth as she spoke.

"But these demigods made a fatal miscalculation. Their seals were breached because they thought the only source of the floodwaters would be torrents of rain from the sky above. They failed to reckon with the great stores of water the Master would release from the fountains of the deep, and the flood did indeed reach them. They drowned as surely as the race of Adam on the surface of the earth, and when the waters retreated, this city was left much as you see it now, ravaged and empty, but not utterly destroyed.

"Fortunately, these ancients recorded their knowledge on stone tablets, which left their records undamaged by the water that filled these caverns for years. These tablets held secrets of nature, of power, of warfare, of signs and seasons, of government, of magical arts of which only a handful on earth have ever known a fraction. Many of these secrets I have uncovered already, but those yet to be discovered are as uncountable as the stars in the heavens. Within these caverns I have learned most of my arts, and I have learned to contact the departed spirits of those who built this civilization. They guide me and impart to me secrets of life and power, and of arts by which one may make himself as the gods. I myself am virtually immortal, for I have lived many hundreds of years.

"I know I cannot deceive you, King Lanson. You know me to be evil and I will not pretend to be otherwise. I tell you frankly that it has been my intention for almost two centuries to rule the Seven Kingdoms, and after them, to conquer other kingdoms as well. Though it may take many more centuries, I expect eventually to bring all the major kingdoms of the world under my power. I am well suited for it. From the tablets within these walls I have gained the knowledge to lead the brotherhood of kingdoms on the island above us to become the greatest nation on earth, rivaling even the civilization that you see lying in ruins about you.

Twice I have come close. I almost won the Seven Kingdoms in the war against Perivale 130 years ago, and I would have won it had not my ancient enemy who calls himself the Master of the Universe supernaturally empowered Perivale by giving him a measure of his own Spirit." Morgultha's face contorted into something like a snarl, and she trembled in rage as she spat these words.

"In that war I lost a priceless talisman of great power when Perivale stole from me the Crown of Eden. Had I retained that treasure, the Seven Kingdoms would already be in my grasp. Even without the power of the Crown, five generations later I almost thwarted your Master's plan to place Perivale's descendant Aradon on the throne. I failed again, but only because I was hampered by men too weak to help me accomplish my plan. Balkert, Brendal, and my own son Lomar all failed me. But none of these had half the mind and strength that you have.

"Even after Aradon's coronation I did not despair. I revised my plans and, with very little help, manipulated events to prevent Aradon's predicted uniting of the Seven Kingdoms. I stirred up unrest among the people in the uncommitted kingdoms and turned the tide of opinion away from Aradon. My plan came near to working, and it surely would have worked had you not inadvertently foiled it by restoring Aradon's daughter to him. But I hold no grudges, King Lanson. I am a pragmatist, and when one plan fails there is always another. After all, I have all the time in the world. And you are just the person who can help me."

"You are insane, Morgultha. Not only do I refuse to help you, I will do all in my power to keep your evil from ruining the Seven Kingdoms."

As Lanson spoke, the tongues of flame that had been licking out from the brazier began to curl and fold in upon themselves until they swirled and boiled like molten embers. Then they settled, placid and still, glowing like a bright orange mirror. Lanson stared transfixed into the pool of liquid fire while Morgultha continued as if he had not spoken at all.

"You are the strongest man to come to a throne in the Seven Kingdoms since Perivale and Aradon. Your enormous talents will be wasted as head of one little kingdom thrust into a mere corner of the coming glory of the Seven Kingdoms. Listen to me, King Lanson. Listen carefully. I possess the power to make you emperor of the entire Seven Kingdoms."

Lanson stared into the pool of fire. For the first time since Morgultha had begun her speech, he felt her words breach the barrier he had erected against them in his mind. He opened his mouth to speak but could think of nothing he wanted to say.

CHAPTER THIRTY-SEVEN

THE THREE TRIALS
OF LANSON

anson and Morgultha stood face-to-face, their eyes locked into a mutual gaze across the brazier of molten fire on the pedestal between them. "Did you hear me, King Lanson? I just offered you the high kingship of the entire Seven Kingdoms."

"That is not yours to give," replied Lanson. "The rulers of nations are in the hands of the Master of the Universe."

"That is not so. You have forgotten something. When Adam was driven from paradise, my master the Dark One became lord of the earth instead of Adam. The thrones of nations belong to him now, and he gives them to those who serve him well. I do indeed have the power to place you on that throne."

"You're talking nonsense, Morgultha. You are the one who craves power. Why do you offer me the throne for which you have fought and striven for two hundred years?"

"I care nothing about the glory of ruling the Seven Kingdoms; I merely want the power. You can be the one to sit on the throne and receive all the honor and riches. I intend to be the one who plots the course and sets the pace for the Seven Kingdoms so they can become all that this once was." She swept her arm toward the ruins about them. "I want the Crown of Eden itself, which is my first step to rul-

ing even mightier empires. You can have the throne of the Seven
Kingdoms and rule under my direction while I continue my quest
for the thrones of the greater kingdoms of the world. I know, of
course, that you, being a servant of the Master of the Universe, are
not driven by a thirst for power as I am. I can accept that. But the fact
that you are good and I am evil does not mean that we cannot at
times walk the same path. As ruler of the Seven Kingdoms, think of
all the good you could do for your Master."

"What good?" said Lanson. "I would be your puppet. I could do
nothing that you did not initiate or approve."

"That is not so. At least, it would not be so after I had expanded
my rule to other nations. I would leave the Seven Kingdoms behind
like a lion leaves a hare to pursue an elk. I would take no further
notice of the Seven Kingdoms, and your rule would be your own.

"Look into the pool of fire between us, King Lanson." She
pointed a thin finger toward the brazier. "What do you see there?"

Lanson looked and wished he had not. He could not tear his eyes
away. He saw himself as clearly as if in a mirror. He was sitting on the
high throne in the magnificent Morningstone Castle in Meridan. The
courtiers, lords, ladies, knights, and even kings of other nations were
gathered before him, all gazing up at him in awe of his majesty. Some
bowed to him; some came forward with requests; others brought gifts
of silks, gold, and exotic foods. Somehow he could hear the conversations of the various groups standing about within the hall, and over
and over the sweet sound of his own name was uttered in awe on every
tongue.

As he gazed into the molten pool the scene shifted, and he saw
himself astride a great charger in the midst of a raging war. His golden
armor gleamed and his bright sword flashed in the sunlight as he
slashed with mighty strokes to the right and left, driving through the
thick of the battle as the enemy gave way before him. Then he saw
himself on his return to the city. The streets were lined on each side
with throngs of adoring citizens, cheering and throwing rose petals as
he led his victorious troops toward Morningstone Castle.

Pride swelled within Lanson's breast and a desire as compelling
as hunger or lust burned in his heart. He watched as the scene in the

liquid fire shifted again and again, showing him the power he would wield, the vast riches that would be his, the armies he would command, the admiration he would elicit, the women who would swoon over him and throw themselves at his feet, the kings who would bow to him, the songs minstrels would sing of him, the books that would be written about his exploits, the art and sculpture that would depict him, and even the generations to come that would hold the name of King Lanson in awe.

He closed his eyes to shut out the pictures, but they continued to boil in his mind as vividly as they had in the fire. Not only could he see himself as the greatest king ever to rule the Seven Kingdoms, he could feel it, even taste it. The glory of it all made his heart beat faster until he became a little giddy. He could no longer find the resistance to push the pictures away. Why should he not do this thing? Perhaps it was his destiny. And if he found later that it was not, he could simply lay down his crown and repent. Maybe what Morgultha was asking was not really so wrong. As she herself had said, he could align with her now, then turn away from her after his power was intact— power that he could use to accomplish great good in the Seven Kingdoms for the glory of the Master of the Universe.

But as these thoughts danced through his mind, another thought, still and quiet, stood behind them, patiently waiting for Lanson to attend it. What of Aradon, whom he would displace? What of the prophecy that had designated Aradon as high king of the Seven Kingdoms? What of simple right and wrong? He remembered his father telling him the importance of being content in the soil where one was rooted—not to long for the richer soil in the garden across the wall. One should accept his own place and fill it with honor and integrity, whether he was a scullery drudge or a king on a throne. Lanson sighed deeply and opened his eyes. The pictures were gone. He knew the answer he must give to Morgultha.

"I will not be a party to your ruthless ambitions."

He tensed, expecting to see the black-clad woman erupt in fury. But instead she smiled, or at least, stretched her lips back to reveal her long white teeth. "I expected just such an answer. The very strength that makes you valuable to me also makes you harder to persuade.

However, I will now show you a compelling reason why you should reconsider. Follow me." She turned from the brazier and began to walk toward the grotesque stone creature behind her. But Lanson did not move.

"I do not choose to follow you. Nothing you show me will change my mind."

"And just what better way have you to spend your time? Do you think you can escape these caverns without my help? What I have to show you will forever alter the way you think about the future of the Seven Kingdoms. Come with me." Again she walked toward the statue, and this time Lanson followed.

She led him to the right of the pedestal on which the stone beast stood. The pedestal alone was over twice Lanson's height, and the back of his neck prickled as he looked up at the two baleful stone eyes glaring down at him. When they reached the back of the pedestal Morgultha struck it with the staff in her hand, and a door opened inward into the stone. She stepped inside and Lanson followed. A stab of panic shot through him at the reverberating boom of the door closing behind them.

They stood at the top of a winding stairway, the steps vaguely visible in the ubiquitous red light glowing from somewhere below. They descended to a depth of a hundred fifty feet or more when the stairway ended abruptly at an irregularly shaped opening in the wall. Lanson peered out at a forest of stony vertical forms, fantastic in shape, thick as trees, and lit with the same lurid light that had illumined the caverns above. The ground about the stalagmites was pocked and scarred with cracks and fissures and orifices through which seeped steam and red magma. Lanson followed Morgultha on a narrow trail that wound through the stalagmite forest. Many of the grotesque columns reached the ceiling, from which hung an inverted forest of stalactites, which seemed to mirror the fantastic shapes that reached up toward them from the ground.

After several minutes Morgultha and Lanson reached a large open space, a hundred yards or more in diameter. Here Morgultha stopped and pointed to an enormous boulder in the center of the space. The stone soared to a height of eighty feet or more, shaped like an inverted pear and balanced impossibly on top of a much smaller wedge-shaped stone some twenty feet high and fifteen feet in diameter. Black cracks in the earth, jagged and forked, reached outward from the stone in all directions like the spokes of a wagon wheel. These fissures were filled with some kind of black pitch.

"I will now explain to you the meaning of these stones," said Morgultha. "The small stone beneath the larger, of which only a quarter shows above the ground, is the staunch of the closed wound from which the fires of the deep once bled. The ancient Nephilim, who lived in these caverns before the great flood, used their arts to shut and seal the fiery fountain simply by plugging it with this stone and filling the cracks about it with molten rock. But the pressures of the fires below still push hard at the stone plug and would spew it from the hole were it not for the huge stone set on top of it. As you can see, the larger stone is precariously balanced. If it were to tip over, the smaller stone would blow from its hole like the lid of a steam kettle. Fires from below would spew upward with such force they would soon rip away the floor of the space on which we now stand, and the earth would disgorge its belly of an endless sea of molten stone. The magma would first fill the caverns of the lost city of the Nephilim. Then it would burst through the peak of Black Mountain and burn every living thing from the entire surface of the Seven Kingdoms, finally covering the dead island with a shroud of ash. The island would become a barren gray desert upon which no life of any kind could survive. Of course, the stone is much too weighty for men to move by their own power, but in the chambers of the temple above us I learned the spell that will topple it."

Morgultha turned toward Lanson and her eyes burned with fierce intensity. "You are my last key to ruling this island. If I can keep you from joining Aradon's federation, the two remaining kingdoms may hold out as well and I can keep my wedge against amalgamation in place as I gather power to coerce the other four. But if you turn from me, it means I cannot keep the Seven Kingdoms from merging into a powerful unity that I will not be able to break for centuries. If I am denied the Seven Kingdoms for myself, I will utter the spell that will tip this stone and destroy them all. You hold in your hand the fate of the Seven Kingdoms, King Lanson. Join me and win them for your own power and glory, or defy me and destroy them."

"It is you whom I will destroy," cried Lanson, drawing his sword and moving quickly toward her, intending to slash her to shreds before she had time to utter the fatal spell. To his surprise she made no move and showed no fear as he approached. Her pale eyes began to take on the color of the sea. The black of her robe began to shimmer with hues of muted green, russet, and amber. A full white beard appeared on her jaw and white hair on her head. Lanson stopped short, his eyes wide and his mouth gaping. Before him stood the figure of Father Clemente, his eyes bearing a look of gravity and deep concern.

"I have never been so glad to see anyone in my life," said Lanson as he sheathed his sword in relief.

"You have done well, King Lanson," said Clemente in his rich bell-like voice. "You have resisted a great temptation that hardly any man on this earth could have stood against. And you have refused to be intimidated by a threat of impending doom. These temptations were sent to test you, my son, and you have passed them well." He looked upon Lanson with eyes bearing an infinite sadness. "But I must tell you that the greatest test is yet before you. You must come with me now and prepare yourself for the most terrible challenge you will ever have to face."

Lanson's joy at seeing Father Clemente faded, and in its place arose a cold dread that stayed with him as he followed the man back through the forest of stone and up the winding stairway toward the temple. They entered the temple through the door at the back of the pedestal, and again Lanson looked out over the vast interior of the stone structure. By the dim glow of the red light, he saw things he had not seen earlier. The sides of the hall were lined with stadium benches, eight rows high. Lanson's spine chilled as he saw that in all the seats sat figures in black robes, their hoods pulled over their heads, hiding their faces in dark caverns. All were still and silent, facing the arena before them like silent judges of doom.

"As I told you, you will soon be put to a test like none you have ever faced. The watchers you see about this hall will be your jury. They will judge whether you pass the test."

Lanson followed Father Clemente toward the center of the arena, where the brazier still stood on its pedestal, again burning with an orange flame. Behind the brazier stood another person, wearing a light, thin robe. As they approached, Lanson could see that the figure was a woman, her wrists shackled in front of her with a heavy chain connecting the shackles to a stone block resting on the floor. He stopped and gaped in sheer consternation. The woman was Evalonne.

"What is she doing here?" he demanded in fury. "Bishop Hugal agreed to spare her from this pit."

"Bishop Hugal did not spare her. He cast her into the pit moments after you entered it."

Lanson rushed toward Evalonne, and in spite of her plight, a look of joy came over her face as she saw him and cried out his name. Lanson reached to embrace her.

"Stop, Lanson!" The voice of Clemente rang out behind him, echoing through the hall. Lanson paused and turned toward him. "Remember how I once told you that you would rid the Seven Kingdoms of a great evil?" He pointed toward Evalonne. "There stands the evil. You must destroy her."

Lanson was utterly baffled. "I do not understand."

"There are things that can devastate a kingdom more readily than a fountain of fire," said Clemente. "Kingdoms are more often destroyed from within than without, and it happens when the will of their leaders becomes too weak to root out the evil that can eat away the foundations of order. This woman is the embodiment of just the kind of thing that can bring down a kingdom. She is a fornicator and a lewd woman who defied the order of society to pursue her own pleasure. Unless such as she are rooted out and destroyed, your kingdom cannot stand. It will be eaten away from the inside and fall like a tree with a rotten interior."

"But, Father Clemente, Evalonne has repented. She is no longer the same woman who committed those deeds. Her life has been renewed."

"Her repentance does not remove her guilt. Her sin is like filth that clings to her, and if she is released, it will multiply like maggots to contaminate all of Lochlaund. The only way to get rid of her sin is to slay her. You must show that you have the strength to do this hard thing, though it tears your heart from your breast. Otherwise, you will be unfit to rule your kingdom, for you will be forever ruled by your own emotions."

"But what about mercy? You told me yourself that mercy is an even greater thing than justice. Strict justice might be served in killing her, but mercy would die with the stroke."

"Mercy is for the Master to grant, not for mortal kings. Your duty is to protect your kingdom from evil. If the Master chooses to mete out mercy in the next world, that is his prerogative. But you must not usurp that right as your own. Your duty is to follow his law."

"I understand the importance of the law, but—"

"Enough talk, Lanson. Each moment you delay, your resolve weakens. Do your duty to your kingdom and waver no longer. You must do it now."

The ghastly watchers in the gallery never moved, never made a sound as Lanson, in terrible agony, turned toward Evalonne. Her eyes were wide with disbelief and terror as he stepped toward her, anguish and uncertainty wrenching his heart. What should he do? How could the Master require of him such a thing as this? Maybe like Abraham his hand would be stayed when he lifted his sword to strike her.

"Why do you delay, Lanson? You must strike now."

The hooded figures in the galleries watched in silence as he slowly approached the chained woman, his sword now drawn, finding it impossible to be assured that the thing he was being asked to do was right. He knew that the right course was often the most difficult, but how could he know that this was the right course? He remembered his father saying that in every dilemma there was always a way to know what is right. Whenever one was deceived or unsure, part of the uncertainty was always due to self-deception. The truth would always find a way to show itself through the fog of a lie, but only the heart that was pure would be able to see it.

He now stood face-to-face with Evalonne and slowly lifted his sword above his head, ready to strike the fatal blow. He looked into the pleading eyes of the woman, and his heart was moved with feelings more powerful than any he had ever experienced. He loved her more than his own life, more than his kingdom. But did he love her more than he loved the Master? That was the question, was it not? It was not right for him to choose his own love over the good of the people the Master had charged him to guide and protect. He must love whom the Master loved and slay whom the Master chose. It was his terrible duty to kill the thing he loved most in the world.

As these words entered his mind, he instantly remembered where he had first heard them. They were uttered as prophecy by the old woman with pale eyes whom he had met in the forest soon after he had found Mossette. She had cursed him and told him he would someday slay the thing he loved most in the world. Suddenly Lanson realized that the woman in the forest was the same as the woman he had met in this very temple. The pale eyes and thin face were exactly those of Morgultha. Father Clemente was now asking him to fulfill the curse of an evil woman. It simply did not fit together.

At that moment Lanson understood what was happening. His expression became hard as stone, and Evalonne, watching him with eyes wide as saucers, blanched in horror. But he lowered his sword and turned away from her, facing the figure of Father Clemente instead. "You are not Father Clemente. Show yourself for who you are."

Clemente's face distorted into a grotesque scowl as he lifted his arms and waved them over the fire in the brazier. Immediately the flame rose to a height of six or seven feet as billows of heavy smoke boiled from it. The smoke quickly hid Clemente and the statue of the monster behind him. Lanson turned toward Evalonne, but she, too, was now hidden by the smoke. He tried to feel his way toward her but lost all sense of direction in the swirling gray clouds and could not find her.

"Evalonne!" he called.

"Lanson," he heard her wail. "I am here. Please hurry! They are coming to get me . . . Lanson!" The last was a shout of utter terror.

Lanson ran about the floor, waving his arms in the smoke about him as he shouted her name over and over. But the syllables merely echoed in the vast hall, mocking his futility. Suddenly a woman's scream split the air, followed immediately by the rising rumble of a roar, deep and throbbing, as from the throat of some monstrous animal. He turned all about, looking into the gray swirls about him for the source of the sound. As he looked, the smoke began to lift, and he saw crawling toward him not thirty feet away the hideous creature of his nightmares. The pedestal behind the monster was empty. He watched the thing crawl toward him, mostly on its powerful hind feet, its knotty and muscular forearms touching the ground lightly for balance. Its body was a bulging hulk the size of a wagon, scaly and blemished all over with wartlike protuberances. Its eyes glowed orange from beneath heavy, frowning brows, and blood dripped from the long fangs of its grinning mouth, running down its legs and smearing in red streaks across the stone floor. A tail, long and reptilian, trailed behind it.

The watchers in the gallery remained silent as the living statue stalked toward Lanson. Though he could hardly take his eyes off the terrible creature, his eyes darted quickly to the trail of blood, and he saw to his horror that it began at the block of stone to which Evalonne's manacles were chained, though they were now empty and splotched with blood.

With a cry of rage Lanson charged the monster. In maniacal fury he hacked at its nose and forearms as it snarled and snapped and swiped at him with razor-sharp claws. He ducked under the deadly strokes and dealt a blow to the creature's thigh, which brought a flow of blood. With a roar of pain, the monster rose up on its back legs and flailed its claws at him in a frenzy. He jumped backward, but not in time to escape a blow to his shoulder that left three gashes in his flesh. Instantly he brought up his sword and beat back the fury of claws, inflicting three or four deep slashes in the flesh of the creature's arms and leaving one claw dangling and dripping blood. The monster drew back and, howling with pain and rage, reached down and grasped the ends of the bloody chains sprawled on the floor. It swung the stone block attached to the chains like a mace about its head, then hurled it toward Lanson. He watched the stone coming toward him, tumbling over and over in the smoky air as the chains flew about it like tentacles. He jumped aside too late to avoid the stone, but it hit the floor inches to the left of where he stood. A flying chain wrapped around his right wrist and wrenched him to the floor, where he slid and tumbled in the wake of the bouncing stone as his sword went spinning across the arena.

Instantly the creature charged at him. He struggled to free his wrist from the tangle of the chain, which had somehow wound itself into a knot that would not come loose. He scrambled toward the stone block and began to beat the knotted chain furiously against the edge of it as the monster's shadow moved across him. The chain loosened, and he pulled free and bounded toward his sword, but he felt claws dig into his back, and his legs flailed in the air as the monster lifted him from the floor and brought him toward its hideous face. He struggled and wrenched and kicked, but the monster's grip was firm. He gaped in horror as the grinning mouth opened, dripping globules of yellow, gelatinous saliva from the huge rows of needlelike fangs.

As Lanson moved slowly toward the mouth, he wrenched and twisted, managing to free his right hand. He reached to his belt and, with fumbling fingers, drew his dagger from its sheath. As the dripping mouth opened to receive him, he reached upward and stabbed furiously at the creature's eyes. With a howl of pain, the monster dropped him to the floor and clutched at its bleeding eye sockets. Falling to the floor, it bellowed and thrashed and writhed in pain and fury. Lanson picked himself up and ran to his sword, then turned to where the monster was threshing about and began to thrust his blade toward its vital organs, dodging its flailing arms and legs all the while. With each thrust the monster howled and convulsed, blood now flowing from six or eight wounds in its chest and abdomen. Lanson wondered what kind of blow it would take to kill the thing. He aimed his sword directly at a place on the creature's breast where he thought the heart must be and raised it to make what he hoped would be the final blow.

"Wait, Lanson. Please, don't kill me."

Lanson hesitated, stunned at the voice. It was exactly that of his father—in every tone, every inflection, even to the slight brogue and the clipped pronunciation of the words.

"My spirit is trapped inside this hideous body," the voice of King Kor continued. "If you kill it, I will be sent out into the void of darkness, forever isolated from contact with any soul in the universe. I cannot bear it, my son. If you ever loved me, spare me this fate and do not strike the final blow."

Lanson lowered his sword. "Father, how can this be? I don't understand that you could be—"

In that instant the creature lunged at Lanson, guided by the sound of his voice, intending to tear out his throat. Caught off guard, Lanson jumped to the side, and the monster sank its teeth into his already wounded shoulder. With all his might, Lanson thrust his sword time and again into the creature's midsection and chest until he felt its body relax and its teeth release their grip.

He stood, panting heavily as he watched the hideous body twitch and jerk before it finally lay silent and still on the arena floor. He started to turn away, when a slight movement of the dead creature caused him to turn back. As he watched, the corpse seemed to become fluid, its outlines slowly blurring and contracting as the color darkened. In a few moments Lanson realized he was no longer staring at the monster of his nightmares but at the body of Morgultha, her eyes a mass of blood and her robe ripped and stained from the wounds inflicted by his sword. As he continued to stare in shock, the skin of her face and remaining hand began to shrink and wither as webs of wrinkles, long and deep, creased the entire surface.

After the change was complete and the body lay still, Lanson shuddered at what he saw—the corpse of an ancient, decayed woman who looked every year of her centuries of age. He lifted his eyes to the galleries about him. All the seats were empty. The hooded figures were gone. He looked toward the pedestal. The stone image of the monster was back in its place, in every detail exactly as Lanson had first seen it.

CHAPTER THIRTY-EIGHT

In The Maze

anson stared at the withered body of Morgultha lying crumpled on the temple floor, his mind struggling to understand all that had just occurred in the arena. Apparently the entire encounter from start to finish had been against only one foe—Morgultha herself. Father Clemente and the monstrous living statue had been only images, either manifestations of Morgultha or illusions controlled by her. But what about Evalonne? Was her image an illusion as well? Or had she actually been present, cast into the pit by Hugal in spite of his promise? If she had been truly present, was it possible that she could have been devoured by the mere image of the monster or by Morgultha in the form of the monster? Surely illusions had limitations on how far they could actually affect reality. But Lanson knew little of such things and began looking about the floor to find Evalonne's blood smeared across the stones as he had seen it during the battle. He found no trace of it. Indeed, he could not even find the stone block or the chains that had bound her.

"Surely she is alive," he murmured, and the walls of the temple echoed the words back to him. The more he thought on it, the more certain he felt that the image of her was mere illusion, and the real Evalonne was still safe on the surface of the earth far above.

There must be a way back to that world. Apparently Morgultha had been able to get in and out of these caverns of the Nephilim, but how would one go about finding the passageway? He thought of returning to the branched maze where he had entered the caverns, but he knew that even if the maze did lead to an exit, he had no hope of choosing the right forks that would take him to it.

He remembered Morgultha speaking of the stores of knowledge she had found in the buildings around the temple. Perhaps he could find something in them that would show the way out. He stood at the top of the temple steps and looked out over the ruined city. On each side of the temple and facing the avenue in front of it were two smaller buildings with pillared fronts, identical to each other. They looked as though they could house archives or a library, and thus were likely places to begin his search. He descended the steps, jumping from one to the next, and by random choice turned toward the building on his left.

As he neared the structure, he heard a distant sound as of something cracking and splitting. He stopped and looked all about, but seeing nothing alarming and hearing nothing more, he continued toward the building. Suddenly a shower of stones and rubble crashed down upon the steps in front of him. He jumped back, dodging an airborne boulder that came bounding down the steps, chipping and shattering as it went. He turned and ran back toward the temple as stones of all sizes cascaded from the ceiling of the caverns high overhead and crashed to the ground with a thunderous roar. When the shower ceased, thick clouds of dust swirled about for several seconds, then settled to reveal a pile of stones and scree that completely covered the steps and blocked the door he had intended to enter.

"Very well, I will search the other building," he muttered as he turned toward the structure on his right, glancing often into the smoky gloom that hid the invisible ceiling of the caverns. He climbed the steps and peered into the door, then cautious as a stalking cat, he stepped inside.

By the dim red light of the cavern, he could barely see that he was in an anteroom of some kind, for doors led off from either side to the interior of the building. He was surprised to see an unlit torch protruding from the wall in front of him until he reasoned that Morgultha must have placed it there. He took it from its sconce and leapt back down the steps to one of the fiery fissures in the floor of the caverns. After lighting the torch, he got back up the steps as fast as he could climb them. Holding the light aloft, he entered the ante-room, then warily stepped through the door into the dark interior.

He found himself in a large room, roughly square, with walls of stone. Ten feet inside the door was a cube of stone about six feet wide, six feet high, and four feet deep. The top of the cube was at eye level to Lanson. Looking around the room, he saw that it was filled with cubes identical to the first, all arranged in rows with ample walking space between each. He stepped into the chamber and wandered among the cubes, counting thirty-two of them. When he turned and looked at the back of them, he could see that they were precisely hollowed out like boxes open on one side. And placed vertically inside each cube like books on a shelf was a row of stone tablets, each four feet high, three feet wide, and no more than an inch thick, each resting in its own slot grooved into the top and bottom of the cube's interior.

Curious, Lanson laid his torch across the top of one of the cubes and grasped one of the slates, intending to slide it out to see if he could determine what it was. He found the task more difficult than he anticipated. The tablets were heavy, and he was breathing hard and his hands were raw before he managed to get the stone out of its slot and leaning against the cube.

He held the torch toward the gray stone. Its entire surface was engraved with a series of markings, mostly in the shape of thin wedges resembling spearheads and crescents, all combined in complex clusters and arranged in precise rows. *So this is the library of the Nephilim,* thought Lanson. No doubt the room contained a vast accumulation of ancient knowledge, but none of it could benefit him, for he could not read it.

He held up his torch and moved to the next room, which was another library exactly like the first. The third room was the same, as were the fourth and fifth. But the sixth room was altogether different. As he looked inside it, he did not at first recognize what he saw. Around the walls of the room ran a smooth stone path, elevated about a foot above the sunken interior. In the flickering light of the

torch, the entire sunken floor seemed filled with blocks and stones
and small pillars of varying sizes, some only a few inches high and
others reaching the level of his waist.

After a moment Lanson realized that he was looking at a precisely
detailed model city carved entirely from stones. Elevated in the center of the room stood an exact replica of the temple where he had
defeated Morgultha. And on each side of it were replicas of the two
buildings he had seen from the temple steps, including the one he
was in at this moment. *This is a model, or a map in relief of the entire
city of the Nephilim,* thought Lanson with awe. His eyes followed the
street from the temple to the gates, which stood in detailed miniature, even down to the two carvings of the monsters guarding the
entrance.

From the gate he traced in reverse the path he had followed to
reach the temple and found that it ended at the foot-high wall of the
elevated walkway that encompassed the miniature city. He went
around the walkway to the place where the miniature path ended.
Falling to his knees and looking over the edge, he found a hole in a
miniature cliffside, representing the opening to the maze from which
he had entered the great cavern. All was carved in uncanny detail,
even to the steps on which he had descended from the mouth of the
maze. Since this was obviously the place where he had entered the
caverns, perhaps there was a corresponding passage where one could
exit. With his heart pumping at the thought, he went around the
entire walkway, holding his torch low, looking for the replica of
another opening that could lead him out of this hell.

But he found nothing. When he had come fully around the
room, he stood above the replica of the cave where he had started and
sighed. His theory had proven false. His next thought was to explore
all other rooms in the building before trying anything else. He took
a step toward the door where he had entered and suddenly fell forward to the floor, dropping his torch in front of him. Something had
tripped him. He picked up the torch and held it to the floor where
he had stood but could see nothing that should have caused him to
stumble. Something strange was going on here. He had the uneasy
feeling that he was not alone.

As he continued to search about, he found the likeness of a large tree carved into the wall of the room exactly above the place where the walkway crossed the miniature cave. He thought it strange that the Nephilim would have carved such a thing as a tree, for he had seen no sign of trees or any other flora anywhere in the underground city. He held the torch higher and saw that the tree reached almost to the top of the wall, some fourteen feet above him. It was a dead tree with no leaves, only branches and twigs of diminishing size as they reached upward and outward from the thick trunk. He could see some round or oblong object carved at the top of the tree just to the left of center. He first thought it was a strange fruit, or perhaps the moon behind the tree, but when he lifted the torch toward it he saw that it was a skull, though somewhat poorly carved compared with the precision craftsmanship of the miniature city. Its mouth was jagged and uneven, and the eye sockets were of different sizes and slightly askew. Yet in spite of the poor quality of the carving, Lanson blanched when he saw it, though he did not know why.

From the moment he entered the room he had been so focused on the model of the city that he had not even noticed the walls. Perhaps there were other carvings on them that would give him some kind of help in escaping the caverns. Again he made the circuit of the walkway, examining the walls as he went. But they were completely blank. The tree and skull were the only carvings on them, which Lanson found baffling. What could the tree mean? Why did the mis-shapen skull give him such an uneasy feeling? Unable to solve the puzzle, he shook his head and turned to leave the room.

Again he stumbled and almost fell to the floor. Bewildered at what could have tripped him, he turned and examined the floor again but found nothing. Once more the sense of another presence in the room weighed heavily upon him. He straightened and looked at the tree, and suddenly his eyes widened in recognition. It was not a tree; it was a map—a map of the maze of caves through which he had entered the cavern. The skull at the top was the stone of the Devil's Mouth. If he could follow the correct branches exactly as they forked on the map, he would surely reach the skull and could exit through it. How could he have been so stupid as to have missed it?

His elation ebbed as he considered the complexity of plotting his way through the maze. It began with one large trunk and continually branched and redivided until it ended in several hundred twigs. At each fork the choice was simply to go to the right or left, but how would one ever remember which choice to make at each juncture? The only answer was to plot his course from the map and record the choice at each fork on a shard of stone that he could take with him into the maze. It would not be easy. While in the caves he would not only have to read what he had recorded, but count precisely how many forks he had entered so he would know which faced him next. He could make no mistakes.

His first need was a shard to write on. He thought of the tables of stone in the library rooms, but even if he could break from one of them a piece small enough to carry, it would not do, for they were already filled with markings.

He started for the door, thinking to descend the steps outside yet again to search about the building for a shard of rubble small enough to carry. Suddenly a cracking sound filled the room as a small section of ceiling stone gave way and crashed at Lanson's feet. Another step and the debris would have hit him on the head. He remembered the enormous fall of stones from the cavern ceiling that had almost crushed him when he attempted to enter the first building, and the two times he had stumbled over some invisible obstacle in this room. He could not shake the feeling that some malignant spirit hovered about determined to destroy him. He lifted his foot to step over the pile of rubble but paused as he looked at it. Lying at his feet was a thin wedge of stone little larger than his hand—exactly what he needed. Again the feeling of something uncanny in the air came strong upon him. But he picked up the sliver of stone and turned back to the carving of the tree.

He placed the torch on the edge of the walkway, faced the tree, and using his knife as a stylus, began to mark on the shard the right or left choices at each fork between the skull and the trunk. He inscribed one mark for a right turn and two for a left. The task was not easy. He had to plot his route backward, beginning at the skull and working his way down to the trunk. This meant he had to invert his thinking, and more than once he had to stop and concentrate on the process before he erred and made the opposite mark than he intended. And soon after he had marked the first two or three junctures, he discovered that each time he looked away from the tree to mark the shard, he lost his place among the limbs and had to rework his route from the top.

Finally he finished the markings, but he would not leave the tree until he had checked them three times, first forward and then backward. He found only one error, which he corrected, then ran his check three times more before he was convinced his map was perfect. Finally satisfied, he took up his torch and left the building, stepping cautiously as he listened for any evidence of his invisible enemy.

He leapt down the steps, proceeded along the avenue to the gates, still guarded by the stone monsters, and picked his way through the fissures and magma scabs of the scarred earth until he reached the cliff wall where he had entered the caverns. He climbed the steps and walked into the trunk of the maze, still bearing his torch. He came to the first fork of the tunnel, checked the carved stone in his hand, and took the left option as it indicated. He repeated the procedure at the next juncture and the next, as the caves narrowed with each forking.

Finally, after proceeding through nine forks, he reached the tenth and last one, which led him into a tunnel so narrow that it would not admit the width of his shoulders, and he had to move sideways, feeling the rugged walls pressing against his back and chest as he inched forward. After he was several minutes into the constricted space, it made a sharp turn to the left, and he started violently as he stared eye to eye into a hideous grinning face. His horror subsided only a little as he realized it was only a gray and mottled human skull, complete with an intact skeleton below it, wedged into the narrow tunnel. With his heart beating like a hammer, he held his torch toward the grisly thing, and it seemed to jerk and quiver as if the flickering light were bringing it to life. Lanson shuddered. Looking beyond the skeleton, he saw that the passage ended immediately behind it. The poor soul had apparently reached the end of the tunnel, turned to retrace his steps, and found himself wedged into the narrow space.

Lanson's heart sank. Somewhere he had made a wrong turn. Or

worse, perhaps the map was false, designed deliberately to mislead. Sick with despair, he began to work his way back through the narrow space, all the while sensing the eerie presence of the hideous bones behind him.

When he arrived at the fork, he checked his stone and found that according to his mark, he had made the correct choice. He decided to retrace his steps to the previous juncture. As he thought on it, he wondered at the purpose of such a narrow channel as the one he had just left. It was much too small to admit the creatures who had lived within these caves. When he reached the previous fork, he checked his stone guide again and found that he had indeed misread it. The stone had a blemish in it, a small furrow that he had interpreted as a second mark, and thus he had taken the left passage instead of the right. Greatly relieved, he entered the right fork and made his way forward again.

When he reached the next juncture, at which the marks on his stone told him to take the right passage, he was surprised to find that the tunnel did not narrow as it had in each instance before. He walked forward freely with at least two feet of space on each side of him. He strained his eyes peering into the darkness, hoping at any moment to see daylight streaming into the tunnel from the outside world.

His heart leapt as he thought he saw a pinpoint of light far ahead. He increased his pace, looking intently at the light all the while. Soon he saw another point of light beside the first, then another and another. Baffled by the multiple lights, yet hopeful, he hurried forward, then stopped in dismay. Directly in front of him, only a few feet away, stood a solid wall of rugged stone embedded with crystals, glistening and dripping with water running from a spring somewhere above. These wet crystals had reflected the rays of Lanson's torch, leading him to mistake them for lights. Instead of finding an opening to freedom, he now faced another dead end.

What had he done wrong? He was certain his marks were accurate, and excepting his one misstep, he felt sure he had followed them carefully. He touched the wall as if to assure himself that it was no illusion. He looked all around him. There was no other opening. He looked toward the ceiling and at first saw nothing but gaping blackness. But when he held his torch high he could see that the tunnel above him went straight upward for about fifteen feet, then curved abruptly forward—that is, in the same direction he had been traveling. He saw no better option than to climb the wall in hopes that the tunnel continued above. It was rugged enough that he was certain he could find handholds and purchase for his feet, but how would he carry his torch? After a moment's hesitation, he decided he would have to throw the torch as high as he could into the tunnel above, hoping there was enough lip in the rock where the tunnel curved that it would stay where it landed. He checked his pouch to be sure he had his flint, then threw the torch upward as far as he could. It came tumbling down again. He threw it once more with the same result, but the third time it did not come back, and he could see the glow of it on the wall of the tunnel above him.

He began to make his way up the wall, his arms and legs spread like a spider's, groping and probing in the darkness for stones and fissures solid enough to support his weight. He found the climb more difficult than he anticipated because of the wetness of the rock, his feet often slipping and his hands groping for holds not coated with mossy slime. He was breathing hard when a quarter-hour later he reached up and felt a lip where the angle of the wall changed from vertical to horizontal. When he pulled himself up another few inches, the light of his torch smote his eyes, and he climbed onto the ledge and sat while he caught his breath.

He picked up the torch and saw before him a flight of steps, high and steep, that must have been hewn from the raw stone when the earth was young. They were cracked and crumbled but seemed essentially intact, ascending at a frightful angle and disappearing into the darkness above. Without hesitation Lanson began to climb the steps, though the height and narrow lip of them required the use of his hands as much as his feet. Often he had to lay the torch on the next step and use both hands to pull himself up. The steps were littered with stones and scree, and twice Lanson came upon one that had crumbled away and had to climb hand over foot to reach the next.

After ascending thirty or more steps he began to hear a faint, continuous sound—a distant murmur as of wind or moving water. Not long afterward he began to find the steps increasingly crumbled and damaged as the angle of ascent became even more acute. Finally the steps ceased to exist altogether, and he was forced to climb a near vertical wall of bare, wet stone. More than once he gripped a rock jutting from the wall only to have it give way in his hand and tumble into the darkness below. And more than once he felt a stone on which he stood waver slightly or begin to sag beneath his weight. The sound he had first heard as a murmur was now a roar. He was becoming exhausted and wondered how much longer he would have to climb before he came to the opening or even a ledge where he could rest.

Suddenly the ridge on which he stood crumbled beneath his foot and he slipped downward. He clutched wildly at the rugged surface of the wall, dropping his torch and watching in horror as it plunged into the darkness below. Finally his foot lodged on a lower ridge, stopping his slide, and he pressed himself against the wall panting heavily until his heart calmed. He resumed his climb in total darkness.

Progress was much slower as he had to grope for invisible holds and test each with painstaking care before trusting it with his full weight. But he moved steadily upward until soon the roar became deafening, and moments later he pulled himself onto a ledge or landing or perhaps the floor of another level of the caverns. He sat still for several minutes catching his breath as the roar, certainly the sound of rushing water, pounded in his ears. On hands and knees, he cautiously crept toward the sound, brushing his hands back and forth across the floor ahead for obstacles or pitfalls. After crawling thirteen paces, his hands groped along the stone surface until it ended and he reached downward into empty darkness. The roar was deafening now, booming up from what was obviously a pit or crevasse of considerable depth. Feeling along the edge of the pit with his hands, he followed it to his right, and after about ten or twelve feet he met a vertical wall. He turned back and followed the edge to the left and found his way blocked by another wall.

Disheartened, he sat with his back to the invisible wall, the roaring pit on his left and the cliff he had climbed on his right, and considered his options. He concluded that in spite of his meticulous care, he had after all made a mistake in the maze. And now he was apparently trapped on the top of something like a dam or a flat ridge with an almost sheer drop on one side and a pit of rushing water on the other, blocked by vertical walls at either end. And he could see absolutely nothing. The walls at the ends of the ridge were too steep to climb, and if he could climb them he had no idea where they would lead. Probably simply to the roof of the cavern. To plunge into the pit of roaring water would be foolhardy. In despair he folded his arms across his knees and laid his head upon them. Unless he could think of some other option, he would end up like the corpse of the woman he had seen when he first entered the maze.

He closed his eyes, and immediately the image of Evalonne filled his mind. Somehow the veil that had shut out all thoughts of beauty and goodness while he was in the city of the Nephilim had been lifted. Evalonne's winsome face and emerald eyes set his heart to longing for her with an ache that was almost physical. And along with her came images of bright sunlight, green fields, golden-thatched cottages, lush, leafy trees, vistas of heather-covered hills cradling lakes of crystalline blue, shepherds whistling as they herded sheep across stone bridges, bees buzzing among flowers waving in the breeze, and voluminous silver clouds rolling across the blue sky. A long, quivering sigh escaped him as the beauty he had known flooded his mind like sunlight bursting through a cloud.

When he opened his eyes again he could see the uneven surface of the floor at his feet as clearly as if illumined by a strong lamp, each pebble casting an elongated shadow toward his feet. Lanson looked up. Startled at what he saw, he scrambled to his feet, drew his sword, and tensed for battle. Standing before him at the center of the ridge was Father Clemente, holding in his right hand a sword with a blade that seemed made of pure flame.

"Who are you?" asked Lanson.

"Have you such a short memory that I am forgotten already?"

"I have not forgotten the false image of Father Clemente that I met only a few hours ago in the caverns beneath us. How do I know that you are not another?"

"How did you know the image of Father Clemente to be false?"

"Because of what he demanded of me. He contradicted the principle of mercy the true Clemente had taught me. I knew the true Clemente would never make such a demand."

"You are exactly right, King Lanson. You can always know a messenger to be false, no matter how godlike his appearance, if he contradicts what you know to be truth."

"But the question remains," continued Lanson, "how can I know that you are not another false Clemente?"

"Do you mean you do not know me after all the help I have given you in these caverns?"

"What help? I've been utterly alone since the moment I arrived in this hell. And I could have used your help."

"I should be deeply offended at your lack of gratitude," replied Clemente, a twinkle in his eye that was lost on the angry Lanson. "Who do you think foiled the aim of Morgultha when she hurled the stone block at you? Who do you think caused the avalanche of stone that prevented your wasting valuable hours searching for direction in the wrong building? Who do you think tripped you to make you see the map of the maze that would get you out of here— and had to do it twice before it sunk into your thick head? Who do you think provided you with a hand-sized stone tablet upon which you could record your directions? Who do you think held numerous loose stones in place as you climbed the crumbling stairway just moments ago?"

"You did all that?" Lanson relaxed his guard. "I thought something was trying to kill me. Please forgive my lack of gratitude. But you must agree that it's sometimes a bit hard to tell your help from harm."

"Severe measures are sometimes necessary—though I seldom need to trip anyone twice."

"You would have done just as well not to trip me at all. The map was wrong. Look where it has got me."

"The map was not wrong," said Clemente.

"Then I misread it or misplotted my course. I must retrace my steps and start over."

"You did not misread the map, nor did you misplot your course. If you return to the caverns you will die."

"How can you say the map was correct when it has led me to this impasse? If to go back is death and I can't go forward, what am I to do?"

"I can get you out of here in moments. But you must do exactly as I say."

"What would you have me do?"

"You must leap into this pit."

Lanson stared at Father Clemente, then looked over the edge into the black, thundering abyss. "There must be some other way. I've spent hours, expended most of my energy, and risked my life climbing out of the caverns below. Why should I waste all that by merely jumping back into the depths again?"

"Because there is no other way out."

Lanson glared hard at Clemente. "That is such an outrageous demand that I wonder if you are not another illusion. How do I really know that you are the true Father Clemente?"

"I am not an illusion."

"Your denial means nothing. An illusion would claim itself to be real."

"You can know that I am no illusion because you slayed the maker of the illusion."

"But how can I know that even that was not an illusion? I've been fooled so many times in these caverns that I wonder how I can know whether anything is real."

"When you start letting your mind play such games, you can never know. You can convince yourself that even your own being is an illusion and all reality is merely a phantom projected by some inexplicable cosmic phenomena. But if you adopt such a belief, you will find yourself living in a world of continual contradiction—a world in which things seem to have substance and seem to have meaning and seem to be true in spite of your assertion that they are not."

Lanson thought long while Clemente waited silent and still as if he possessed an eternity of patience.

"I leapt once into a pit. It seems hard that I am now required to do it again."

"Nothing in this fallen world is ever once and for all. It is the nature of things that you must choose daily and risk yourself over and over again."

"How can I know this leap will not kill me?"

"But for the assurance I have given, you cannot know. You can only know that to return to the caverns of the Nephilim is death."

"Is there no other way?"

"There is no other way. You must leap."

Lanson turned from Father Clemente and gazed down into the pit. He could see nothing but darkness. The thunderous waters must be far, far below. He stepped to the edge and closed his eyes.

Then he leapt into the abyss.

CHAPTER THIRTY-NINE

ṬḄE ĘNḊ OF ṬḄE VIGIL

valonne sat on the stone huddled in her cloak against the cool night. The rain had ceased hours ago, but the air was still damp and puddles dotted the stone floor. Sir Maconnal sat on a rock three feet from hers, his head bowed, his eyes closed, and his lips moving occasionally, though no sound came from them. For the entire night she had sat on the stone, hardly noticing the cold or the many watchers gathered around them, some standing and talking quietly with their neighbors, others sitting on the ground in contemplation, a few asleep. She knew from occasional glimpses of their faces that their hope had begun to wane. No one spoke the thought that had crept like a lengthening shadow into the minds of all—that no one had ever returned from the Devil's Mouth. And it was beginning to seem that no one ever would.

Evalonne had not slept at all. She had seldom even looked away from the craggy skull above them, though she could hardly see it in the darkness, and only as a looming, black, featureless mass. But as she stared toward it now it grew slowly grayer as the sky behind her began to glow with the approach of the sun. Soon she could barely make out the chilling black hollows of the eyes and mouth.

As the blackness of the heavens turned to gray, Bishop Hugal, sitting with his two guards on the ledge at the base of the Devil's Mouth, arose stiffly and addressed the watchers below.

"Citizens of Lochlaund, the sun is about to break over the horizon. The prescribed duration of the ritual watch is ending, and it is time for you to end this fool's vigil and return to your homes. All along your hope of King Lanson's return has been without substance. You have wasted a night, and there is no need to waste daylight as well. King Lanson has perished by the will of the Master of the Universe. He will not return. Go to your homes and take up your lives."

Evalonne glanced at Sir Maconnal, expecting him to stand and refute the bishop, urging the people not to heed him. But Maconnal did not move and gave no sign that he had even heard Hugal's voice. Others had heard, though, and she could tell by their uncertain looks and whisperings that hope was flickering low and that the first rays of the sun would extinguish it altogether. A few watchers turned and began to make their way toward the path that led down from the stone. Maconnal made no move at all. Evalonne lifted her eyes toward the grim skull and continued her watch.

ℒ

Lanson hurled straight downward into the abyss, utterly helpless, feeling the air rushing over him as the roar from the darkness below rose to meet him. In moments he plunged deep into the water and felt himself swept into the rushing current as he fought his way toward the surface. He broke from the water and gulped for air before the current tugged him under again and shot him forward like a bolt from a crossbow. Bouncing helplessly from one side of the channel to the other, he occasionally managed to get his head above water and draw a breath before a change in direction or a sudden downward turn sucked him under again.

Suddenly he felt himself propelled out of the tunnel and tumbling through the air amid a wet spray. His fall ended with a splash as once again he plunged deep into a body of water and swam back up to the surface. There was no longer any current, though the surface rippled with the force of the waterfall that fed it. And to his great relief, he could see. Everything was bathed in a dim orange light. He was floating in a pool bordered on three sides by the walls of a cave. The rushing waterfall that had delivered him spewed from an opening high above the back wall. The pool emptied through a black opening in the wall to his right, and the wall to his left was sheer and featureless. On the fourth side of the pool a pebbly bank lay before him, and beyond the bank stretched a rocky tunnel, and at the end of the tunnel, perhaps seventy yards distant, was an opening through which he could see an orange glow.

Lanson's heart sank. Apparently he was back in the deep caverns of the Nephilim. He swam to the bank, dragged himself from the water, and, with dread weighting him like a stone, began to plod toward the orange light. Bitterness welled up within him. The Father Clemente he had met above the abyss was apparently either false or outright evil. Why had he trusted the strange man? He could not answer that question, except that this Clemente had exuded an aura, an attitude, an air of authenticity that invited trust. But it was all for naught. He had been betrayed and his despair was deep. He was so exhausted that the very air he breathed seemed heavy in his lungs, yet he plodded on toward the orange glow, which grew brighter with every step.

As Evalonne gazed up at the skull, she suddenly tensed and became alert. She thought she had seen a flicker of light in the blackness of the right eye. The rim of the sun had just broken above the horizon behind her, but its rays were not yet strong enough to account for what she had seen. She straightened up to look more intently, and as she gazed she became sure that the eye was filling with light. She reached over and touched Maconnal's shoulder.

"Sir Maconnal, look yonder at the devil's eye."

Maconnal raised his head and looked to where she pointed. The eye now glowed with a strong light coming from somewhere inside it. As they gazed, a figure appeared in the eye—a tall, robed being with hair and beard shining white in the light of the sword he held, which dazzled like a flash of lightning.

"It's Father Vitale!" said Evalonne.

A moment later another figure appeared beside the first, and Evalonne's heart leapt, bringing her to her feet. "It's Lanson! He's come back! Look, Sir Maconnal, King Lanson has returned." She wrung her hands, cried, and laughed all at once.

When Maconnal saw Lanson join Father Clemente in the eye of the skull, he closed his eyes and silently mouthed a prayer of thanksgiving. By now the other watchers had seen the two figures standing in the eye and stood gaping in awe and disbelief.

Z

When Lanson reached the opening, it took him a moment to comprehend what he saw. Countless points of flame blazed some hundred feet below him, which he took to be fires of the deep breaking to the surface of the caverns through a honeycomb of small craters in the stone floor. He lifted his eyes to the orange glow far in front of him and, after a moment of confusion, realized with a start that he was looking not into a cave but out over the landscape of Lochlaund. The orange glow on the horizon was the rim of the sun, just beginning to show over the distant highlands. And standing tall on the horizon just to the right of the sun he saw the towers and spires of his own Macrennon Castle.

As he gaped in dazed awe, a sound rose from the darkness below that nourished him like milk and honey. Human voices, raised in exultation, cheered him and drove from his mind the last remnants of the darkness that lingered from his ordeal in the caverns. He looked down again and realized the points of light were torches. A crowd of hundreds filled the stone plateau below him, cheering and shouting his name with all their strength.

At Sir Maconnal's command, men took up the ladders and ropes that always accompanied the ritual watch and carried them up the ramp toward the skull. Maconnal followed close behind, but Evalonne, now strangely shy, remained on the stone platform below. The men hoisted the ladder up to the eye and held it steady as King Lanson descended to the ground, where he clasped Maconnal to his breast in silent gratitude.

Maconnal looked up at the eye of the skull, now dark and empty. "Where is the man who was with you?" he asked.

"What do you mean? No one was with me."

"But he was. We saw him beside you in the eye of the skull. He held a flaming sword in his hand."

"Father Clemente!" said Lanson. "It's strange that I did not see him, though I have no doubt that he was there with me. Where is Evalonne?"

"With the watchers below. She has not taken her eyes off the devil's eye all night."

As Lanson and Maconnal walked down the ramp, the people below began to clap their hands as they took up a rhythmic chant, "Long live King Lanson!" which they repeated over and over until he reached the stone, where they thronged about him, cheering and laughing with sheer joy. Lanson acknowledged their adulation with waves and handclasps and by touching every hand that reached toward him, smiling broadly all the while and looking all about the crowd for the face of Evalonne.

So focused was Maconnal during the long night of the vigil, it had not occurred to him to tell Evalonne that Lanson had called off his wedding to Lady Lamonda. Or he may simply have assumed that she had heard. But she had not. In fact, she assumed the opposite, thinking the wedding had proceeded after her own trial. In her mind, King Lanson was already married.

She watched as he walked down the stone ramp toward the plateau where the people waited, filling her heart with his noble image for the last time. Now that the vigil was over, she turned away, still resolved to remove herself from his life and get on with her own. As he began to mingle with the exultant throng, she tore her eyes away and no one noticed as she slipped through the crowd toward the road to Macrennon.

Lanson made his way across the stone table, and the people continued to press about him—lords, ladies, knights, farmers, tradesmen, and laborers alike expressing their heartfelt gladness at his unprecedented return. He was deeply grateful for such an outpouring of goodwill, for he knew it meant the people would support him in his challenge to the kirk. But he continued to search the crowd for Evalonne, wondering why she was not among his greeters.

"Where is Evalonne?" he asked Maconnal, who had kept close beside him.

"I do not know," Maconnal replied. "She was here all through the night. She was the first to see you looking out of the devil's eye."

Lanson began to scan the crowd in earnest. When he became convinced she was not on the stone table, he looked down at the watchers thronged at the base of the mountain but caught no sight of her there. Then he looked beyond the crowd and saw her—a lone figure walking away on the path that led to the road to Macrennon, the rising sun rimming her hair with burnished gold. Lanson pointed to her and bellowed to the watchers below.

"Stop that woman!"

It took a moment for anyone to comprehend the command.

"Stop that woman on the road and bring her to me," he cried again.

Three men on the far edge of the crowd ran toward her. Everyone on the upper table and in the flat below turned to watch as the men caught up with the woman, stopped her, and pointed up to where the king stood. She shook her head and began to run, but they caught her by the arms, turned her about, and walked her back toward the king. The crowd parted to make way as the men marched her up the path to the stone plateau where their king waited. They set her before him and backed away. The crowd went silent, waiting to see what kind of drama was about to play itself before them.

Evalonne stood before King Lanson with her head bowed, staring at his feet, mortified to have all eyes looking at her. They knew who she was—a fallen, immoral woman condemned by the kirk, saved only by the heroic sacrifice of their king. Surely they must hate her for putting their beloved monarch in such jeopardy. Lanson stepped close and placed his hands on her shoulders. She closed her eyes and almost swooned.

"Evalonne, why did you run away?" he asked.

The people clustered around the couple listened in dead silence, their ears straining to hear every word.

"All right, let's back away, now," Maconnal chided the eavesdroppers. "Let them have a bit of privacy, if you please." He began to shoo the crowd back from the pair, giving them an open circle of some ten feet all around.

Evalonne still could not look at Lanson. "I ran away because I . . . I had caused enough harm to you. You had done so much for me, I didn't . . . I couldn't face you again. I had to leave while I could so you could . . . to let you get on with your life."

"But I was hoping our lives would no longer be separate," said Lanson.

"I . . . I don't know what you mean. You are now married to Lady Lamonda."

"Married? Oh, I see; you do not know. I wonder why Maconnal did not tell you. Yes, I was about to marry Lady Lamonda, but only because I thought the woman I loved was dead. When I learned she was alive, I called off the wedding."

His words hit Evalonne with such impact that she could not readily grasp their meaning. "You . . . you did not marry Lady Lamonda because you are in love with someone who is dead?"

"No, no. I *thought* she was dead. And so I agreed to marry Lady Lamonda to honor my father's wishes. I saw it as my duty. But I have come to realize that mere duty is a poor foundation for a marriage."

"But if you loved someone you thought was dead—"

"Evalonne, it is you whom I love. Please say you will marry me."

"You want *me* to say that I will marry *you?* Oh, Lanson, I think I must have loved you from the moment you came into the Red Falcon Inn with little Mossette in your arms. I have never in my life known anyone, man or woman, like you. But . . . but . . . ." Evalonne put her hands to her face and covered her eyes, which were filling with tears, and shook her head.

"But what, Evalonne?"

"A woman such as I cannot wed a king. The people know who I am and what I have been, and they would not have me as their queen. It would not do, Lanson. You must let me go." She turned to leave, but Lanson grasped her again by the shoulders.

"Yes, you are unworthy to be a queen. And I am unworthy to be a king. No one is really fit to sit upon the throne of a kingdom, yet someone must do it, and the task falls to me. Now I have chosen you for my queen, and fit or not, I beg you to accept the task."

"But the people—"

"I am certain by what I have witnessed in the reception of the people this morning that they will readily accept you. Your past is past. You are no longer what you were, and you must take up a new life now."

"A new life, yes . . . but to be a queen . . ."

"Remember the ancient women Rahab and Tamar, one a harlot and the other guilty of incest. Yet both became forebears of illustrious kings. Evalonne, I ask you again, will you marry me?"

Unable to speak, Evalonne looked up at Lanson, her eyes bright through the streaming tears. "Yes, King Lanson, I will marry you," she whispered.

Without a word he wrapped her in his arms, lifting her from the ground, and kissed her full upon the lips as the crowd cheered and applauded. He took Evalonne's hand and pulled her through the crowd and halfway up the ramp to the Devil's Mouth, where he stopped, still holding her hand, and turned to face the watchers.

"Men and women of Lochlaund," he cried, "I have something of great importance to tell you. The woman standing beside me has just agreed to become my wife. We will be wed in two days. I introduce to you Evalonne, your new queen-to-be."

Cheers burst forth from all the commoners and most of the nobles in the crowd as they applauded in wild abandon.

"Two days?" repeated Evalonne, still in shock but smiling broadly and blushing deeply. "How can we plan a wedding in two days?"

"Oh, you women make too much fuss over weddings. I almost told them it would be this afternoon."

After a moment Lanson held up his hands to quiet the crowd.

"Hear me, citizens of Lochlaund. I cannot find words to express the depth of my gratitude for your vigil of the night and your petitions to the Master. But as a token of my appreciation, I invite each of you to a wedding feast to be held right here at the base of Black Mountain immediately after Evalonne and I are wed. I require only one thing of you as admission to the feast. Each person who attends—man, woman, or child—must bring to the feast a stone, the larger the better. I will give prizes for the ten largest stones. Please come, each of you, and honor my queen and me with your presence. And do not forget to bring stones."

"What be the purpose of the stones?" yelled a man from the crowd below.

"That I will not tell," replied King Lanson. "But I assure you that they will be put to good use."

Lanson took Evalonne's hand and descended the ramp into the crowd. Though the vigil was over and their king had returned, the people seemed reluctant to leave, choosing rather to stand about chatting and laughing in pure good fellowship. As Lanson moved among the people he kept Evalonne close to him, seldom letting go of her hand. "I'm not letting you get away again," he told her. She had never felt more cherished.

ℒ♥

Midmorning had passed before the celebration settled down and the people began to disperse. Bishop Hugal, flanked by his two guards, had watched the proceedings silently from the ledge of the Devil's Mouth, anger and frustration churning his belly like a nest of vipers. From the darkness of his hood he scowled at the remainder of the watchers clustered about King Lanson as he lifted Evalonne to her saddle, mounted his own horse, and flanked by Sir Maconnal, rode off toward Macrennon, the rest of the crowd trailing behind him.

"This is not over yet," muttered Hugal as he descended the plateau and returned to the abbey.

CHAPTER FORTY

THE CHARRED LETTER

ishop Hugal sat alone in his chambers, sunk deep in his heavily padded chair. The only light came from a small candle, now burnt low and flickering feebly in the heavy darkness as if overwhelmed by a task too great for it. The only movement in the room was the wavering of the candle's dim rays on the stone walls, the only sound the rasp of Hugal's breathing. An observer would have thought the bishop asleep, but he was not. He had sat without moving for more than two hours, his mind smoldering with the embers of vengeance, which he was about to heap upon the hated King Lanson. A knock sounded at his chamber door.

"Come in," rasped the bishop's voice from the cavern of his cowl. The door swung open and a gray-robed monk entered the room.

"Everything is ready, your grace," said the monk in a hushed voice.

"You have brought the exact wine I told you to select?"

"I have," replied the monk, bringing out from the folds of his robe a stoppered bottle of dark liquid.

"And you have added to it the contents of the vial I gave you?"

"Exactly as you instructed," said the monk. "The carriage is ready and awaits us at the gate." With the monk's help, Bishop Hugal eased himself out of his chair and, leaning heavily on his cane, shuffled stiffly to the waiting carriage. When he was comfortably seated, the monk took the seat beside him and instructed the driver to take them to Macrennon Castle.

                                             ✦

Alenia bent over her trunk, rummaging through the blankets, dresses, parchments, stockings, scarves, and other fragments of her past packed inside it. *Men!* she thought with a frown. *They are all stupid brutes. Even the king. Two days to plan a wedding! And a queen's wedding at that. What was the man thinking? I know exactly what he's thinking, but it's no excuse. Should a man with no more sense than that even be allowed the throne? Where could I have put that veil?* She closed the trunk and turned to the several baskets stacked in a corner of her room. Surely the queen's veil was in one of them.

When Evalonne returned from her vigil at the Devil's Mouth, she had sent for Alenia immediately. Alenia went to the chambers Lanson had assigned to Evalonne and found the girl exhausted but too deliriously happy even to think of sleep. Evalonne had told her of all that had occurred at the Devil's Mouth, including King Lanson's startling announcement that he would wed her. The girl was giddy with awe. "Isn't it wonderful?" she had said over and over. "Can you imagine a man like Lanson loving a girl like me? Think of it, Alenia. I, of all people, to be desired and cherished by a king! It is almost unbelievable. I wonder if I am dreaming."

Alenia, with a face as serious as a judge, had reached out and pinched the awestruck young woman on the arm. "You seem to be real, so I presume you are awake."

Evalonne had begged Alenia to help her prepare for the wedding, and Alenia had readily agreed. The two had begun to chat as women do about dresses and colors and flowers and veils and décolletage, and giggled at delicate intimacies not meant for the ears of men.

Then Alenia had asked when the wedding would be, and when Evalonne told her it was two days away she had fumed and ranted at the ignorance of men. "Did he tell you who would coordinate the wedding? Who would select the music and hire the musicians? Who would officiate? Who would plan the banquet? Where you would get a dress? How you would find bridesmaids and dress them? No! He told you nothing, did he? I thought as much. And do you know why? Because not one of these thoughts has entered his fool head, that's why. It's the way men are, Evalonne. Get used to it. Lanson may be the king, but he's still a man, and about some things that means stupid as a mud hen." But nothing she said could penetrate the happy fog that enveloped the young queen-to-be.

There would be no time to make a wedding dress tailored expressly to Evalonne's proportions. They must find a gown already made and alter it to fit. Alenia remembered seeing the gown of Queen Lawannon, Lanson's mother, hanging in the wardrobe near the king's chambers. She took Evalonne to the wardrobe and, after a little searching, found the gown and held it against her to check the fit.

"It is beautiful," Evalonne had whispered. And Alenia had to agree. The color was a creamy beige trimmed with burgundy and outlined with gold piping. The bodice was covered with intricate patterns of embroidery. The sleeves were of silk, and the dress, gathered in tiny pleats at the waist, billowed full as it reached the floor. The veil and headpiece were not with the gown, and the two women spent several minutes looking for it before Alenia slapped her forehead.

"I have the veil. The queen gave it to me shortly before she died in hopes that I would wear it in my own wedding someday. A vain hope that was!" With the problem of the dress solved, she had led the giddy Evalonne back to her chambers, firmly insisting that she sleep now while she could. She would send word for the tailor and seamstress to be at the castle early in the morning, and by the end of the day the dress would look as if it had been made for her. Leaving the young woman, she had returned to her own quarters to find the veil.

Where had she put it? Alenia finished looking through one basket and emptied the next on her bed. She rummaged through the contents—rags, gloves, an old bonnet, a partially burnt parchment, three or four worn-out aprons—why did she keep such things? She gathered up the pile and dumped it back into the basket. The charred parchment slipped out and fluttered to the floor. She wondered why she had kept it. As she picked it up, she remembered. She had rescued it from the fireplace after King Kor had been murdered, though at the time she had not known he was dead. She had kept the parchment, intending to give it to the king when he recovered. By the time it was known that he was dead, she had forgotten all about it. She hoped it was not important. She should have given it to King Lanson long before now. She quickly scanned the document, and as she read, her eyes grew wide and her hands began to tremble. She tucked the parchment inside her dress and, upsetting the basket in her rush, ran out of her room and through the castle hallways toward King Lanson's chambers.

&v

King Lanson sat on his throne, the hall full of nobles, knights, ladies, and commoners milling about waiting for their names to be called. He was tired to the bone. He had gotten only two hours of sleep since returning from the Devil's Mouth, and he could see that he would get no more until nightfall. Before assuming the throne, he had thought kings to be the freest of men. They set their own agendas and answered to no one. But he found that the duties of kingship held him like the bars of a prison, and he had returned to his throne by mid-afternoon to hear the most pressing of the cases on his docket.

He had just awarded title to a small farm to the daughter of a recently deceased farmer after lawyers for the kirk, hoping to confiscate the property, had tried to deny her right to inherit because of her sex. The farmer's will had stipulated his son as heir, but the son was dead and the daughter had claimed rights as next of kin. As the grateful woman left the hall, Sir Maconnal approached the throne and told the king that Bishop Hugal waited outside requesting immediate audience with him.

"He is not on the docket. What do you think he wants?" said Lanson.

"From the looks of things, he comes with a peace offering," replied Maconnal.

"Let him enter."

The doors opened and the herald announced the bishop's entrance. Hugal, cowled as always, hobbled into the hall on his cane, followed closely by a robed monk carrying a tray containing a bottle of wine and two glasses. When Hugal reached the foot of the dais, the hall grew silent and all eyes turned toward the throne as the bishop addressed the king.

"King Lanson, I congratulate you on your successful return from the Devil's Mouth."

"Thank you, Bishop Hugal," replied the king.

"Though you and I have often differed, sometimes sharply, over matters of justice and authority, your return from the caverns makes it clear to all that you have the favor of the Master of the Universe. It ill behooves me as head of the Kirk of Lochlaund to be in contention with you, the head of the Kingdom of Lochlaund. In spite of our past differences, we must find our way toward accord within the will of the Master."

"I agree with you fully," said the king.

"I thank you for that, your majesty. And now, before you and all the people assembled in this hall, I wish to confess to the Master of the Universe my error in opposing your reign, and I pledge to you the full support and cooperation of the kirk as you continue as Lochlaund's king. Do you accept my contrition, King Lanson?"

"Of course I do, Bishop Hugal. And I commend you for your courage and humility in coming to me with your confession. Let me pledge before all these witnesses that I will do all within my power to honor the will of the Master of the Universe from this day forward."

"May the Master strengthen you in that resolve, my king. I have brought with me the last bottle of the finest vintage ever to rest in the cellars of the abbey, bottled over a century ago by monks in the vineyards of the valleys of Rhondilar. As a token of this renewed spirit of cooperation between the kirk and the kingdom, will the king join me in sealing our pledge with a ritual drink from the wine of accord?"

"I will happily drink to our accord," replied King Lanson.

Bishop Hugal turned to the monk standing behind him, uncorked the bottle, and poured the two glasses half full. He took them in his hands and turned toward the throne. Sir Maconnal came forward, took one glass from the bishop's hand, and carried it up the steps to the king. As King Lanson and Bishop Hugal lifted the glasses to their lips, the sound of angry shouting and scuffling broke from the great doors at the far end of the hall. The two men lowered their wineglasses, yet unsipped, and looked toward the uproar. A woman broke past the guards into the hall, running full speed toward the throne, holding in her hand a piece of charred parchment.

"Alenia!" exclaimed Sir Maconnal as he stepped down the dais and stopped the woman with a firm grasp of her shoulders. "What in thunder do you think you are doing?"

"The king must see this," she gasped, breathing hard from her run through the hallways.

"Not now!" said Maconnal. "You are interrupting a moment of critical importance to the future of the kingdom. Now go back and—"

"No! The kingdom has no future unless I see King Lanson now!"

"You must wait," said Maconnal sharply as he began to force her away from the throne toward the doors at the end of the hall, though she struggled and resisted every step. She turned to look over her shoulder as the king again held up the glass, ready to bring it to his lips.

"No!" she shouted. "King Lanson, you must not drink that wine."

But Lanson, ignoring her in the interest of regaining decorum in the hall, had the glass almost to his mouth. Alenia twisted with all her might and, wrenching free from Maconnal's grasp, ran up the steps of the dais and knocked the glass away from the king's lips, sending it shattering to the floor. King Lanson glared at her dumfounded as Maconnal stared in disbelief.

Before anyone could recover his tongue, Alenia held the parchment in front of Lanson's face. "Read this, King Lanson. You must read it now!"

Lanson took the parchment from her hands and began to read. Slowly his face turned hard and pale, his brow furrowed, and his eyes glared in icy fury. After a moment he stood and pointed his finger toward Bishop Hugal. He spoke in a voice low and firm but cold as steel. "Arrest that man for high crimes against the Kingdom of Lochlaund, namely, the murder of my father King Kor."

Immediately two guards moved from the sides of the hall and stood on either side of Bishop Hugal. A third guard took the arm of the monk standing behind him and led him from the floor. King Lanson, his face set like stone, gazed hard at Hugal.

"The evidence of this letter is clear, Bishop Hugal. You conspired with the traitor Sir Brendal to murder King Kor of Lochlaund. What have you to say for yourself?"

"I may seem guilty of the charge by ordinary standards," said the bishop, "but extreme maladies demand extreme remedies. Kor had begun to show signs of heresy. His commitment to justice was weakening. His resolve to make examples of lawbreakers had begun to soften. He was drifting from the truth and had begun to question the policies and advice of the kirk. I, as bishop of the kirk, the Master's representative in Lochlaund, am justified in doing whatever necessary—even if my action does not comply strictly with your concept of law—to see that the Master's ways remain intact in the kingdom. King Kor's death was not a murder but a war casualty in the ongoing battle between good and evil. By reason of my position and my duty to defend the Master's will, I am not guilty of the charge."

Sir Maconnal stepped forward. "Your majesty, will you grant me a word of refutation?"

"You may speak, Sir Maconnal."

"Although the bishop is a kirkman and pledges allegiance to a power higher than the kingdom, he is, nevertheless, a citizen of the kingdom and therefore subject to its laws. The Master of the Universe himself ordained human law and expects even citizens of the kirk to be subject to it. Therefore, I deem that Bishop Hugal has committed a crime not only against the kingdom but against the Master of the Universe as well."

"There are levels of laws, Sir Maconnal," interrupted Hugal. "The higher must sometimes supersede the lower."

"Your majesty," replied Maconnal, "such a defense shows that the bishop's thinking has become twisted, for it places his own judgment above the law of the kingdom, and thus above the law of the Master."

Bishop Hugal pointed a finger toward Maconnal. "You, Sir Maconnal, are the ultimate source of all the troubles that have come upon this kingdom and the house of Kor. You are the father of all heretics in Lochlaund—the foul sore from which the infection has spread. You corrupted King Kor, and now you have corrupted his son. I did what I had to do to save Lochlaund from a good king who was polluted by the vomit of your heresy. And if I must forfeit my life for my efforts, so be it."

"I have heard all I need to hear," said King Lanson. "Bishop Hugal, bare your head and receive your sentence."

"I will take no orders from a heretical king," replied Hugal.

At a nod from King Lanson, the guard reached out and forcibly pulled back the bishop's cowl, and everyone in the room recoiled in horror. Hugal's head and face were covered with scabrous sores and wartlike tumors.

"Replace the cowl," said Lanson, and the guard complied. "Bishop Hugal, I deem your crime to be deserving of death. However, it is clear that a punishment far greater than any the law can inflict has befallen you. Therefore, I hereby commute the sentence of death and lay upon you two punishments: first, by the power of the king to remove from office a kirk official who has committed a felony, I proclaim that from this moment you are no longer the Bishop of Lochlaund. Guard, please remove from Hugal the emblem of his office." The soldier unclasped the chain about Hugal's neck and brought it to the king.

"Secondly," Lanson continued, "I hereby banish you from the city of Macrennon and the towns of Lochlaund. You will spend the rest of your days as a homeless wanderer. You will be given the bell and staff of the unclean, and you will be shunned by all men. But you will be protected by the law that you have disdained, for if anyone lays a hand on Hugal, he will answer to the law and will be punished to its full extent."

From the darkness of his cowl, Hugal glared at the king. "You have won the day, Lanson, but tomorrow it may be you who suffers death or banishment. As long as Maconnal's heresy lives, the head that wears the crown of Lochlaund will be ever uneasy. Indeed, you almost drank your death moments ago. Had you sipped from the glass I gave you, in thirty days your own body would have been ravaged by the same plague that is slowly sloughing my life away. Such is your future, son of Kor, unless you return to the law of the Master. He will not long abide one who takes his law lightly."

"You accuse me of taking the law lightly," King Lanson replied. "The charge is false. The nation of Lochlaund will find me an ardent defender of the law, to which I am also subject. What I will not defend are the appendages you and your predecessors have attached to the law, or your narrow interpretations of the law to which you have given the force of law. And this kingdom will learn that within the law are provisions for mercy, which you have steadfastly chosen to ignore. Now, Hugal, depart from the presence of men, and in the life remaining to you, may your sufferings lead you to the heart of the Master."

A page brought a staff to Hugal and tied a small bell to his sash. Without another word Hugal turned and walked stiffly from the hall as the assembly looked on in stunned silence. The only sounds were the tapping of his staff and the jingling of the bell as he passed through the great doors and out of the castle.

When the bells and staff could be heard no more, King Lanson called Maconnal to the dais. "Sir Maconnal, it is the will of the crown to designate you the new Bishop of Lochlaund. Will you accept the appointment?"

Maconnal was stunned. For a moment he said nothing, looking as if he had been stricken with paralysis. Then he found his voice and his conscience and said, "I will accept the charge, your majesty."

King Lanson took the chain of office and hung it about Sir Maconnal's neck. He turned his friend toward the hall and announced, "Ladies, gentlemen, lords, knights, and citizens of Lochlaund. I present to you Bishop Maconnal, servant of the Master of the Universe and shepherd of the Kirk of Lochlaund."

Immediately the roar of applause and cheering voices filled the hall. Alenia, who had slipped back into the crowd, could not hold back tears of pride as she watched the king place the chain on this man she admired so much. As the applause waned she began to walk toward the doors when she heard her name called from the throne. She stopped and turned. King Lanson himself had descended the dais and was walking swiftly toward her.

"Alenia, wait a moment," said the king as he approached her. He took her gently by the arm and led her back to the dais and up the steps. He turned her to face the hall and said, "Men and women of Lochlaund, it pleases me to honor this brave and loyal servant to whom I owe my very life. Alenia, today you saved me from death, and I will ever be grateful. You have been a faithful servant to my mother, my father, and now to me. I wish to honor you. Is there any desire in your heart or boon you would like to ask? Please ask it now, and if it be reasonable and within my power, I shall grant it."

Alenia crossed her hands upon her breast and curtsied deeply to the king. "Indeed there is such a boon, your majesty. In these few days since you have brought to this castle your betrothed, Evalonne, I have come to love her as a daughter. I ask that you grant me the privilege of becoming her personal servant."

"Only this and nothing more?" asked the king.

"Only this, your majesty. I can think of nothing that will make me happier."

"Very well, your wish is granted. Though in the granting of it I think I have given my chosen queen as great a gift as I am granting you. Not only shall you be a servant to Queen Evalonne, you shall be first among her ladies-in-waiting. As a lady of the kingdom I grant you title to Glenncroft Manor, which has recently come into the possession of the crown, as well as your own apartments in this castle adjacent to that of the royal couple. Please rise, Lady Alenia."

Alenia stood, her eyes brimming. "I thank you, your majesty."

Bishop Maconnal came to her side and beamed on her a smile that filled her heart with sunlight. He offered his arm and escorted her through the hall as the people applauded. When they had passed through the doors, Maconnal turned to her and said, "You saved the king's life. He would have given you half his kingdom. Yet you asked only to serve one whom you love. I must say that never in my life have I known a woman of such loyalty, determination, selflessness, and courage. You well deserve the honor the king bestowed upon you today."

Lady Alenia, overwhelmed by such high praise from the man she idolized, could contain herself no longer. Her happiness overflowed in a flood of tears as she began to weep uncontrollably.

Poor Maconnal was taken aback. "What did I say? I'm sorry, Alenia. I didn't mean to hurt—would you tell me what I said?"

Alenia shook her head as she leaned against him, still crying, and he enfolded her in his arms and stroked her hair until her tears subsided.

CLOSING THE GATES OF HELL

n the next morning the sun rose over Lochlaund to one of the strangest days in the kingdom's history. Men from Macrennon and the countryside around the city were busily gathering stones. What made the day so strange was that they had no idea why they were gathering stones, except that the king had commanded it. The common people of Lochlaund had never been invited to a royal wedding feast, and if stones were the price of admission, they would gather stones.

Some got their gathering done early and went on about their usual business. Others got into the spirit of things and spent the day finding the largest stones they could carry. Wagons were piled with all they could carry. Stout carts with heavy wheels were filled until the sideboards bowed outward like the ribs of a gorged hog. Some carts were so heavily loaded that additional dray horses were harnessed to pull them. The stones were of all sizes, from that of a fist to that of a man's body. Some were even larger. One the size of a bull's torso was strapped to its own oaken wheels and rigged to a team of oxen. Even children got into the spirit of things, filling the bottoms of buckets with as many walnut-sized pebbles as they could carry.

As Alenia had promised, the tailor and seamstress arrived early and got about the fitting and measuring of Evalonne's wedding dress. Still grumbling about the stupidity of men, Lady Alenia organized servants and pages and badgered King Lanson into charging the steward

to mobilize men to ready the hall for the wedding and the cooks to
ready the food for transport to the site of the feast at Black Mountain.
By the end of the day she was exhausted but confident that all the
details of the celebration were under control.

On the next day Lady Alenia let Evalonne sleep as late as she
would, then insisted that she rest quietly for the remainder of the
morning. "Who knows how much sleep you will get tonight," she explained with a wicked smile. She had lunch sent to Evalonne's
chambers, and after the girl had dined, pages brought her a wooden
tub large enough to sit in and filled it with warm water. In spite of
Evalonne's protests, Alenia and four maidservants disrobed her,
bathed her, and dressed her in Queen Lawannon's wedding gown.

When all buttons were buttoned, all ties tied, every seam straightened, and every hair combed until it glistened lustrous as crimson
filaments of gold, Lady Alenia led Evalonne to the mirror. She was
stunned by what she saw. She had never seen herself so beautiful. She
delighted unabashedly in her beauty, for she knew it would bring joy
to Lanson. Her beauty was a gift from the Master, not to her, but to
her husband. That such a gift could flow through her from the Master
whom she loved to the husband whom she loved filled her heart with
unspeakable joy. She felt that she was, indeed, a queen.

A half-hour before the wedding the great hall of Macrennon
Castle was filled with the nobility of the kingdom—lords, knights,
earls, and their ladies, along with selected tradesmen and officers of the
kingdom who were closest to the king. A minstrel backed by a small
band and a choir of eight filled the air with ballads and love songs until
Bishop Maconnal and King Lanson strode in from the side and
mounted the dais. All heads turned as the oaken doors opened at the
end of the hall, and Lady Alenia entered and marched to the dais.

Then all breathing stopped as Evalonne appeared in the doorway
on the arm of Lord Kenmarl, smiling and blushing lightly. The band
struck up a march and she moved with a grace natural and elegant
down the center of the hall, her hair glowing like flame as she passed
through the beams of sunlight streaming from the high windows. She
stepped up the dais and stood beside King Lanson as Kenmarl placed
her hand in his, then retired and blended with the crowd. Many of the

guests claimed afterward that when it came to beauty, they would put Lochlaund's queen up against Volanna of Meridan any day.

The new bishop could have used the occasion to impress his flock with his wisdom and oratory, but he did not. He kept the ceremony mercifully short, using the simplest language, devoid of the phrases and linguistic formulae the people were accustomed to hearing. But long or short mattered little to the two lovers. Each gazing entranced into the eyes of the other, they lost themselves in the eternal realm of love, and time had no meaning. They uttered their vows, then Lanson turned back her veil, wrapped her in his arms, and lifting her off the floor, kissed her full upon the lips as the men cheered and the women blushed and tittered. Pride swelled in the people's hearts as their strong young king and his stunning new queen marched from the hall to the thunder of enthusiastic applause.

Shortly after the wedding a steady procession of carts, wagons, carriages, and riders mounted on horses and donkeys lined the road to Black Mountain, pouring from Macrennon and the countryside around it. Some of the carts lumbered slowly along the uneven trail because of their weight of stone. One wagon broke an axle, another lost a wheel, and one cart lost half its load when a sideboard gave way.

As the people arrived at the base of Black Mountain, row after row of makeshift tables were already set in place on the grassy meadow and under the shade of the oaks. They were loaded with beef, mutton, leeks, nuts, corn, and potatoes, along with kegs of wine and mead. As the guests looked up to the devil's skull, they were surprised to see ladders and scaffolding in place at the eyes and nostril and some kind of wooden apparatus just outside its mouth. A half-dozen oxen were tied near the base of the mountain. The arriving guests wondered at the meaning of it all, but they could get nothing from the king's men who were supervising the event but a smile and a cryptic "wait and see." They directed all carts and wagons containing stones to gather near the natural ramp just beneath the skull. Instructions would come later.

Most of the guests had already arrived when the carriage bearing the king and his new queen rolled into the clearing. Lanson and Evalonne, their faces still lit by smiles they could not extinguish, mixed with the people, acknowledging their good wishes with thanks and blessings. When the steward gave the word, Lanson mounted the bed of a wagon, thanked the people for their presence, and invited them to join the feast.

"What about the stones?" shouted someone from the crowd.

"I will tell you after we've all had our fill," replied King Lanson. "Eat well. You will need the strength."

The guests took their king at his word and put themselves fully into the feast. Families loaded their plates and trenchers with food and sat at the tables, on blankets spread on the grass, or on the rocks scattered here and there in the grassy meadow. Laughter and banter filled the air as friends mixed and mingled, young people clustered among themselves separate from their parents, and children, laughing and squealing, chased each other through the grass.

Lady Alenia filled her plate and spread her blanket under the shade of a spreading elm. She sat alone, but after only a few bites, a masculine voice above her asked, "Lady Alenia, is this place taken?"

She looked up into the face of the new Bishop of Lochlaund. "No, it is not taken," she replied, her mind in turmoil. She dearly wanted Maconnal to sit with her and had to bite her tongue to keep from offering the invitation. But he was now a kirkman and any indication of interest in a woman was forbidden. She would not be doing him a favor by encouraging the contact.

"May I sit here?" he asked, taking the dilemma out of her hands.

"Well, of course you may, but should you?"

"Why should I not?"

"Because you are now a kirkman and I am a woman."

"Dear Lady Alenia, it is muchly because you are a woman that I desire your company."

Alenia suddenly felt warm and her face flushed. "But . . . but it is forbidden for you to—"

"Forbidden by whom? Certainly not by the Master of the Universe. He has never denied to any of his servants the joys of conjugal love . . . uh, not that I am suggesting that you and I, uh, that is, that we are about to . . . uh . . ." It was Maconnal's turn to blush.

"Then why don't kirkmen marry?"

"It is merely a longstanding tradition that the kirk has solidified into law. There is no law against it in the early documents. The kirk must stop elevating such traditions into absolute prohibitions. Where the Master has made no rule, neither should his kirk."

Alenia thrilled at his words, and the bud of hope that she had closed blossomed and filled her heart. "Bishop Maconnal, you are welcome to sit on my blanket."

Lanson and Evalonne, much too filled with each other to be hungry, moved from one cluster of guests to the next, entering briefly into the conversation of each, often laughing at some joke, holding a new baby, or swinging a giggling toddler about like a slingshot. When the feast began to wane, the steward came to the king and whispered in his ear. Lanson nodded and again mounted the bed of the wagon.

"Honored guests," he called, "while we were feasting, my servants have been busy measuring the stones you have brought. As I told you, I will award prizes of gold to the ten largest. The winners have been determined. Let us proceed with the awards."

The people gathered about the wagons. The winner was obvious—the bull-sized boulder that had been outfitted with its own wheels. The burly, blond-bearded farmer who had brought it beamed a gap-toothed grin as he came forward amid cheers and applause to receive a pouch of coins from the king. The remaining winners were called and King Lanson gave each a smaller yet generous pouch. With the prizes awarded, the king instructed the winners to line up their carts and wagons behind the prize stone. Then he pointed upward to the skull of the devil. "We shall take the stones up there," he said. Those with the largest stones rubbed their chins and gazed at the angled roadway up the side of the mountain.

"I fear the road may be a bit steep for the weight we carry," said one of the winners.

"We have anticipated that problem," replied the king. "We have extra oxen, complete with harnesses, heavy ropes, and chains. Rig them as you need." The men wasted no time. They harnessed two additional oxen and attached them with ropes to the prize-winning boulder. The oxen strained at the start of the slope, and several men got behind the stone and bent their shoulders to it until King Lanson called them away. "It's much too dangerous," he explained. "If a rope were to break, men could be killed. Let the oxen pull the stone." After a moment the oxen found their footing and the boulder moved ponderously up the slope.

When the stone reached the Devil's Mouth, Lanson instructed the men to detach it from its wheels and roll it into the funnel of the steaming pit inside the mouth. Using poles as levers, coupled with sheer muscular strength, nine men rolled the stone to the edge and tipped it over into the steaming orifice. It scraped and slid downward, stopping with a thud that shook the earth as it lodged in the narrow throat of the mouth. Immediately the steam stopped. The other wagons followed, and their stones were dumped on top of the first. Stones kept coming until soon the original stone was covered. After several more wagonloads of smaller stones, what had recently been a pit was now a level floor, then a heap, and then a mound reaching to the roof of the mouth. Stones kept coming until the mouth was filled, then several masons, who had been mixing mortar in troughs outside the mouth, began to seal off the opening with a stone wall.

On the day before, a beam fitted with a rope and pulley had been rigged on top of the skull, and it was now put to use hoisting stones from the ground to fill the two eye sockets. The sun was hovering above the western treetops when the last stone was sealed in place, closing up the sockets and the nostril. The fabled stone was no longer a skull, but merely a round, jutting boulder of no particular distinction.

As the masons and carpenters dismantled their scaffolds and hoist, Lanson and the men who had been handling the stones descended the road back to the meadow where the guests remained assembled. Again he mounted the wagon.

"Men and women of Lochlaund, the Devil's Mouth will swallow no more victims. I have witnessed with my own eyes the remains of those who suffered the horror of slow death in the pit, accompanied by unspeakable terrors from creatures that exist only in the worst nightmares. This does not mean that justice will be lacking to those who commit capital crimes. The punishment will be swift and certain, but without the unwarranted torture and agony in the caverns of the Nephilim."

Once again the people cheered and applauded. "King Lanson,

you have closed the gate of hell," shouted someone in the crowd. Instantly Lanson remembered the prophecy of Father Clemente. He had used almost the same words: . . . *and you shall close the gates of hell.* For the first time he understood what Clemente had meant.

"Well then, what is to keep us from dancing?" said Lanson. He called for the musicians to take up their instruments; then he jumped from the wagon, grabbed Evalonne's hand, and led her into the meadow. When the musicians struck up a lively jig, he took his bride by the waist and the two began to step and whirl with zest as Evalonne, her hair flying about her face and shoulders, laughed for sheer joy. Other couples quickly followed, and soon the meadow came alive with skirts and tunics billowing and weaving in the fading sunlight as the air rang with music and laughter.

Maconnal got up from the blanket and pulled Alenia to her feet. "Come on, let's join the dance," he said as he took her hand and pulled her toward the field.

"But, Maconnal, you are forgetting who you are."

"Oh? And just who do you think I am?"

"You are the Bishop of Lochlaund now, remember? King Lanson appointed you only yesterday."

"The Bishop of Lochlaund is not who I am; it is merely my office. Who I am is Maconnal. What I am is a man—a man who is enjoying immensely the company of an extremely fair and lovely woman with whom he desires to dance. Now quit making excuses and come on."

"But the people will think—"

"The people must learn to think differently about the Master of the Universe, and you and I must help them. Come."

Maconnal put his hand to her waist and they stepped and whirled about the meadow, weaving in and out among the other couples as Alenia, breathless and dizzied, clung to him like a sailor to a mast in a pitching sea. When King Lanson saw his friend whirl past him, Alenia in his arms, he stopped and stared in disbelief.

"Would you look at that!" he said to Evalonne. "I had no idea Maconnal could dance."

A few other couples saw that the king had stopped dancing and ceased as well to look in the direction of his stare. When they saw their new bishop dancing with a woman, they were as shocked as their king. Soon most of the couples had paused to watch the spectacle and began to clap their hands to the rhythm of the music. Maconnal and Alenia, absorbed as they were in their unfolding discovery of each other, did not notice for several moments that they were the only couple still dancing. When they did notice, they stopped and looked about, nonplussed and blushing sheepishly as the audience surrounding them broke into laughter and applause. When the couple realized they had been the butt of a good-humored joke, they laughed as well. Lady Alenia grabbed Maconnal and the unlikely pair took up the dance again with renewed zest. The others followed and danced until the last rays of the sun dropped behind the distant silhouette of Macrennon Castle.

Exhausted but happy, the people loaded their wagons, and soon a line of torches marked the procession back to Macrennon. Horses plodded slowly along as young men sang the songs that still lingered in their minds. Wives sat on the boards with their heads resting on the shoulders of their husbands as their children slept sprawled on blankets in the wagon beds behind them. Maidens sat in carriages and carts, gazing at the stars above as they relived the rhythms of the dance and the touch of young masculine hands on their waists.

That day was never forgotten in Lochlaund. Not only was it a day of joy and laughter, it was known ever afterward as the day that King Lanson closed the Devil's Mouth. It was said in later years that this day set the course from which his reign never wavered. Just as King Tallis of Valomar was known for wisdom and Aradon of Meridan for strength of character, King Lanson of Lochlaund was known for justice tempered with mercy.

On that night the people fell in love with their new queen as well, though it was true that a handful never forgave her past and deplored the thought that a woman so tainted should be their queen. But these naysayers were few and knew to keep their disapproval mostly to themselves. For on that day in the meadows below Black Mountain, Evalonne won the hearts of her people, and from that day forward she was known to all as Queen Evalonne the Joyful.

epilogue

Having so quickly gained the confidence of his people, King Lanson had no dissenters on the week following when he asked his Hall of Knights to ratify the treaty with Aradon, bringing Lochlaund into the federation of the Seven Kingdoms. Instead of sending emissaries to Corenham to deliver the treaty, Lanson and Evalonne made the journey themselves. Aradon and Volanna received them warmly, and a close friendship was forged between the royal couples that lasted throughout their lifetimes.

On hearing that Lochlaund had signed the treaty of federation with Meridan, Morgamund of Sorendale sent word to Aradon that he was ready to join the confederation as well, completing the uniting of the Seven Kingdoms predicted by prophecy over 120 years before.

ABOUT THE AUTHOR

THOMAS WILLIAMS, long an aficionado of medieval literature, has authored fifteen published plays. *The Devil's Mouth*, the sequel to his acclaimed novel *The Crown of Eden*, is his sixth book. As the Executive Art Director for Word Publishing, his cover designs have won the Christian Booksellers Association Best Jacket Award five times, and his painting of C. S. Lewis hangs in the Wade Collection at Wheaton College. He and his wife, Faye, live near Nashville, Tennessee.

Also Available from Thomas Williams

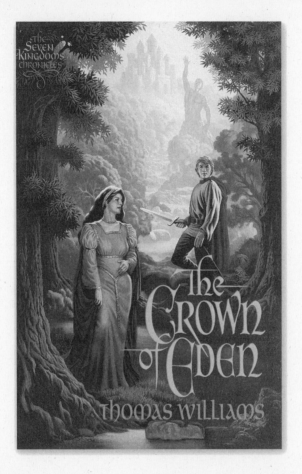

An epic tale of love, courage, and honor, *The Crown of Eden* will transport
you to a medieval world of breathtaking beauty threatened by an ancient evil.
A blacksmith's apprentice must choose between his deepest desire and his
integrity, knowing that the fate of the kingdom hangs on his decision.

WORD PUBLISHING